Protecting WHAT'S MINE

USA TODAY & WSJ BESTSELLING AUTHOR

SIOBHAN DAVIS

This paperback edition © May 2025
ISBN-13: 978-1-917550-32-1

Edited by Kelly Hartigan (XterraWeb) editing.xterraweb.com
Edited by The "Write" Editor
Proofread by Imogen Wells of From Beginning to the End
Research and critique by The Critical Touch
Cover design by Shannon Passmore of Shanoff Designs
Cover imagery © bigstockphoto.com
Interior imagery © depositphotos.com
Formatted by Zsuzsanna of Midnight Readers Book PR using Vellum

Book Description

He doesn't realize he's sleeping with the enemy…

Our dream vacation turned into a living hell when Mom and I were kidnapped.

The cartel wants to use me to exact revenge on La Cosa Nostra, and my mother is the collateral damage.

To save her, I agree to their vile plan and return to New York, faking my way into Don DiPietro's home as a nanny to his adorable son.

Seducing my boss is the goal. I need to gain his trust and then betray him.

Except the longer I'm around Cristian and Elio, the more I realize I can't hurt them.

Especially when I develop genuine feelings for the hot single dad who has sacrificed so much for his adopted son.

The attraction isn't one-sided, but Cristian seems determined to maintain boundaries.

Until we both reach a breaking point and cave to our desire.

One touch, one taste, is all it takes to fall desperately in love.

Cristian is everything I've ever wanted, but he doesn't know of my deception.

I'm on borrowed time.

And when it all comes crashing down, I'm not the only one who pays the price.

Note from the Author

This is an interconnected stand-alone dark romance set in the *Mazzone Mafia* universe. While you don't need to read any other book to enjoy this one, I recommend reading the other interconnected standalones in this world in the suggested reading order for maximum enjoyment.

For readers who are familiar with the *Mazzone Mafia* universe, please note that this book is set two years after the epilogue in *Taking What's Mine*.

This is a dark romance with mature content only intended for an adult audience. Some scenes may be triggering for readers. Please refer to the content warning list on my website: www.siobhandavis.com/triggers

Happy reading!

Mafia & Italian Glossary

Meanings are listed per the context of this book.

- Bambino – baby.
- Capo – Italian for captain. A member of a crime family who heads/leads a crew of soldiers.
- Capocrimine – another word for don, meaning the head of a crime family.
- Cosa Nostra/La Cosa Nostra – A criminal organization, operating within the US, comprising Italian American crime families.
- Consigliere – Italian for adviser/counselor. A member of a crime family who advises the boss and mediates disputes.
- Don/Boss – The head of a crime family.
- El Rey – In Spanish, it means The King. It is how the cartel members refer to their boss Pablo Fuentes.
- La famiglia/famiglia – Italian for the family/family.
- Made man – A member of the mafia who has been officially initiated/inducted into a crime family.
- Mafioso/Mafiosi – An official member of the mafia.
- Nipote – used to refer to one's granddaughter or grandson in Sicily.
- Nonna – Italian for grandma.
- Nonno – Italian for grandpa.
- Omertá – The mafia code of silence. Breaking omertá usually means death.
- Soldato/Soldati – Italian for soldier/soldiers.
- Soldier – A low-ranking member of the mafia who reports to an assigned Capo.

- The Cartel – Sinaloa Cartel from Mexico and a competitor for the drug supply business.
- The Commission – The governing/ruling body of Cosa Nostra, which sits in New York, the organized crime capital of the US.
- The Five Families – Five crime families who rule in New York, each headed by a boss.
- Underboss – The second in command within a crime family and an initiated mafia member who works closely with and reports directly to the boss.

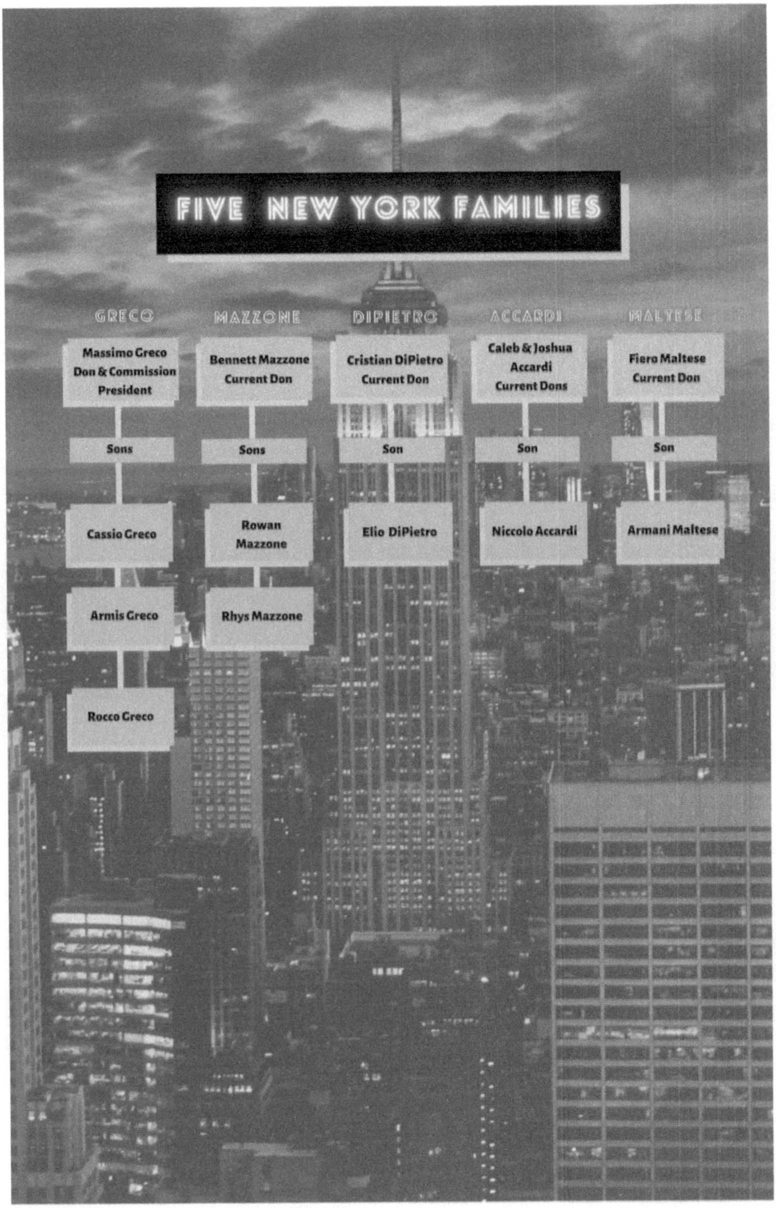

FIVE NEW YORK FAMILIES

GRECO

Massimo Greco
Don & Commission
President

Sons

Cassio Greco

Armis Greco

Rocco Greco

MAZZONE

Bennett Mazzone
Current Don

Sons

Rowan Mazzone

Rhys Mazzone

DIPIETRO

Cristian DiPietro
Current Don

Son

Elio DiPietro

ACCARDI

Caleb & Joshua Accardi
Current Dons

Son

Niccolo Accardi

MALTESE

Fiero Maltese
Current Don

Son

Armani Maltese

THE COMMISSION BOARD

CURRENT PRESIDENT

Massimo Greco
New York

BOARD MEMBERS

Bennett Mazzone New York	**Fiero Maltese** New York	**Cristian DiPietro** New York	**Joshua Accardi** New York	**Caleb Accardi** New York

Dario Agessi Philadelphia	**Rodolfo Volpe** Pittsburgh	**Dominic Mantegna** Chicago	**Louis Pagano** Detroit

Rocco Greco

DIPIETRO FAMILY

ACCARDI FAMILY

Caleb Accardi
Current Don

Twins

Joshua Accardi
Current Don

Married

Married

Elisa Accardi
Nee Salerno

Gia Accardi
Nee Bianchi

Children

Children

Niccolo Accardi

Chiara Accardi

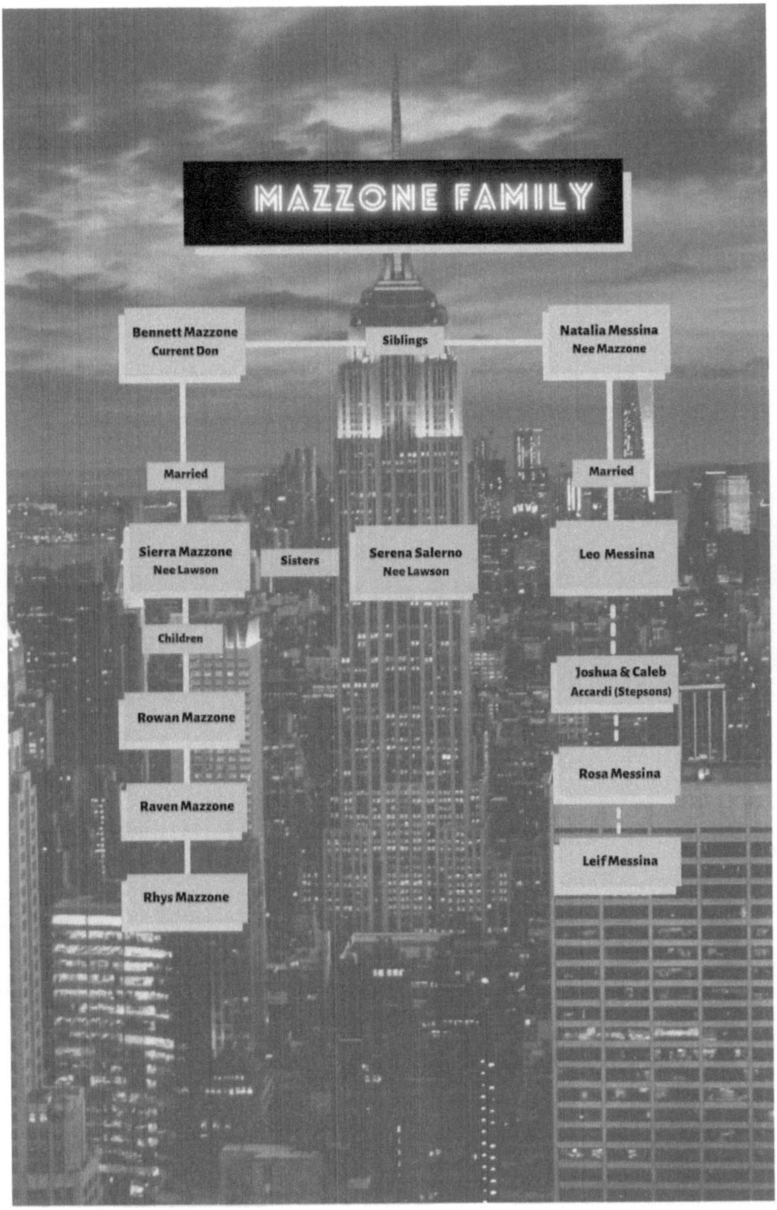

MAZZONE FAMILY

Bennett Mazzone
Current Don

Siblings

Natalia Messina
Nee Mazzone

Married

Married

Sierra Mazzone
Nee Lawson

Sisters

Serena Salerno
Nee Lawson

Leo Messina

Children

Joshua & Caleb
Accardi (Stepsons)

Rowan Mazzone

Rosa Messina

Raven Mazzone

Leif Messina

Rhys Mazzone

MALTESE FAMILY

GRECO FAMILY

Protecting WHAT'S MINE

Prologue
Sloane

I frown as I read the message on my cell. "Thiago isn't coming," I say, setting my phone down on the glossy black tabletop.

"Oh?" Mom tilts her head to one side. "That's a shame. How come?"

I shrug, not caring too much either way. My little fling with the hot waiter at the resort has a looming end date, and it's not like I'm attached. Although it was Thiago's idea to come here tonight, and I should probably be pissed he's ditched us, it's not like it's his fault. If he has to work, he has to work. "One of his colleagues is sick and he was on call, so the hotel made him come in," I explain.

"That's too bad." She combs her fingers through her chin-length dark hair, nervously scanning the busy cocktail bar. "We should go back to the resort."

"We're here now, and we might as well stay since we've already ordered drinks."

My gaze swings to the bar on our left. Three barmen are busy tending to a long line of thirsty patrons. A dazzling array

1

of booze is displayed in illuminated shelving behind them. Music pumps out of speakers, and the guys sway their hips and flirt with the female clientele as they mix drinks. One of the barmen locks eyes with me, flashing a flirty wink and a matching grin. My smile is automatic. Latino men are fun, flirty, and hot in my—limited—experience.

This is my first Mexican vacation, but it won't be the last. I've loved it here. The five-star resort we're staying at is incredible, the food is delicious, the beaches are stunning, and we went on an amazing day trip yesterday to Chichén Itzá, learning all about the Mayan and Toltec culture and history, before stopping at a cenote—an ancient sinkhole—for a cooling swim on the way back. I wish we weren't going home in a week. I could easily spend all summer here in blissful luxury—if I had the money to fund it.

My college bestie has been begging me to come to Mexico for spring break since freshman year, so when I messaged Rory to say I was down for spending our last spring break here, she was thrilled.

Tearing my gaze from the hottie at the bar, I cast a glance around the rest of the plush space. High gloss tables with matching stools comingle with smaller tables and larger booths. Huge potted plants are dotted around the dimly lit room. Overhead, twinkling string lights drape the industrial-type ceiling and flickering candles reside on every table alongside bowls of nuts.

This Russian-owned bar is a relatively new addition to downtown Cancun, according to my online research, and it's a welcome one, judging by the crowd. There seems to be a mix of tourists and locals, and the servers are working nonstop delivering yummy cocktails around the room. There isn't a single table free, and we only got one because Thiago comes here regularly and he reserved it for us.

"It's safer at the resort," Mom says as I spy a waitress heading our way carrying a tray.

"Mom, we're perfectly safe here. You need to chill and stop reading shit online."

"The state department advisory said all travelers need to exercise increased caution," she retorts, wisely clamping her lips shut when the waitress reaches our table.

I thank her, and Mom pays for the drinks, her not-so-subtle way of telling me we're leaving after this round. "Cancun is one of the safer areas, and there are plenty of US states with a higher crime rate." I pat her hand. "Stop worrying. Relax and enjoy yourself."

"I can't help it." She slides a cocktail in front of her. "It's my natural disposition."

"I have lived with you for most of my twenty-one years on this planet." I cock a brow and grin as I grab my drink. "I'm well aware."

"I think it comes with the territory when you're a single mom."

I don't remind her of the seven years she was married because it's a touchy subject. "I'm an adult, Mom. You did good raising me. Now it's time to let loose and have some fun." I lift my glass to hers. "A toast. To enjoying our second week and having lots of fun!"

"I think my idea of fun and yours are vastly different," she teases, clinking her glass against mine.

"No kidding." I waggle my brows before bringing my drink to my lips. I'm guessing I got my little wild streak from my father, though I have no way of verifying it as I've never known him. Then again, Mom got pregnant with me after a one-night stand when she was twenty, during a backpacking trip around Europe, so she definitely had some wild in her at one point.

"Oh, that's good," Mom says after tasting her gin cocktail.

"Yummy," I agree. "Thiago said these are the best cocktails in all of Cancun." The cocktails at our hotel are the one letdown. They're clearly using cheap booze and far too much juice or mixer. These drinks are on a whole other level.

We chat as we drink, and I successfully coax Mom into a second round, glad she has relaxed and is enjoying herself. The irony is I probably worry about her as much as she worries about me. She's only forty-two with her whole life still to live, but she seems to have closed herself off to the possibility of love. She has close friends she goes out with, and she adores her job as a teacher at the local middle school, but she refuses to entertain the idea of a relationship, and that makes me sad for her. I know her ex-husband broke her faith in men, but she's been divorced over eleven years. It's more than enough time to get back in the saddle. I decide I'm finding her a hot guy to have some fun with before we leave Mexico in a week.

"Sloane." Mom clutches my arm. "I don't feel so hot," she slurs, slouching in her chair.

A stabbing pain pierces my skull the same time my stomach churns unpleasantly. "Fuck." I have a bad feeling about this, but I'm damned if I'm letting us become a statistic. My panicked eyes dart around the room, my gaze connecting with the same barman from earlier. This time, the look he gives me sends ice-cold chills racing through my body, and I know my assumption is correct.

"We need to get out of here." I toss some bills on the table to cover our last round and help Mom out of her seat. She sways on her feet, clearly in a worse state than me, and I wrap my arm around her back, keeping her close as I guide her toward the door, praying the bouncers don't try to stop us. My head is pounding, and nausea swims up my throat. I hope I have enough strength to get us to our car before I collapse. Thank fuck I organized a car and driver with the hotel and made arrangements for him to wait for us while we were in the bar.

I feel eyes trailing my every step the closer we get to the door, and I'm trembling all over. My breath falters when the security guys at the door take one look at Mom and start speaking to one another in Spanish. "Excuse me," I say, pushing past them. My vision blurs in and out, and I need to get us the fuck out of here now before we both pass out.

One of the guys moves to touch my arm, and I yank Mom past him. I'm almost fully propping her up now. "Don't touch me!" I snap, and the guy holds up his palms. I maneuver Mom out onto the sidewalk, grateful when they let us go without further interference.

Our driver is parked across the road at the curb, and upon spotting me, he gets out and rushes over to help me with Mom.

"We've been roofied," I explain as we each take one of Mom's arms.

He cusses in Spanish, glancing all around as we walk Mom over to the car. Her head is lolling from side to side, she's moaning, and little beads of sweat have formed on her brow. My legs almost give out when I'm helping her into the back seat. Pain is pummeling my skull, and alcohol sloshes uncomfortably in my stomach as I climb in beside her.

My fingers fumble as I try to buckle Mom in. She's fully passed out now, and my panic has reached coronary-inducing territory. Our driver wastes no time hanging around, quickly taking off. When I get Mom secured, I buckle my belt and drop my head against the window. I'm seeing two of the driver as he talks rapidly in Spanish into his phone, in a clearly aggravated, high-pitched tone, while his eyes constantly scan his mirrors and the back window.

I can't even lift my head to look, and I'm struggling to keep my eyes open. I doze in and out, and I'm only vaguely aware of being jostled forward when our car slams to a halt. The driver is screaming, and I try to focus my vision, but my eyes won't cooperate. Two loud popping sounds barely reach my eardrums. My heart is pounding so fast, and I know this is bad, but I can't do anything to stop whatever is happening because I have no control over my body right now.

I almost hit the asphalt when my car door is suddenly yanked open. Large hands grip my shoulders, and then I'm hauled against a warm body. I open my mouth to scream, but nothing comes out, and then everything turns dark.

When I wake, I'm on a plane, surrounded by unfamiliar men. I'm confused until it starts to come back to me. I don't see Mom. Panic crawls up my throat, and my body reacts instinctively, my legs flailing and my arms thrashing around. A tall, broad figure looms over me. A sharp pinch in my neck stings before I succumb to nothingness again.

When I wake the next time, the first thing I register is the crying. My head hurts as I move it toward the sound. Mom is lying beside me on a bed propped against a wall covered with peeling paint. She's sobbing and staring at me with terror evident in her eyes. "Mom." My throat scrapes as the word leaves my lips, and my mouth is as dry as the Sahara. My arm feels like a dead weight as I attempt to touch her.

"You're awake," a strange man says. "Good."

A tight pain spreads across my chest as fear has a chokehold on me. Callused fingers grip my ankle, and I'm tugged down the dirty mattress. My heart slams against my rib cage as I stare in horror at the five men standing around the bed in the small, windowless room. All are armed, coated with a myriad of ink and piercings, and sporting similar dark, lust-filled glints in their eyes.

"No," I croak as the man holding my ankle starts moving his hand up my bare leg. It's only then I realize I'm completely naked and totally vulnerable. Adrenaline supercharges my veins, and I kick out, trying to wrench my leg free.

"Leave her alone!" Mom cries, crawling to my side and wrapping her fingers around the man's wrist, trying to force him off me. She's naked too, and the full horror of our new reality is only now dawning on me.

Another man backhands her, sending her flying back. Her head hits the wall with a loud crack.

"Mom!" I scream, continuing to kick at the monster feeling me up while I arch my neck and look back at my mother. She's cradling her head in her hands and softly moaning. I cry out when fingers touch my pussy, and tears automatically leak out of my eyes.

"You leave her alone!" Mom shouts, clambering off the bed and swaying on her feet. She rounds on the man, slapping him across the face before pummeling her fists on his chest. The hand leaves my body to wrap around Mom's throat.

"Bitch, you dare to attack me?" he snarls in heavily accented English.

Mom's fingers claw at his hand as he exerts more pressure on her neck.

"Please, stop." I sit up, wrapping my arms around myself as if that will stop the vicious trembling that's seized my body. A strangled sob rips from my lips as the other men ogle me like I'm their next meal. I stand on shaky limbs. "Let her go. I'll do what you want if you don't harm her." His meaty hand eases his grip on Mom's throat a little. "Please. She's my mom."

"Aw." The asshole reaches out with his free hand, cupping my bare breast and squeezing it. "That's cute, but no bitch gets to disrespect me without punishment." He tweaks my nipple hard, and it takes every ounce of self-control I have not to react. Bile fills my mouth, and acid churns in my gut. "And *Mom* has bigger tits." He makes fun of my voice, releasing me to paw at my mother instead.

"Don't be too hasty," one of the other men says. He grabs both my boobs in his hands and fondles me. I want the ground to swallow me. "They may be small, but they're perky." I close my eyes as his mouth lowers over my tits. Tears stream down my face, and inside, I'm dying.

"Take me," Mom pleads, and my eyes pop open. She's rubbing at her neck while the main asshole gropes her everywhere. "I'll take my punishment. Just leave my daughter alone. Do what you want to me, but don't touch her."

"You don't get to call the shots, slut," the man says, roughly shoving his fingers inside her.

Mom is shaking as badly as I am.

"I'm sorry," I mouth as tears continue to fall freely down my face.

This is all my fault.

She didn't want to leave the resort, but she wouldn't let me go on a date with Thiago alone. She didn't want to stay at the bar after he canceled, and I should have listened to her. If I had, our drinks wouldn't have been spiked, and we wouldn't have been kidnapped. I ignored her fears and safety concerns, downplaying them when she was right. Mom is only in this mess because of me, and if I could die to save her, I would.

"I love you," she mouths back, silently crying while the man violates her.

Hands paw at my body while different hands grope hers. I can't watch, so I stare blankly ahead, trying to numb myself to everything happening.

Mom screams, and I drag my gaze around in time to see her being pushed down over a table. The main monster kicks her legs apart before lowering his zipper.

"Don't, please don't! Fuck me, not her," I cry out. "Please."

The other men laugh. "Well, if you insist," a man with a bald head and a skull tattoo says, shoving me down on my back on the bed.

Mom screams again, and chills crawl all over me despite the stifling heat in the room. I buck and writhe while trying to fight the man crawling over me.

The door slams against the wall, and a dark shadow fills the doorway. "Enough," a man with a deep masculine voice says, the cadence booming around the small room. Authority is evident in his tone, and the men defer to him as he stalks inside. This man is clearly the one in charge. The man on top of me is lifted off and thrown to the floor. "No one touches the girl." The newcomer wears army fatigues and a neutral expression as his eyes roam my body. He pulls me to my feet and hauls me around in front of him. "Lift the woman," he commands, and the bastard hurting my mom pulls out and yanks her to her feet.

Mom stares vacantly at me with tear tracks streaking her pretty face.

I want someone to pinch me and drag me from this nightmare because this cannot be real.

"I'll make a deal with you," the boss says to Mom. "We won't touch your daughter as long as you spread your legs and do as you're told."

"Why are you doing this to us?" Mom whispers.

"We have our reasons."

"Please let us go," I say. "We won't tell anyone anything. Just let us go home, and we will forget all about this."

"That's not how this works." His hot breath fans over my ear, and my legs almost buckle in disgust. "The big boss has important plans for you. You cooperate, and we'll let you live. Refuse, and we'll keep you alive, but you'll wish you were dead."

"What plans?" Mom asks, her voice cracking.

"Do you agree to my deal?" he says, ignoring her question.

Mom's gaze meets mine, and everything I see reflected in her eyes mirrors how I feel. Steely determination radiates from her face when she returns her gaze to the boss. "You promise she won't be touched?"

"Yes. I give you my word. We need her unmarked and as pure as a non-virgin can be."

Mom eyeballs him before calmly agreeing. "Okay."

"No, Mom!" I cry. "No, please no." I wriggle against my captor, but his arms lock around my chest, caging me in place. "I won't do it!" I screech. "Whatever you want, I won't do it. If you hurt my mom, I refuse to cooperate!" Lifting my legs, I swing back, trying to hit the prick in the balls, but my feet only land midway up his thighs, and they lack a punch.

Shoving me to my knees on the cold stone floor, he bends down and clamps his hand around my throat. Not enough to restrict my breathing, but it's enough of a threat to control me. "You will obey," he says in a cold, clinical tone. "My men have needs that must be met. Cooperate, and I'll restrict it to once a week. Disobey, and your mother will bear your punishment. If you cause continuous problems, you'll both become cartel sex toys, and you'll be fucked every hour of every day for the rest of your miserable lives."

"Cartel?" My voice shakes, and my lip wobbles as he secures a leather collar around my neck, locking it into place.

"You're the property of the Sinaloa Cartel now," he says, straightening up and yanking on the chain attached to the collar. My head whips back involuntarily. He stares down at me with emotionless black eyes. "Forget your old lives because they no longer exist. The quicker you accept that truth, the easier it will be for everyone."

"Fuck. You." The words slip out before I can trap them.

He folds the chain around his fist, stretching my neck and

body back at an awkward angle. "That's two infractions your mother now has to pay for."

Icy fingers tiptoe up my spine, and nausea floods my mouth.

He looks across the room. "Continue and fuck all three holes." He relaxes the chain, and my body falls back into position. Mom cries, and I squeeze my eyes shut. "Watch," the boss commands. Slapping sounds and grunts mix with Mom's quiet whimpers and sobs. I don't want to watch, but I don't want Mom punished further either, so I compel my eyes to open.

Pain obliterates every part of me as I'm forced to watch my mother being assaulted by multiple men in multiple ways. It seems to last for hours, and my heart is a torn, bloody mess by the end of it.

"Don't worry," the boss says as Mom collapses on the floor when the last man pulls out and closes his zipper. "Your turn to sacrifice will come."

Chapter One
Cristian

Scrubbing my hands down my face, I sigh heavily while Isa escorts the last candidate to the door. Swiveling in my chair, I turn to face the large window in my spacious office at DiPietro Freight Management & Logistics. The stunning views of the waterfront from one window and the sprawling uptown from the other are things I love about my office. As I stare at the gently rolling water, my frustration recedes a little. I know Isa is doing her best, but she strayed too far from the brief, and I'm annoyed at the time she's wasted. She's finishing up in a month, which means we're running out of time to find a replacement.

I turn around when I hear footsteps approaching in the hallway outside, my gaze snagging on the framed photo on my desk. Gia took it last year at Chiara's and Niccolo's joint second-birthday party. My smile is instant. Elio's twinkling green eyes and mischievous smile send a flood of warmth through my body. I can't believe he's four now. Time is moving way too fast, and I want to slow it down, to imprint every precious moment with my son in my heart so I never forget how special these early years have been.

"I think she's the winner," Isa says, reentering my office with a wide smile and a confident swagger.

"Close the door." I sit straighter in my chair, preparing to battle with Elio's biological aunt.

Her smile doesn't falter as she sinks into the chair across from me. "Regina has the best qualifications and the most experience, and she has a calmness I love."

"I don't disagree with that assessment. She's a lovely woman, but she's sixty-two, Isa."

Her eyes narrow. "Her age shouldn't matter, Cristian."

"In theory, no. But practically, it does. You have taken care of Elio for the past three years. You know he's high-spirited and super active. I need a nanny who is young and energetic to keep up with him. I need someone who doesn't have other outside commitments yet, someone who can devote their time solely to Elio. All these women we interviewed today are wonderful, but they do not fit the brief I gave you." I should've screened the candidates myself, but life has been hectic recently with the expansion I'm overseeing here at my family business and attending to my *mafioso* responsibilities. When my current nanny offered to help find her replacement, I didn't hesitate to accept the offer, but now I'm regretting it. "I'm looking for a *mother* figure for my son, Isa. *Not* a grandmother figure."

Her lips pinch, and her eyes narrow. "That is so discriminatory, Cristian. I thought better of you, and I really think you need to reconsider your position."

God, grant me patience. Isa has been a godsend with my son, but she has tested my patience on more than one occasion. I love that a relative was taking care of Elio while I had to work, but Isa pushed those boundaries any chance she got, and her interfering ways have caused many arguments between us.

Things were tense at first when I adopted Cruz and Bettina's son in the aftermath of my brother's demise because the Da Rosa family wanted to adopt him, and they weren't happy I planned to raise him as a single parent. Not that the single parent part was by choice. Back then, I had hopes of proposing to my girlfriend, believing her to be the one. But Aliya showed her true colors after I brought Elio to live with us, walking out on me, *on him*, only two months later, just as I'd been about to propose.

It's been a familiar pattern since then, which is why I have now given up on dating. It's easy to find a woman to fuck when I need to let off some steam, and I've been darkening the doors of Club H far more regularly these past two years. I'm done with women bailing on me because they don't want to raise another couple's son.

I don't see it like that.

Elio is *mine*.

We share blood, and I'm the only parent he'll ever know. It'd be nice if he had a mother too, but that wasn't meant to be. Which is why finding the right nanny is so important. A young nanny will have the energy to keep up with my little boy and hopefully will stick around through the formative years before they settle down and start their own family.

Maybe I am being ageist, but I won't apologize for putting my son first. I know what he needs, and Isotta Da Rosa does not get to overrule me, no matter how much I appreciate all the love and care she's shown Elio. She's getting married soon, and I'm sure a family of her own is in the cards. While I don't think Isa will fully abandon Elio, he won't be her priority for much longer. "With the greatest respect, Isa, I know what my son wants and needs, and none of those women are suitable. Kindly thank them and advise them they have not been successful."

"You're making a mistake, Cristian. A young nanny will be

more concerned with partying and having fun, and Elio will just be a job to them."

"Now who's being discriminatory?" I arch a brow and drum my fingers on the armrest of my chair.

"You know I'm right. You're simply too stubborn to admit it."

"Pot, kettle, black, Isotta. Does your husband-to-be know about your legendary stubbornness?"

"Carmine is well aware of what he's getting." She worries her lower lip between her teeth. "Maybe I'll talk to him again. See if he'll reconsider letting me stay on."

I bite back a retort. I've made my feelings known about her arranged marriage to a man thirty years older than her. Arranged marriages continue to be tradition in *La Cosa Nostra*, but they are no longer officially sanctioned or controlled. The Commission, the governing body for all Italian American *mafioso* in the US, has changed many of the old ways, granting greater freedoms and flexibility, especially when it comes to women. Rather than dictating how things should be, we leave a lot up to individual families to decide.

Much of the older generation is still stuck in the old ways and traditions. The Da Rosa patriarch being one. His three older daughters were all married off to men of his choosing. I don't know what his view was on Bettina. It was widely known among the *mafioso* in New York that she was Cruz's mistress, and she'd borne him a child outside his marriage. Rafaelo Da Rosa hadn't denounced his second-youngest daughter, but I doubt he condoned it either. Anyway, it's no surprise he lined up a marriage contract for his youngest daughter. I'm just surprised Isa agreed to it.

"Don't stir trouble on my account," I say. "I still have a month to find a suitable replacement."

"I don't want to leave him. Or you."

"I'm grateful for all you've done, but you've got your own life to lead, and it's not like we'll be strangers. We'll still see you."

"I know." Her lower lip wobbles. "I just love Elio so much. He's more like my son than my nephew. I will miss his cute little face and the way he digs his toes into my leg when he's all snuggled up against me on the couch."

"He will miss you too, but we'll adjust. I won't stand in the way of your happiness."

Her face contorts, but she disguises it fast.

I lean across the desk. "You don't have to marry him if it's not what you want," I softly remind her. We had this conversation previously, but maybe it's worth repeating now that she's only one month from her wedding day.

"I can't bring shame to my family by backing out now." She knots her hands on her lap.

"I wouldn't let that happen."

Steely-blue eyes stare at me. "I know you're a powerful man, Cristian, one of The Five and on the board of The Commission, but even you can't promise that. Papa is old school. He expects me to trust he's making the best decision for me, and I need to respect his choice."

By marrying a woman of twenty-eight to a guy in his fifties? Not fucking likely. I keep those thoughts to myself though because I already know verbalizing them won't get me anywhere. Isa is Daddy's little princess, and she trips over backward to please him. It's been frustrating to witness.

Rafaelo Da Rosa doesn't hold me in high regard, and a part of me doesn't blame him. My elder brother treated his other daughter like trash. Bettina loved Cruz, but he used her as a surrogate, murdering her in broad daylight after she'd delivered his son and heir. I understand why the DiPietro name is mud in the Da Rosa household, like I understand why they didn't want

Elio to come live with me. But they should know by now I'm nothing like my dead brother. I abhorred the things he did, and I could never treat people as carelessly as he did, so their continuing to bear a grudge is petty and frustrating.

"What about your choice? Why don't you get a say?" I ask.

"I have always known this is the way it would be. Father made this arrangement with Carmine when his wife's diagnosis was confirmed. No one expected her to battle bone cancer as long as she did, so I guess I can count myself lucky I had years of freedom before my duty kicked in. I've been luckier than most."

"I still don't think it's right, but I see your mind is made up."

"There is nothing to decide, Cristian. What's done is done."

"You know where I am if you ever change your mind."

"I appreciate that, and I'm grateful you care. Elio is lucky to have you as a dad."

"I'm lucky to have him as my son, and I won't fail him." I push back my chair and stand. "I know the kind of nanny he needs. I want to see the rest of the applications." I slip my jacket off the back of the chair and pull it on. "Please email me the files so I can review them at home tonight."

Chapter Two
Sloane

Staring at myself in the mirror is like staring at a stranger. My hand lifts, toying with the long, dyed golden-blonde strands of hair curtaining my face. Months of forced cosmetic surgery have altered the structure of my face, though it's subtle. My nose is thinner, my cheekbones higher, my lips fuller. The only thing that is unchanged is my wide blue eyes.

The reflection is stunning, but I don't feel like me.

I'm *not* me.

I'm trapped in a body crafted to ensnare a powerful man.

I have no control. I'm a puppet, and the cartel is the one pulling the strings.

Looking down at the monstrosities perched on my chest, I pine for my small breasts. That sick fuck Pablo Fuentes—leader of the Sinaloa Cartel—made me undergo months of transformation so there is minimal risk of anyone discovering my real identity.

"We need to leave shortly," Diego says, barging into my bedroom without knocking. You'd think after seven months of enduring a living hell with no privacy that I wouldn't care, but it's the small things I took for granted before that matter so much now. "El Rey wants to speak to you first." He thrusts a cell at me.

Bile coats my tongue as I hold the phone out in front of me. Video, of course. It's not enough I have to listen to Pablo's slimy voice; I'm also forced to look at his ugly face.

"I want to see all of you," the leering asshole says, and I grind my teeth to the molars as I drag the cell up and down my body.

"What the fuck is this?" Fuentes snarls. "I told you to dress sexy!"

"I'm interviewing to be a *nanny*. If I turn up in a sexy dress, he'll dismiss me before I've even opened my mouth." I gesture at my conservative black pencil skirt and white silk blouse. I've paired them with plain black stilettos and a string of fake pearls.

"I told you the interview is only a formality. My inside contact will ensure you get the placement," he snaps. "Do I need to remind you of what's at stake?"

"I don't need a reminder," I say in a clipped tone.

"Maybe you need additional incentive."

Pain spears through me when he grabs Mom, hauling her onto her knees in front of him. "Take it out and suck it, whore."

"That's enough." I rub a hand across my queasy tummy. "I don't need additional incentive. I understand the stakes." My mother's life is literally in my hands. If I don't deliver for the cartel, they will kill her. The fear of fucking up has kept me awake for hours every night since I returned to New York. Thank God for concealer.

"You ignored a direct order." Fuentes smirks as Mom unzips him and pulls his disgusting cock out.

She has a dazed expression on her face that's familiar.

Hurt flays the flesh from my bones as effectively as if my skin were physically being carved up. The thoughts of everything Mom has endured lay siege to my tortured brain, like always. I live with constant guilt and regret. It's quite possible she's addicted to the shit he keeps pumping into her neglected body, but how can I criticize or tell her to resist it when the drugged haze she slips into numbs some of her pain?

"*Mommy* will continue to pay the price for your disobedience, Sloane. The fact you're there and she's here doesn't change shit."

"I'll wear a sexy dress," I blurt, panicking as Mom lowers her head.

"No, what you're wearing is better."

I open my mouth to protest the "punishment" but clamp it shut again. The look on his face dares me to challenge him. I've learned from experience that I never win; he'll only see it as further grounds to hurt my mother. Shame rattles my insides as I think of all the ways I have failed her. But I won't fail her now, even if I detest what I'm being made to do. I don't like that I'll be responsible for this man losing his life, but it's his life or my mother's, and there's no contest.

"Good girl," Pablo says, looking at me as he pats Mom's head while she bobs up and down.

Knots twist in my gut. I've been forced to blow that prick daily for months. Yes, I wasn't violated regularly like Mom, but that didn't mean my body wasn't misused in ways that didn't physically mark me.

Fuentes' men nicknamed me "The Blowjob Queen." They joked that their cum in my belly sustained me. Fuentes' favorite hobby was blowing his load over my enhanced chest after the surgery, and I couldn't hate my fake boobs any more if I tried.

"Have you memorized the file?" he asks, spreading his

thighs and leaning back in his chair as he knots Mom's longer hair around his fist.

Someday, I am going to gut that prick and make him choke on his vile cock. "Yes," I grit out, clenching my jaw.

"I expect the performance of a lifetime, my little American Barbie." He grins at his own pathetic excuse of a joke.

"I'll deliver." I often wonder if he targeted me because I was studying drama at Yale or if it was because I'm from New York. My gut tells me Thiago set the whole thing up, but it could just be we were in the wrong place at the wrong time. I guess I won't ever know because the prick refuses to answer any time I ask him.

"See that you do." Grabbing the back of Mom's neck, he forces her mouth lower. Garbled sounds rip from her throat as she struggles against his firm grip, trying to breathe over a mouthful of cartel cock. "If you blow this, you won't ever see your mother again. I'll video her final minutes and send it to you, ensuring you never know a minute's peace. Her death will always be on you."

"I won't blow it."

"Don't even think of confiding in Don DiPietro or begging him for help. My contact will know, and that will be the end for dear mom."

"I know what I need to do and what's at stake. I won't fail my mother."

Loosening his grip on Mom's neck, he leans into the screen. "See that you don't fail *me*."

The screen goes black, and my hand shakes as I give the cell back to Diego. In some ways, I've become desensitized to all the horrors that are my new existence. I've had to numb myself to a lot of it to survive. Mom needed me to be brave and smart, and I've tried, but it's not easy. I will never stop fearing that man and the things he can do and has done to my mother and to me.

Protecting What's Mine

Mom is counting on me. The only way she's getting out of this alive is if I get Don DiPietro to hire me, bed me, and confide in me. Failure isn't an option. Otherwise, we're both dead.

———

I read through the file on my lap one more time as Diego rides in the taxi with me to the DiPietro Freight Management & Logistics building, where my interview is scheduled to take place. I don't know how he pulled it off, but Fuentes says this fake background will be corroborated when the Italian mafia conducts their regular checks. The fact that I already have an interview confirms I passed. Fuentes has crafted a false identity that is as close to my real one as possible, so there is less margin for error, but not enough similarities to lead anyone to my true persona.

I'm dying to check online to see what was reported when Mom and I went missing, but I have no access to the internet. Diego and Alvaro have been all up in my business since we arrived in The Big Apple two weeks ago. I am only allowed out of the tiny apartment to shop for clothes and cosmetics or to exercise on the roof. My meals are carefully calorie-controlled. God forbid I put on weight. I've been slender all my life, but I was always a healthy weight. I've got to be at least ten pounds lighter by now, if not more.

I hate my thinner frame. Fuentes seems to think all American men want blondes with big tits and skinny frames. Or perhaps that's Don DiPietro's type. I wouldn't know. I've been told the bare minimum about the man. I know he's powerful within the Italian mafia in New York, he is a single father to his nephew, and he is the CEO of his family business. The cartel wants me to spy on him to discover the transportation routes for their drug distribution network within the US and, when the time is right, to deliver Cristian DiPietro to the cartel so they can kill him. I don't know why they have beef with him personally, because that information wasn't forthcoming.

How has my life come to this? Getting mixed up between a cartel and the mafia with my mother's life hanging in the balance and everything resting on my ability to seduce a dangerous man. I can't even enjoy the fact I'm back on US soil because I'm not free. My every move is watched and controlled, and I can't contemplate stepping out of line because Fuentes will make Mom suffer for my mistakes.

Resting my head against the window, I close my eyes and allow myself one brief moment to be human. To throw a pity party. To wish I had never agreed to meet Thiago outside the resort. To lament the life I've been forced to leave behind. To mourn the future that no longer awaits.

"We're here," Diego says a few beats later, and my reprieve ends. He pays the driver in cash, and we get out onto the heaving sidewalk in the Financial District. "The building is around the corner. You're on your own from here because they have cameras outside, but don't try anything." His eyes drill into my skull as his fingers dig into my arm. "I'll be watching. One false step and it's lights out for your mama."

I yank my hand out of his grip. "I'm well aware."

He stares at me for a few minutes. "Go, you don't want to be late."

I'm cursing him in my head and visualizing gruesome ways to kill him as I walk off in the direction of the DiPietro building. Although it's futile, I run over scenarios in my head again, ways in which I can reach out for help. If I could get my hands on a cell, I could call Rory or give my bodyguards the slip and go to the police or the FBI, but those options only save me. They'd be a death sentence for Mom, and I can't pull my best friend into this mess in case they target her too. So, I need to let thoughts of escape go and stick with the program. I have no choice but to do as Fuentes says, and hope he'll let us go like he's promised after I've played my part.

The impressive building rises majestically ahead of me when I round the corner. Tipping my head back, I stare at the looming building with multiple floors stretching farther than I can see. Nerves fire at me from all angles, and I wipe my clammy palms down the side of my skirt as I walk toward the entrance doors. There is so much resting on this first meeting, and I cannot fuck it up.

Shoving my shoulders back, I lift my chin and adopt my new persona. Sloane Barton isn't here to be interviewed. Sloane Clark is, and she's about to give the performance of her life. Nothing less will do.

I sit confidently in the small waiting room as I prepare to be called. Heels clicking on the polished floor claim my attention, and I turn my head, watching a tall brunette approach, wearing a tight smile. "Ms. Clark. Mr. DiPietro will see you now," she says, pursing her lips as she rakes her gaze up and down me with clear derision.

Wow. Judgmental much? I get that I don't look like the stereotypical nanny, but it's rude to judge me for my looks when she hasn't even heard a word I have to say. Forcing a fake smile on my face, I rise gracefully, pleased I have the height advantage by an inch or two. Normally, I avoid heels because it means I tower over the average guy, but on this occasion, I'm glad to be taller. "Thank you." I cast a quick look over her, but I'm not as obvious or bitchy as she was. Her small chest is at odds with her tall frame, curvy hips, and rounded butt, but I envy her all the same.

She stalks ahead of me, her spine rigid and an air of haughtiness surrounding her. I wonder who pissed in her cornflakes this morning or if this is her usual personality.

I smooth a hand down the front of my skirt when we stop in front of a door. She enters the large office first, pausing by the door to usher me inside before closing it after me. She gestures toward the desk at the far side of the room. A man is standing in front of the window, looking out at the waterfront in the near distance. I'd say the view is spectacular in the summer from this vantage point. I study Don DiPietro as I walk across the room. Broad shoulders taper to a slim waist, narrow hips, and a shapely butt behind his black dress pants. My steps falter when he turns around and I get a look at his face.

My god, he's stunning.

Dark hair is slicked back from his face in a classic American style. Vibrant green eyes study me as I approach, flaring slightly as he examines my face. He gets brownie points for not looking below my chin. His olive complexion complements the layer of stubble on his chin and cheeks. Cristian has a strong nose and full lips, an ode to his Italian American heritage. Ink peeks out from under the wristbands of his pale blue dress shirt and above his collar. A small diamond earring loops around one ear.

He's older than me, but I anticipated that. I didn't know what to expect, really. It's not like I've ever crossed paths with the Italian mafia. But I wasn't expecting a man in his thirties, and I certainly didn't imagine he'd be so hot. I can't decide if it's better he's attractive or if it makes my planned seduction worse.

A throat clearing snaps me out of it, and a natural blush stains my cheeks when I reach his desk.

"Ms. Clark. I'm Cristian DiPietro," he says, rounding the

desk and smiling pleasantly. "It's nice to meet you. Thank you for coming in."

I smile shyly, remembering my role. "The pleasure is all mine, sir. Thank you for letting me interview for the position."

His arm extends, and I shake his hand. His palm is callused but warm, and heat travels up my arm from his touch, alongside a trail of fiery tingles. "Call me Cristian. We don't stand on ceremony around here."

"Is this your son?" I ask, spying the framed photo on his desk. It's a fabulous picture. Cristian's pride in his son is obvious in the adoring expression on his face.

"That's Elio." The same pride radiates in his tone.

"He's adorable. The resemblance is strong."

"Have a seat." He motions toward the empty chair in front of the desk as the woman sinks into one of the chairs on the opposite side. "This is Isotta. She is Elio's current nanny, and she's helping me with the interview process."

Well, that's just swell. I can tell the woman dislikes me, and if she holds any sway, I might have already blown this. I nod and smile in her direction. "It's good to meet you."

"We should get down to it," she says in a clipped tone, opening a file in front of her.

Cristian leans back a little in his chair and smiles in my direction. "Before we begin, you should know Elio is my adopted son. He's my biological nephew. His father was my only brother. Both his parents died before he was one."

"I'm sorry to hear that. He's lucky he has you."

"Adopting Elio has given me the greatest joy. My world revolves around my little boy." His face softens as he glances briefly at the framed photo. "Isotta is Elio's aunt, on his mother's side, and she has selflessly given of her time to care for him while I work. But she's getting married shortly, and that's why we are interviewing for her replacement."

"How exciting," I say, smiling pleasantly at the dour-faced woman. "Congratulations."

Silence greets my statement until Cristian pointedly clears his throat.

"Thank you," she says. "I'm very attached to Elio, and I'll still be around a lot, so whoever we hire will have access to ask me questions. Elio is a delightful child, but he can be a handful."

"What Isa means," Cristian says, drilling her with a look, "is Elio is a very active child. He has lots of interests, and he's well-rounded. He's into sports, art, reading, science, and he loves learning about the world. He isn't the kind of child to sit for hours in front of the TV, not that I'd permit it. He will need to be entertained and enlightened. He starts pre-K in September, but until then, his nanny will need to plan his days in advance to keep him busy and active."

"That won't be an issue. As you're aware, I have a degree in early childhood education, and I have CPR and first aid certification." The former is a lie, but the latter isn't. "I'm pretty good at arts and crafts. I babysat regularly for different parents during high school, and I was on the school's basketball team and cross-country team. I led an active lifestyle growing up in Lake Placid, and I love the outdoors." All of that is true except where I come from. I was raised in Ithaca, New York, but the Lake Placid experience would've been similar.

"And yet your previous employer dismissed you after eight months. That's hardly a ringing endorsement, and your actual nanny experience is limited." Isotta arches a brow, and while she might think she's concealing her smugness, I read it all over her face.

I don't like this woman, and I'm not going to let her rattle me. She clearly doesn't want to relinquish the role, and I'm betting no one will be as good as her in her eyes. Folding my hands in my lap, I smile pleasantly as I calmly reply. "My employer relocated to Europe. Mr. Smithson's company transferred him to Switzerland, and though his wife wanted me to travel with them, the company was providing a nanny, and it was already arranged."

I purposely swing my gaze to Don DiPietro. "I understand I might not have as much experience as other candidates, but I make up for it in other ways. I adore children, and I seem to bond naturally with them. There is nothing quite like seeing the world through the eyes of a child. Nurturing their inquisitiveness and supporting their individuality is important to me, while setting boundaries and maintaining discipline is critical so they feel safe and grow up with a healthy respect for adults and the rules. I think I strike the right balance." My eyes flit to the sullen woman sitting beside my would-be employer. "At least that's what my former employer has said in their reference. If you have doubts, you can always reach out to them."

"That won't be necessary. Your references have already been verified," Cristian says, glancing sideways at his current nanny. He shoots me an apologetic look before smiling. "Tell me about the kids you were taking care of and what their day-to-day routine was."

The interview progresses naturally from there, but it's an odd experience. Isa's obvious aversion to me comes through in the questions she asks and her aggressive probing style. Cristian is more laid-back, and his questions are more intelligent. He doesn't give as much away, his manner affable and warm. I can tell he's growing increasingly irritated by Isa's behavior, but he doesn't call her out on it.

When the interview wraps up forty minutes later, I pray I've done enough to secure the job and that Fuentes is right and his contact will make sure the position is mine.

Chapter Three
Cristian

"I believe congratulations are in order," Elisa Accardi says, smiling as she hands me another beer. I came up to Glencoe for the weekend to check on the progress of the house I'm building, and I'm staying with Elio in Elisa's and Caleb's guest wing. Dinner earlier was a lively affair with three kids under the age of four, but they're all sleeping now, so the adults finally get to talk.

"Sloane looks perfect," Gia Accardi says, flopping down on the couch beside her husband. "When I saw you'd requested a recheck of her background, I personally went through her file." Gia works in intelligence gathering and analysis for *La Cosa Nostra*, and she's one smart lady. I wasn't aware she'd looked at Sloane's file, but it reassures me she did.

Joshua and Gia live in the house next door to Caleb and Elisa on the grounds of the vast estate they co-own in Connecticut. The Accardi twins have been my best friends since we were kids. They were more like my brothers than my actual brother growing up. That they ended up married to best friends and continue to do everything together is no surprise to anyone who knows them. Caleb and Joshua are tight, and no one comes between them.

The twins bought this huge plot of land the year before their kids arrived. It's not too far from where their parents live, which is handy when they need a babysitter. When I told them I was house hunting in the area, they didn't hesitate to offer me the opportunity to build on their grounds, and I jumped at it.

They have a secure setup, and it'll be good for Elio to grow up with friends. My plan is to permanently relocate here when our house is built. Right now, my penthouse in the city is home, but I want Elio to have a yard to run around in. While we have Central Park at our doorstep in Manhattan, it's not exactly safe. None of us has forgotten the Sinaloa Cartel or their threat to come after us. All because of a loose cannon in Miami who is now dead.

Dominic Ferraro and his son Cesco created this war with the cartel, leaving behind a mess we are trying to clear up. The only reason the cartel hasn't come at us yet is because the US government wants their heads on spikes for causing so many fentanyl deaths in Florida a few years ago. All the cartel leaders have had to lie low while the FBI and Homeland Security search for them. They know the instant they set foot on US soil, they'll be arrested.

So, we have a reprieve, but it won't last long, and we all need to be vigilant. Me more than most because my brother Cruz set everything in motion with the cartel before he died, and I'm guessing the DiPietro name is as heinous to the cartel as it is to Rafaelo Da Rosa. Which is why I'd prefer my son grows up safely guarded here in Glencoe. I already have him enrolled at the local private school, and he'll attend pre-K here too.

"Oh, she's perfect, all right," Caleb says, wearing his signature smirk. "At least Cristian thinks so."

"Shut up." I level him with a warning look as I raise my bottle to my lips. I shouldn't have said anything to Caleb about my concerns or how gorgeous Sloane is.

"What don't I know?" Elisa's gaze dances between me and her husband.

Caleb slides his wife into his side, wrapping his arm around her shoulders. "Cristian didn't want to hire her because he's afraid he won't be able to keep his hands to himself. Apparently, she's stunning and far too tempting."

I narrow my eyes at my best friend. So much for keeping my confidence.

"Is that why you requested a recheck? Were you hoping to find something she lied about in her application to justify not offering her the position?" Joshua asks, swirling whiskey in his glass.

"Not really. It was more she seemed too good to be true," I say. She has the perfect credentials, and though she doesn't have a ton of experience, Elio loved her when she came by to meet him yesterday, and that's what matters the most.

"Is that the truth, or is it the fact Isa is dead set against her?" Gia inquires.

"How do you know that?" I didn't mention the huge argument Isa and I got into after Sloane left my office on Wednesday to anyone.

"I'm a good judge of character. I can read that witch like a book."

Gia has not held back on her opinions of Isa. She has visited here with me a few times, and Isa and Gia butted heads right from the start. If I didn't know Gia, I might think it's connected to Bettina—Isa's older sister, who was Elio's mom and Joshua's ex. But I do know Gia, and she's not the spiteful type. She simply doesn't like or trust Isa.

"Well, you're right. Isa doesn't like her at all for the job, but she doesn't get to make the decision. If I weren't short on options and time, I would find someone else, but there is no one. Sloane ticks all the boxes. I can't not hire a nanny just 'cause I think she's hot and I'm worried I'll be tempted to make a move on her." I had actually offered a different woman the position, but she turned me down because she'd accepted another nanny job.

"There's no law that says you can't." Gia tucks her knees up onto the couch and snuggles in closer to Joshua.

Sometimes, it's difficult to be around my friends and not feel envious. I'm happy they're happy, but being married and having kids is something I've wanted for a long time, and it doesn't appear to be in the cards anymore. Not that I'd change the decision I made to raise my nephew as my own. I have no regrets. I'm just lonely, and I wish I could've found someone to share our lives. But it's not meant to be, and most of the time, I've made my peace with that. It's only odd moments, here and there, that are hard.

"Joshua was my boss, and that didn't stop him," Gia adds with a saucy wink.

"You had my twin breaking all kinds of rules for you, Gigi," Caleb teases.

"There are some rules worth breaking," Joshua agrees, smiling. At one time, we all would have keeled over to hear our strait-laced friend say something like that, but Joshua is more like his old self these days. Gia's love has cracked through the hard shell he had erected, and she's softened all his rough edges. I love that for my friend.

"Love you." Gia brushes her nose against Joshua's before lightly kissing him.

Joshua holds her tight. "Love you too."

"Barf." Caleb fake gags, but he's ridiculous. He's as loved up as his twin and equally into the PDAs.

Joshua flips his brother the finger, and I knock back more of my beer.

"When do we get to meet Sloane?" Elisa asks.

"We can put her through her paces," Gia offers. "Make sure she's as good as she seems to be."

"I don't want the girl scared off, and it'd be nice if you all got along." When we move in here, we'll all be spending lots of time together, so it'd make it easier if everyone gelled.

"When does she start?" Joshua asks.

"A week from Monday. Isa is going to train her for her last couple weeks."

"I already feel bad for Sloane," Gia says. "I can't manage one hour in Isa's company without wanting to claw her eyes out. I still stand by what I said. She wants you, Cristian. She wants you bad."

"She isn't interested in me like that," I protest, like I have every time Gia has mentioned this. "And she knows I have no interest in her like that either."

"She's getting married soon, Gigi," Elisa says. "If she wanted Cristian, she'd have made a play for him already."

Four pairs of eyes land on my face. "Fuck off," I say, but there's no heat behind the words. "I told you she hasn't made a move on me, and it wasn't a lie. No offense, Gia, but you're wrong on this occasion."

"I'm happy to be in this instance, but seriously, Cristian, if anything should develop between you and Sloane, it wouldn't be a bad thing as long as it doesn't interfere with her care of Elio. Don't close yourself off to it. Sometimes love finds us when we're least expecting it."

"She's Elio's nanny. I wouldn't risk messing that up, which is why she will remain firmly an employee and nothing else."

"This is your room," I say, depositing Sloane's suitcase on the hardwood floor in the large guest bedroom. My new nanny didn't bring much stuff, which I hope isn't a sign she doesn't see this as a long-term move. I made it very clear I wanted someone who would be with Elio for the long haul. While I can't stop Sloane, or anyone, from resigning and leaving, I hope I conveyed how much of a disappointment that'd be. I don't want Elio having a succession of nannies. He needs security and permanency, not a revolving door of different women taking care of him. "You have a walk-in closet and an en suite bathroom," I explain, gesturing around the room.

"It's a beautiful room, thank you."

Her soft, dulcet tone stirs longing inside me, but I stamp it down, reminding myself of the pep talk I gave myself this morning.

Sloane is Elio's nanny. Period.

"I'll let you get settled. Dinner will be at six."

"Sounds great. Thanks, sir."

My dick jerks, loving that more than it should. "It's Cristian, Sloane. Please just call me Cristian."

"Okay, Cristian." Her lips twitch.

My dick jerks again—fuck my life. How can every word out of her mouth sound so seductive?

"I'll see you at six." I back out of the room and close the door, leaning against the wall for a second to catch my breath.

"Cristian?" Isa stares suspiciously at me from the end of the hallway.

"Yes." I pull myself together and walk toward her.

"Is everything all right?"

"Yes. Why wouldn't it be?"

She crosses her arms. "It's okay to admit you made a mistake. I can talk to Carmine and—"

"Stop." I rub my aching temples. "I'm sick of having this argument with you. The decision has been made. Sloane is here, and you will make her welcome for Elio's sake."

Her lips pull into a thin line. "I see the way you look at her, you know."

"Isa." My tone carries a warning. "Enough." I walk past her, counting to ten in my head.

"Just be careful, and remember you hired her to be Elio's nanny, not your plaything."

I whirl around and glare at her. She's pushed me too far this time. "You are way out of line, and I think it's time you were going."

Hurt splays across her face. "I know when I'm not wanted." Removing her apron, she shoves it into my hands. "Your dinner is keeping warm in the oven, and Elio is drawing in the living room."

"Thank you."

"I'll be here in the morning unless you've changed your mind about me training her?"

I run a hand through my hair. "I would still like you to show Sloane the ropes, and it would be better for Elio if there's a transition from you to her, but let's just do it for the next couple days, yeah? I'm sure you could use the extra time to prepare for your wedding. You'll be paid in full, of course." I don't want Isa around Sloane any longer than necessary because I can't be sure she won't run her off.

I think Isa is jealous because Sloane is drop-dead gorgeous. But I've been pondering if maybe Gia is right, even if it doesn't seem to make sense, because Isa hasn't ever hit on me, and she's marrying Carmine by choice. I've concluded she's one of those women who is naturally competitive with other women. I dated a girl like that once, but the relationship didn't last long. I ditched her fast because I can't stand catty women.

"Fine." Isa glares at me. "I'll just say goodbye to Elio, and then I'll be out of your hair."

Why did I say I wanted a woman again? Honestly, at times like this, I'm glad I'm single.

Chapter Four
Sloane

"This is delicious," I admit after tasting the first mouthful of my chicken pasta dish. Isotta may be a nasty bitch, but she's a fantastic cook.

"It's yummy," Elio agrees from his seat across the table beside his dad.

He's a gorgeous little kid and a future heartbreaker with those big green eyes, cute dimples, smooth olive complexion, and thick, dark hair. I don't know if Isotta resembles her dead sister or not, but I don't see much of his mother in the little boy. He's so much like Cristian, and he clearly takes after the paternal side of the family. I don't know what happened to his bio parents, and though I'm curious, there's no way I'm asking.

"Why did Auntie Isa leave? She always has dinner with us." Elio looks expectantly at Cristian.

"She is having dinner with Carmine from now on, and Sloane will be having dinner with us."

Elio's nose scrunches up. "Carmine's a poop."

My lips fight a smile.

"That's not very nice," Cristian says, ruffling his son's hair. "Your auntie is marrying him soon, and he'll be your uncle."

"I don't need other uncles. I have lots and lots of them." His arms expand, and I smile.

"Which uncle is the most fun?" I ask in between bites of the scrumptious dinner.

"Uncle Caleb!" he shrieks. "He flies me like I'm Superman, and he plays guns and wrestling with me, and he's awesome."

"Caleb is one of my best friends," Cristian explains. "He's basically a big kid, but Elio loves him."

Elio pops a piece of chopped-up chicken into his mouth. "I love Uncle Zumo too," he says over his food. "He's funny."

"Don't talk with your mouth full. Remember." Cristian rubs some tomato sauce from his son's cheek. "It's rude, and you could choke. Chew first. Talk after."

"Okay, Daddy," he says while still chewing his food.

I can't help grinning. He's such a little cutie. "Another friend or family?" I ask, meeting Cristian's attentive gaze.

He sets his silverware down on his empty plate. "Friend. My sister Sabina is my only other sibling. She lives in North Carolina with her husband, but we rarely see them."

"That's a shame." I finish my dinner and reach for my glass of water.

"Yeah. My friends are more like my family."

"I look forward to meeting them." His lips twitch, and I almost choke on my water. "I didn't mean for that to sound...I, um, just meant—"

"It's okay, Sloane. You *will* meet them in due course. I have a few things to update you on after Elio is in bed."

"What things?" Elio pipes up. His mouth and chin are covered in sauce, and I swear there's more dinner on the table than on his plate or in his belly.

"Grown-up things, nosey." Cristian boops his son on the nose.

"I'm getting bigger." Elio puffs out his chest. "I'm almost a grown-up."

Cristian chuckles. "Don't be in such a rush to grow up, son. Trust me when I say things are much easier when you're a kid."

"For sure," I readily agree, standing with my plate and silverware in hand.

"You're really tall," Elio says, peering up at me.

"I am." I lift Cristian's plate. "I was one of the tallest girls in my high school, and I got to play on the basketball team."

"I love basketball!" Elio almost bursts with excitement. "Will you play with me?" His eyes are brimming with happiness.

"Sure will."

"Yay!" He bounces around in his seat. "Can we go tomorrow, please, Daddy?"

"We can go to one of the courts tomorrow evening," Cristian says, smiling at his son before he directs his attention to me. "Elio attends a weekly youth basketball clinic, and I try to take him to one of the courts in Central Park or the local indoor court, if it's cold, at least once a week, so he can practice." He stands. "Let me get those." Before I can argue, he takes the stacked plates from my hands.

"It's gonna be so much fun," Elio proclaims before popping another piece of chicken into his mouth. I sit down beside him while Cristian is in the kitchen, and Elio babbles away, in between eating, filling me in on all the things he likes to do.

"All done, bud?" Cristian says a few minutes later, materializing at the table. He's wiping his wet hands on a towel.

Elio nods, patting his stomach. "My tummy is full."

Removing a wipe from the box in the center of the table, I take his little hands in mine as Cristian leans down to pluck up his son's mostly empty plate. "I'm just gonna clean you up because someone got tomato sauce everywhere," I tease.

"'Kay." He's fidgety in his chair as I methodically wipe his face and hands, removing all traces of his dinner from his skin. His clothes are a different story.

"Your hands are so soft." He runs his finger over the back of my hand.

"So are yours." I smile at him.

"You're really pretty," he says. "Like a princess." He looks over my shoulder. "Isn't she, Daddy?"

"Very pretty."

Cristian's deep tone does funny things to my insides, and my cheeks warm. "You will have all the girls swooning someday, Elio."

"Girls are gross," he says, and Cristian chuckles. "Except my aunties and you."

"High praise indeed," Cristian says with amusement underscoring his tone.

"Can Sloane give me my bath?"

"Of course."

"Yay!" He jumps off his seat, grabs my hand, and pulls me up from my chair. "Come on, Slowpoke Sloane."

I burst out laughing as his small, soft hand clamps around mine. This child is a hoot.

"Be gentle, Elio, and be nice." Cristian drills him with a warning look.

"I'm always gentle and nice, Daddy." He waggles his brows.

"Lead the way, my little prince," I say, almost tripping over my feet as my energetic charge moves full steam ahead.

Before dinner, after I'd unpacked my things, Cristian and Elio gave me a tour of my new home. I've never lived anywhere this fancy or had such a large bedroom to myself. If I wasn't shitting myself over the things I'm going to have to do, I'd probably enjoy living here and looking after Elio.

We have to pass through the kitchen to get to the other side of the large penthouse, where the bedrooms and bathrooms are, and as we walk by, I notice Cristian has fully cleaned up, which is a bit of a surprise. I watch him walk over to the sink with Elio's plate, silverware, and our glasses. "I'll do those when Elio is in bed," I call out. While Cristian explained he has a housekeeper who comes in a couple of times a week, it's part of my job to clean up after activities and cook meals on days she's not here.

"I've got it," he says, depositing the dishes in the sink and walking after us.

Elio races into his bedroom to get undressed, and I help him while Cristian starts the bath.

"These are my favorite pajamas." Elio thrusts the blue, black, and green top and pants at me.

"Cool." They have rockets, planets, the moon, clouds, and the words "Blast off to bed" on them.

"I'm gonna be an asonaut when I grow up," he says, taking my hand.

"An astronaut?" I say as I fold his pajamas and place them on the end of his bed.

"That's what I said." He looks at me like duh, and my lips curve at the corners. "I'm gonna fly into space and get moonrock to bring home to my daddy and Auntie Isa," he explains as we walk from his bedroom to the large family bathroom.

"Wow, they're lucky."

"I'll get some for you too," he adds when we enter the bathroom, and my heart melts. He's such an outgoing little boy and so affectionate. I'm already completely enamored with him.

The tub is half full, and Cristian is pouring some bubble bath into the water.

"That is very kind, and I'd love some."

"I'll make you a deal," he says, and Cristian chuckles. "You play basketball with me, and I'll get you moonrock."

"You strike a hard bargain, buster," I say over a grin as Cristian lifts his son into the tub. "But you got yourself a deal." I lift my hand and we high-five.

"Where's Quack-Quack?" Elio asks, running his hands through the water.

"Here he is." Cristian hands him a large yellow rubber duck. "He won't take a bath without it," he whispers to me. His warm breath fans across the side of my cheek, heating my skin, and his whispered words in my ear send little tremors racing through my body.

"Noted," I say, pleased my voice comes out even.

"He has a touch of eczema," Cristian adds, handing me a large container. "That is shampoo and a body wash for sensitive skin, and it's the only one I've found that doesn't aggravate him."

"I'll be sure to only use this."

Cristian sits on the closed toilet seat, staying close by but not interfering as I bathe his son. After Elio is clean, he lifts him out, bundling him in a large fluffy white towel. "Daddy?" Elio says, stifling a yawn. "Can Sloane read me my story tonight?"

"If that's what you want."

Elio lifts his tiny palm to his dad's cheek. "You won't be sad?"

"Of course not, silly." He peppers Elio's face with kisses and Elio squeals, wriggling in his dad's lap. "I usually read him his bedtime story," Cristian explains, looking over at me. "But I'm happy to hand over the reins tonight if you don't mind."

"If you don't, I don't."

His eyes probe mine, and a spark ignites the space between

us. "I'll just get him settled," he says, standing. "And then I'll leave you to it."

I trail Cristian into Elio's bedroom, watching as he dries his son and helps him into his pajamas. Cristian tucks him in and leans down to kiss his brow.

"Love you, Daddy." Elio wraps his arm around Cristian's neck. "To the moon and back."

"Me too, buddy." Cristian holds his son close, and my heart is equally swelling and cracking.

The relationship they have is beautiful, and I've only caught a glimpse of it. What the hell has Cristian done that the cartel wants to kill him, and how am I going to go through with this knowing I'll be depriving a kid of his father for the second time in his short life?

Chapter Five
Cristian

"He's fast asleep," Sloane confirms when she appears in the living room. "He could barely keep his eyes open while I was reading to him."

I mute the TV and swivel on the couch so I'm looking at her. "It never takes him long to fall asleep," I explain. "As soon as his head hits the pillow at night, he conks. I never get to read him more than a page or two of his book. We've been reading *The Cosmic Diary of a Future Space Explorer* for months, and we're still only halfway through it."

"It's an interesting book, and he was fascinated, smiling in between yawns." Sloane hovers in the doorway, running a hand through her golden-blonde hair.

"He's determined to be an astronaut when he grows up."

"He mentioned that." She smiles. "He's an amazing kid, sir. Uh, Cristian."

"He's definitely taken a liking to you." I lift one shoulder. "Come sit. We have some things to discuss."

I turn around, purposely not watching her walk across the room toward the couch. She's only wearing leggings under an oversized sweater with slides on her feet, but she still looks utterly gorgeous. Living with her will really be a test of my self-control. I can't remember the last time I was this strongly attracted to a woman. I'm already constantly reminding myself she's Elio's nanny and way too young for me.

Sloane sinks onto the couch a few feet away from me, smiling shyly. Tucking her hands between her knees, she gives me her undivided attention. There isn't a scrap of makeup on her face, and she's absolutely flawless. Almost too perfect to be real.

I clear my throat and cross my leg over my knee as I settle back into the couch. "While we have covered most things already, there are a few key items we need to talk about. You've signed an NDA, but it's worth repeating that anything you are privy to during the course of your work for me is highly confidential and must never be discussed with anyone, ever, at any time."

"I understand. My previous employer was a diplomat, and he had similar concerns. I would never breach confidentiality, and I understand the importance of signing an NDA. Contrary to what a lot of people assume, I know it's a legally binding document and there are significant consequences if I break it. You don't have to worry, Cristian." Her big blue eyes remain fixed on mine as she speaks. I'd like to trust her fully, but that trust must be earned. For now, I need to be circumspect in how I word things.

"The business I run is a lucrative business that's been in the DiPietro family for generations. Like all successful families, we have our fair share of competitors, enemies, and people who would like to take us down. Security is of the utmost concern, especially when it comes to my son. Two armed bodyguards will shadow you and Elio at all times, as I previously mentioned, but I'd also like to request you take a security detail with you anytime you go out during your free time. You could be targeted because of your association with me."

Sloane nibbles on her lip, looking deep in thought.

"I can't force you to have a personal bodyguard," I add, "but it's in your best interests. To keep you safe."

"Am I in danger?" Her eyes widen.

"Not directly, but I won't lie and say you aren't in danger when it's possible you could be. But my men will keep you safe, so you shouldn't worry. My son is my world, and you'll be way safer as his nanny than any ordinary person walking the streets of New York."

"I don't mind taking a bodyguard with me during my downtime. If it helps to put your mind at ease, then go for it." She shrugs as if it's no biggie. I wonder if she has heard anything on the street. There is little on the internet these days about any of our *mafioso* ties, thanks to Caltimore Holdings' IT efforts.

Caltimore Holdings is the organization headed up by Bennett Mazzone. Mazzone was the first president in the newly reformed Commission, and he has almost single-handedly transformed *La Cosa Nostra*. Ben is a shrewd player, and he recognized years ago that investing in technology was the way forward. The tech we have at our disposal these days is next level, and it's saved our asses more times than I can count. Part of the work the IT division does, on behalf of all mafia in the US, is removing all mention of our illegal activities from the internet. So, if Sloane has learned something, it's come from word of mouth. That's harder to control, but most people are fearful of crossing us and usually keep their mouths shut.

"Okay, good. I'll introduce you to the three men tomorrow." I swivel on the couch, angling my body in her direction. "You should know there are cameras in the penthouse." Her brows climb to her hairline. "Don't worry, there are none in the bedrooms or bathrooms, but all the main living spaces have audio and visual cameras."

I had most of them installed just before the adoption went through, and Elio moved in with me. I didn't trust any of the Da Rosas, and I wanted to watch Isa with Elio to ensure he wasn't being harmed in any way. I also wanted the added security in case anyone should breach the sanctity of our home. Two birds, one stone.

Her eyes instantly lift to the ceiling and the tops of the walls. "You won't find them. They're the latest technology and almost invisible to the naked eye."

"That's kind of creepy, but I get it, and I'm sure I'll adjust."

"I take security very seriously. No one gets past the front desk downstairs without prior approval, and all visitors must sign in and produce identification. Armed guards man the reception area and building twenty-four-seven. You need a code to get into the elevator, and the code is changed weekly. Same with the code to the penthouse alarm. The penthouse has a comprehensive security system with an impenetrable panic room. I'll show you where it is and how to access it tomorrow."

"It sounds like I'm definitely in danger." Her voice pitches a little higher, and she knots her hands on her lap.

"It's precautionary. Surely, your previous boss had security measures in place?"

"He did, but it was nothing like this."

"You have nothing to be scared about. Like I said, you're safer working for me than anyone else, and I'll keep you well protected." I alluded to some of this during the interview and hiring process, but I hadn't spelled it out because I couldn't. Not until she'd signed on the dotted line and her confidentiality was assured.

Guilt prods at me because she currently looks like a deer trapped in headlights. She's only twenty-one, and it's a lot to take in, especially when she doesn't know the half of it yet. Maybe I should've said nothing, but I don't want her blind to the dangers either. "I'm mentioning this so you aren't blind-sided. You need to be very aware of your surroundings. Trust your instincts. If you think anything is off, tell your bodyguards immediately. Give me your cell, and I'll plug my numbers into it." I hold out my hand for her phone. "My secretary is aware you have unfettered access to me, no matter what. Call me anytime if you need me. Nothing is more important than Elio's safety, and that provision now extends to you."

Red spots appear on her cheeks. "I dropped my cell this morning, and I haven't had the time to replace it."

My hand lowers to my thigh. "I'll organize a phone for you. Do you need anything else?"

"Do I have access to a tablet or a laptop while I'm here? It would be good to research excursions for Elio, and I'd like to sign up on a few arts and crafts apps to get ideas for things we can do together."

"I'll organize a device for you. Anything else?"

She shakes her head, sending waves of blonde hair cascading over her shoulders. "I can't think of anything. Thanks, Cristian."

"Give Mrs. Peake a list of foods you like and any toiletries you need. She'll include it with the weekly grocery order. Isa has a list of meals she cooks on set days, and my housekeeper knows what to order, but if you want to change anything, just inform her in advance."

Sloane slips off her slides and tucks her legs up onto the couch. "I don't want to change anything at first. Routine and familiarity are important during the transition period, but gradually, I might like to introduce a few different things, if that'd be okay?"

"Of course. Nothing is set in stone, and Elio is adaptable."

Her nose scrunches. "I don't want to tread on Isotta's toes. I'm guessing she'll still be around a lot?"

"Isa has been amazing with Elio, and she was a lifesaver for me when I first adopted him, but she's no longer Elio's nanny. You are."

"She's still his aunt."

"Yes, but as his aunt, she doesn't get to dictate how he's brought up. That is my job as his father. I don't want you to feel like you can't change things. Do whatever is in Elio's best interests, and don't worry about Isa. She'll be a newlywed soon, and she'll be busy with her own family. She takes Elio to spend time with his cousins on Saturdays, and that will continue, but I doubt we'll see her more often than that."

"Okay." She smiles, but it seems a little uncertain.

Internally, I sigh. It's not surprising Sloane has picked up on the animosity radiating from Isa because she's as subtle as a tornado. Elio loves Isa, and I don't want to deprive him of his aunt, but new boundaries will need to be established. I won't have Isa undermining Sloane or sticking her nose in where it's not wanted. The next few weeks should be fun.

"Talk to me if you encounter any issues, and I'll smooth it over." I slide my arm around the back of the couch.

"I will." Untucking her feet, she slips them back into her slides. "Was there anything else?"

"Just one more thing. We'll be moving out of the city in due course. I'm building a house in a small, quiet town a few hours away. The plan is to move there before Elio starts pre-K in September. You'll have a self-contained apartment within the house, and I'll supply you with a car. It's a secure property close to a couple of my friends. You'll meet them in due course. They have kids a little younger than Elio, and it'll be good for him to grow up with playmates on his doorstep and his own yard to run around in. I trust this won't be an issue?"

Again, I hadn't mentioned this during the hiring process because I'm keeping this intel on the down-low for good reason. From her file, I know she doesn't have any living relatives, but I don't know if there is someone she'll miss in the city.

"That won't be an issue. It sounds nice and perfect for Elio."

"You'll have your weekends free, of course, and should you wish to come back to the city to see friends or your boyfriend, you can stay here."

She opens her mouth but promptly snaps it shut again. Her tongue darts out, wetting her lips, before she clears her throat. "There, ugh, isn't anyone serious, but I might want to return to the city some weekends."

An uncomfortable feeling churns in the pit of my stomach at her insinuation. It shouldn't matter if there *is* someone in her life, so why do I suddenly feel like some other kid has stolen my lunch money?

"Do you..." She chews on one corner of her mouth as her words trail off. "Is there a girlfriend I should expect to meet?"

"Not currently."

"Oh, okay." Her cheeks pinken before she averts her gaze, glancing at the floor.

A tense undercurrent charges the space between us.

"Do you have any other questions for me?" I ask, attempting to put things back on a professional footing.

"Not at this time." She smothers a yawn as she stands. "If it's okay with you, I'm going to grab a shower and an early night."

"Of course. Your nights are your own after Elio is asleep unless I'm out late." I try to get home for dinner every night, but occasionally, meetings run over, and there are some nights I meet friends or head to Club H to fuck a random stranger. It's in her contract that she's required to babysit on nights when I'm not home. I never abused it with Isa, and I won't abuse it with her either.

"'Kay. Goodnight then, sir. I mean Cristian." Her blue eyes spear mine, and I'm glad she's focused on my face and not on the growing bulge in my pants. I swear, every time she calls me *sir*, it stirs my dick to life.

"Goodnight, Sloane. Sleep well."

Chapter Six
Sloane

I should have slept like a princess in this uber-comfortable bed in this beautiful bedroom fit for royalty, but of course, I was awake half the night tossing and turning as my brain refused to switch off and give me a minute's peace. The strain involved in wearing a façade is more stressful than I thought. I'm having to think on my feet, and it feels like I'm a double agent, which I suppose I am. Guilt is a permanent weight on my shoulders, and I suspect that's only going to get worse.

When my alarm goes off, I feel like crying, but I peel the comforter back and swing my legs out the side of the bed. Can't be late on my first official day as Elio's nanny. My little charge is an early riser, and I predict a lot of early nights in my future. Except heading to bed before nine p.m. is not exactly conducive to seducing my boss. I probably should've stayed up with Cristian last night. Maybe watched some TV and opened conversation, but I was exhausted, and I wanted to retreat and mull over everything I learned.

Pablo won't be pleased I have a full-time security detail,

but if it means Diego and Alvaro can't easily get to me, then it's a win. I've no doubt they'll be following me everywhere I go, like I've no doubt they're somewhere close by now, staking out the building, but them not having access to me is a relief.

When Cristian asked me about a boyfriend, it was on the tip of my tongue to say no. Pablo wants me to make it clear I'm single so there are no obstacles in my boss's path if he makes a move. But Pablo has also demanded I keep his goons updated weekly, and my permanent shadow may not be a full deterrent. Should Diego or Alvaro find a way to ambush me, I can always claim they are someone I'm casually dating.

I wish there was a way of eradicating all contact with Pablo, but I know that's an impossibility. Just as the thought lands in my mind, my cell vibrates with a new message. Considering this is a cartel phone and the only people who know the number are Pablo and his henchmen, I can guess who the message is from and what it contains. I squeeze my eyes shut for a few seconds before I summon the courage to open it. It's from the Sinaloa boss, as I thought. A video message, of course. Because nothing drills the point home harder than watching him abuse my mother on film.

Mom wears the same dazed, drugged-up expression on her face that always kills me. She's tied to the bed, naked, her skinny frame littered with scars, some older, some fresh. The asshole hammers between her thighs while glancing back to whomever is filming the sick scene. "A reminder, my little American Barbie." He drives into her with brutality, and nausea swims up my throat. "Every time you fail me, you fail your mother." The man holding the camera moves forward. One hand reaches out and gropes Mom's breast.

Bile coats my tongue, and anger replaces the blood flowing through my veins. I want to hack his hand from his arm so he can't ever touch her again. I want to kill them all—every male in that compound who has touched her, hurt her.

"I have a long list of associates waiting for their turn with my American whore," Pablo pants, dragging me away from my murderous inner monologue. I'm forced to look at his gross, sweaty face as he pumps into my mother. She's barely coherent underneath him, and I'm glad she's zoned out. How much more of this can she take? Acid churns in my gut as I rub my stomach while my heart splinters behind my rib cage. "I want intel before Sunday. Don't disappoint me, Sloane. You know what'll happen if you do."

The video cuts out, and I delete it as I've been instructed. I'm guessing they have access and can tell if I disobey. I'm terrified to do anything in case they find out and Mom ends up paying the price. My instructions were to keep the phone with me always because it has a location tracker installed, but I'm to keep it permanently on silent and ensure no one knows I have it, especially my new boss.

I'm sick to my stomach as I slowly climb to my feet, my limbs so heavy I feel ancient.

Resting my head against the tile wall in the shower, I let the warm water cascade over my head and down my back while I contemplate how the hell I'm going to get intel that fast. Cristian has cameras all over this penthouse, which means I can't do any fucking snooping. I can't even detect the cameras to see if I could dismantle them, but who am I kidding? I'm a drama major, not a tech major. I have no clue how to deactivate and reactivate a camera without getting caught.

Silent tears mix with the water as it rolls down my face. This already seems like an impossible task. Cristian DiPietro is like the Jason Fucking Bourne of the mafia, and I am no match for his experience or his skill.

Slumping to the floor, I pull my knees into my chest and

release the pent-up emotion that's been bottled up for months. Sobs wrack my skinny frame, and I stuff my fist in my mouth to stifle them. The last thing I need is my boss barging in here wondering what's wrong.

I cry for a little while longer before I shove my pain back inside and get a grip. I'm resourceful by nature, and I've survived this far against all odds. I'm not going to adopt a defeatist attitude before I've even tried. This might seem impossible, but I'll find a way. I've got to because my mother is depending on me, and I can't let her down.

"These are for you," Cristian says, entering the kitchen as I'm cleaning up after breakfast. Isa was already here when I came out of my room, and she wasted no time laying down the law. As soon as Cristian left the table, she demanded I tidy up while she took Elio to clean up and get dressed. My boss sets a brand-new cell phone and tablet on the island unit.

"Wow, that was quick." I try not to ogle him, but it's hard because he looks sexy as sin in a black shirt and black pants. He's not wearing a tie, and the top few buttons are open, show-casing a hint of tanned, inked skin.

"My team is very efficient." He points to the number on the outside of the cell phone box. "I've added your number and sent you a text with all my contact details. I included the Wi-Fi logins too."

"Thank you."

"I'm working from home today," he explains, brushing past me on his way to the scary-looking coffee machine that seems like it belongs in a top-notch coffee shop.

My nose twitches as his cologne wafts around me. It smells expensive and all man, but I'm not surprised. Cristian is an alpha male to his core, from his good looks to his custom-fit clothing and the expensive watch on his wrist I'm betting cost a small fortune. Seducing a man like him will not be easy, and I've got to up my A-game.

"But I've got a few back-to-back calls, so I'll be busy until lunch. Isa will show you the ropes this morning."

More like tie one around my neck if she got the chance. "She's been great," I lie as he fixes his coffee like a seasoned barista. "I'll be fine, and we'll take good care of your son. Don't worry about anything, sir." I deliberately use the endearment because I've seen how he reacts to it. It's subtle, but his eyes always flare with heat for a split second whenever I say it. I lick my lips, and his eyes lower to the movement. "Have a great day, and we'll see you later."

His gaze remains on my mouth for a beat longer before he lifts his eyes to meet mine. Tension bleeds into the air, but it's not the negative kind. The same crackling energy that sparked between us last night in the living room flexes and writhes in the gap separating our bodies, and I hope I'm not the only one feeling it.

"Disturb me if you need to," he says in a gruff tone before taking his delectable self and his aromatic coffee out of the room.

I sag against the counter, smoothing a hand over my racing heart. I'm grateful I don't have to seduce some overweight, ugly-ass, middle-aged man, but being so attracted to Cristian presents different problems. I can't afford to like him, want him, or care for him because that'll complicate an already compli-cated situation.

"If you took this job to seduce your boss, you might as well quit now," Isa says in her aggravating nasally tone.

I wonder how long she was listening and watching. "I don't know what you're talking about," I calmly reply, holding my head high. "I took this job because Elio is an adorable kid, and the deal was sweet. Like you said, I need more experience, and this is a dream job."

Folding her arms across her chest, she scoffs. "I'm not buying it."

"I don't know what you want me to say, Isa. I have no ulterior motives." I look her straight in the eye as I lie to her face.

"It's Isotta to you," she snaps, putting herself all up in my face. "Only my family and friends call me Isa, and you're neither."

I grind my teeth to the molars before plastering a fake smile on my face. "I meant no offense, Isotta, ma'am. Apologies."

Bitch.

Her mouth pulls into a hard line as her gaze sidles to the packages on the counter. "What is this?" She leans down, examining the items with a building scowl.

"Cristian organized a cell phone and tablet for me."

She rakes her furious gaze over me. "So, this is your game, huh? Act like the diplomat didn't pay you handsomely. Play the poor, needy nanny part to perfection and get Mr. DiPietro to buy you things. You're nothing but a—"

"Where is Elio?" I ask, frowning as I look behind her and don't see my little prince.

"He's in the playroom drawing." She waggles her finger in my face. "If you memorized his schedule, you'd know it's art time this morning, and don't try to distract me from—"

"I memorized it." I cut across her again. "I'm just surprised he's been left alone in there. He should be supervised at all times." I examined the storage and supply cupboards last night, and there are scissors, glitter, glue guns, Play-Doh, and other small craft items a little kid could choke on or hurt themselves with.

I move on autopilot, striding around her with purpose.

"He's sitting in a chair drawing," she hisses, following hot on my heels. "He can't come to any harm."

I stalk down the hallway, past Cristian's sealed office door, the home gym, and the old-school library, to the large playroom with the wide window overlooking CP in the near distance. Elio is muttering to himself as he sits at a double-sided desk in the middle of the space, drawing a picture with a multitude of colored pencils spread out around him.

I breathe a sigh of relief when I spot the locked cupboard doors. It's possible I overreacted, but taking care of Elio is my responsibility now. I don't like Isa, and I don't know her. Would she resort to putting the child in danger to get me fired? Because I'm beginning to think that's her goal.

Chapter Seven
Cristian

A rap on my door claims my attention, and I tear my eyes from the email I'm in the middle of writing to look over my shoulder.

"Cris." Isa pokes her head into the room. "I brought you some lunch." Without waiting for an invitation, she strides into my home office carrying a plate and a mug. I lock my screen and swivel in my chair. "I'll eat with all of you."

"We've already eaten." She sets the plate and mug down on my desk. "I told Sloane to tell you. Didn't she say anything?"

"No one said anything, but it's fine." I gesture toward my screen as she props her butt against the side of my desk and stretches her legs out in front of her. "I have a lot on my plate today anyway, and I want to finish early so I can take Elio to the courts." I lift the sandwich from the plate.

"Don't expect much," she says, scrunching her nose and glaring at the sandwich as if it's personally offended her. "How anyone can mess up a sandwich is beyond me, and I wouldn't hold out much hope for the coffee either. She's clueless."

I silently count to ten. "I hired Sloane to be a nanny, not a chef or a barista." I examine the sandwich in my hand. "Looks good to me." I take a huge bite out of the pastrami salad sandwich, finding no fault with it.

"I've probably spoiled you with my superior cooking skills. I guess you'll have to lower your standards now."

Fucking hell. "It's not a competition, Isa." It takes effort to soften my tone and keep my words kind when I'm tempted to throttle her. "Elio loves you. He'll still love you even when you are no longer his nanny. You don't need to worry about being ousted from his life."

"I'm not." She moves in closer and leans down. "I'm worried about *you*. That girl has ulterior motives, Cris, and you're already playing right into her hands."

I really hate when she calls me that. "If you've got something to say, just say it," I demand in a clipped tone, struggling to hold onto my legendary patience.

"She's not even on the job twenty-four hours, and you're buying her things!"

"Careful, Isa. You're beginning to sound like a jealous girlfriend."

"She's taking advantage of you, and you can't even see it!"

I stand, beyond incensed. "I provided her with the tools she needed to perform her job. You are reading far too much into this, and you are way out of line. I know you don't like her. You've made that blatantly clear, but you don't get a say in how I run my life or the decisions I make for *my son*."

"What twenty-one-year-old doesn't own a cell, a tablet, or a laptop? You can't tell me she doesn't have the money. She was well paid by the diplomat, and she's single with no financial commitments. Like I said, she's playing you, and you need to open your goddamned eyes, Cristian!" She's getting all worked up for fucking nothing, and I'm at my wit's end with her. I don't know why she is acting like this.

"Not that it's any of your business, but the financial check I ran confirms the girl is broke." Isa wasn't privy to the financial reports of any of the candidates, as it had no bearing on their suitability for the role. I like to be thorough, and I had the full gamut of checks performed, only sharing the pertinent information with my former nanny.

"And that's not suspicious." She snorts, and it's very unattractive. I'm seeing a side to Isa I really don't like.

"Connect the dots, Isotta! Her mother died of cancer seven months ago. She was her only family. The bank foreclosed on her family home, and she was left with a mountain of other debt. It's obvious where her money was and is going." Sloane has requested her salary be paid into two bank accounts. A small amount is going into her personal bank account, with the bulk going into an account that debtors are paid from. The girl literally exists on nothing. Of course, she can't afford a new cell and tablet. "You're the only one who thinks this is suspicious."

I think Sloane's meager personal possessions are further indication of her dire situation. Yesterday, I was afraid it meant she wasn't planning to stick around, but after thinking about it last night, this is the obvious conclusion. Sloane doesn't have the funds to buy herself things. I have more money than I know what to do with. So I plan to add a clothing allowance to her contract, and I've already notified my housekeeper to buy whatever toiletries and cosmetics Sloane needs. If she questions it, Mrs. Peake knows to lie and say I did the same for Isa.

I'd outright offer to help if I didn't think Sloane would refuse. I vow to find other ways to support her without making her feel like a charity case. While she's in my employ, Sloane will not want for anything. A happy nanny means a happy Elio, and I'll do whatever I can to alleviate stress in Sloane's life.

"I'm not buying her act, Cris." Isa pushes off my desk, crossing her arms over her chest. "You'd do well to be on your guard. Don't let her pretty face and cosmetically enhanced body distract you from her true agenda."

She's like a broken record, and I'm sick of hearing it. "I'm not having this same argument with you." I rub at my throbbing temples, barely resisting the urge to grab Isotta and shake her. "I've got work to do."

"I'm only trying to protect you." Her hand lands on my arm. "You're a man. It's natural you're led by your dick, but you're smarter than this."

I step back, letting her hand fall away. It takes colossal effort not to lash out at the woman. It's clear she feels threatened, and I'm trying to understand it, but she doesn't get to speak to me like this. "You need to leave, Isa. Go now before I say something we'll both regret."

Hurt splays across her face, taking the edge off my rage but only slightly.

"We're taking Elio out on his bike in a bit, just in case you come looking for us."

"Take Clint and Umberto with you."

"Of course. You don't need to tell *me* that." She huffs before finally taking the hint and exiting my office, taking her envy and disdain with her. The door slams shut, and I pray for patience that is in limited supply.

Flopping down in my chair, I rest my head back and close my eyes for a few seconds. Then I pick up my sandwich and wolf the rest of it down. My mouth pulls into a grimace when I gulp back a mouthful of coffee. Goddamn. It's awful. All Isa had to do was show Sloane how to use the machine, but I guess that's asking for too much.

Taking my empty plate and the almost full mug, I head out of my office toward the kitchen to make myself a fresh cup.

"It's clear you didn't grow up in a good Italian American family." Isa's cutting tone reaches me in the hallway, and I slow my steps to eavesdrop. "More like dragged up," she spitefully adds.

"How dare you." Sloane's voice is level, but I hear the simmering rage behind her words. "My mother was a single mom, and she sacrificed a lot so I never went without. She raised me right, and there is nothing wrong with this kitchen. It's perfectly clean. Last I checked, I was the *nanny*, not the housekeeper."

"We have standards here. Standards you're already failing to measure up to, and I'm not just talking about the kitchen. You will stay here and properly clean the kitchen while I take Elio out to the park."

"I don't answer to you, and Cristian made it clear Elio is *my* responsibility now. I'm not staying behind. I'm going with you."

"Listen here, you little gold-digging witch."

I've heard enough. I'm seething as I stalk into the kitchen and face the warring women. "A word, Isotta."

My stern tone brooks no argument as I glare at Elio's maternal aunt. Elio is stalled in the doorway on the other side of the room, his little brow furrowed as he looks between his former and current nanny. "Hey, buddy." I purposely soften my tone and smile at my son.

Horror washes over both women's faces, and it's clear they were too busy arguing to notice him.

"Sloane will get you ready for the park. Show her where your coat and boots are."

"Okay." His tone is meek, and I'm livid.

"I'm so sorry," Sloane whispers, looking distraught. "I didn't see him there."

"We'll talk later. Isotta won't be going to the park with you. Clint and Umberto will escort you. They know the way." I introduced her to Elio's bodyguards this morning and to John Angelo, the *soldato* I've assigned as her personal bodyguard.

He's one of the older men on the security team, but he's experienced and solid, and he'll take good care of her.

"I really don't—"

I shake my head, cutting Isa off mid-sentence, pinning her with a warning look I usually reserve for my enemies. Her lips clamp shut, and I'm glad to see she still has a modicum of sense.

"Buddy, say goodbye to Isa for now. She'll be back on Saturday to collect you."

Elio races across the kitchen and throws his arms around Isa's legs. "I don't want you to go," he cries, clinging to her as tears roll down his face.

Pain stabs me in the chest. This isn't the way I wanted things to be. I had planned a handover that would run for two weeks to gradually acclimate my son to the change. But Isa has left me with no choice. It's clear the two women do not get along, and forcing them to work together will only cause more problems in the long run. As much as I hate hurting Elio, it's time to rip the Band-Aid off.

Isa's pain-filled pleading eyes latch onto mine. I shake my head again. She has brought this on herself. She has orchestrated a situation that's hurt my son, and it's unforgivable. While Sloane should not have retaliated while Elio was watching, I believe her when she said she didn't know he was there, and I don't blame her for standing up for herself. But the hard truth is, while they were throwing down, no one was thinking about my son, and that is unacceptable.

Sloane stands in the corner, looking heartbroken as she watches Elio sob. Isa lifts him into her arms and hugs him close, whispering reassurances into his ear.

"You'll still see Auntie Isa, buddy," I remind him, extracting him from his aunt after a few minutes. I set him on top of the island unit. "It's okay to be sad, but she's not going away. You'll be going to your *nonna*'s house every Saturday with Auntie Isa to see all your cousins."

"And *Nonno*?" he asks in a trembling voice.

"And *Nonno* too." I brush his dark hair out of his eyes. "All that's changing is that Sloane will be with you during the week, and you're going to have lots of fun with her. Right?"

He sniffles and nods. "Can you come to the park, Daddy?"

I've got a shit ton of work to do and people expecting emails and calls, but they'll have to wait. My son always comes first. I can't let him go off with his new nanny when he's upset. He needs reassurance and stability. "Absolutely." I press a kiss into his hair, inhaling the sweet strawberry scent of his shampoo. "How about this?" I ease back, cupping his handsome little face. "We'll go for a bike ride and then head to the courts, and what do you say to pizza at Mr. Papas?"

"Yay!" Elio's screech is so loud it almost bursts my eardrums. He flings his arms around me. "You're the best daddy ever."

My heart swells with love. "Love you, bud." I wrap him in my arms, hugging him to death before I set his small feet on the ground. I give him a little nudge. "Go with Sloane for now."

He races off before slamming to a halt and spinning on his heel. He comes flying back, throws himself at Isa briefly, and beams up at her. "Bye, Auntie Isa. See you on Saturday." He takes off again, running toward Sloane.

"Bye, champ. Love you." Isa's voice cracks a little.

"Love you too!" he calls out without stopping. His tiny hand slides into Sloane's hand as he tugs her around the corner.

I wait a few beats to ensure they are out of range before I round on Isa. "I heard what you said to Sloane, and it's completely unacceptable. I think it's best you go now, and we limit your engagement to Saturdays for the moment. Elio needs time to bond with Sloane, and that won't happen if you're constantly here."

"Don't do this, Cristian. Please." She grips the sleeve of my shirt. "You know how much I love him."

"You should've thought about that while you were lashing out at Sloane in front of him." I remove her hand from my shirt and take a step back.

"That wasn't on purpose."

"No, I don't think it was, but the fact is you both forgot about my son, and it's inexcusable, as are the things you said to Sloane." She opens her mouth to protest, but I cut her off before she spews more of her vitriol. "You have made your feelings known, Isotta. I don't need to hear it again. This isn't the way I wanted the transition to go, but this is the best option for everyone."

"You're making a big mistake, Cris," she whispers.

"We'll see you Saturday morning." I shove my hands into my pants pockets, drilling her with a look that confirms this discussion is over for good. "Remember, I need him back by twelve."

"I haven't forgotten."

She moves to walk off, and I can't let her leave like this. "I'm grateful for everything, Isa, and I don't want things to be awkward between us. You're important to Elio and me."

"It sure doesn't feel like that now." Pain is etched upon her face.

"We all need time to adjust, and you've got a wedding to plan. Focus on that. You deserve to be happy."

She smiles, but it doesn't meet her eyes. "You do too."

Chapter Eight
Sloane

I'm shaking as I help Elio into his puffer jacket, gloves, and scarf. I think I've blown it. It's quite possible I'm about to be fired, and I wouldn't blame Cristian if he does. I'm ashamed Elio was witness to that. I should have bitten my tongue and not retaliated, but no one gets to insult my mother and get away with it. "Are you okay, my little prince?" I ask, brushing hair back off his face.

"I'm awesome." He flashes me a toothy grin, and I'm reminded of how forgiving children are. "This is the best day ever! I love my daddy so, so much." His eyes sparkle with blatant joy and love for his father, and memories of similar outings with my mom resurrect in my mind, which only adds to my pain and current anxiety.

Panic swirls in my gut as I zip Elio's jacket up and move on to his feet. Mom is dead if I lose this job, and I'm as good as dead too if that happens. Sweat rolls down my back, and it's an effort to keep a smile on my face as Elio regales me with tales of previous bike rides and basketball games while I help him into his boots.

"Ready, bud?" Cristian says from behind me, and my spine automatically stiffens. I finish lacing his boots and straighten up.

"We're ready, ready, ready!" Elio squeals, jumping up and down.

The resilience of kids is remarkable. "Could I just talk to you for a second?" I ask in a hushed voice, forcing my gaze to hold Cristian's.

He stares at me for a few beats before slowly nodding. "Grab your coat while I take Elio to Umberto and Clint. They can bring the bikes around the front of the building."

I nod and take a step forward. "Sloane." Elio grips my hand, and I look down at him. "You're not going to leave me too, are you?"

Oh my god. I crouch down in front of him and kiss his soft cheek. "I hope not," I quietly say, not wanting to lie to the child.

"Sloane will see you downstairs in a few minutes," Cristian says.

"Okay." He smiles a happy smile, showcasing the gap in his lower teeth.

Cristian clutches his hand and nods at me. I walk toward the hallway leading to the bedrooms.

"Hurry up!" Elio shouts after me. "You don't want to be Slowpoke Sloane again!"

I smile despite my fear, wiggling my fingers at him as I back up out of the room.

I'm on autopilot as I head to my bedroom and into the walk-in closet. My measly clothes barely fill one-fifth of the available space, and it's as pathetic as I am. I pull my black woolen coat off the hanger and switch out my sneakers for boots. As I walk back to the kitchen, I'm devising all kinds of reasons in my head to present to Cristian not to fire me. Yet when I'm confronted with his stern figure, all my calculated composure evaporates, and I burst out crying.

I stand before my new boss like a wet noodle, hugging my arms around my body as tears stream down my face. "I'm so sorry, Cristian," I say over sobs. "That should never have happened. I hate that it upset Elio."

"Hey, hey." Cristian walks toward me, hesitating for a second before he gently pulls me into his arms. "Don't cry, Sloane."

"Please don't fire me." I beseech him with my eyes, and I'm not opposed to begging on my hands and knees. "If I'd known Elio was there, I swear I wouldn't have snapped back at her. It's not an excuse, but she'd been winding me up all morning. Nothing I did was right, and then she insulted my mother, and..." A sob rips from my mouth, and I can do nothing to stop the meltdown. It's been a long time coming, and while now is not the time to fall apart, I can't halt it.

"Sloane. Shush." Cristian presses my head to his chest and runs his hand up and down my back. "Calm down, sweetheart. You're shaking all over."

"I can't lose this job. I need it so badly."

"I know you do."

I go rigid in his arms. Surely, that doesn't mean...

"I know about your mother and the debts," he adds in a soothing voice. "I'm so sorry you lost her like that, and I can't begin to imagine how hard it's been to grieve and lose your home and have all these financial commitments hanging over your head."

Whoever Pablo hired to create my fake identity and backstory has really done a stellar job. "You must think I'm pathetic," I mumble against his chest, snuggling in closer. I feel safe in his arms, and I need to cling to that right now. Cristian smells so good, and he's so warm and solid and strong. I might be imagining it, but his arms seem to hold me tighter.

"I think you're a young woman who's had far too much to deal with, and you're doing the best you can."

I peer up at him, instantly ensnared by his mesmerizing emerald eyes. I haven't known the man long, but he has a way of looking at me that is wholly intense and all-consuming. I could easily get addicted to the way it makes me feel. "I promise I will always put Elio first, and nothing like that will happen again. Please don't fire me, Cristian. Give me a second chance, and you won't regret it."

"I'm not firing you, Sloane."

The second the words leave his lips, my legs try to go out from under me. I collapse against him, and he sways a little as he adjusts his hold on me to keep me upright. "Whoa, careful there, beautiful."

My eyes pop wide at the same time his do. I don't think he meant to say that.

"Can you stand?" he says, his deep, gruff voice doing funny things to my insides.

"Yes. Of course." I shuck out of his arms the same time he steps back, examining me carefully before he fully lets me go. I instantly miss the safety of his arm, though it's only an illusion. But it's one I enjoyed for the brief interlude I had it. "I'm sorry for acting so unprofessional. I promise I'm not normally like this."

"Sit down for a bit." He gestures toward one of the stools. I pull myself up onto it as he retrieves a few bottles of water from the refrigerator. He hands one to me. "If you're not feeling up to an outing, I can take Elio myself."

Our fingers brush as I accept the bottle from him, igniting delicious tremors across my skin. I've never had such a strong, visceral reaction to any man before, and it scares me a little.

"No, I'm fine." I swipe at the moisture under my eyes, embarrassed and relieved in equal measure. "I'm sorry for falling apart like that, and I'm really, really sorry about arguing with Isa in front of Elio. It's unforgivable."

"Nothing like that can happen again." He leans back against the refrigerator.

"It won't. I swear."

"You won't have to worry about Isa. It's in everyone's best interests that she leaves now. She will be here on Saturdays to collect Elio, but that's it."

"I don't want to deprive Elio of his aunt. He clearly loves her a lot. I don't know why she dislikes me so much, but I will hold my tongue for Elio's sake if you want to change your mind."

"I appreciate the offer, but it wouldn't work, and maybe a clean break is better anyway. Kids bounce back quickly."

"They do, but she's important in his life, and if he needs her, I'm okay with that." I have learned a big lesson today. Who cares what that snotty bitch thinks? Let her insult me, insult my mother, all she likes. She doesn't matter. Protecting Mom and ensuring we both get out of this alive is the priority. I shouldn't have let some jealous cow get to me.

"It's a hard adjustment for Isa too. She feels threatened by you, but it's no excuse for the way she spoke to you. I'm sorry for the hurt it caused."

"You don't need to apologize for her, and I guess I need to develop thicker skin."

"You're still so young. It'll come in time."

"I'm not that young," I protest because the last thing I need is him thinking I'm a weak little girl. I need him to see me as a desirable woman because my only chance at getting the intel Pablo wants is getting close to this man. "Everything I've endured this past year has aged me beyond my years."

"It wasn't an insult." He glances at his watch. "We should go. I'm betting Elio is driving Umberto and Clint insane by now."

When we reach Central Park, we climb out of the blacked-out SUV while the bodyguards retrieve the bicycles from the roof. The three of us depart on one of the cycle routes, with Umberto and Clint jogging on the sidewalk behind us. It's a brisk January day, and biting-cold wind slices across my face as we travel at a leisurely pace.

The park is more subdued this time of year. No light-pink blossoms adorn the cherry trees, and I miss the lavender-pink buds of the Eastern redbuds in full bloom. But there's something about winter with the crisp chill in the air, the trees bare of leaves—except for the evergreens—and the abundance of trampled foliage covering the sidewalks and pathways that soothes me. Lingering traces of snow cling to the uppermost branches of the trees we pass by, painting a pretty picture.

The frigid wind on my face reminds me I'm alive, and right now, there's a lot to be said for that. So, I try to live in the moment and not dwell on the terrible predicament Mom and I are in. Maybe that makes me a selfish daughter, but I'm clinging to my sanity by my fingernails right now.

After the bicycles are packed away, we get coffees from a cart and a hot chocolate for Elio and sit on a bench to drink them. The bodyguards make zero attempt to blend in, leaning against the trunks of trees and scanning every passerby as if they're a threat. It's comforting. I wonder where Diego and Alvaro are. I'm sure they're lurking somewhere close by, as the cartel cell in my jeans pocket would have notified them I'm on the move.

If I didn't think Mom would be punished for it, I'd consider drawing attention to them in the hopes Cristian's men might beat the shit out of the two assholes. That's something I'd gladly root for.

"Your nose is all red, Slowpoke Sloane," Elio says, grinning that toothless grin.

"Look in the mirror, little dude." I boop him lightly on the nose. "I'm gonna start calling you Rudolph."

Elio bursts into song, and Cristian and I join in, garnering our fair share of curious looks from passersby.

"Christmas was last month," some know-it-all spotty-faced teenager shouts as he whizzes past on a skateboard.

"Don't care!" Elio shouts back, poking his tongue out. "What a grinch," he mutters under his breath when the teen is out of sight.

My lips twitch at the corners, and Cristian chuckles. I shiver as a gust of wind whistles past us, lifting stray strands of hair from my ponytail.

"You're cold." Cristian's gaze roams quickly over me. "That coat isn't warm enough, and you need a hat and gloves."

"I'm fine." I pull the collar of my coat up, shielding my neck.

"We can play at the indoor court, Daddy." Elio is sporting a hot chocolate mustache, and I didn't think the kid could be any cuter, but he is. "I don't want Sloane to freeze."

"I won't freeze." Removing a wipe from my purse, I gently clean his mouth. "Besides, running around will heat me up. Hope you're ready to go up against the champ," I tease.

"Nuh-uh." Elio shakes his head repeatedly. "No one beats my daddy. He's The Big Apple basketball champ."

Cristian coughs. "Pretty sure that crown belongs to Brunson or one of the other Knicks guys, but I'll take the praise where I can get it." He smiles adoringly at his son.

Elio thrusts his empty cup at me before crawling into his daddy's lap. "I want to see the Knicks play again."

"I'll check out tickets." Cristian snuggles his son and looks at me. "Have you ever been to The Garden to catch a game?"

I nod. "I caught a few games with my team when I was in high school. Those were fun times."

"I'll get you a ticket if you'd like to join us? A few of my buddies usually come too."

"I'd like that. Thanks."

"Can we go shoot hoops now?" Elio hops up, holding his dad's hand and trying to drag him to his feet.

"I wish I had a tenth of his energy," I joke as I stand.

"You and me both," Cristian says over a grin, leaning down and scooping his son up and onto his shoulder. "Let's go put Sloane through her paces."

Chapter Nine
Cristian

"Go, Sloane, go!" Elio shouts, jumping up and down as Sloane maneuvers around Umberto, heading toward the net. Her moves are sharp but elegant, and she dances around my teammate with effortless skill. Her aim is true, and Elio shrieks in excitement when the ball drops through the net, and Clint declares Team Rudolph the winners.

Elio races toward Sloane, and she kneels, opening her arms wide for him. Elio flings himself at her, almost causing her to lose her balance. "That was awesome! I'm so happy you're my nanny. Will you always be on my team?"

"Always, buddy." She raises her palm for a high five. "Teammates forever."

He slaps his tiny hand against hers. "Yay!" His fingers curl around Sloane's as she stands.

"I don't think you have anything to worry about, boss," Umberto remarks as he materializes at my side, holding the ball tucked under one arm. "She's a natural with him, and he already loves her."

"I'm relieved. It's more than I hoped for."

"Don't be sad, Daddy," Elio says, approaching with his hand firmly enclosed in Sloane's. "You can't always be the champ."

I muss up his hair. "I'm winning every day I have you in my life, bud. I can handle losing this time." I smirk at Sloane. "Next time, we won't go so easy on you."

"Yeah, right." She snorts. "Bring it, dude. We'll rise to the challenge every time. Right, Rudolph?"

"Yes! Let's go again now!"

Laughter tumbles from my chest. Elio is always full of energy and so enthusiastic about life, and it's infectious.

Mom says Cruz and I were both live wires when we were kids, so I guess it runs in his genes. I hope that's all he's inherited from his bio dad. That he's more like his mother. Bettina made bad choices in life, but she was a good person. Isa said she never forgave herself for hurting Joshua the way she did, and she fully believes my brother groomed Bettina from a young age and bewitched her.

I don't have much difficulty believing it. Cruz deliberately caused pain and suffering to others with no regrets or remorse. People were pawns to him. Tools to use to achieve his agenda, and he didn't care who he hurt. In fact, from what Valentina has told me, he got off on hurting others, especially women. I shudder as I consider how many women could be out there with kids fathered by my brother as part of his nefarious breeding plan to infiltrate *La Cosa Nostra*. I used to think there was some goodness in Cruz, but by the end, he was evil to his core. I don't think my parents will ever recover from the legacy he left behind. In particular, my father has taken it hard.

"Daddy?" Elio tugs on my pant leg. "Can we play another game? Puh-lease."

I cup his handsome little face. "It's getting dark, son, and I don't know about you, but I'm hungry for some pizza."

"And garlic balls and ice cream!" Elio shrieks. "I want everything! Can I, Daddy? Puh-lease?"

My heart mushrooms with love for my son. "Sure thing, bud." I lean down and kiss his brow. "It's a special occasion, and we can't take Sloane to Mr. Papas and not have garlic balls and ice cream."

"This isn't Mr. Papas," Elio proclaims as Clint pulls the SUV in front of Saks Fifth Avenue.

"We're making a quick pitstop, but you can stay in the car. Continue watching your movie, and before you know it, Sloane and I will be back."

His lip juts out. "I want to come too."

I press a kiss to his soft cheek. "Next time, buddy."

"It's not fair." He plants his hands on his hips and scowls at me. "I wanna go to the kids' floor and get a toy."

"It's not your birthday or Christmas, and you have tons of new toys. Be a good boy for Umberto and Clint, and I'll let you get the ice cream sundae at Mr. Papas."

His brow furrows in concentration before smoothing out. "Okay, deal!"

I trade a smile with Umberto as I kiss my son on the head. "Behave. We'll see you in a bit." Clint will drive around while we're shopping.

"What's going on?" Sloane asks, looking confused.

"You'll see." I gesture toward the door as Umberto swings it open. He steps back to let Sloane hop down, and I slide out behind her.

She blows Elio a kiss. "See you soon, my little prince."

Elio blows her a kiss in return, and it's super sweet.

"I think you'll have quite the little charmer on your hands when he grows up," she says, waving as Umberto closes the door.

"Don't I know it." My hand winds around Sloane's back as I escort her toward the entrance, my gaze scanning our surroundings as we walk. I keep my hand on her slender waist until we enter the elevator and separate.

"I still have no clue why we are here," she says in a low voice, keeping our conversation away from prying ears.

"You need a warmer coat."

Her face drops. "My budget doesn't stretch to a new coat, and this one is fine," she says, glancing at the thin woolen coat she's wearing.

"I'm issuing you a clothing allowance, and this coat is on me."

"Absolutely not."

"I insist," I say, moving my arm around her back again when the elevator opens on our floor. I steer her out toward the section where Kate is hopefully waiting. "You'll be outside daily with Elio, and the weather won't warm up for some time. Consider this part of your work uniform."

She opens her mouth, about to protest again, but she must think better of it. Her slender frame feels fragile against me, and I wonder if she's this slim because she hasn't had enough money for food. Spotting Kate up ahead, I walk us speedily in that direction.

"Mr. DiPietro, how lovely to see you. It's been a while." The older woman smiles as she extends her arm.

I shake her hand. "It's great to see you, too, Kate. This is Sloane."

"It's lovely to meet you, Sloane." Her assessing gaze rakes over my nanny from head to toe. "You have exquisite skin and a gorgeous figure. There are a few pieces I've chosen that I think will look stunning on you."

"Thank you." Sloane bites down on her lip. "This is all new to me, and I'm not sure what to expect. Cristian just sprung it on me."

"Mr. DiPietro is one of the good guys. He knows how to treat his lady friends, and don't worry, sweetie. I'll take good care of you."

"Sloane is my son's new nanny," I confirm in a sharp tone, pissed at the insinuation and her indiscretion. She makes it sound like I've taken tons of women here when that's not the case. I hadn't mentioned who the clothes were for when I called Kate earlier to make an appointment, and I shouldn't have to.

"I'm so sorry. I only assumed..." Her cheeks stain red, and panic widens her eyes. "Please forgive me, Mr. DiPietro. That was most unprofessional." She turns to Sloane. "I apologize for jumping to conclusions."

"It's fine, Kate," I say, not wanting to make a bigger deal out of it even if I am annoyed. Perhaps I should've gone elsewhere, but it was a last-minute decision. I used to take Aliya here for clothes, and she was always delighted with the items Kate chose for her. "Do you have a dressing room set up? We're taking Elio for pizza, and he's not known for his patience when it comes to his favorite food."

"Say no more. We wouldn't want to keep the little cutie from his pizza. Come with me, Sloane. I have a suite all ready, and I'll show you the things I've picked out, though I may need to revise the sizes." She gestures for Sloane to follow her, but my nanny looks uncertainly at me.

"Go on. It's okay. I'll stay right here until you're done."

While I wait for Sloane, I take a seat on one of the couches and check emails on my phone.

"Mr. DiPietro." Kate drags me away from my screen. "We're done, but the young lady is insistent she doesn't need anything. I thought you might like to talk with her."

"Of course." I put my phone away and stand.

"She noticed the prices, and I think it shocked her," Kate explains as she leads me to the dressing room where Sloane is.

"I'll handle it." Walking into the large space, I find Sloane standing in front of the large mirror wearing a pastel pink short puffer jacket with a belt and a fake-fur-trimmed hood. "That looks lovely and warm."

"It's gorgeous," she admits, pulling the hood down and turning to face me. "But it's too expensive. I don't need a Moncler jacket for work, Cristian."

"Do you like it?"

"I love it, but—"

"We'll take it," I tell Kate before refocusing on Sloane. "You need a full-length coat too. Did you pick out something else?"

"What about this one?" Kate says, holding up a hanger containing a long black wrap wool coat. "You liked it, and it looks fabulous on you. Plus, it's fifty percent off today."

"It's still far too much money."

"We'll take that one too, and can you add matching scarves and gloves for both coats, please?"

Kate's warm smile radiates relief. "I'll get everything together and meet you at the register." She moves to help Sloane out of the jacket she's still wearing.

"Could I keep this on?" Sloane asks, glimpsing herself in the mirror. "It's so warm I don't want to part with it."

"Of course, dear. I'll just take the tag to ring it up."

Kate hurries away, leaving Sloane and me alone.

"This truly is too much, but thank you, Cristian. No one has ever done anything so nice for me before."

"Please tell me that isn't true."

She shrugs. "I've never had much luck with men. Most of the guys I dated were poor students or too self-obsessed to even consider doing anything nice for me."

"I want names," I growl, flexing my knuckles, as irrational anger surges through my veins.

"What?" she whispers, and I silently curse myself for acting like a jealous boyfriend or husband.

"What about the guy you're seeing now? Doesn't he do nice things for you?"

Her eyes lower to the floor. "It's, ah, super casual with him. And not exclusive," she blurts, lifting her gaze to meet mine. "It's not serious at all."

"Does he treat you right? Take you out to nice places and pay? Send you flowers and gifts? Run you hot baths? Cook you dinner? Give you a massage when you've had a bad day? Listen to you when you're stressed or upset, and do everything and anything to cheer you up? Does he make you laugh and give you multiple orgasms while worshipping every inch of your beautiful body?"

Sloane's eyes widen, and I drag a hand through my hair, shocked at my outburst. *What. The. Actual. Fuck, Cristian??* I guess I haven't let go of all my bitterness toward Aliya. I treated her like a fucking queen, and she threw it all back in my face.

"Pretty sure what you've just described is pure fantasy. Maybe if I was dating a book boyfriend," she teases.

"I've done all that," I blurt, because it seems I'm not done with the verbal diarrhea. "Not that it was appreciated."

"Wow." She walks slowly toward me. "I didn't think guys like you existed in real life, and whoever the woman was, she clearly didn't deserve you."

"She left two months after I adopted Elio. Said she couldn't be a mother to another couple's child."

Sloane's nostrils flare, and fire flashes in her eyes. "What a bitch. Anyone who gets to be a mother to that little boy is the luckiest woman alive. How could she not want him? That hurts me so much."

"My sentiments exactly." I rub a hand along the back of my neck.

"Like I said, she didn't deserve you, and it sounds to me like you and Elio had a narrow escape."

I bob my head. "I'm glad Aliya showed her true colors when she did. Saved me from making the biggest mistake of my life. I'm a firm believer that things happen for a reason."

"I used to believe that, but now I think things happen with and without reason. There are some things that happen that make no sense. You can be a good person, live a good life, and bad shit happens for no fucking reason."

"You're thinking about your mom."

She nods, gulping audibly. Pain mixed with sadness washes over her face. "She didn't deserve what happened to her."

"It's hard to make sense of illness, especially losing one who is so young."

"Yeah." I watch as a mask shrouds her pretty face, and she shrugs it off. "We should go. Elio is waiting."

Chapter Ten
Sloane

"Bye, champ. Love you," Isa says, her voice filtering into the kitchen from the hallway.

"Bye, Auntie Isa. Love you to the moon and back. Thanks for taking me to see Nonno and Nonna and my cousins."

"I'll see you next week, cutie, for your final suit fitting."

"Ugh. Do I have to?" Elio complains, raising a smile to my face.

"It won't take long," Cristian says. "Being a ring bearer is a big honor and a serious responsibility. You need to look your best."

"All right, I suppose."

I quietly chuckle to myself. Good luck to whoever the tailor is. Getting Elio to stay still for any length of time is a challenge. Today is my sixth official day as his nanny, and it's safe to say I'm worn out. Elio keeps me on my toes every day, but I welcome it. Pablo is sending me daily pics and videos reminding me my first deadline is approaching, and I've still got fuck all to offer him. I'm hoping I might get an opportunity to do some snooping this weekend, but I'm not overly hopeful. I have barely slept a wink all week worrying about the consequences for Mom if I don't produce *something*.

"Sloane. Did you hear me?"

Cristian's deep, sultry voice drags me from my head. I didn't even hear them come in or Isa leaving. "Sorry, I was daydreaming. What did you say?" I try my best not to ogle him, but it's hard when he looks so delicious. Today, he's wearing an expensive-looking black woolen sweater over ripped black jeans and boots. It makes him look younger and hot as hell.

"We're leaving in five minutes, Sleepyhead Sloane." Elio wraps his arms around my legs. "I missed you."

Crouching down, I pull him into my arms. Tears prick my eyes. I'm already so in love with this little boy. "I missed you too, my little prince." I dot kisses into his hair before clasping his face in my hands. "Did you have fun at your grandparents' house?"

He nods vigorously. "I played on the trampoline with my cousins, and Nonna made me apple cake." He rubs his belly, thrusting it out. "Look how big my belly is 'cause I ate so much cake."

I chuckle, mussing up his hair as I stand.

"Go to the bathroom before we leave," Cristian tells his son. "And wash your hands after!" he calls out as Elio races out of the kitchen.

"There are a few things I want to run through before we leave," Cristian explains, rounding the other side of the island unit.

I'm not sure if he's putting a physical barrier between us on purpose or not. He's been more guarded since Tuesday, and I'm guessing he regrets telling me so much personal stuff. He's worked in his home office after Elio is in bed every night since, and it's given me next to no time to work on my seduction plan.

"Okay." I lean back against the kitchen counter.

"Firstly, you're technically not on duty on the weekend, and you're not obligated to come with us. I should have asked instead of assuming you were okay with it. I'd like you to see the new build and to meet my friends, as you'll be spending time with them in the future, but if you have plans with your boyfriend, it's fine for you to stay behind."

I don't have to consider it. There is nothing to be gained from staying behind. I can't go snooping with all the cameras, and Cristian keeps his home office securely locked when he's not in there. I have more of a chance of getting intel if I'm with him. And more of a chance to get to know him on a personal level if I'm with him as often as possible. Separating myself from him will not support my goal.

"I have no plans, and I want to come with. I'm excited to see the house and meet your friends, and I don't think I should be apart from Elio during these important early stages."

"Okay, great." Stress visibly leaves his shoulders. "Just know you aren't tied to us for the weekend. The grounds are vast, and you are free to go walking, running, swimming, or biking, or to do your own thing while we're there."

"It's fine, Cristian. Spending time with Elio and you isn't a chore." I peer up at him with doe eyes before shyly averting my gaze.

"There's one other thing." The dark, decadent quality of his tone sends shivers racing up and down my spine. I love the sound of his voice. It constantly does wicked things to my insides I shouldn't be keen to encourage. "Once we leave the city, you'll have to wear this." He holds out a black eye mask, looking a little sheepish. "My friends have gone to a lot of trouble to protect the location of their property."

"I understand." He explained a bit before.

"They are very protective of their wives and kids and have

made an enormous effort to keep their property secure. All visitors who aren't family are required to wear a blindfold. It's nothing personal."

"It's fine, Cristian. I get it. I can't fault anyone for going to such lengths to protect their loved ones." The words imprint on my heart as they leave my mouth, and a sour taste crawls up my throat.

"Elio's father wasn't a good man, and he pissed a lot of people off before he died. The consequences of his actions are far-reaching. His enemies may target Elio. I will die before I'll let anything happen to my son, and I won't apologize for the measures I take that may seem unnecessary and an overreaction. I won't take any chances with that little boy."

His words are like a dagger slowly driving into my heart. Cristian doesn't know he's already opened his door to the enemy. Nausea swims up my throat, and I couldn't hate myself any more than I do in this moment. "You don't need to explain it, Cristian. I get it. Elio is so lucky to have you in his life." Tears prick the backs of my eyes, and I'm seconds from losing it again. I can't fall apart before my boss a second time. "If that's all, I'll just finish packing my weekend bag."

Cristian's eyes bore into mine, and I hope he doesn't see the truth behind the veil I wear. "That's all. I'll grab Elio and meet you at the front door."

Pressure settles on my chest to the point of pain as I walk to my bedroom to get my bag. As soon as the door is closed, I race to the bathroom and divest the measly contents of my stomach. I'm an awful person. This entire situation is my fault, and I'm only in this mess because I trusted the wrong person. If it'd resolve things, I'd put a bullet in my skull right now.

Slumped on the floor of the bathroom, I rub at the pain spreading across my chest. Inside, I'm waging a silent war. How am I going to do this? How can I sign this man's death warrant?

I don't want to, but it's him or Mom, and there really isn't a choice.

But there is a choice when it comes to Elio. I'm going to protect that kid with my life. Which means I can't bring my cartel cell with me this weekend. Pablo can't know the location because he could target Elio or Cristian's friends. It's bad enough I'm living with the knowledge they are going to come for Cristian. I couldn't bear it if they went after his son or his friends too.

However, if I don't take it, Pablo will punish my mother. That's the simple hard truth, and I hate I have to hurt my mother to protect the little boy who already means so much to me.

Scrambling to my feet, I brush my teeth and wash my hands before sitting on the bed. As I hold the cell in my hand, it feels like a ticking bomb while I wrestle with my conscience. I'm still mulling it all over when Elio calls out for me. "Come on, Slowpoke Sloane. It's time to go!"

Mom's students spring to mind suddenly. They all adore her, and she adores them. She's a natural with kids, and I think that's where I get it from. Her disappearance must have hurt them so much. My heart aches with a fresh wave of pain.

I know what Mom would want me to do.

She wouldn't want me to place any kids in harm's way for her.

Her instinct would be to protect them, and that's what I need to do, so I slip the cartel cell in the hidden pocket of my black purse and leave it in the closet. Then I grab my weekend bag and my spare purse and exit the bedroom.

"Wakey, wakey, Sleepyhead Sloane." Elio's teasing little voice rouses me from sleep, and I blink my eyes open, my lashes brushing against soft black silk. Pulling the eye mask off, I rub my sore neck as I push my head off the window and straighten up.

A pool of dried drool stubbornly clings to the window I was sleeping against. It's gross and highly embarrassing. "We're here already?" I ask in a sleep-drenched tone, smothering a yawn. My eyes meet Cristian's amused gaze through the mirror. He drove today, and the bodyguards are following us in the SUV. Glancing over my shoulder, I spot the vehicle trailing us along the winding, seemingly endless driveway. Tall trees loom over us like otherworldly guardians as we maneuver past expansive empty fields on both sides of the road.

"Yes, we're here." He looks apologetic. "You'll need to keep the mask on for a little longer."

"Oh, sorry. No problem." I slide it back over my eyes, wondering when he put it on me in the first place.

"You were asleep the whole time," Elio proclaims. "And you were snoring!" He giggles, and my cheeks heat with mortification. I'm actually glad I can't see Cristian right now.

"Oh my god." I lean my head back and silently berate myself. "That's so embarrassing."

Cristian chuckles. "It was cute."

"Don't lie; it only makes it worse."

"You haven't been sleeping since you moved in, have you?"

"It's that obvious?" I subtly rub at my mouth, hoping there is no dried drool clinging to the corners.

"Not really, but I'm observant. I've noticed."

Well, that's not good. I can't have him being *too observant*. If he figures out my agenda, Mom and I are both finished.

"I've had trouble sleeping my entire life," I say, but it's completely untrue. I'm the type who conks out the second her head hits the pillow. I sleep like the dead usually, but that was before. Now, sleep is an illusion as much as this new life is. "Even as a baby, Mom said I never slept for more than a couple hours at a time." The mask makes it easier to deceive him because I don't have to look him in the face while I spin a web of lies.

"That's not good. It's hard to function if you haven't had a good night's sleep. Have you seen a doctor?"

"I don't want to take sleeping pills, and that's what they'll push on me."

The car slows down, and the engine idles. A soft whirring sound tickles my eardrums, and a cold breeze lifts strands of my hair. A beeping sound rings out as Cristian punches in a five-digit code. I'm glad I can't see shit through the eye mask. I don't want to know the entry code. I want to know as little as possible so it can't be tortured out of me at a later stage.

"You can remove the mask now," Cristian confirms as a little hand tugs on my arm.

"Quick, Slowpoke Sloane. You gotta see the playground."

I whip the blindfold off in time to see the large play area off to the side, equipped with an obstacle course, climbing frame, swings, slides, and a zipwire that runs from the playground into the woods that seem to border the rear part of the property. "Wow, that's amazing. You're a lucky little boy." What I wouldn't have given for something like that when I was a kid.

"Daddy says that all the time too. Will you push me on the swings?"

"Absolutely. We'll have lots of fun this weekend for sure." Removing a wipe from my bag, I scrub at the patch of drool on the window of Cristian's expensive sports car.

"That is Caleb and Elisa's home on the right," Cristian supplies as we drive toward two impressive properties.

"That is a stunning home." My gaze skates over the ranch-style house with greed. This truly is how the other half lives. The gorgeous home has a variety of different peaked roofs and an abundance of gray-framed windows, some arched and some rectangular. A few balconies abut the windows on either side. At first sight, it looks like the house is only on one level, but that's because the ground level is almost hidden by the front pathway and gardens stretching majestically on either side of the wide property. Manicured hedges border pristine flower beds, and the small water feature in the center of the front path is also bordered by hedges. "It's exquisite."

"The twins have great taste, albeit very different." He swings past that house to a more industrial-type modern build beside it. "That is Gia and Joshua's home."

"It's equally stunning in a more simplistic way." The two-story building has flat roofs and wide rectangular windows on all sides. The structure is propped up by several tall, wide white pillars, and the gardens at the front adjoin the other house.

"That's my house!" Elio points excitedly out the window as Cristian drives farther along the road in the direction of the construction up ahead. "Can I show her my bedroom, Daddy?"

"Not today, bud. We can't enter the house without the fore-man." Cristian's eyes dart to mine again through the mirror. "I'll bring you back sometime when the crew is here. Although they are mostly working on the interiors now, it's still considered a construction site and not safe to go inside without hard hats."

I nod as I drink it all in while the car slows down on our approach. A pang of longing hits me square in the chest. "It's beautiful, Cristian. It has a real Mediterranean feel about it." The two-story mansion is painted a muted terracotta color, and the dark wooden door and window frames perfectly complement it. A few double doors on the second level open to high balconies with wrought-iron railings. Archways wrap around the ground level, offering enclosed seating areas for cover during the warmer weather and providing an unparalleled view of the front gardens. I look behind me, and you can see the playground in the distance from here.

Cristian stops the car, and we climb out onto a beige paved driveway. "That will be a six-car garage," Cristian explains, jerking his head to the half-built structure on the left, while he takes a firm hold of his son's hand. "No running off, Elio. It's dangerous." His son pouts but stops wriggling under his father's stern gaze.

Cristian appears to have struck a good balance between setting boundaries and allowing Elio's spirit to blossom. The more I'm around the man, the more impressed I am, and the harder my task seems. Cristian DiPietro is a good man. A good father. I'm more convinced than ever that he's done nothing to earn the wrath of the cartel. I'm certain their beef was with his brother. Why should the good brother be punished for the sins of the bad one?

"All those dug-out sections will be flower beds," he explains, yanking me out of my inner thoughts. Cristian jerks his head toward various-sized and shaped areas that have been carved out in the ground in front of the house.

Walking along the short path toward the house, I imagine what it would be like to live somewhere like this. Pain fills my heart knowing I won't make it that far. I won't ever get to experience the joy of living in this Wonderland, and it saddens me. If things were different, I would be very happy with this life. Content caring for the most amazing little boy, and maybe falling in love with his father. I can see it. But it's out of reach, and daydreaming will only add to my suffering. So, I try to harden my heart and shut down my feelings as Cristian and Elio proudly show off their new home.

Chapter Eleven
Cristian

"The build is progressing nicely," Caleb says, arriving outside my house with his son Niccolo in his arms.

"It is. At this rate, we might be in by early summer." I lift my arms, and little Nico comes to me. "How's it going, rascal?"

"Elo!" Nico wriggles in my arms, trying to jump down when he sees my son, but I hold him tight.

"This is my bestest friend Nico," Elio tells Sloane as they approach hand in hand. "He can't say my name, so he calls me Elo. I like it. It's like a superhero name."

"Totally," Sloane agrees. Her eyes widen when she gets a look at Caleb, and I don't like it. I don't like it one little bit.

Caleb chuckles. "Partner in crime." He leans down to my son, holding his hand out for a high five. "Been up to any mischief lately?"

"Team Rudolph beat Daddy and Umberto yesterday, Uncle Caleb." Elio is quick to rat me out as he slaps his hand against Caleb's.

"And Team Rudolph would be?" Caleb asks, straightening up and flashing Sloane the kind of smile that has all the ladies swooning.

I'm suddenly visualizing strangling my best friend with my bare hands.

"Sloane and me." Elio beams up at her. "She's my nanny now, and she's the new basketball champ."

"That is something I wish I'd seen." Caleb grins at Sloane as he extends his arm. "It's great to meet you, Sloane. We've all been dying for you to visit after *everything* Cristian has told us about you."

The insinuation is blatant, and I glare at his irritating head, close to swinging my fists in his face.

"That doesn't sound ominous or anything." Sloane grins, and is she *flirting* with him?

"Trust me, you have nothing to worry about," Caleb adds, nudging me in the ribs. "Cristian had nothing but the very best things to say about you, and I can see why."

Oh my god. I'm going to kill him before this weekend is over, I just know it. "Don't mind Caleb. He loves sticking his nose into things that are none of his business."

Caleb chuckles, and my hands curl into fists at my side. "Nice deflection. Good luck keeping that up all weekend," he says in a hushed voice so only I can hear.

"Knock it off, asshole," I quietly say. "I told you the score. Quit stirring shit."

"Not a chance in hell, man." Caleb smirks before redirecting his attention toward Sloane. "Come over to the house and meet my wife, Elisa. My Lili is the sweetest human on the planet, and she's excited to meet you."

"Daddy, I wanna go to the playground," Elio pleads as Caleb lifts Nico into his arms.

"Me too, Papa!" Nico shrieks.

"We'll drop off our bags and head to the playground for a little while before dinner," I tell my son, and it thankfully appeases him.

Caleb, Nico, and Elio head to the house on foot while Sloane and I drive alongside them.

Elisa, Joshua, Gia, and their little girl Chiara are all waiting for us when we arrive, alongside a surprise guest. "Hey, man." Walking up to Giulio Accardi, I drop our bags on the ground and drag him into a hug. "Long time no see. I didn't know you were visiting this weekend." Giulio is part of our crew, and he's Joshua and Caleb's older cousin, as well as being the official Accardi *famiglia consigliere*.

"It was a last-minute thing. We thought we'd play a four-ball tomorrow if you're interested."

I shuck out of his embrace. "I'm game as long as Sloane is okay to look after Elio."

"We're dropping by Nat and Leo's tomorrow. They want to see the kids," Gia explains. "We can take Elio with us." She steps toward Sloane. "You can join us too, if you like." She thrusts out her hand. "I'm Gia. We're glad you could visit this weekend."

"Thanks for having me. It's good to meet you, and that sounds great." Sloane lifts her eyes to mine. "I'm happy to watch Elio while you go out. It's no biggie."

"Thanks. I haven't played golf in ages."

Elisa brushes past Gia, pulling Sloane into a warm hug. "I'm Elisa, and you're so pretty. We're going to be the best of friends."

"Um, thanks." Sloane looks a little overwhelmed at Elisa's obvious enthusiasm, though not unhappy about it. The girls separate, and Sloane smiles at Caleb's wife. "Your husband said the sweetest things about you, and I can see he wasn't wrong."

"He's the love of my life, and he treats me like a princess."

Elisa leans into Caleb's side, swooning at him in a way that's completely normal for her. The way those two love one another is something else. "I've worshipped the ground he walks on since I was a little girl."

"True story." Giulio steps in front of Sloane. "I'm Giulio. Cousin to these two idiots." He gestures toward the twins. "Pleased to meet you, Sloane." Clasping her hand, he raises it to his lips, where he slowly plants a kiss on her soft skin. "I'm single by the way," he adds, waggling his brows and clearly flirting with her.

I add him to my kill list as I fix him with a lethal look he's pretending not to see.

"Dude, don't." Caleb shakes his head at Giulio. "If you value breathing, do not hit on Sloane. Cristian is uber protective to the point it might warrant further probing."

I want to tell them all to fuck off, but there are innocent little ears present. "Knock it off. You're being rude." I face Sloane. "I apologize for my friends. None of them have grown up yet."

Gia snorts. "Hey, leave my husband out of that assessment."

"Cristian isn't wrong," Joshua says, smiling politely at Sloane. "They're really just big kids. Shocking considering one of them is a father." He smirks at his twin. "I'm Joshua, by the way."

Sloane smiles. "Good to meet you." She peers down at the little girl playing peek-a-boo behind her dad's legs. "Nice to meet you too." She wiggles her fingers at Chiara, who shyly wiggles them back.

"You two seriously need to *get laid*," Caleb says, whispering the last two words as his gaze bounces between Giulio and me.

"Thanks for the concern, but I have no trouble in that

department, and Cristian does all right too," Giulio says. "Been darkening the doors of Club H quite regularly from what I've heard." Giulio smirks, and I'm seriously regretting taking Sloane to meet my friends.

"It's a private club for a reason," I say through gritted teeth, mouthing "jerk" at one of my oldest friends.

"What's Club H?" Elio asks. "Why don't you take me there?" He pouts.

"Fuck." Caleb's lips twitch, and I'm tempted to flip him the bird.

"You said a bad word, Papa." Nico holds out his tiny hand. "A dollar for the cuss jar."

"This is only going to get more ridiculous," Gia says, looping her arm through Sloane's. "Let's get you settled into your rooms. Cristian, you're all staying with us. Giulio is staying with Lise and the manchild."

"I heard that, Gigi." Caleb pouts, and it's an almost carbon-copy look of the expression on his son's cute little face.

"I wanna go playground, Papa!" Nico screeches.

"Me too!" Chiara pipes up in her soft little voice, emerging from the shelter of her father's legs.

"Me three!" Elio adds.

"We'll take the kids to the playground, and you can follow us," Elisa says, holding her hand out to Elio.

"Sounds like a plan." I pat the top of Elio's head. "Be a good boy, and do what your aunt and uncles tell you."

"Scout's honor." He salutes me, and Giulio chuckles.

The others walk off with the kids while I trail behind Gia and Sloane, carrying our three bags.

"You have a beautiful home," Sloane tells Gia as she leads us through the large open-plan layout on the ground floor.

"Thank you. I still have to pinch myself every time I step

inside. Some days, I can't believe I live here. I grew up a lot more humbly."

"Same. This is all like something from a fairy tale." Sloane's eyes are out on stalks as she drinks in her surroundings.

Gia and Joshua's place is incredibly sophisticated with luxury furniture and fittings. Though it's minimalist in style, it's homey too.

"It truly is. I'm living a life I never imagined I could have, and I never take it for granted. Every day, I say thanks for Joshua and Chiara, and getting to share it with my best friend is the icing on the cake."

"Cristian told me you and Elisa have been friends for years." Before Sloane fell asleep in the car, I filled her in briefly on the friends she'd be meeting.

"Since we were little kids. Our moms are friends, and they're both super close with Natalia— Joshua and Caleb's mom."

"You're all so tight-knit. That must be nice."

"It is." Gia squeezes her arm. "You're part of it now too," she adds, leading us up the stairs to the bedrooms. "Cristian told us about your mom," she lies, and I wonder if she can feel the daggers embedding in her back.

The last thing I want is Sloane believing I've told everyone everything about her. That would be a massive invasion of her privacy. Gia only knows this intel because she personally conducted the second background check. Not that she can explain it, considering Sloane doesn't know anything about *La Cosa Nostra* or our involvement in it. At some point, I'll have to tell her because it's not something I can hide forever. It's why we usually hire from within *la famiglia* and avoid having to explain who we are and what we do. While we aren't like the mafia of the past, we still get our hands dirty as needed.

I wonder what Sloane would think if she knew how many men I've killed.

For some inexplicable reason, the thought troubles me.

Gia shows us to our rooms, which are all situated beside one another, and we deposit our bags before heading out to the playground to meet up with the others.

We spend an hour outside chatting while pushing the kids on the swings and supervising them as they move around the other parts of the playground. Gia and Elisa are engaged in conversation with Sloane while I catch up with my buddies.

"How are things going with Sloane?" Joshua asks.

"It was a bit of a shit show at the start until I told Isa to leave. The girls don't get on, but all is good now."

"You mean Isa doesn't like Sloane," Joshua surmises.

"Yep." I lean back against the tree, watching Sloane laugh as she runs over to catch Elio at the bottom of the slide.

"Isa must hate her. Sloane's the Margot Robbie to her Anna Kendrick," Caleb says as we all watch my nanny scoop a laughing Elio into her arms.

"Brutal, man." Giulio shakes his head, fighting a smile. "You shouldn't insult Anna Kendrick by unfairly grouping her with Isotta Da Rosa. Anna's a babe."

Joshua scrubs a hand over his smooth chin. "I'd watch out for Isa if I were you. You know my thoughts on the Da Rosa women, and it's not that I'm bitter. I put it all behind me when I fell in love with Gia. Isa is an even bigger snake than her sister, and I wouldn't trust her."

Joshua might think he's not biased, but he always will be. "Isa was a great nanny to Elio, and he loves her. She's his aunt, and I can't stop him from seeing her. She has no access to Sloane, and that's how it'll stay."

"No one who knows you could ever call you soft, Cristian,

but you've definitely got a soft spot for Isa. We don't want to see it coming back to bite you in the ass," Caleb says.

"He's *definitely* got a *hard* spot for this one though." Giulio grins, tipping his head in Sloane's direction. "Don't try to deny it, man. You haven't taken your eyes off her once."

"Don't pretend like you haven't been watching her either," I reply, working hard to keep things light.

"I'm not. She's a smoke show, and if you weren't already obsessed with her, I'd ask her out."

"I'm not obsessed with her," I blurt.

"Yeah?" Giulio shares a look with Caleb. "So, you won't mind if I ask her out?"

"Fuck no. She's my nanny. That means she's off-limits to me and you." And every other male in existence.

"Don't see how my dating her would be an issue."

"It's a conflict of interest. If it ends badly, she could quit."

Caleb snorts. "You're stretching, buddy. Admit you're hot for her. It's just us here."

"You're a worse gossip than any woman, Accardi."

"Not gonna deny it, but I've never betrayed your confidence, Cristian. I might tease, but it's in your best interest. You're getting in your own way, and I wouldn't be a friend if I didn't try to help you out."

"I can't get involved with her. She's Elio's nanny, and things need to be kept strictly professional."

"So, I can date her?"

"No. Fuck off, Giulio. Touch her, and I'll rip every last remaining hair from your head before I slit your throat and gut you from chest to cock."

"Wow, very creative. I've really struck a nerve, huh?" Giulio grins, and I quickly look around before flipping him the bird.

"Stop winding me up. You want to hear the truth? Fine.

She's beautiful, and I'm insanely attracted to her. She's also super sweet, a lot of fun, and very easy to live with. If the circumstances were different, I'd have asked her out a thousand times already. But they're not. Stop busting my balls for prioritizing my kid over my needs. Elio comes first. Always. Period."

"None of us ever doubts that," Joshua says.

"You're an amazing father," Caleb adds. "And I get why you don't want to complicate things, but don't shut yourself off to the possibility. Look at what I did? I wasted years denying what I felt for a bunch of reasons that seemed valid at the time, but in reality, they were bullshit. I don't want you to do the same."

"Out of all of us, you were the one most suited to getting hitched and having a family. I hate what that bitch Aliya did to you, but not all women are like her," Giulio adds. "I don't regret my short-lived marriage. I'm upset it didn't work out, but I don't regret it, and I will remarry at some point. I hate seeing you so determined to abandon any hope of a relationship. You dated a few rotten eggs. Probably got them out of your system now. There are lots of good women out there who will love Elio like their own."

Caleb gestures toward Sloane and Elio. She's holding him up while he scales the monkey bars, laughing and cheering him on, and he's grinning like it's his birthday. "She adores him. It's plain to see."

"And he adores her right back," Joshua says.

"I've seen the way she looks at you," Giulio supplies. "The attraction is not one-sided."

"It still can't happen. I'm tempted. So fucking tempted, but I can't risk it. If I went for it and it didn't work out, she'd have to leave, and Elio would be devastated. He's just lost one nanny. I don't want him to lose another."

"He might lose a nanny but gain a mother," Joshua quietly

says. "I understand your reservations, and it's too early to know if it's worth taking a risk, so I think you're right to hold back for now. But if you develop feelings for her, don't deny them, Cristian. If I'd done the same, I wouldn't be married to the love of my life now. Don't shut her out if there's a possibility you two could have a future together. You'll only regret it if you do."

Chapter Twelve
Sloane

Laughter and raised voices greet me when I reach the bottom step of the stairs in Gia and Joshua's palatial house. Following the sound, I discover the adults congregated in the large, plush living space, spread out across the two white leather sectionals in front of a blazing open fire.

Everyone is here tonight. Little Nico is having a sleepover because his parents didn't want to leave him in the house next door, asleep on his own, even if this estate has the best security systems and they have a baby monitor. I can't fault Caleb and Elisa for wanting their kid to be close by. From the things Cristian has said, the Italian mafia has their fair share of enemies, and if it was me, I'd be overprotective of my kid too.

It only reaffirms I did the right thing leaving my cartel cell behind, even if I'm sick to my stomach knowing my mother is paying that price right now. Nerves prod at me as I stand back, feeling like an intruder. They've all been so nice and welcoming; making sure I'm included in every conversation and I don't feel left out. Shame has a stranglehold on my insides, warring with the usual guilt and fear. I'm the enemy in their midst, and they have no clue. I hate what I'm being forced to do, but it is what it is, and I've got a part to play. Time is ticking, and if I don't produce something tomorrow, Pablo will seriously hurt my mother to make a point.

I clear my throat, and every head whips in my direction. "They're all asleep," I confirm, standing awkwardly behind the couches.

"You're an angel," Elisa says, scooting up and patting the empty space beside her. "Come sit. We have wine."

"You didn't have to do that, Sloane." Cristian's intense attention sends fiery shivers tiptoeing up and down my spine as I walk toward the girls. "Thank you."

"Our kids already have you twisted around their little fingers." Caleb grins as he lifts a bottle of beer to his lips. "It was manipulation at its finest."

"What would you like to drink?" Gia asks.

"Wine is good. Thanks," I say, sinking onto the couch in between Gia and Elisa. "I didn't mind," I tell Caleb, looking over at him. He's seated at the end of the other couch with Cristian on his left. "They're the sweetest kids. Adorable and so well-mannered. You should all be proud." I was flattered the kids wanted me to read them a bedtime story, and it wasn't a chore.

"We're honored to be their parents." Elisa hands me a glass of lush red wine. "I just love being a mother."

"Do you want kids, Sloane?" Caleb asks, his eyes boring a hole in the side of my head.

"Caleb! That's a really personal question." Elisa shakes her head, warning him with her eyes. "Ignore him, you don't have to answer."

"We're all friends here," Giulio says. "You'll quickly discover that means nothing is sacred and no topic is off-limits."

"It's an invasion of Sloane's privacy." Cristian glares at his friends. "Drop it and stop being rude."

"I want kids," I truthfully admit, because answering seems the best way to avoid an argument. "Though it's not in the cards for a long time."

If at all. It's not like I can plan anything anymore. The thought is sobering and upsetting. On several occasions this past week, I've fallen into the fantasy, almost forgetting the reality of my situation. Every time I crash-land into the nightmare of my current existence, it's like stabbing myself through the heart. I'm trying to stay focused, to remember I'm doing this to save Mom, but it's hard sometimes not to let my mind wander to all the plans I had for my future. A future that evaporated in an instant the moment I stepped foot in that Russian bar that fateful night.

"You'll make an amazing mother," Elisa says, yanking me out of my head. "If our kids are any indication, children naturally gravitate to you because you have a warm, nurturing, and fun side."

"That's very kind of you to say." I sip my wine, fighting the growing turmoil inside me.

"So, Sloane." Giulio's eyes twinkle with mischief as he stares at me. "Are you dating anyone right now?"

"Giulio." Cristian manages to convey such menace with that one word—it's impressive.

"I'm casually dating, but it's not serious at all," I say before lifting the wineglass to my lips.

"You failed to mention that, my friend." Caleb arches a brow in Cristian's direction.

"Like I said earlier, Accardi, Sloane's private life is no one's business but her own."

"Are you exclusive?" Giulio leans forward with his elbows propped on his knees, flashing me a flirty grin.

A laugh bursts from my chest. "What part of *casually dating* and *not serious* gave you that impression?" I want Cristian jealous, but the lie could backfire if I'm not careful.

"Great, so if I was to say...hypothetically ask you out to dinner, you might not be opposed to it?" Giulio asks with an expanding grin.

Holy fuck, this is so not helping. "Umm." It's not that Giulio isn't dateable. He's a good-looking guy. Well dressed with good taste, obvious money, and charm, and he seems to have a fun personality. But he's not my target, and I don't think going on a date with one of my boss's friends will positively support my goals in any way. I glance briefly at Cristian. Steam is practically billowing from his ears, but I'm not sure if he's offended on my behalf or if he's jealous. "I'm flattered, Giulio, but I don't think that would be appropriate given my position as Elio's nanny."

Relief is written all over Cristian's face. Caleb is grinning like he's privy to some private joke. Elisa is eyeballing her husband and issuing some silent warning. Joshua is sitting back on the couch, with his ankle resting on his knee, looking unfazed as he takes it all in. Gia is drinking her wine and watching all our reactions carefully, and I get the sense nothing gets past her.

"You're too old for her anyway," Cristian says.

Giulio's lips tease into another grin. "I'm only a few years older than you."

Cristian's shoulders stiffen. "What has that got to do with anything?"

"Age is just a number," Caleb says. "Look how happy Valentina and Fiero are, and the age gap between them is much larger."

"Change the subject," Cristian barks, tightening his grip on his beer bottle.

"So, back to kids, Sloane," Caleb says, and Cristian snaps, jumping up and jabbing his finger between Caleb and Giulio. "You're both meddling pricks." He drains his beer and sets it down on the table. "I'm going out for a walk." He storms off, leaving tense silence in the air.

"That was cruel," Elisa says, staring at her husband. "You should go after him."

"Let me." I climb to my feet, putting my wineglass down. "I could use a walk too." I rush off in the direction Cristian went, grabbing my new coat and gloves on the way.

When I step outside, my boss is nowhere in sight, and I haven't got a clue where he might've gone.

"I know where he is," Gia says, appearing at my back. "Come on. I'll walk you over to him."

"Thanks." I fall into step beside her, and we don't talk for a few seconds until Gia breaks the silence.

"I'm sorry about those idiots back there." She rubs her bare hands together. "It might seem like they're stirring up trouble, but it's only because they care about Cristian. We all do. He's one of the good guys, and he deserves all the happiness in the world."

"I get that, and you don't need to apologize." My breath forms little puffy clouds in the chilly nighttime air as we take a left and step onto a path that cuts across the large shared garden at the rear of both properties. "I'm guessing his ex did a real number on him," I add, throwing out the bait.

Surprise splays across Gia's face. "He told you about Aliya?"

I nod. "She sounds like a selfish bitch."

"Aliya disappointed us all. They were dating for two years, and I thought of her as a friend. She was fun, smart, ambitious. We all thought she really loved Cristian, but she showed her true colors when he adopted Elio. She didn't say anything at first. We think she thought he wouldn't go through with it or that the Da Rosa family would take him in. But as soon as the adoption papers were signed and Cristian took Elio home, she changed her tune. I've never been so disgusted in another woman. None of us speaks to her anymore."

"At least she didn't pretend. That would've been worse." The irony isn't lost on me.

"True. She spared him that pain, Elio too."

"I don't know how anyone could reject either of them. I haven't known them long, but it's long enough to know the truth. Any woman would be lucky to have them in her life."

"Does that sentiment extend to you?" she asks, slowing down as we reach the woods.

I purposely frown. "I'm not sure I follow."

"Don't do that. We've all seen the looks passing between you. The attraction is obvious."

"I'm the nanny, Gia. Cristian is *my boss*."

"I didn't let that stop me when I was Joshua's employee." She shoves her hands in the pockets of her coat. "I won't tell you what to do. Cristian is right; it's no one's business but your own, but I will say this. Don't hurt him, and don't mess him around."

Before I can even try to form a response, she points to a path on the left. "Follow that trail. He'll be in the gazebo at the end." Gia spins on her heel and walks off, leaving me drowning in a pool of guilt and pain.

It takes a few minutes to compose myself before I set off in the direction of the gazebo. Lights border the stone path all the way, helping to guide me. Giant evergreens form a forested arch overhead, and mottled fallen leaves crunch under my feet as I walk, surrounded by nocturnal sounds of the woods. I'm lost in thought, plotting different strategies and wondering which angle is the best to play.

"You shouldn't be out here," Cristian says from behind me, and I almost have a coronary on the spot.

My heart jumps into my mouth, and a scream tears from my lips. I stumble on my feet as my knees buckle. Warmth seeps through my coat, heating me all over, when Cristian slides his arm around my waist and pulls me up against him. "Sorry. I didn't mean to startle you."

"Holy fuck." I slap a hand over my chest, rubbing at the anxiety mushrooming there. "You shouldn't sneak up on people like that!"

"Come sit down." Keeping me tucked into his side, with his arm firmly holding me upright, he guides me over to the gazebo and down onto the couch inside.

The cushion dips when he sits beside me, and I feel his intense gaze on me as I examine our surroundings. String lights creep up the four wooden posts, helping to illuminate the space alongside the spotlights embedded in the circular stone patio the gazebo is positioned on. The long rectangular coffee table plays host to a myriad of candles and diffusers. Various flower beds with different shrubs, flowers, and stone decorations border the structure on all sides. "It's pretty out here."

"You should see it in June or July. It's magnificent during the day with an abundance of colorful flowers, but at night, it's magical when the fireflies come out to play. I like to come here when I visit to think."

"I'm sorry. I didn't know you preferred to be alone. I only wanted to check you were all right." I stand, praying he stops me.

I look down at him, watching some inner battle wage upon his face. "Stay."

His dulcet tone invades every nook and cranny of my being, lighting me up from the inside. I let my tongue peek out, wetting my lips, watching him trace the movement with his eyes, and I settle on a game plan. It's risky, but I don't have months to seduce him. *Mom* doesn't have months. I have to work with what I've got. I wasn't sure if I was imagining the looks he throws my way when he thinks I'm not watching, but Gia just confirmed it. "How long are we going to ignore this thing between us, Cristian?" I deliberately lower my voice, piercing him with a sultry look as I wait for his reply.

He stares at me for what feels like an eternity. This time, I can only guess at the inner battle taking place because he's wearing a carefully constructed neutral expression on his face. "I don't know what you're talking about."

I stare him straight in the eyes. "Don't embarrass me, Cristian. At least have the balls to face up to it."

He holds himself rigidly still, and he doesn't break eye contact as he replies. "Having this conversation is not in either of our best interests."

"Your friends don't seem to think so." I sit back down, deliberately letting my knee brush against his leg. "Unless I've mistaken what that was all about back at the house."

"My friends spoke out of turn, and you'd do well to forget it."

Tentatively, I reach out and touch his arm. "Tell me I'm wrong. That I'm imagining the way you look at me." My fingers trail up his arm, and he doesn't move a muscle to stop me. His gaze is fixed on my face, and electricity crackles in the air. "That you don't feel the same electric pull between us. That your heart doesn't speed up when I enter a room like mine does with you." My hand touches bare skin at his neck. His pulse thuds steadily under my fingertips, and his Adam's apple jumps in his throat as I slowly caress his neck and his jawline. I move a little closer, letting my thigh snuggle against his. Fire burns in his eyes, and his nostrils flare as his hungry gaze dips to my mouth. "That you don't imagine what it'd be like to kiss me when your eyes linger on my mouth like they are now."

My fingers trail a path over his lush lips. My heart is pounding behind my chest, and butterflies are running amok in heady anticipation. My mouth waters as I fixate on his mouth, silently pleading with him to kiss me. "I know you want to kiss me, like I know you're longing to touch me the way I'm touching you right now." I press a kiss to the underside of his jawline, my nose touching the silky layer of stubble residing there.

Cristian hops up, and I almost face-plant the couch. "It doesn't matter what we feel. Nothing can happen, Sloane. You're my son's nanny. We can't let anything get in the way of that."

"I can be Elio's nanny and mean something to you too," I say, though I know it's a lost cause from the expression on his face. He looks tortured, like he's writhing in pain. I rise to my feet. "I've never felt such a strong connection to any man before, Cristian. Maybe it's not the same for you, but something that feels like this can't be wrong."

"To cross that line would not be right, Sloane, and let's face it. I'm way too old for you."

"How old are you?" I ask, leaning against one of the gazebo posts.

"I'm thirty-two and already far too jaded. You should be with someone your own age."

I push off the post and close the distance between us, pressing my hands to the front of his jacket. "Guys my age are immature and self-obsessed. None of them could compare to you. Your age doesn't matter a bit to me, Cristian." I place my hand over his heart. "All that matters is what's in here." I peer deep into his conflicted eyes. "You're a good person, Cristian. The most incredible father. I can't help how I feel, and—"

He steps back, letting my hand fall to my side. "No, Sloane." His tone is authoritative, brooking no argument. "This cannot and will not happen. You are Elio's nanny, and he is your sole priority. If you can't put your feelings aside, we may have to reconsider your position. I don't want to do that, but this isn't happening. Do you hear me?"

Fuck. I've overplayed it, and now all seems lost. "Yes, Cristian. I hear you loud and clear." My voice cracks, and it wasn't intentional.

His features soften, and his voice is gentler when he speaks. "I don't want to hurt you, but you've got to let this go. We can forget about it and start over."

"Forgive me. I shouldn't have said anything."

"I blame my friends, not you, okay?"

Pain lashes me all over as I nod.

"Come on. It's freezing. Let's go back to the fire."

Chapter Thirteen
Sloane

I watch Gia and Elisa bundle the three kids into the back of a sleek black SUV from my hiding place at the window. I was supposed to go visit Leo and Natalia with them, but I faked PMS to get out of it. I hated lying to them, especially after we had a great night last night, chatting for hours about everything and anything, but I need to snoop, and this is the only chance I'll get. The guys left an hour ago for golf, and I've no idea when they'll be back.

When the car disappears out of sight, I grab the letter I wrote and head out of the bedroom. I haven't seen any cameras in the house, but I'm assuming they're all part of the Italian mafia—the names are a dead giveaway—and privy to the same technology Cristian uses. Maybe Gia and Joshua don't have cameras inside their house because the estate is like Fort Knox, but I can't take silly risks. So, this is the best idea I could come up with.

I walk into Cristian's room, closing the door behind me. I'm trusting they don't have cameras in the bedrooms. The bedroom is tidy, the bed neatly made, and Cristian's weekend bag is already packed and resting in the corner. Placing the letter on the bed, I head to the bag to search it. My heart plummets as I inspect the carefully folded clothes and his toiletries bag. But that's the sum total of the contents. There is nothing of relevance, nothing that is of any use to me. Tears prick my eyes as I sit back on my knees. I wasn't overly hopeful, but it's still a blow. I rub at my eyes and check the bag is how he left it before pulling the zipper closed. Then I place my decoy apology letter on top and leave his bedroom.

I walk to the kitchen in a bit of a daze. I'm failing my mother. I'm a lousy spy. An ineffectual seductress, and I don't know where I go from here. I don't know what to do, and I wish I had someone to talk to. Finding some peppermint tea in the cupboard, I put the kettle on to make a cup, hoping it will help to settle my nerves. I must keep my wits about me if I'm to come up with a new plan.

My eyes skim over the island unit as the kettle whistles in the background, and my gaze returns to the large, padded brown envelope sitting on the counter. My feet move on autopilot before I can track the motion. *Cristian* is written on the front of the sealed envelope. Feeling around it, I detect what I think are multiple folders inside. The kettle reaches a crescendo before clicking off, and my brain fires into action. Bringing the envelope to the kettle, I hover the sealed side over the steam, rejoicing as the edges of the flap start lifting. It takes another round with the kettle before the flap is loosened enough for me to open it without breaking it.

I glance out the large window on instinct, but there are no cars approaching. Too late, I wonder if there are cameras in here. Panic jumps up and slaps me, but I've come this far, so I might as well continue. Carefully extracting the contents, I separate the three files and place them flat on the counter. There's a note too:

Cristian,

This is all I've managed to find so far, and we won't know for sure until we speak to these women. Given the need for discretion, I felt it more appropriate to provide this in print rather than risk leaving a digital footprint. Let's meet for coffee during the week to discuss after you've had a chance to review the intel.

Best, Gia.

I frown as I flip open the files, finding personal information on three women and their young kids. One of the ladies is American, the other two are European, and they're all single mothers. What is this? Could Cristian be searching for a wife? Or a new nanny? Did I completely fuck it all up last night? No, it can't be the latter. Gia would have prepared this before my failed seduction attempt. The first option makes more sense. I'm guessing arranged marriages are commonplace in their world. It's also an additional reason why Cristian rejected me last night and seems determined not to pursue the attraction between us.

Pablo has requested information on Cristian's business and mafia dealings, and I'm fairly sure this intel is completely unrelated, but it's all I've got. I snap pictures of all the files, hoping Cristian doesn't have access to the content on my cell phone or, if he does, that I can transfer it to my cartel cell and wipe it in time before he checks. I google how to reseal the envelope, happy to find the glue has become sticky again, and it secures easily. Then I reposition it where I found it, make myself a peppermint tea, and hightail it back to my room.

The tablet I asked Gia for before she left is staring temptingly at me from the top of the dresser in my bedroom. I've been too afraid to use my cell to search for news of Mom and me, in case Pablo's contact somehow has access to it, but he won't have access to this. Still, I need to be cleverer than I was back in the kitchen. I can't search for that in the off chance Gia somehow finds it, but I figure it's safe to look up my best friend.

I input the password Gia gave me and log in. Creating a fake Gmail account, I use it to set up an Insta profile. Barely breathing, I pull up Rory's profile, and tears instantly sprout when I see my friend's beautiful face. My heart thuds painfully in my chest, and I wish I could write her a message, tell her what happened, and beg her for help. My finger hovers over the message button for far too long. Tears stream down my face as I contemplate the pros and cons, but ultimately, I know I can't do it. I can't risk Pablo going after Rory, period.

I read through her posts with a heavy heart, happy she's out there living her best life, but sad she's doing it alone. I should be by her side as she parties, goes to yoga, jogs around campus on our regular route, and attends classes as a senior. In less than four months, she'll graduate with her degree. That was supposed to be me, too, and anger crashes through my despair. I want Pablo Fuentes to pay for what he's done to me, to Mom, to all the other women he's got trapped in his enclave.

My tears reappear when I discover she posts weekly, asking for news of me and Mom and tagging various state agencies. Rory's posts have been shared thousands of times, and there are so many supportive comments.

In the immediate aftermath of our disappearance, it looks like the mainstream media picked up the story, and my face was splashed everywhere. I watch the brief clip of the CNN report Rory has pinned on her page with a massive lump in my throat. If I were to google my name, I bet tons of articles would pop up.

My crying gets louder when I see pictures and videos from Ithaca. Our community seems to have rallied around our disappearance. Everywhere Rory walked in town, there are posters tacked to walls and light posts pleading for help in finding us. The mayor even released a statement, and a GoFundMe page was created to raise money for a private investigator and a reward to offer to anyone with information. I can barely see my old high school friends through the tears blurring my vision. I recognize several people holding posters as they walk up to the town hall to join other protestors.

Rory's most recent video post is a heartfelt, frustrated condemnation of the authorities and their failure to protect American women. Rory states that a quarter million American women go missing every year, and hundreds go missing in Mexico while on vacation, and the government does not do enough to find them. She vows to continue pushing for intervention, promising she won't give up until she has answers. The online petition she's set up has over twenty thousand signatures so far.

My bestie is the absolute best, and I miss her so freaking much. Without her efforts, I wonder if anyone would've even known we were missing or cared.

My heart hurts, the pain so extreme it feels like I might stop breathing. I hug the tablet to my chest as I purge more tears. As if I needed other reasons to love Rory. I knew she wouldn't forget. I knew she wouldn't let me down. I want to contact her so badly, but my selfishness and recklessness got me into this mess, and I have zero desire to tangle Rory up in this nightmare.

It pains me to exit her page and delete my account and the Gmail, but I do it. For Rory. I permanently delete all traces of my activities from the tablet and curl up into a ball on top of the bed, clutching a pillow and hugging it for dear life. My tears dry as I let my melancholy go. I have to find a new plan. I can't give up just because my first seduction attempt failed.

I don't know at what point I fell asleep, but I wake with a jolt when I hear Cristian calling me.

"What's wrong?" I sit upright, resting my back against the headrest as I brush knotty strands of hair out of my eyes. Cristian is sitting on the side of the bed, so close I can count his eyelashes. Warmth emanates from him in waves, and the urge to wrap myself around him is strong. I'm vulnerable right now, and I long for the safety of his strong arms.

"I should be asking you that." His gorgeous green eyes radiate compassion as they study my face. I can only imagine what he sees—splotchy skin and swollen eyes—and the obvious conclusions he'll draw. He holds up the small envelope I left in his room. "I read your note. Your apology isn't necessary. Clean slate, remember?" he softly adds.

"I feel like I keep messing up, and it's only a matter of time before you fire me."

"I'm not planning to, Sloane." He stands and lifts one shoulder. "Come with me."

"Are we leaving?" I swing my legs off the side of the bed, stifling a yawn as I rise.

He shakes his head. "Elio is with the others at Nat and Leo's place. The guys went there after our round, but I didn't stay. Elisa said you weren't feeling well, and I wanted to check on you." His eyes peer deep into mine. "Is that the truth, or have I done this?"

"You haven't done this," I truthfully reply. "I'm not feeling great. Being around your friends, your family, reminds me of everything I no longer have." I force a smile. "For so long, it was only Mom and me, and now she's gone, and I feel so lost and so alone." It's probably the most real I've been with him. I work hard to trap more tears. I cannot keep crying in front of this man. I slap a hand to my chest. "It hurts so much sometimes it feels like I can't breathe."

Cristian envelops me in his arms, and I go willingly. I don't cry, and we don't speak. He just holds me, and it's everything.

"I'm sorry you're hurting," he says before breaking our embrace.

I wrap my arms around myself. "Thank you for being so understanding."

"You don't have to thank me for that. Come. I have something for you."

Curious, I follow him out of the room and down the hallway till we come to the master bathroom. A delicate floral fragrance tickles my nose as I step into the opulent room. A freestanding tub occupies pride of place under the window, offering an expansive view of the rear gardens and the woodland behind it.

"I thought a bath might help." He dips his fingers in the water. "It's still warm."

My cheeks flush, wondering if Elisa told him I had my period or if he guessed. He knows now it's not the truth either way.

"It smells lovely in here."

"I found some scented oil and put some in, and I left towels for you by the sink."

"This is really thoughtful. Thanks, Cristian."

"You're welcome." He backs up. "Take your time. We're not leaving for a couple hours yet." He lingers in the doorway.

"Okay." My smile is genuine, and fresh hope is tentatively building as he remains in place, staring intently at me, almost like he wants to say more and he's reluctant to leave.

He clears his throat, and his expression is tender when he says, "I can't relate to what you're going through as I've never lost anyone I loved more than life itself, but it's totally normal to grieve, and it's always better to let it out than keep it bottled up inside."

I may not be grieving in the traditional sense, but I am grieving for everything Mom and I have lost. Even if we somehow manage to get out of this alive, we will never be the same people again. Our lives have been permanently altered in an irrevocable way. "You must think I'm a basket case."

"No, Sloane. I think you're human."

I don't deserve his compassion, but I'm too selfish to refuse it. "I swear I'm not usually this much of a mess."

"You don't need to make excuses, and you're not alone, Sloane. My friends have already adopted you, and you have Elio." He runs a hand through his hair, messing up the styling. "You have me," he adds. "I know things are a little strained between us, but you can lean on me, Sloane. You can be Elio's nanny and my friend, if you want."

I see it for the lifeline it is, and I fully grasp it with both hands. "I would like that, Cristian."

His lips curve ever so subtly. "Good." He finally steps back. "I'll leave you to your bath before the water goes cold."

Chapter Fourteen
Sloane

"Stay put," Cristian says after parking the car in the basement parking lot of his apartment building. His eyes soften when they land on his sleeping son. Elio is out cold, fast asleep with his head resting against my side. I have barely moved a muscle in the past hour, afraid I might wake him. "I'll get him," he adds before climbing out of the driver's side.

Cristian is careful opening the back door and unbuckling his son's seat belt before gently lifting him into his arms. Elio mumbles in his sleep as he snuggles against his father's chest. Cristian jerks his head for me to follow, and I get out of the car, still clutching the eye mask in one hand, acknowledging the bodyguards as they open the trunk and retrieve our bags.

No one talks while we ride the private elevator to the penthouse. Removing my shoes inside the front door of my new home, I slip my feet into my slides and trail Cristian to Elio's bedroom, quietly watching him undress his son and tuck him into bed. Elio's eyes open for a few brief seconds, and he sleepily smiles at his father before succumbing to slumber again. Cristian stares at him for a few beats before tenderly kissing him on the brow.

Pressure settles on my chest as I watch the sweet moment between father and son, and I slip away to my room before my boss sees me. Leaning back against my door, I squeeze my eyes shut as my chest tightens in pain. After I slump to the floor, I raise my knees and cradle my head in my hands.

I can't do this. I can't take that man away from his son.

Tears prick my eyes, but I don't let them fall. I can't keep breaking down like I have been. The journey back to the city was agony as I battled with myself. Cristian ran me a bath, and he gave me a box of melatonin to help me to sleep. He'd gone to the pharmacy after golf, especially to pick them up for me. Then Gia gave me an Italian cookbook that was her mother-in-law's. She said Natalia wanted me to have it so I could learn a few staples. Elisa handed me some essential oils her Aunt Sierra had given her to help with my fake PMS.

These are good people. The best people. They barely know me, and yet they welcomed me with open arms, and they went out of their way to help me. How can I betray them? It would be the worst way to repay their kindness.

The photos of the files are sitting on my cell phone taunting me. I don't even know if sending them to Pablo will do any good. He wants intel on drug shipping routes, not random single mothers Cristian is considering marrying. If I send these pictures, will I put those women at risk? And will it be for nothing if Pablo still punishes my mother? But if I don't at least appear to look like I'm trying, he might kill my mother.

I'm damned if I do and damned if I don't.

I don't know how long I sit on the floor contemplating it before I get up and go to my closet to grab my cartel cell. My heart is heavy as I turn it on, knowing what I must do. Fear has an ice-cold grip on my heart as the phone vibrates with a slew of messages and missed calls. There are two new videos, and without looking, I know what I'll find. It pings with a new message, proving Pablo is getting alerts on my phone activity and always watching.

Intel now or your mother is dead.

The message is accompanied by a picture of my mother with her head yanked back and a knife held to her throat. Mom is barely recognizable under the multitude of bruises and cuts to her face. Stuffing my fist in my mouth, I try to muffle my anguished cries.

I did this.

She's hurting because of me.

I should be the one all bloody and bruised, not my mother.

I'm not a religious person, even less so since Mom's precious God let this happen to us, but I pray now as I send the files to that Sinaloa monster, begging God to spare my mother and these innocent women.

If there is a price to pay, let it be me who pays it because everything that has happened is all my fault.

My entire body shakes as I wait for a reply. It comes five minutes later. An instruction to meet Diego and Alvaro at a diner two blocks away. I don't want to go, but he'll kill my mother if I'm a no-show. I change into jeans and a nice top and put some makeup on as if on autopilot. All the blood has leeched from my skin, and no amount of blush or bronzer disguises it. The uncontrollable shaking hasn't gone away either, and I need to get a grip before I give the game away. I concentrate on my breathing, slowly inhaling and exhaling, feeling the pull deep in my belly as I attempt to lower my heart rate.

When I'm as composed as I can be, I grab my purse and my cartel cell, leaving the cell Cristian gave me behind in case Pablo's goons have any ideas of putting tracking software on it. Then I leave my bedroom and hope it's not the last time I'll see it.

"Going out?" Cristian inquires when I reach the kitchen. He's standing in front of the coffee machine, wearing a slight frown.

"Yes, if that's okay."

"Of course. You are free to do whatever you want in your downtime," he says, offering a smile that doesn't seem entirely genuine. "I made you a coffee. I can put it in a takeout cup if you want to bring it with you?"

He is such a thoughtful man. I can barely speak over the painful lump clogging my throat. "Thanks."

His eyes pin me in place as his frown returns. "Is everything okay?"

I force a smile. "Yes. I'm just meeting a...friend." I almost choke on the word. "I shouldn't be too long."

His probing gaze continues to stare at me as his frown deepens. "It's dark out. You should take John Angelo with you."

"I was planning to." I want Pablo's goons to see my bodyguard. To know if they try to murder me, they might end up losing their lives too. I'm not planning on going any-fucking-where without John Angelo. He may be the difference between life and death.

"Good." He doesn't look happy as he transfers my coffee to a travel mug. "Here. This should keep you warm."

My hands barely feel the warmth as they wrap around the mug. "Thanks, Cristian." I fake another smile before walking off, hoping it's not the last time I see him.

"Sloane."

Cristian stops me when I reach the archway into the entrance hallway. I glance over my shoulder, willing my hand to stop shaking. "Yes?"

"Are you sure you're okay?"

No! Help me! Help my mother! End this nightmare for both of us. "I'm fine," I lie. "I'll see you later."

"Enjoy your night," he says, but his tone and his eyes lack all trace of his usual warmth.

* * *

John Angelo walks by my side as we head in the direction of the diner. His towering frame, broad body, and alert eyes offer some comfort, but it's only fleeting. I drain my yummy coffee in record time, but it does little to warm my icy bones. I pepper my bodyguard with questions to keep myself distracted. He gives me short, clipped answers, and I'm probably annoying the shit out of him, but the older man is too polite to tell me to shut up.

The closer we get to the diner, the more my nerves fire at me. By the time we reach the door, I'm a certifiable mess, and I need to get my shit together. I work hard to pull a mask over my features. To slip into the role of Sloane Clark, but it's challenging. Perhaps it's just as well I didn't get to finish my studies. I'm not sure I have what it takes to be an actress.

"Do you want me to come in or wait outside?" he asks, and I dither over how to respond.

Sloane Barton wants him to come in and protect me, but would Sloane Clark ask a bodyguard to come inside when she's on a date? I worry my lower lip between my teeth before making my decision. "If you could stay out here, please." I'm trusting he'll still keep a watchful eye from outside.

"No problem."

"Thanks," I whisper before I pull my big-girl panties on and open the door.

Once inside, I scan the room for the two assholes, but they aren't here yet. A waitress seats me in a booth facing the window upon my request. Being able to see John Angelo gives me a small modicum of relief. I order a chai and a muffin and try to steady my nerves as I wait for them to show up.

I'm on edge as the waitress carries my order to my table. Where the fuck are they? I want to get this over with. I sip my tea and force a few mouthfuls of muffin down, but it tastes like sandpaper, and my stomach churns unpleasantly as the seconds tick by.

My heart jumps into my mouth a couple of minutes later when my phone vibrates with a new message. I open it under the table, nearly spewing the contents of my stomach when I read the command to go to the bathroom.

My legs almost go out from under me when I slide out of the booth, but I force one foot in front of the other and make my way to the bathroom, feeling John Angelo's eyes on me from outside. Opening the door, I encounter a long, narrow hallway with four doors. I'm heading toward the female restroom when an arm reaches out from the wheelchair-accessible bathroom, and I'm yanked inside.

A hand clamps over my mouth to smother my startled cry. The lock clicks as Diego circles the front of my body. His hard eyes warn me not to shout. Alvaro's arm wraps around me from behind, tugging my back to his chest. I'm trembling all over and incapable of stopping my body's natural reaction.

"El Rey isn't happy with you," Diego supplies, tilting my chin up with the tip of his gun.

"We have her," Alvaro says, keeping his arm around me

while he thrusts his free arm out, showcasing that sick fuck on the screen of his cell.

"Who is the man following you?" Pablo grits out, glaring at me from the phone.

"One of Cristian's men. He's my personal bodyguard. I tried to get him to stay behind, but Cristian is insistent I take him whenever I go out alone."

The two goons chuckle, and I hate them with the intensity of a thousand suns.

"Cristian, huh?" Pablo arches a brow.

"It's what he told me to call him."

Pablo purses his lips for a moment. "What is this shit you sent me?"

Diego keeps the gun pressed into my chin, and a cold sweat breaks out over my body. "It's all I could get, but it must be important because it was classified, and I had to steam the envelope open to get at the contents."

"Who are these women?"

"I don't know, but they must be important." Please forgive me. I send the thought out to the universe, praying someone keeps those women safe.

"You have disappointed me, my little American Barbie." Pablo's glacial tone spears through me like an actual dagger. "Where were you this weekend?"

"At their friends' house out of town. I had to wear a blindfold the entire journey, so I don't know where it was, only that it took over six hours to get there." I lie on purpose, hoping to thwart any efforts they may make to find the property.

"Why was your cell not on you?" he snaps.

"Cristian warned me security would be tight and I would be searched upon arrival. I had no choice but to leave the phone behind. If I'd taken it, they would have it in their hands, and the game would be up. I didn't have any time to consult with you, and I had to act fast, so I made the only decision I could. Please don't punish my mother for it. I had no choice, Pablo, please."

"You don't seem to understand the seriousness of the situation."

"I do!" I blurt. "I understand, but you've got to give me more time. It's only been a week. Cristian is smart. If I make a move too soon, he'll figure it out." I'm not telling him I crashed and burned already. "Please, Pablo, I'll get you what you want, but it will take time."

Pablo stares at me for so long I wonder if he's even breathing. "Okay," he says after an indeterminable time, shocking me. He usually goes out of his way to disagree with me, purely for an additional reason to punish my mother. "You have one month, but no longer. That is enough time to seduce the prick and get me what I need. In the meantime, you will install the cameras Diego gives you."

"I can't. He has cameras all over his house. They are really sophisticated and completely hidden, but he told me they are everywhere, and they have audio and visual functionality. If I try to plant anything, I will be caught."

"How do I know you're not lying to me?" Pablo leans into the camera, his menacing sneer filling the screen.

"Check with your contact. I'm not lying."

"You'd better not be."

"I know what's at stake. I would not gamble with my mother's life."

"I think you need additional incentive," he says before switching to Spanish and talking directly to his men.

Diego grins, removing his gun from my chin and placing it down on the counter beside the sink.

"You will do what you are told," Pablo says, switching back to English. "You will also meet Diego and Alvaro every Sunday here at the same time for the usual debriefing." He fixes me with a lecherous smile. "You have one month and not a day longer. Do not disappoint me."

The call ends. My anxiety skyrockets when Diego takes a step closer and his dark eyes fill with lust. My trembling accelerates as he rakes his gaze over me. Terror tightens my chest, and bile crawls up my throat. Alvaro grinds his hips and thrusts against me, and I'm grateful for my jacket blocking his hard-on from pressing into me.

Two sharp raps sound on the door. "Sloane, are you in there?" John Angelo asks.

Diego lifts the gun, pressing it to my temple as he warns me with his eyes.

My life literally depends on how convincing I am, so I slam my mask down and project calm as I reply. "I'm here and I'm okay."

"Are you sure?"

"Yes, I'm just dealing with some, ah, women's stuff, but I'm fine."

"Oh, okay. I'll wait outside." I barely hear his footsteps as he leaves.

Diego punches out a message on his cell, and it vibrates with a reply. Lifting his head, he nods at Alvaro, and his buddy removes his arm from around me and shoves me at Diego. "You go first. Watching you blow your load in her mouth will get me really fucking hard."

"No." I move to step back, but Alvaro grabs my arms, yanking them behind my back. "Please don't do this. Let me go, and I won't say anything to Pablo."

"Has our little Blowjob Queen forgotten her place?" Diego taunts, dragging my zipper down the front of my jacket.

"And it's El Rey to you," Alvaro adds, cupping my crotch through my jeans. "Show the boss the respect he deserves."

Never. "Please don't." I plead again, knowing it's futile.

"Remove your clothes. I want to come on your tits," Diego says, groping me through my top and bra.

"Cooperate and we'll tell El Rey you were a good girl, and maybe he'll go easy on your mama," Alvaro adds, fully removing my jacket and rubbing his disgusting crotch up against me from behind.

I zone out as I remove my upper garments, drop to my knees, and open my mouth wide.

Chapter Fifteen
Cristian

"Come in, boss." Umberto opens the door, letting me inside the bodyguards' apartment that is on the floor below the penthouse. Spotting the man I came to see, I walk toward the kitchen. "I'd like a word, John Angelo."

"Sure thing, boss." He sets his bowl of cereal down and follows me into the hallway that leads to the bedrooms where it's quieter. "Is everything okay, sir?"

"I'm not sure." I lean against the wall and eyeball him. "Where did Sloane go on Sunday night?"

If he's surprised I'm asking, he doesn't show it. "To a diner a couple blocks away. The one on the corner, opposite the phone store."

I know the spot. It's not a bad place. They do a mean apple pie, but it's not somewhere I would ever take anyone on a date. "Did anything happen while she was there? She's been a little off since then, and I'm worried about her." I asked her once if she was okay, and she assured me she was, but I'm not buying it. She's been a lot quieter this week, and when she's not working, she holes up in her bedroom and rarely comes out. I can't shake the feeling that something is wrong.

"Ah, I think I know why." Compassion splays across his face. "I didn't want to say anything because it wasn't a security risk, but she mentioned she was meeting a guy, and he failed to show. She locked herself away in the bathroom for ages. Gave me a bullshit excuse when I checked on her, but when she came out, she was clearly upset."

"That explains it." She said it was casual and not serious with the guy, but it's not unsurprising she was upset when it happened the day after I rejected her advances. Fuck. I hate that I contributed to her melancholy mood. What kind of asshole would stand a girl up like that? Especially one as amazing as Sloane. I will never understand some men. "Thanks."

"No problem, boss. She's a sweet kid."

Internally, I wince. She might seem like a kid to an older man like John Angelo, but she's all woman to me. I haven't been able to stop thinking about her since she hit on me. I know I did the right thing stopping it before we crossed a line, but I can't help imagining what it might've been like to kiss her and touch her. To call her mine. I sure as shit would not be arranging a date in a diner and then standing her up. I'm tempted to make her tell me his name so I can acquaint him with my right hook, but her private life is none of my business, and I've really got to get a grip.

Perhaps Caleb is right, and I need to get laid. Maybe getting some woman underneath me will cure me of the illicit thoughts I can't shake from my brain.

"We might have a problem," Don Fiero Maltese says, claiming the attention of everyone around the table. It's our weekly early-morning board meeting of The Commission at Commission HQ in the heart of Manhattan. So far, we've just been gossiping like women over coffee and pastries, but now shit's about to get real.

"You have the table," Don Massimo Greco says, nodding at his best friend to proceed.

For a long time, it was a given that Fiero would succeed Massimo as Commission president. But that ship has sailed. He muddied his reputation a couple of years ago when he kidnapped his now wife Valentina from her then husband. Dominic Ferraro was a total piece of shit who initially sold his wife to Fiero for a weekend. Fiero, the consummate bachelor of the *mafioso*, fell head over heels in love and refused to give her back. But that's a story for another time. Suffice it to say, while protecting Valentina, he ruined any chance he might've had of becoming the next president. Not that he cares. He's blissfully happy, all loved up with his wife and his one-year-old son Armani, and they've got another *bambino* on the way.

"One of my men came to me Monday with some alarming news." Fiero scrubs a hand along his prickly jawline. "He received an anonymous request to meet. A legit threat was made against his family. He was told to tell no one and attend the meeting alone. He came straight to me, and I put protections in place to safeguard his family and encouraged him to go to the meeting under the guise of cooperation."

"Let me guess." Bennett Mazzone says. "The cartel is making their move."

"Correct." Fiero bobs his head.

"What did they want him to do?" Caleb asks.

"Obtain details of the Cali operation and shipping routes from Mexico to New York."

Fiero and Massimo own a drug production plant in Cali and a shipping hub on Staten Island. They provide *Cosa Nostra* across the US with the high-class narcotics we supply to VIP clientele, mostly through our network of clubs. Joshua and Fiero manage the smaller street-supply operation in New York in conjunction with our Irish mafia partners, purely to ensure no one encroaches on our territory. It's often more hassle than it's worth, but it's a necessary evil to protect our turf.

"It's not surprising they're trying to go after our drug trade," Caleb says, leaning back in his chair.

"We hit their business, so they'll try to retaliate by hitting ours," Agessi agrees.

"I still think they'll come after my family too. Cruz promised them something he didn't deliver. They're not going to let that go." I smooth a hand down my tie as I level my colleagues with a neutral look.

"We don't disagree with you, Cristian." Massimo taps his pen on top of the table.

"That's not how it seemed to me." Caleb lifts a brow in Massimo's direction.

My buddy is loyal. Joshua too. They were both as pissed off as me when the board voted against my proposal to create a team to track down women Cruz might have impregnated as part of his master breeding plan. Aside from the personal reasons for wanting to track these women down, I want to ensure they are all safe and well taken care of and that none of the children ever become targets because of the DNA they share with me and Elio.

Fiero, Joshua, Caleb, and I were the only ones who voted to find these women and children. The others all voted no, and we were outnumbered. They don't consider it a priority. They think it's safer for the kids to remain blissfully unaware of their heritage and by reaching out we'll draw attention to them.

While it's a valid point, I think they're making a mistake. These women and children are part of our *famiglia*. Not checking to ensure they are safe is failing to meet the most basic of obligations, in my opinion. The only ones who know I haven't dropped it are Caleb, Joshua, and their wives. Gia is putting herself at considerable risk helping me on the down-low in her spare time, and I couldn't love her any more for it.

"Allocating considerable resources to tracing women and children who may or may not exist is not viable. This intel proves it. The cartel is targeting us at grass-roots level, and we've all been put on warning now." Massimo rakes his gaze around the table. "We cleaned house not too long ago, but that doesn't mean some can't be turned. Meet personally with your men. Make it a priority. Tell them we know this is happening and to come forward if they are approached. Reassure them we can protect their families and keep them safe."

Heads bob around the table.

"This is a priority, and I want a weekly update from now on." Massimo's gaze swings to mine. "You should take additional precautions, Don DiPietro, though they may not attempt to infiltrate your *famiglia* as it's the obvious ploy."

"Unless it's a double bluff," Mantegna says.

"I think everyone should be extra vigilant," Ben says. "While Fuentes and the other members of the Sinaloa leadership can't step foot on US soil without risking arrest, there is nothing stopping their crew from going after us. We have to assume they've been biding their time and making plans they are now are putting in motion."

"You should put additional security measures in place to protect your parents," Massimo says, staring down the table at me.

"That's already in place. I upgraded their security system and installed a panic room at the house two years ago. They have every tech available protecting them, and a team of guards watches the cameras and walks the perimeter twenty-four-seven. No one is getting near them." I knew this time would come, like I knew our family would be the cartel's first targets. I have been prepared for this moment since my brother died.

"Good." Ben runs a hand through his hair. "It's been a while since I talked to the old man. I'd hate anyone to target him because of that bastard Cruz." My father represented our *famiglia* during the time Ben was Commission president. There's a lot of mutual respect between them.

"I'll see them on Saturday at Isa's wedding. I'll warn Papa to be on his guard."

"What's next with your *soldato*?" Joshua asks Fiero.

"He's agreed to go along with the ruse. We're going to feed them some fake information. Lure the guys into a trap, and then we can interrogate them."

"It's a good plan," Massimo agrees. "I want to be apprised of every step going forward. Run everything by me first."

"Consider it done," Fiero says.

The meeting moves on to regular business, finally wrapping up ninety minutes later. Fiero approaches me as we're all gathering our things, preparing to leave for our respective offices. "Valentina wants you to come to lunch on Sunday. She misses Elio," he says.

"We'll be there."

He clamps his hand on my shoulder and lowers his voice. "You can tell me how the hunt for Cruz's kids is going."

"You're not supposed to know about that," I coolly reply, slinging my laptop bag over my shoulder.

"They're your flesh and blood. I know you well enough to know you couldn't rest easy without confirming they were okay, and I get it. Valentina needs that same peace of mind."

"We shouldn't discuss this here," I say, noticing Massimo frowning as he glances at us from the top of the room.

"Agreed. We'll talk Sunday. Come around three." He steps back. "And bring the new nanny. Valentina wants to meet her."

I'd throw something at his smirking face if I wasn't in the conference room with President Greco's suspicious scrutiny already directed at me.

Chapter Sixteen
Sloane

I tiptoe out of Elio's room, careful not to wake my little prince. We had a very busy day, and the little guy is all tuckered out. Stopping in the doorway, I turn and stare at him. He's so precious. I've only been in his life for ten days, but I already love him so much. Quietly closing the door, I head along the hallway and back to the kitchen to clean up. Cristian didn't join us for dinner tonight. He's out, and he said he'd be late. He didn't mention whether he had eaten or not, so I plate the leftover lasagna and cover it with Saran Wrap in case he wants to reheat it later.

It was my first attempt at making it, following the recipe in the cookbook Natalia gave me. The sauce is a little watery, but the flavors are good. Elio seemed to like it anyway.

After I clean the kitchen, I walk toward my bedroom, like usual, but think better of it. While I have my own TV, I'm sick of looking at the four walls in there and I'm not in the mood to sketch tonight. Grabbing an unopened bottle of white wine from the refrigerator and a wineglass from the cupboard, I head into the living room and get settled on the couch.

Kicking my slides off, I snag a blanket from the back of the plush leather sectional and position myself in the corner with a large soft cushion at my back. I pour a large measure of wine into my wineglass and sink into the couch with the blanket covering my lower half.

I flick through the movie options and choose *Goodfellas*. It came out way before I was born, and I've never seen it. I don't know if Italian mafia movies are anything like real life, but at least I'll get to watch a few villains slaughtered in cold blood, and I can imagine it's Diego, Alvaro, and Pablo getting their just desserts.

Knots twist in my gut, and bile crawls up my throat like every time I think of Sunday. I've been really struggling to keep it together this week, hiding from Cristian every night because I don't trust I won't crack in front of him. I squeeze my eyes shut, but it doesn't expel the scene from replaying repeatedly in my mind. It's a miracle I lasted the journey home without breaking down in front of John Angelo. I spent way too long in the shower that night, trying to scrub Diego's disgusting dried-in cum from my chest and using the water to shield my cries. Retching repeatedly didn't soothe my pain either knowing Alvaro's vile seed was already deeply embedded in my stomach. At least they didn't strip me down below or force themselves inside my vagina. That is something to be grateful for.

A strangled sound rips from my mouth unbidden as the movie starts. Is this what my life has come to? Being grateful to monsters for not assaulting me in worse ways? Memories of the beating Mom was subjected to because of my failure resurrect in my mind to add to my agony. He's going to kill her, and it will be all my fault.

Draining half my wine in one go, I wish it would anesthetize me. I want someone to remove my brain and scrub it free of all the hideous memories that keep me up at night.

I've taken the melatonin Cristian bought me at bedtime, but it isn't helping. I still can't sleep, and I'm running on fumes. I have forced food down my throat each day purely because I need to eat to keep my strength, but it's challenging when all I want to do is give up. I want to crawl into a black hole, cover myself in a blanket, and block out all the light. I want to retreat inward and numb myself to everything.

But I don't get to be that selfish.

Mom is counting on me, and I can't ever forget that.

Wrapping the blanket fully around me, I drink my wine and try to concentrate on the movie. It's good, and eventually it sucks me in, and I forget reality and lose myself in the violent world exploding on the screen. I'm so immersed I don't hear Cristian walking toward me until it's too late.

"Good choice," he says, and I jump about ten feet in the air, spilling the dregs of my wine over myself and the couch. Good thing it's leather and it'll wipe off easily.

"Oh my god, Cristian!" I shriek. "You scared the hell out of me."

"Shit, sorry. I thought you heard me come in." His gaze lands on my chest, where the wine has made the material almost see-through.

"I'll get out of your way." Putting my glass down, I swing my feet onto the floor.

"Come back after you change," he says, meeting my eyes. "I haven't watched this movie in years, and I could do with a drink."

"Sure, okay." I leave the room and return to my bedroom, removing my wet shirt and wiping the sticky layer clinging to my chest. I'm lost in thought as I fix myself up. One good thing about moping all week is I've decided the best strategy with Cristian is to just be myself. Well, as much of myself as I can risk being. I know he's attracted to me, and I pray he'll cave at some point. He said we could be friends, so I'll be his best friend and let things develop more naturally. I don't know if I can make him fall for me in a month, but deliberately trying to seduce him won't work, so this is all I've got.

I hope it's enough.

After changing, I return to the living room.

"I got you a fresh wineglass," he says, pointing to it on the table as I walk toward him. "I also paused the movie, so you didn't miss anything."

"We can go back to the start if you want," I suggest, eyeing the glass of wine with apprehension. I should probably take it easy. I've already had a large glass, and I'm afraid my tongue will loosen and I'll say something I shouldn't if I drink much more.

"Nah. I'm good. I watched this movie a lot with the twins when we were kids."

I settle back into my corner, and Cristian hands me a different blanket. "The other one is a bit wet."

"Sorry." Accepting the blanket, I unfold it over my legs.

"What for? I'm the one who startled you and caused you to spill your wine. It's no biggie. Mrs. Peake will send it out to the dry cleaners."

"She's a really sweet lady," I say, taking a small sip of my wine. "She's been very kind to me."

"She used to work for my parents, but she came to work for me when I bought this place ten years ago. In a lot of ways, she's been like a second mother to me."

"She speaks very highly of you. It's obvious she loves you like a son."

"The feeling is mutual. As much as I don't want to be without her, I've been encouraging her to retire for a couple years now," he admits, lifting the wineglass to his lips.

I watch his throat bob as he swallows, and there is something so incredibly sexy about it. The layer of stubble on his chin and cheeks is a little thicker than usual, and it really suits him. Visions of running my fingers through the soft bristles dance through my mind, and lust stirs deep in my belly. It's been a long time since I've been turned on by a man, and it's good to know I haven't been completely ruined by recent experiences.

A longing for Cristian to hold me coasts over me. His arms offer security, warmth, and strength, and I pine for it. I've been extra vulnerable since Sunday, and I wish I could crawl into his lap and let him comfort me.

"I can't imagine that went down well." I run the tip of my finger over the rim of my glass. "I get the feeling she loves looking after you and Elio. She told me her husband died years ago, and she didn't have a family of her own. I imagine her identity is fully tied up with her work here."

"You're not wrong, which is why I haven't pushed it. But I worry about her health. She has worked hard her entire life, and she should be enjoying herself now."

"She enjoys taking care of you. That's all she needs," I say, because it's blatantly obvious. As is the way Cristian cares for her. She told me he bought her a bungalow with a massive garden a few years ago, and he pays for a car and driver to take her anywhere she needs to go. "Will she be coming to the new house?"

He nods. "I'm building her a self-contained apartment within the house, too, but I haven't given up hope she might use the opportunity to retire or at least cut back to one day a week." He swirls wine in his glass. "Ultimately, it will be her choice." He shrugs before taking another mouthful of wine.

"I thought you were staying out late tonight." I pull my knees into my chest.

"I changed my mind." He scrubs a hand along his chin as his gorgeous green eyes stab into mine.

Electricity charges the air, and he can't not feel it. The chemistry is potent between us. There's an intensity to it I've never experienced before. His Adam's apple bobs in his throat when he finally tears his gaze from mine. "What made you choose this movie?" he asks, focusing on the paused image on the screen.

"I'm not sure. I wanted something with action or suspense, and this caught my eye." It's not exactly a lie, but it's not the full truth either. I hope my choice of movie hasn't triggered any suspicion in his mind. In hindsight, it probably wasn't a smart decision.

"You don't like romantic movies?" He moves a little closer.

"I do, but I have to be in the right mood."

His lips kick up at the corners. "And tonight, you're in more of a murderous mood?" he teases.

"Something like that." I take a gulp of wine, hoping he drops the subject. Thankfully, he does.

"Let's get to it then." He presses the play button, ending our conversation.

Gradually, we move closer and closer until we're sitting side by side. "Damn, that's vicious," I say at a particularly gruesome part.

"Does it disturb you?" His inquiring gaze flicks to mine.

"The scene or the fact it happens in real life?" I risk asking.

"You think this happens in real life?" His eyes are subtly probing, and I'm conscious of just how close we are.

"You don't?" I volley back.

"I know there are plenty of evils in this world. Unfortunately." His eyes dip to my mouth for a nanosecond.

"Unfortunately, I know that too."

His brow puckers. "Did something happen to you?"

I want to tell him everything. But I can't risk it. He has a rat in his midst, and I don't know who it is or how much access they have. I wonder if they are being blackmailed by the cartel too. "Something doesn't need to have happened to know about the evils in this world. I've watched my fair share of documentaries. Heard stories at college. A girl at my high school was murdered by a sick pervert when I was a junior. Mom tried to raise me to be aware of the world around me, both positive and negative."

If only I'd been more aware when it counted.

"Your mom sounds amazing."

"She is." I almost choke on my wine. "I mean, she was."

Compassion floods his face.

"Sometimes, I forget she's not here anymore," I add.

"I can't imagine how tough it must be. It sounds like you and your mother had a very close relationship." He leans forward to grab the wine bottle, and a whiff of perfume tickles my nostrils.

My stomach lurches, and I gulp over the lump that appears in my throat. He was out with a woman tonight. It hurts more than it should, and not for all the right reasons either.

"What's wrong?" he asks, stalling with the bottle in his hand.

"Nothing," I croak before clearing my throat. "Just thinking about Mom."

He doesn't look convinced, but he lets it go. "I've been thinking a lot about my relationship with my son since you came into our lives. I shudder to think what it'd do to him to lose me so young. It makes me more determined to always be around for Elio."

Guilt shreds my insides at his words.

Cristian refills his wineglass before moving the bottle toward mine. There isn't much wine left, but I know when I've reached my limit. Slapping my hand over the top of the glass, I shake my head. "You finish it. I won't be in a fit state to watch your son tomorrow if I drink more."

"You're good with him, Sloane. Thank you."

"Please don't thank me." He'd be sick if he knew the truth. "Taking care of Elio doesn't even feel like a job. I love being with him," I say with sincerity.

A loud pop on the screen interrupts our conversation, and the movie reclaims our attention. Tommy falls forward with a bullet hole in the side of his head.

"He had it coming," Cristian says. "He was too much of a loose cannon, and he didn't abide by *omertá.*"

"*Omertá?*" My brows lift.

"It's a code of silence and a code of honor within the Italian mafia. Tommy was never going to be initiated."

"Sounds like you know your mafia movies."

His eyes bore into mine. "Something like that."

I don't know if it's smart to pursue this conversation, but I don't have time to play it safe. "Do you know how to use a gun?" I ask.

Shrewd eyes examine my face. "Why do you ask?"

I shrug casually. "You've spoken about having enemies, and you have a top-notch security system with armed bodyguards."

"You caught that?"

"I'm not naïve, Cristian. I don't need to see the guns to know your guys carry them."

His knee brushes against mine. "Does it bother you?"

I vigorously shake my head as my eyes latch onto his lips. He has a gorgeous mouth, and I bet he knows what to do with it. Shivers cascade over my body at the thought of Cristian's mouth all over me.

"Sloane?" Cristian snaps me out of it, and I realize I've been staring at his mouth like a lovesick fool.

My cheeks heat in embarrassment. "It doesn't bother me. It's the opposite, in fact. I feel safe knowing I'm protected."

He nods slowly. "New York is a dangerous city, and yes, I have a gun, and I know how to use it. My father took me to the shooting range from a young age."

"How young were you, and will you do the same with Elio?"

"I was six, and yes."

"Wow, that's super young."

"Maybe." He shrugs, knocking back the last of his wine.

This could backfire, but I've got to ask it. "Will you teach me? I want to know how to use a gun."

Chapter Seventeen
Cristian

"Why?" I ask, working hard to mask my surprise. Has Sloane figured some things out about me and my position within *La Cosa Nostra*? I come home to find her watching a mafia movie, and now this? Is it just coincidence? Or am I reading too much into it now I know for sure the cartel is targeting us?

"I think every young woman should know how to defend herself. Like we've agreed, there is a lot of evil in the world."

"You could attend a self-defense class," I reply. "There are plenty of them in the city."

"I've already taken self-defense classes, but I'd like to know how to shoot. I want to get a firearm, but I don't have a clue how to go about it."

I study her pretty face, but I don't detect any lies. It's been a long day, and I'm way too cynical. Of course, it would be natural for any woman of her age to want to know how to fully defend herself. Watching a popular mafia movie means nothing. Sloane is smart, and she's drawn natural conclusions. I'm pretty sure she has zero idea I'm one of the leaders of *La Cosa Nostra* in the US.

"I can get a gun registered for you," I offer, "and I'll teach you how to use it. There are a few ranges in the city, or we can use a private range close to the twins' place on weekends."

"I like the idea of a private range," she says, her eyes lighting up. "Thank you."

"We can't go this weekend as Isa's wedding is Saturday and friends have invited us to lunch on Long Island on Sunday, but I'll organize a gun and take you for your first session the following weekend if you like?"

"That sounds great." Her tongue darts out, wetting her tempting lips. "So, uh, does that mean I'm not needed this weekend?"

"Come to the wedding with me," I blurt without engaging my brain. "As my nanny," I add, cringing on the inside. "You know how energetic Elio is. I could use a second set of eyes on him." That's a perfectly logical reason for her to attend, and I should have asked her earlier. It's got absolutely nothing to do with not wanting Sloane free to meet up with that asshole who stood her up last week.

"I'm not sure Isotta would like that."

"There's a plus-one on my invite, and she wouldn't cause a scene at her own wedding. Besides, she'll be too busy to even notice." I hope. I don't pull rank often, but I'll do it on Saturday if I have to. She should be expecting Elio's nanny to attend, and I'm not going to rescind my invite just because Isa has taken a dislike to Sloane.

"I don't know. I don't want to make an enemy of her or cause any trouble for you."

I fear it's too late for that. "I'll smooth things over. Trust me, it'll be fine."

"Okay. If you're sure?" She nibbles on her lips, and I've never been jealous of teeth before.

"I am, so that's settled." My arm slides along the back of the couch, dangerously close to Sloane's shoulders. My every instinct implores me to lean closer and claim that lush mouth. I don't know why I bothered wasting my time going to Club H tonight when there is nowhere else I'd rather be than at home with her.

Exactly, fuckface. My inner voice doesn't hold back. *You were supposed to fuck some random stranger and get Sloane out of your head.* Except she's already dug her way under skin and bone, and despite several tempting offers, none of the women who approached me tonight raised even the slightest interest. My dick stayed soft all night, and in the end, I gave up, frustrated and horny as hell, and came home to the one woman who only has to glance at me and my cock gets hard.

This could be a real problem.

I'm reminded of a conversation I had with Caleb, back when he was falling for Elisa, and he tried to fuck her out of his system to no avail.

I drag a hand through my hair and retract my wandering arm from the back of the couch. Fuck. I can't let myself fall for Sloane. She's not the one for me. The sooner I get that message through my thick skull, the better.

"Are you feeling okay?" Concern underscores Sloane's tone as she yanks me out of my worrisome inner monologue. "You look a little flushed. Did you eat?"

"I had a late lunch but skipped dinner." Loosening my tie, I pull it over my head, before unbuttoning the top two buttons of my shirt and running a hand around my neck.

"Stay right there." Sloane hops up and disappears for a few minutes while I pause the movie. There's still a decent amount left after the scene where Tommy got whacked.

Sloane returns holding a tray with a pasta bowl and silverware. "I saved you some dinner," she says, setting the tray down in front of me. "It's my first time making this recipe. I hope it's okay." She shuffles shyly on her feet. "It should fill the hole in your stomach at least," she jokes. A pretty blush stains her cheeks.

"Thank you." Leaning down, I sniff the steam rising from the bowl. "It smells delicious," I truthfully admit.

A hypnotizing smile spreads across her decadent mouth, and we stare at one another for a few seconds.

"I'll just grab you some water and a napkin," she says before hurrying out of the room again.

I dive in, suddenly ravenous, and it's pretty damn good for a first attempt. Sloane comes back, handing me a glass of water and a napkin. "This is really good."

She positively blossoms with my praise. "I'm glad you like it," she says, sitting beside me. I restart the movie and watch it while I eat. The instant I'm finished, she swipes the tray up, refusing to let me lift a finger. Dabbing my mouth with the napkin, I watch her leave the living room, thinking a guy could get used to having her around the place.

I come home early on Thursday night, wanting to spend some time with my son before bedtime. I hadn't called Sloane to let her know, wanting to surprise Elio, but I'm the one surprised when I step foot in the penthouse. My nostrils twitch at the scent of vanilla and butter in the air as I unbutton my coat and hang it up. High-pitched squeals come from the direction of the kitchen, and the sounds of racing footsteps tickle my eardrums as I approach the room.

"You're too slow, Slowpoke Sloane," Elio shouts in between giggling.

"No, don't," Sloane cries before dissolving in a fit of laughter.

I stop in the doorway, amusement covering my face when I see the state of the place. The counter is littered with the evidence of baking, and there is flour everywhere. It's sprinkled on every surface and dotted all over the floor. Elio and his nanny are engaged in a tickling contest on the floor, and they are both coated with flour and what looks like dough on their clothes and in their hair.

"Having fun without me?" I inquire, walking toward them with a big smile on my face.

"Daddy!" Elio shucks out of Sloane's arms and heads toward me.

"Elio, no!" Sloane warns, but it's too late.

My son barrels into me, wrapping his sticky flour-coated arms around my legs. White handprints mark my black pants, but I couldn't care less. It'll wash out.

"I'm sorry, Cristian." Sloane stands before me, cringing as she surveys the mess Elio has made of my pants.

"Don't be. I like seeing my son having fun."

"Even if we made a mess of your kitchen, ourselves, and your pants?"

"Kitchens, people, and pants can be cleaned."

"We made torch cookies!" Elio squeals.

"Torcetti," Sloane confirms with a smile. "They should just be done," she adds, her steps hastening toward the stove as she glances at the clock.

"I'm surprised any made it into the oven," I quip.

"We were supposed to be making biscotti next, but *someone* thought it would be a good idea to have a flour fight instead." She eyeballs Elio with nothing but pure joy on her face.

"It was so fun, Daddy," he says before removing his arms from around me. He grabs my hand. "You need to try my torch cookies. They're gonna be yummy."

"Careful, my little prince," Sloane says, cautioning Elio to hold back as she opens the oven door. A blast of steam shoots out, blowing over her face. "Wow, that's hot." I hold Elio back a safe distance, and we watch Sloane remove the tray with an oven glove. She carefully sets the tray down on a wooden board. "Wash your hands if you want to help coat them with sugar."

I lift Elio up to the kitchen sink and help him to fully wash his hands. Then I dry them with some paper towels and set him standing on the chair Sloane has propped up against the island unit. After washing her hands, she shows Elio how to dip the looped golden-brown cookies in powdered sugar and place them on a wire rack to cool.

"I want to eat one," Elio proclaims, rubbing a hand over his tummy. "They smell delicious!"

Sloane laughs. "How about we clean ourselves and the kitchen, and then the torcetti should be cool enough to eat?"

"I want one now." He pouts, jutting his lower lip out.

"They are too hot, and they'll burn your throat and hurt your tummy." Sloane holds out her hand. "We need to get the dough bits out of our hair before it becomes a nightmare. Come on." She lifts one shoulder. "Clean up, then we get a treat."

He's moody as he presses his hand in hers, but he goes willingly enough, and I'm impressed. "We'll be back, but this could take a while," Sloane says over her shoulder before they leave the room.

I steal a cookie before I slip out of the room, almost burning my tongue as I devour half of it in one go. The buttery flavor explodes in my mouth, taking me back to my youth when Mama spent every Saturday morning making an array of Italian baked goods. Cruz and I used to fight to be the first one to reach the kitchen and claim the first almond biscotti. Those were my favorite, but torcetti were a close second.

Stripping out of my ruined pants, I place them in a sealed bag before pulling on some jeans. I drop the bag in the laundry room for Mrs. Peake to take to the dry cleaners before I head to the kitchen to clean up. I'm chuckling as I listen to Elio's shrieks coming from the bathroom.

When they still haven't materialized thirty minutes later, I go to investigate, discovering Elio crying where he's sitting in the middle of the tub. Sloane is carefully combing his hair while trying to comfort him. "It's okay, sweetie," she says. "I got it all out now." She presses a kiss to his cheek as I lean against the doorway watching her with him. "I just need to shampoo it once more and give it a final rinse."

"My head hurts," he whines, sobbing again.

"I know, my little prince, but the quicker we get this done, the sooner you get that cookie," she reminds him, and it's the magic word. Elio dutifully tips his head back.

I grab a large towel and watch while Sloane gently washes his hair. Compassion splays across her face as she tends to my son. "He dunked his head in the water before I could comb it out," she explains to me in a whisper. "The flour congealed and stuck to his hair. Removing it was not pleasant. The poor little guy."

"Don't think he'll be in a hurry to do that again," I whisper.

When he's done, I lift him out and bundle him up in the towel before sitting on the closed toilet seat and cradling him in my lap.

"I don't like flour fights anymore," he proclaims, sniffling a little.

Sloane and I share a knowing look as I bite back a smile. "It's always good to try something once."

"Daddy?" Elio looks up at me with trusting eyes, and it's like being punched in the heart.

Every time he looks at me like this, I want to bottle the feelings it invokes in me. I hug him a little tighter. "Yes, buddy?"

"Can I have hot chocolate with my cookie?"

"Sure thing, son."

"Yay." He jumps off my lap and runs naked out of the bathroom. Sloane moves to go after him, but I take her elbow, stopping her.

My fingertips are on fire where they make contact with her skin, and I yank my hand back as if burned. "Get yourself cleaned up." I eye the mess in her hair. "I've got this."

The delicate column of her throat moves as she stares wordlessly at me, slowly nodding.

That familiar static electricity fizzes in the small space between our bodies, and I'm cursing under my breath as I hightail it out of the bathroom, knowing I'm totally fucked and unsure what the hell to do about it.

Chapter Eighteen
Sloane

My cartel cell pings with an incoming message on Friday morning, instantly slaughtering my good mood. Cristian and I watched a movie again last night, and we spent hours chatting with both of us pretending the searing-hot chemistry sparking between us didn't exist. I went to bed with a big smile on my face. Should have known it wouldn't take long for reality to come calling.

Pain scrapes my throat dry as I look at the photo of Mom's bruised body. My punishment on Sunday clearly wasn't enough. Pablo took it out on Mom too. The video he sent me Monday night showed him savagely beating her while a few of his men cheered from the sidelines. It's haunted me all week.

The phone vibrates with an incoming video call, and I check my bedroom door is locked before racing into my bathroom to answer it.

"The clock is ticking, my little American Barbie," he croons as he forces Mom to her knees in front of the camera. She's naked, but it's nothing new. I've almost forgotten what it looks like to see her clothed. "I thought you might need an added incentive." His dark grin sends chills creeping up my spine. "Watch."

Pushing Mom on all fours, he parts her ass cheeks and shoves his hideous cock inside. Mom cries out, lifting her head and staring forlornly at the camera. The usual glazed look is vacant, and it's the first time I've seen Mom lucid in months. It's clear someone else is in the room, recording the assault. Tears roll down her pale cheeks, and her face contorts in pain as Pablo thrusts and grunts behind her.

Pain eviscerates me, and I wrap my free arm around my middle, struggling to hold back my tears. Mom's eyes focus on the screen as the animal continues to hurt her. "I love you," I mouth, hoping it registers.

"Save yourself," she mouths back. "It's too late for me."

I shake my head repeatedly. I know what she's saying, but she can't ask that of me.

I hear Cristian calling me from outside my bedroom, and panic seizes me. "I need to go," I whisper. "Cristian is looking for me."

Pablo's lust-drenched face fills the screen as he continues thrusting. "Three weeks, Sloane," he pants. "You have three weeks to deliver, or it's lights out for Mommy Dearest." The last image I have is his hand circling Mom's neck from behind before the screen dies.

"Sloane? Are you awake?" Cristian asks, and I don't even have time to compose myself.

I walk on autopilot toward the bedroom door and unlock it.

"Shit, sorry." He averts his eyes, but not before snatching a quick look at my flimsy tank top and sleep shorts. "I wanted to let you know I made an appointment for you this morning. John Angelo will drive you."

"An appointment?" I ask in a flat tone.

"Yeah." His eyes scrutinize my face. "Is everything okay?"

"I'm fine," I lie. "Just another bad night's sleep."

"The melatonin isn't helping?"

"A little," I lie again.

He doesn't look convinced, but I'm wrung dry. I don't have any more juice to fake it. Inside, I'm a mess, and it's a miracle I'm standing.

He clears his throat. "I booked some treatments at a spa for you, but I can cancel if you're not feeling up to it."

"What?"

"I thought you might like a little pampering before the wedding tomorrow. Gia and Elisa will be joining you there."

"What about Elio?"

"My mother is watching him until you're finished. I'm driving him over to my parents' place before work." His brow furrows. "Are you sure there's nothing troubling you?"

"I'm sure." I force a half smile. "A spa outing sounds perfect. Thanks, Cristian." Though curling up in a ball, screaming and crying, is what I feel like doing, I'm better off trying to distract myself because I'm very close to losing my shit and blowing my cover.

He examines my face again. "You're welcome." He walks off but stops and spins around halfway down the hall. I haven't budged. "If you need me for anything today, call my cell. No time is a bad time, okay?"

He is such a good guy, and I wish I could tell him, but I just can't risk it. Tears prick the backs of my eyes, but I manage to hold them at bay. I nod, swallowing the messy ball of emotion clogging my throat. I slouch against the doorway long after he's gone, despondent and in so much pain it feels like I'm suffocating.

"We have champagne!" Elisa says when I arrive at the luxury hotel spa to discover her and her best friend waiting in the reception area for me. She gets up from the plush velvet couch and thrusts a flute at me. "Who cares what time it is, right? It's never too early or too late for champagne." She waggles her brows as she sits back down, and I take the empty tub chair across from her. Elisa's infectious, bubbly personality is the first thing to lift my dejected mood today, and I'm grateful for it.

"That's a mantra I can get behind," I say, tipping half the glass into my mouth.

Gia laughs. "I knew we were going to be the best of friends." She looks around the swanky salon. "This is super sweet of Cristian, isn't it?"

I quirk a brow. "It wasn't your idea?" On the way here, I assumed the girls must have organized it and asked Cristian if I could come.

"Nope." Elisa grins. "Cristian called to ask if there was a spa in the city we could recommend."

"Then he offered to book us in too, and he organized it all," Gia adds. "If I wasn't already completely in love with my husband, I might be tempted to make a move on Mr. DiPietro."

Elisa cracks up laughing. "Don't mind her. She's full of it. Gia had ample opportunity to make a move on Cristian and didn't go there because they were only ever meant to be friends."

Before I can ask what she means, a staff member appears to take us to the changing area.

Ten minutes later, we are drinking our champagne in the Jacuzzi and picking up our conversation. "What did you mean back there, Elisa?" I ask before swinging my gaze to Gia. "Were you interested in Cristian at one time?"

Gia narrows her eyes at her bestie. "Elisa shouldn't have

said anything. I was merely trying to encourage you to make a move on him."

"Been there, bought the T-shirt, and have egg all over it now," I deadpan before swigging the last of my champagne.

Elisa almost chokes on a mouthful of bubbly.

"Tell us everything," Gia commands, giving me her full attention.

So, I do, explaining what happened the night at their place when I went after Cristian into the woods.

"Cristian is an honorable man, and Elio means the world to him," Elisa says. "I'm not surprised it went down like that."

"It's pure Cristian," Gia agrees. "Don't take it personally. I know he likes you. It's way too obvious to hide."

"It doesn't seem to matter." I stretch my arms back against the edge of the Jacuzzi. "He wants to keep things uncomplicated and stick to professional boundaries, and I only respect him more for it."

"But you like him," Elisa probes.

"More than I should." I don't see the point in hiding the truth. Where I can be honest, I want to be.

"There's no such thing." Gia finishes her champagne, putting her glass down on the ledge. "You can't force yourself to like someone less or not like them at all. Chemistry exists for a reason, and I can relate. Joshua and I were in a similar situation, and we both tried to fight it but couldn't. I'm betting it will be the same with Cristian."

"I pined for Caleb for years," Elisa admits. "He only saw me as a friend until I started dating, and that forced him to take his head out of his ass."

Gia's eyes twinkle. "I know you said it wasn't serious with the guy you're seeing, but maybe you should tell Cristian the guy wants to become exclusive. Make him jealous, and it might spur him into action."

"Or maybe you should take Giulio up on his dinner offer," Elisa says.

"Oh, yes!" Gia's eyes are positively gleaming with excitement now. "That will definitely light a fire under Cristian. He'll go crazy."

"I don't want to lead Giulio on or cause any trouble in their friendship."

Elisa giggles. "Knowing Giulio, he'd agree to it just to wind Cristian up. The guys are always playing pranks on one another."

"You should do it. We can talk to him and help set it up, if you like?" Gia offers.

"I'll think about it." I'm still not convinced it will work. "But back to you and Cristian," I say, eyeballing Gia. "What happened?"

"Do you really want to know?" She leans back, arching a brow. "The guys like to remind Joshua from time to time, to mess with his head, and it always pisses him off."

"You can't not tell me now."

"Sorry." Elisa chews on the corner of her lip. "I shouldn't have said anything."

"If it's in the past, it doesn't matter. I'm more curious than anything."

"If you insist." Gia shrugs. "I lost my virginity to Cristian."

She just puts it out there like that. "Oh, okay, wow."

"And then some." Her lips twitch.

"He made it good for you?" I ask, even as jealousy rears its ugly head.

"He did."

"Did you two date then?"

She shakes her head. "It was a one-time thing, and it never went further. Neither of us was interested in more."

"I see."

Gia sighs. "I knew I shouldn't have said anything."

"No, it's fine. I'm glad I know. I wouldn't like being the only one in the dark."

"I'm sure Cristian will tell you himself at some point," Elisa says. "He's not the kind of man who plays games."

Three beauticians arrive then to escort us to the treatment rooms for our facials, followed by massages. I doze on the table during both treatments for a little while, and I'm more relaxed than I have been in months when I head out to the communal area for my manicure and pedicure. I'm seated between the two best friends, and we chat away as the salon staff attends to us.

I decline more champagne in favor of herbal tea, which I enjoy with some complimentary fruit.

The conversation is casual until the subject switches to Isotta's impending wedding. "I wish you were both going," I admit. "It'd be nice to see some friendly faces."

"She would never invite me," Gia says, admiring her finger-nails. "We have a mutual hate-hate relationship."

"Maybe she has a dislike for blondes," I say. "Because she never even gave me a chance."

Gia snorts. "That's her all over. She would've taken one look at you and been insanely jealous. I'm convinced she wants Cristian, though he tells me I'm ridiculous."

"I wouldn't be surprised if that was true," I agree, sipping the last of my tea. "She's very territorial with Elio and Cristian. She accused me of being a gold digger."

"She did not!" Elisa's shocked gasp turns a few heads.

"I don't know why you're so shocked, Lise. That is pure Isa," Gia says. "She considers every female her competition, and the claws always come out."

"Cristian says she'll be fine with me at the wedding, but I'm not so sure. If it were my wedding, I wouldn't want her at it."

"She won't cross Cristian," Gia says. "He's an important man in our social circles," she cryptically adds.

Anytime I feel guilt building at all the things I'm concealing, I remind myself these ladies are keeping secrets from me, too, and I don't feel so bad. I wish all the cards could be put on the table because I'd love to claim these girls as my friends for real. But wishes usually don't come true, especially in my case.

"Speaking of the wedding, how dressy will it be?" I ask, thinking of the paltry clothing in my closet. "I don't have a huge selection of wedding-appropriate dresses, and I'm wondering if I need to go shopping." I don't have much money, as most of my weekly salary is going into a fake bank account the cartel controls. However, I'm sure I can get a dress if I tell Pablo, but I'd rather not divulge my plans in advance. The less that asshole knows, the better.

Elisa and Gia share a smile. "You don't need to worry about that," Elisa says.

I frown. "I don't?"

"Cristian has it covered," Gia replies in another cryptic display.

"And you don't need to worry about hair or makeup either," Elisa adds. "We've organized a girl to come to the penthouse tomorrow as our treat."

"Why would you do that?" I blurt.

"You're our friend, and it's what friends do," Elisa says.

"It's too much," I protest, blown away by their thoughtfulness and generosity.

"Cristian insisted on paying for today," Elisa adds. "So, the least we could do was ensure you look like a million dollars tomorrow. I always feel amazing when I get my hair and makeup professionally done."

"Isa will throw a hissy fit when you rock up on Cristian's

arm looking like a fucking supermodel," Gia says with a mischievous glint in her eye.

"You're so wicked sometimes, Gigi." Elisa fights a grin.

"That stuck-up cow has it coming," Gia replies. "And don't you dare say you'll feel guilty if you upstage her," she adds, noticing my mouth opening to say that very thing. "She's not a nice person, Sloane. Just remember the way she treated you, and it's not your fault you're beautiful and she's a jealous bitch."

A laugh bursts from my mouth. "I so wish you guys were coming tomorrow."

"Trust me, you'll do fine," Gia says, pinning me with an assuring smile.

Chapter Nineteen
Cristian

"**D**addy! You're home early again!" Elio shucks out of Sloane's reach, racing toward me with one arm in his coat and the rest of it dangling free.

I chuckle as I dip down and gather him in my arms. "I wanted to come with you to your lesson."

Truth is, I couldn't concentrate at work after Sloane sent me a gushing text, thanking me for the dress and the treatments. I got Kate to send me pics of the outfit before she organized delivery to the penthouse, and I haven't been able to stop visualizing Sloane wearing the stunning gold and silver lace gown. More worrying are the fantasies I've been imagining where I rip it off her gorgeous body and worship her smooth skin with my mouth, my tongue, and my cock. I've been half hard most of today, and I was practically useless at the office. Not that I need an excuse to come home early and take Elio to basketball, but I definitely had added incentive today.

"This is the best day!" Elio jumps up and down and dances.

"Thank you so much, Cristian." Sloane stands alongside

me as my son throws all kinds of funny moves. "I can't believe you went to all that trouble for me." Her cheeks are flushed, and her eyes are bright, and I'm relieved to see it. Her pale, vacant stare from earlier concerned me. I think Sloane is struggling with grief much more than she's letting on. I'm glad I could help to lift her mood, even if it's only temporary.

"It's no trouble, and you already thanked me."

"The dress fits perfectly, and it's spectacular. I love it."

"Kate took your measurements last time, and she's very skilled at her job. I'm glad you like it."

"I do, but are you sure it's not too much?" She worries her lower lip between her teeth, and I long to pry it free and suck it into my mouth.

Not helping, Cristian. I silently chastise myself. "All the women will be wearing nice dresses," I reassure her.

"Oh, good. I don't want to stand out or draw attention."

Has she truly got no idea how impossible that is? Sloane could show up wearing a sack and she'd still garner all the attention. She is exquisite even when dressed casually with no makeup on and her hair in a messy ponytail, like now.

"Daddy." Elio tugs on my leg. "Can we go now?"

"Let me get changed, and I've got something to show you first." I retrieve the tickets from my jacket pocket and hold them up. "Who wants to see the Knicks play tonight?"

"Me! Me! Me! This is the best day ever!" Elio squeals, bouncing up and down.

Sloane's smile is affectionate as she watches my son.

"So, I thought we might grab some food after Elio's basketball lesson before we head to the game, if you're up for it?"

"You want me to come too?" she asks.

"Of course, unless you have plans." My mood dips at the thought she might have plans with that asshole she's seeing.

"I don't have plans, and I'd love to come."

"Great." I press my mouth to her ear so Elio doesn't hear. "I thought it might help to wear him out a little today. Hopefully, he'll sleep in late and be slightly less energetic at the wedding tomorrow."

Sloane huffs out a laugh. "It's a nice thought, but I doubt it'll work. He has boundless energy, and he's already excited for tomorrow. He's been telling me all about his cousins."

"It's worth a try," I say, shrugging even though I know Sloane is probably right.

The night is magical, and I can't help wondering what it'd be like if Sloane was a permanent fixture in both our lives. She just fits seamlessly into our world. I can easily imagine building a life with her if only I had met her under different circumstances.

But I didn't, and she's still off-limits, I remind myself though it doesn't stop my mind from wandering as I wrap my dick in my fist in bed and jerk off to visions of my sexy nanny sliding up and down my cock as I fuck her hard against the wall.

When I get up the following morning to let the stylist in, I almost collide with a sleepy Sloane in the hallway. "I've got it," I say, quickly skimming my gaze over her face. The bags under her eyes are becoming more pronounced, and I've got to do something to help with her sleep issues. She's wearing a knee-length ivory silk robe that is clinched tight around her slender waist. Her nipples salute me through the thin material, and blood rushes south to my morning wood. Guess I'll have to deal with that in the shower.

Sloane rakes her gaze over my bare chest, her attention lingering on my tattoos and the ripped muscles on my stomach.

I work out regularly, and I know I look good, but her obvious pleasure as she takes her time ogling me does wonders for my ego. My cock leaks precum, and I really hope she doesn't notice the damp patch on my sleep pants. "Go. I'll show her to your room," I say, angling my body so she doesn't see the bulge I'm hiding.

"I checked on Elio," she says, and her voice has a dreamlike quality to it as her gaze latches onto the deep V on either side of my hips. "Your plan worked. He's still sleeping."

"Good. Hopefully, he'll stay like that for a while."

The bell chimes again, and I drag myself away from my nanny, striding down the hallway and adjusting myself in my pants before I open the door and let the stylist in.

I take a long hot shower while Sloane is getting ready, jerking off in record time to visions of her on her knees with my cock in her mouth. I dress in sweatpants and a T-shirt before ordering fruit and pastries from a local diner, along with pancakes for my son. Then I wake Elio and give him a bath, redressing him in his pajamas just as our breakfast order arrives. I feed myself and my son and take a tray to Sloane's bedroom, adding a mimosa I made for her. Figure a little Dutch courage might be in order, given the day.

Breaking my usual rule, I plonk Elio in front of the TV to keep him occupied while I get dressed. I plan to dress him in his little ring bearer's suit at the last minute.

After trimming the stubble on my face and styling my hair, I slap on some cologne and get dressed. Choosing my favorite black Prada suit, I pair it with a white shirt, gold tie, and black dress shoes. My cufflinks are the ones Mom bought me when I turned eighteen. It's become a kind of tradition to wear them for formal events.

The stylist is leaving as I make my way back out to the kitchen. I see her out and close the door before retrieving my son and taking him to his room to get dressed. Isa's pushy mother has already messaged me several times to ensure we are running on schedule and won't be late.

"This feels scratchy." Elio tugs at the collar of his white shirt. "I don't like it."

"You can get changed after the church and all the photos have been taken," I promise, having already packed a change of clothes for him. Isa's mother will probably throw a hissy fit, but I don't care. As long as he plays his official part, it shouldn't matter what he wears. He's a kid, for fuck's sake. Who gives a shit what he's wearing as long as he's having fun and behaving himself.

"That will take ages," he grumbles.

"You love Auntie Isa, and this is her special day. Just remember you are doing this for her," I say, fixing his tie into place.

"She's going to be so happy when she sees you," Sloane says.

My head whips around, and I find her standing in the doorway like an angel who's been heaven-sent. My mouth slackens as I drink in the vision in gold and silver before me. The lacy dress hugs her upper body to perfection, showcasing her exquisite curves where it molds around her tits, slim waist, and shapely hips. The neckline is low but not indecently so. The little cap sleeves are elegant, and the soft golden layers that flare out from mid-thigh give the dress a whimsical feel. Strappy gold sandals adorn her feet, and her pretty pink toes match her fingernails.

"Is it okay?" she asks as a delicate flush crawls up her neck.

"You look like a princess," Elio says, stealing the words right out of my mouth.

My gaze roams her stunning face, noting every single detail of her flawless features. She's gone for a more understated look with natural lips and a rosy-pink blush on her cheeks, but it's her eyes that undo me. The stylist has made her eyes the focal point, and they appear bigger, fanned by long, thick black lashes, and the blue in her irises is more vibrant. Her hair is smooth and sleek, styled into a simple classic chignon.

She is perfect. Utterly captivating. The most gorgeous woman on the planet.

When her eyes lock on to mine, it's like being sucker punched in the heart. I have never seen any woman more beautiful. She is completely stunning, and I'm speechless.

"Cristian? Is this okay?" she repeats, worry filling her gaze, and I snap myself out of it.

"You're stunning. I'll be the envy of every man there today."

Two red spots darken her cheeks, and I love how unassuming she is.

"Thank you." Her eyes sweep over me and my son. "You both look very handsome."

"My suit is scratchy." Elio tugs at his collar again.

"Remember what I said? This is Auntie Isa's special day, and it's important."

He sighs dramatically. "Okay. I'll do it for Auntie Isa."

"You're a good nephew." Sloane extends her hand toward him and lifts her eyes to me. "We should probably make tracks."

"Let me take a picture," I say as Elio places his hand in hers. They pose in the doorway, both smiling happily, and I snap a couple of pics.

"I'll take one of you two," Sloane offers, holding her hand out for my cell.

We switch places, and I slide my arm around my son and smile for the camera.

"My turn!" Elio rushes toward Sloane. "I'll take a photo of you and Daddy."

"Um." Sloane shuffles awkwardly on her feet.

"Here, let me show you what to do." Crouching beside my son, I demonstrate how to use the camera on my phone. Then I take Sloane's hand and move us back a little, circling my arm around her waist from behind. Heat from her body rolls over me in sumptuous waves, and the heady scent of her spicy perfume tickles all my senses. The urge to bury my face in her neck and just soak her in is almost overwhelming. My cock stirs in my pants, and it's becoming a huge problem around her. Pun intended. My fingers tighten a little at her waist, and I pull her closer. We smile as Elio snaps away, wearing a gleeful grin.

"You're trembling," I say, turning my head to look at her when I feel her shaking. She's only a couple of inches shorter than me in her heels, which I love.

"I'm nervous," she admits, peering deep into my eyes.

The world outside fades as we stare at one another. My heart thumps frantically against my chest wall as I'm ensnared by her gorgeous, big blue eyes. They hide deep chasms and endless depths, and I want to dive in and drown in them—in her. I'm not fully cognizant when I draw her body flush against mine or when her hand gravitates to my chest, and I'm not aware that Elio is still taking pictures. I'm completely under her spell as we get lost in one another. My gaze lowers to her mouth, and her eyes fixate on my lips. It would take nothing to close the scant distance between us and claim her. I want to. I want to so badly, but I can't. I wish things could be different. Those thoughts are like a sledgehammer to my heart and my head, and I pull back, letting her hand drop off my body as I put much-needed distance between us. "Sorry."

"For what?" she whispers.

"For getting so lost in you," I truthfully admit. "Sometimes, it's way too easy to forget there are boundaries when it comes to you."

Sadness glistens in her eyes as she nods. "Then I'm sorry too, for I'm guilty of the same thing."

"Here." Elio shoves his way in between us, smiling as he thrusts the cell at me. It's a timely intervention I'm grateful for. "I took lots and lots of pictures. I might be a photo man instead of an asonaut," he proclaims.

"It's photographer, bud, and you can be whoever you want." I playfully ruffle his hair before smoothing it back out. Don't want to risk the wrath of the Da Rosa women.

"Can you send those to me?" Sloane says, peering at the phone. "If that's okay?"

"Of course." I select all the photos, purposely not looking at them, and send them to her cell. "Come on, let's go." I clasp Elio's hand. "Clint and Umberto are waiting downstairs for us."

Chapter Twenty
Cristian

I'm right. Every pair of eyes turns to stare as I walk Sloane up the aisle toward our seats at the front. Elio is waiting at the back of the church with his nonna and the rest of the bridal party. Isa isn't here yet, but according to her mother, she's en route with her father. I nod at my *consigliere* and underboss as we pass by them. Both are here with their wives to show respect to one of the DiPietro capos.

I only promoted Rafaelo a few months before Elio was born, at my father's request. Papa said it was the right thing to do, even though he doesn't much like the Da Rosa patriarch. Isa's father was one of our longest-serving senior *soldato* at the time, so it was probably the right call. He should be retiring in a few years, and hopefully leaving it to his sons to follow in his footsteps.

"Everyone is staring," Sloane whispers, clinging more tightly to my arm.

"It's hard not to. You look incredible today, Sloane."

"Thank you." She smiles at me, and the expression is similar to one of the photos where we're gazing at one another like we only exist for each other. I couldn't stop sneaking looks at it on the car ride here. A lot of Elio's photos are blurry or cropped, but he took a couple of incredible pics. I should probably delete them, but I know I won't.

"This is us," I say, stopping at the third pew where my parents are already seated. I make quick introductions. "This is my papa, Josef, and my mama, Beatrice. This is Sloane."

"It's very nice to meet you," my mother says, nudging my father to move down and make room. "Elio didn't stop talking about you yesterday. You have made quite the impression on my little *nipote*."

"The feeling is completely mutual." Sloane slides onto the bench beside my mother. "He already has me wrapped around his little finger."

"I'll be right back," I say, trusting Sloane with my parents. I should probably take her with me to greet the groom and his groomsmen, but I promised to protect her today, and I intend to keep my word. The last thing she needs is a bunch of older men perving on her.

Nodding at my parents, I stride to the front row and thrust out my hand, shaking the much older groom's hand. "Congratulations, Carmine. I hope you and Isotta will be very happy together." His hair has more gray than the last time I saw him, and his black jacket is straining to contain his considerable girth. Frustration wells inside me. What father would force his daughter to marry a man so much older than her? I hate this still happens in our world. You will never convince me it's not wrong. I understand when it happens to forge alliances, but in a scenario like this, it doesn't make sense.

"Thank you, Don DiPietro. You honor us by being here today. Your mama and papa too."

I shake hands with his groomsmen, all men from our *famiglia*.

"Is that the new nanny?" Carmine asks, blatantly staring at Sloane as she chats with my parents.

My spine stiffens as I narrow my eyes on him. "Yes. What of it?"

"Maybe I should've held out for the replacement." He laughs at his own joke, and a couple of his groomsmen join him. His tone might sound teasing, but the way he's undressing Sloane with his eyes is anything but trivial.

"Watch your mouth, and quit eye fucking her," I say through gritted teeth. "Remember your place. You're in a church about to marry your best friend's youngest daughter. Show some respect," I hiss, close to throttling the bastard.

"Apologies, *capocrimine*. I did not mean any offense. It's just my nerves getting at me." He dabs his sweaty brow with a monogrammed handkerchief, and I work hard to hide my disgust. There's a reason this man never advanced beyond the *soldato* ranks, and right now, I'm glad for it.

A commotion at the back of the church is a welcome interruption. "I believe the bride has arrived. Congratulations again," I say before spinning around and walking toward my seat, my jaw clenching the entire time.

"Is everything all right?" Sloane whispers when I slide onto the bench beside her.

"It's fine." My facial muscles relax the instant I look at her stunning face.

She leans in closer, placing her mouth close to my ear. "This might be bad of me to say, but I cannot believe Isotta is marrying *him*."

I smother my laughter, but my lips twitch as I turn my head toward her and whisper in her ear, "That makes two of us."

"Why?" she asks, as the "Wedding March" starts.

"It's complicated," I whisper back as we join the congregation in standing. Thankfully, she can't ask me any more questions I'd struggle to answer because the ceremony is underway.

The flower girls lead the procession, scattering petals on the ground as they walk toward the altar. Elio looks proud as punch as he follows them, holding the ring cushion and swaggering up the aisle. The guests all ooh and aah at the children, and they're lapping it up like mini celebrities.

"He has so much confidence," Sloane says, leaning around me to snap a picture. I take a few myself before turning my cell off and slipping it into my pocket.

"Look, Daddy!" Elio shouts when he reaches us, earning a few chuckles. "I'm carrying the rings."

"You're doing a great job, son." Warmth blossoms in my chest as I watch him stride confidently to the altar and hand the cushion off. Then he runs back and slides in beside me. "Well done. You make me proud," I say, hugging him against my side.

"Grandma." Elio leans across me. "Did you see me?"

"I did, *nipote*. You were the best ring bearer I've ever seen."

"I wanna sit beside Grandma and Sloane," he says, pushing past me without delay.

I turn to watch Isa coming up the aisle with her father. Rafaelo walks proudly with his daughter on his arm. The Da Rosa patriarch stops to acknowledge me and my parents, and I wonder what Sloane is making of all this. Perhaps I should've said something to prepare her for today. I'm not sure I'll be able to hold much back after the wedding, and maybe it's time I told her the truth.

Although Isa is hidden behind a traditional lace veil, I sense the daggers she points in Sloane's direction, and I feel a sliver of guilt for not taking her feelings into account. But what's done is done, and she should have realized I'd be bringing my new nanny as my plus-one.

Rafaelo moves on, handing his daughter to Carmine before taking his seat beside his wife.

The ceremony is long, and trying to keep Elio seated and quiet is an effort. When I take him outside to use the bathroom, I let him run around for a few minutes to expend some energy before we return.

Finally, the union is sealed, and the ceremony ends. We trail out after the wedding party, the other guests holding back out of respect for my family. Shit. I can't keep Sloane away from Isa for this part, and it's bound to be awkward. However, it'd be worse if she didn't line up beside me to pay her respects to the happy couple, so she'll have to suck it up and fake it.

"Crap," Sloane mutters under her breath as we approach the church doors, spotting the bridesmaids and groomsmen moving in a line, offering their congratulations to the married couple.

"It'll be fine," I say, tucking her arm in mine. "Just wish them well, and we'll move on."

I let my parents go ahead of us, squeezing Sloane's arm in reassurance as we inch up. Isa's eyes are like laser beams watching us, and her eyes spit fire when she looks at Sloane. Her gaze drags up and down her body with obvious envy. Maybe I should feel guilty for bringing her with me and buying her such an exquisite gown, but I honestly can't find it in me to care. Isa made an enemy out of Sloane when it didn't have to be this way.

"Congratulations, Isa." I lean in to kiss her cheek as Elio barrels past me, running after my parents.

"Hi, Auntie Isa," he sings as he dashes past. "Bye, Auntie Isa."

Warmth softens her stern face as she smiles after Elio. There is no doubting how much she loves her nephew.

"You look lovely," I say, "I hope you'll be very happy."

Before I can pull back, Isa grabs me, making a meal out of kissing both my cheeks. "Thank you for coming, Cris, and thanks so much for your very generous wedding gift. It was truly too much."

I upgraded their honeymoon flights to first class and I purchased a crystal wine decanter and matching glasses set from their wedding list.

"It was indeed most generous," Carmine agrees, pulling his much younger wife into his side.

"Congratulations, Isotta," Sloane politely says. "You look stunning."

"Thank you," Isa says in a clipped tone, and I can tell it killed her to offer that insincere thanks.

"We haven't met." Carmine grabs Sloane's arm, yanking her toward him.

I haul her back to my side, pinning him with a warning look. He is not putting his grabby hands anywhere near her. "This is Sloane. Sloane, this is Carmine."

"It's nice to meet you," she says, clinging a little harder to me. "Congratulations on your marriage."

"Thank you for coming." His eyes briefly land on her chest, and I don't like it. I already warned him inside, and this is the height of disrespect to Sloane, his wife, and to me. "Perhaps you'll honor me with a dance later."

Over my dead fucking body. Before I have a chance to put him in his place again, his bride does it for me.

"Perhaps she won't," Isa snaps, glaring at her husband.

"We'll leave you to your guests," I clip out. I'm seething, and I need to get Sloane out of here before I murder the groom in front of her.

Sloane visibly relaxes against me as I guide her away from the happy couple, heading in my parents' direction.

"Cris?" Sloane inquires under her breath when we're far

enough away. "I didn't realize it was that friendly between you two."

Jealousy is obvious in her tone. It should please me, but I'm trying hard to keep things professional and uncomplicated between us, and the lines are only blurring further. "It's not. I hate when she calls me that."

"Then it's disrespectful of her to keep using it."

"I know." I've been more lenient with Isa than I probably should've been.

"She really hates me," Sloane says over a sigh. "I feel bad that I came. As much as I don't like her, it's not fair. This is her wedding day. I should go home."

"Absolutely not." I turn to face her, stalling our forward trajectory. "I will smooth things over when we get to the hotel. You're here as my guest, and that's final."

We join my parents, chatting with them as I keep an eye on where Elio is running around playing chase with his cousins. We move on to the church grounds for the photos after most of the guests have departed for the wedding reception. Sloane helps my mother to wrangle Elio into position for the various photos while I stand off to one side with my father.

"Sloane is a fine young woman, and she seems to have a good head on her shoulders," my father says.

"She's mature for her age and really good with Elio."

"What about you?" my father asks with a glint in his eye.

"What about me?" I play dumb on purpose.

"Come now, Cristian. Don't try to fool an old fool. She's a very beautiful young woman. Smart, kind, and good with your son. Surely, you know what I'm suggesting."

"She's twenty-one, Pops."

"And?" He stares at me like I'm making no sense.

"And most twenty-one-year-olds don't want to be saddled

with a husband and son. They want to party and enjoy life before settling down."

"It's ridiculous," he scoffs. "My mother married my father at eighteen, and they'd been courting since she was fourteen. I don't know why all the young people make such a fuss these days. Why waste life partying or pursuing careers when you can be a wife and mother?"

"Come on, old man, don't pretend like you're that much of a traditionalist. You were one of the ones who championed for women to have greater rights and freedoms in our world." He also supported Catarina Conti when she first showed up in New York, but I don't mention that because it was Cruz who initially asked my father to give her his backing. Mentioning my brother will only send my father wallowing in a pit of despair and depression. He blames himself for the shame Cruz brought on our family, and nothing any of us says will ever change his mind.

"And I stand over it. Women should have choices, but it doesn't mean my personal views have changed. I don't see anything wrong with wanting to marry young and start a family early."

"This is a pointless conversation." I smile as Sloane bends down to sweet-talk Elio into one more picture. I don't know what she's saying, but it's working. He stops fidgeting with his collar and moves back in front of Isa. "Sloane is my nanny, period. Quit with the matchmaking. I'm getting enough of that shit from my friends."

"It's past time you took a wife, Cristian."

"Please don't start this again."

"I know you don't want to consider an arrangement, but maybe it's the best option for you and Elio. You're not getting any younger, and Elio needs a mother."

"Elio is doing fine, Pops. He's not wanting for anything,

including maternal love. He is doted on by his grandmothers and his aunts, and Sloane adores him."

"I don't want to argue with you. I'm just saying you should consider all options." He squeezes my shoulder and stares earnestly into my eyes. "You're doing a fine job with Elio, Cristian. Your mother and I are so proud of the man you've become. You're an amazing father, as we knew you would be. We only want you to be happy and to have love in your life. You deserve that." His gaze bounces to my mother as she talks with Sloane. "My father chose Beatrice for me, and there isn't a day that I've regretted it. I love your mother more than my life, son. Do not close yourself to it."

My anger fades as fast as it came on. "You got lucky, Pops." My parents have a great marriage, and it's the benchmark I've set for myself.

"You could be lucky too." Papa smiles affectionately at Sloane as he slaps me on the back. "Don't rule anything out. Fate has a funny way of working."

Chapter Twenty-One
Sloane

"Here, you look like you could use this," Mrs. DiPietro says, topping off my wineglass.

She isn't wrong. It's been a long, tiring day, and I'm sick of everyone staring at me, especially the older men. I've even caught the bride's father glancing in my direction a few times. No doubt Isotta has been badmouthing me to her family, and they probably all think I'm a gold-digging slut who doesn't care about their nephew and grandson. Thankfully, Isa has been too busy to approach me, but she shoots daggers in my direction any time we cross paths, and I'm so ready to call it a night.

Forcing my gaze from the dance floor where Cristian is dancing with the bride, I smile at Cristian's mother, hoping my jealousy isn't too obvious. "Thank you." I'm tempted to knock the whole thing back, but I've already had a couple of glasses, and I need to pace myself. I've been too busy hopping up and down with Elio to drink too much, but I don't mind. My little prince is in a side room now with his cousins watching a magic show. The babysitters Isotta hired are taking care of all the kids, so I get a reprieve for a while. I spotted a few men who are obviously bodyguards standing watch outside the kids' room and around the ballroom of the plush golf resort and hotel where the reception is being held. Security seems tight, but maybe this is the norm for mafia weddings.

Cristian has been busy chatting with various men throughout the day, but he makes sure to check in with us regularly. He seems to know everyone here. His dad too. Thank God for his mother. I'd be miserable if it weren't for Beatrice. She's been super kind and attentive, and I'm enjoying getting to know her.

"I think the bride has probably had too much wine," she surmises, watching Isa paw at Cristian in a way that's incredibly disrespectful to him and her new husband. Every time Cristian stops her wandering hands, she starts all over again.

"Or she's just always like that," I say, unable to retract my claws in time.

Beatrice smiles. "Ah, I see you've noticed what my son is far too blind to notice."

"What I don't understand is why she married Carmine if she wants Cristian."

Sympathy splays across her face. "There are certain traditions within our social circles that dictate the way things happen. It's rarely black or white."

She's as cryptic as her son and his friends, but I can't fault the mafia for being guarded around outsiders. Reading between the lines, it seems obvious this is an arranged marriage. Why else would Isotta marry a man old enough to be her dad? I know her personality is hideous, but she's young and pretty, and I can't believe she couldn't find a more suitable man to marry.

I shudder at the thought of being tied to someone like Carmine, which I know isn't a charitable thought, but the guy gives me the creeps. I've spotted him watching me several times today, and I don't like how he looks at me. I've gone out of my way to avoid him, and I'm praying he doesn't try to make good on that dance because I'd rather walk over hot coals than dance with that man.

I have sympathy for Isotta. I can't stand her, but I truly wouldn't wish this on anyone. Every woman should get to choose their life partner. It's disgusting she's been forced into this.

"Josef to the rescue," Beatrice says, gesturing to where Cristian's father has intercepted the amorous bride, slotting into his son's place so Cristian can make his escape. Cristian's eyes find mine across the dance floor, and he stalks toward us. We don't break eye contact as he approaches, and butterflies are skipping around my chest at the intense way he's staring at me.

"Are you okay?" he asks, his eyes probing mine.

"Funny. I was going to ask you the same thing." My eyes flit to Isotta.

"I'm fine." He dismisses it casually. "I need to take care of something, but I'll be back in a few." His expression is tender when he looks at his mother. "Can I get you anything, Mama?"

"More wine is always good, son," she says, waggling her brows.

Cristian chuckles. "Say no more." His eyes linger on me for a few beats before he takes off. My gaze follows him until he leaves the room.

"He's a good son. A good man," Beatrice muses, squeezing my arm.

"A good father," I add.

"The best," she agrees, smiling. "He stepped up for Elio when he needed him." Her smile fades. "Cristian and Sabina are the best people. Kind, loving, hardworking. I don't know where we went wrong with their brother." Pain fills her eyes, and my heart swells with compassion.

Thoughts of my mother and the evil men who have hurt her swarm my mind. "I doubt you did anything wrong. Sometimes, people are just born evil," I blurt before I realize what I've said. My eyes widen in horror. "Oh my god, I'm so sorry, I didn't—"

"You speak no lie, Sloane." Beatrice rubs a hand across her chest. "Cruz was..." Tears pool in her eyes. "Cruz *was* evil." She swipes at her eyes. "It pains me so much to say it, but it's the truth. Josef and I gave him everything. He grew up with lots of love and laughter. He had so much opportunity in life, and he made all the wrong choices. We still struggle to understand it. How it got so bad. How he could do the things he did."

"I don't know what he did." I take her wrinkled hands in mine. "But you shouldn't blame yourself. He was a grown man, and he made his own decisions."

"It's hard not to look back and wonder if we could've done something different. Josef hates that he didn't intervene sooner. Maybe it might've changed things."

I can relate. How many times have I gone over what happened and wished I'd made different choices? "It's natural to think like that, but it doesn't help. What's done is done, and you can't change the past."

"No, we can't." Removing a tissue from her purse, she dabs her eyes and clears her throat. "Today is a day for celebration. No more depressing thoughts."

"For what it's worth, I think Cristian and Sabina are lucky to have you and Josef as parents." I haven't been in their company for long, but you can tell.

"Thank you, sweet Sloane. I can't ever replace your mother, but if you need me for anything, I'm here for you. Even if it's only to talk." She asked me earlier about my parents, and I told her my situation.

"I appreciate that, Mrs. DiPietro. More than you know."

"Beatrice, please." She squeezes my hand before standing. "I'm just going to check on Elio."

"I should do that." I climb to my feet.

"I've got it." Her eyes twinkle when she says, "You should hunt down my son and drag him onto the dance floor. You youngsters should be out there having fun." She points toward the crowded dance floor where couples and groups of women are having the time of their lives. The band is great, and they're playing a mix of old classics and current songs, which is a big hit with the wedding guests.

"I'm going to the bathroom," I say, not touching her Cristian comment.

As I meander through the tables, smiling politely at the strangers around me, I wonder what it would be like if Cristian was mine. If my nightmare didn't exist, and this dream was the reality. We'd probably be scandalizing the crowd with our dirty dancing and would have already found time to sneak out for a quickie. A potent longing surges through my veins, and oh, how I wish his arms were around me.

The music mutes behind me as I exit the room and head down the corridor in the direction of the bathrooms. I slap a hand over my mouth to startle my gasp when I round the corner and find Cristian in some sort of confrontation with Carmine. My boss has the older man shoved up against the wall with his hand wrapped around his throat. Neither of them has noticed me, so I press my back against the wall at the corner and strain my ears to listen.

"I warned you back at the church, Carmine, and you continue to disrespect Sloane and disrespect me." This is about *me*? He doesn't include Isotta in that statement, and I'm guessing it's because she's disrespecting her husband as much as he's disrespecting her. It's not exactly the best way to start a marriage, and I wonder how long it might last. Though if it's an arranged marriage, it's probably for life with no get-out clause.

Carmine splutters something that might be "Can't breathe," but I'm not sure.

There's a bit of shuffling, and then Carmine grunts. Glancing behind me, I do a quick check to ensure no one is coming this way before I resume eavesdropping.

"Listen up good," Cristian says in a cold tone that raises all the fine hairs on the back of my neck. "You're an idiot if you think I haven't noticed what you're doing. You are not to look at Sloane, talk about her to anyone, or go anywhere near her. If you step one foot in her direction, I will blow your fucking head off and not give two shits about it. Have I made myself clear?"

My heart pounds like crazy as Cristian threatens the groom. He's not joking either. Holy fuck.

"Crystal," Carmine pants.

"Get the hell out of my sight," Cristian snaps, and Carmine comes stumbling around the corner before I've had a chance to escape.

Chapter Twenty-Two
Sloane

Carmine's sneering look as he passes by me has ice replacing the blood flowing in my veins. If looks could kill, I'd be six feet under by now. Wow. Perhaps he and Isotta are a perfect match after all.

"Fuck."

My head whips up, and my gaze collides with Cristian's.

"How much of that did you hear?"

"You threatening him if he even breathed near me," I choke out.

"You weren't supposed to hear that." His brow creases as he studies my face.

"I was heading to the bathroom, and I didn't know what to do when I came across you," I truthfully admit.

"I'm sorry you witnessed that." He visibly cringes. "It shouldn't have been necessary, but I've seen the way he's been watching you, and I don't like it. I told you I'd protect you today, and I meant it."

"I'm not angry, Cristian," I say, pushing off the wall.

"Are you scared?"

I know why he's asking. I shake my head. "I'm not angry or scared, Cristian. I'm grateful. I don't like how he's been looking at me either. It's made me very uncomfortable. Isa already hates my guts, and this will only make it worse." What I can't say is how his words actually *comfort* me. Should I tell him the truth? Should I ask him for help?

"I've spoken with Isa. She won't give you any trouble today."

"Oh, I don't doubt it. Seems she's set her sights on someone else."

Cristian splutters, and his eyes pop wide. "Whatever you're thinking, stop. She's had a little too much to drink, that's all."

"You're a smart man, Cristian. Please tell me you don't really believe that. Everyone in that room saw her and knows she wants you."

"It doesn't matter if she does." Taking my arm, he moves me around the corner as two guests approach. He nods at the couple as they pass by before fixing his gaze on me. "I'm not interested in her."

I pull up my big-girl panties and say what's on my mind. "Then you won't mind dancing with me."

"It's probably not wise."

"It's a party, Cristian. You can dance with the nanny, and no one will think anything of it." That's probably not true, but I'm not leaving here without a dance. If the bride gets one, then so do I. Feeling brave, I place my hand on his impressive chest. "I just need to use the bathroom. Wait for me?"

His callused palm cups my cheek, and heat seeps into my skin as I arch into his touch. Fiery tingles race across my face, and I want to fling my arms around him and never let go. He looked so hot today in his suit, but he looks even more gorgeous now he's ditched the dress jacket and rolled up the sleeves of his shirt. I'm addicted to his arms and fascinated with the ink covering his smooth, muscular, tanned skin. I want to lick them all over and trace the veins with my tongue.

"Sloane."

His breathy tone drags my gaze back up to his amused face. "What?" I rasp.

"I'll wait here for you."

"Okay." I feel like crying when his hand pulls away from my face, but I hold it together and walk on autopilot to the bathroom.

I attend to business and quickly touch up my makeup before I rejoin him outside.

Tension bleeds into the air between us as we walk silently side by side down the corridor and back into the ballroom. Cristian procures a chilled bottle of wine and checks in with his mother to ensure Elio is okay. "He's perfectly fine. Having the time of his life with his cousins." Snatching the bottle from her son's hand, she shoos us with a flap of her hands. "Go dance, enjoy yourselves."

Cristian looks torn as he threads his fingers in mine and leads me toward the dance floor, and I can guess why. It might be my imagination, but I think he's already fighting a losing battle with his conscience.

The band is playing a fast number when we reach the packed dance floor, and we find a space off to the left and start shimmying. Damn, Cristian has moves, and any awkwardness is quickly forgotten as we both give it our all. It's not long before we're smiling, laughing, and flirting, and I'm thoroughly enjoying myself. Cristian lets go of his reservations, twirling me around the floor, reeling me into his chest, dipping me down low, and syncing his moves to mine. We draw closer with each new song, and by the time the band slows it down, we're already in one another's arms.

"Sloane, Sloane," he says, banding his arms tightly around

my waist and holding me flush against his strong body as we sway in tune to the music. His brow presses to mine, and then his eyes close. "What are you doing to me?" he whispers over my mouth as I feel his hard length brush against me.

"The same thing you're doing to me," I earnestly reply.

His eyes open and pierce mine. "I'm trying to stay away from you," he admits as his hand moves higher, finding the bare skin of my back. His touch lights a fire inside me, and I shiver in his arms. "But it's so fucking hard."

I want to tell him to stop denying what we both obviously want, but laying it all on the line didn't work out great for me last time, so I trap the words. It has to be him. Cristian needs to be the one to tear down the boundaries he's erected. "You know how I feel," I softly say.

"I feel it too." He subtly rotates his hips, ensuring I feel his erection. "Fuck. I'm going to hell."

"Then I'm right there wi—"

"In case either of you is even remotely concerned with Elio, the show is over, and the babysitters are leaving," Isa hisses, putting herself all up in our faces.

We separate instantly, and Cristian rearranges his face into a calmly polite expression that's more familiar. "Thank you for telling me. We'll go get him." His arm slides around my back, and he steers me around the seething bride.

All the previous intimacy is gone from his tone and his expression, and whatever moment we were having has been effectively ruined thanks to the bride. I'm positive that was her intention anyway.

"Daddy!" Elio charges toward us. "The magician made his hat disappear!" His green eyes pop wide. "Like puff, it just went away."

"Wow, that sounds amazing." Cristian bends down, ruffling his son's hair.

"He made balloon animals too. I got a lion. Grandma has it." Elio takes each of our hands. "I wanna dance."

"We can stay for a few dances, but we'll be going home then. Okay?"

"Deal." Elio is already dragging us toward the dance floor before the word has left his mouth.

We dance for a few songs, earning plenty of stares from other wedding guests, but Cristian ignores their nosiness, and I follow his lead.

"Lift me up, Daddy." Elio raises his arms, and Cristian scoops him up. Elio wraps his legs around his dad and reaches out a hand for me. "Come on, Slowpoke Sloane." We dance as a unit, and my heart is so full it feels like it could burst. Cristian has his arm around me while he carries his son, and there's no hiding the emotion shining in his eyes.

I want this.

I want this so badly.

My heart is splintering as reminders of my hideous reality crack through my happy shell.

I'm yanked forcibly away from Cristian as the bride interrupts for the second time tonight. "You are making a scene," Isa says, glowering at me as she reaches for Elio. "People are talking."

"Let them," Cristian coolly replies, keeping a firm hold of his son. "It's time we were going home anyway."

She backtracks immediately, panic replacing the previous pissed-off look on her face. "You don't need to go yet. It's only a little past nine thirty."

"It's way past Elio's bedtime, as you know, and he's exhausted," Cristian replies. He leans in and plants a quick kiss on her cheek. "Thanks for inviting us. I hope you and Carmine have a wonderful honeymoon."

Isa glares at me like I'm the devil incarnate, and I'm so sick of her obvious jealousy.

"Say goodbye to Auntie Isa," Cristian says, nudging Elio, who now has his head resting on his dad's shoulder. Sleep seems to have crept up on him fast.

"Bye, Auntie Isa. See you after your moonhoney."

Cristian and I share a smile that only seems to anger Isa more, but she hides it well as she smiles at Elio and kisses the top of his head. "I'll miss you, champ."

"Same," he says over a yawn.

"Enjoy the rest of your wedding, Isa," Cristian repeats before artfully steering me away and off the dance floor. "I'll just tell my parents we're leaving." He removes his hand from my back. "They'll probably want to come with."

"Of course."

We head to his parents' table in silence, Isa having ruined the moment again. "We're heading home," Cristian says.

"Good," his father says, standing. "It's time we left too. It's way past this old man's bedtime." He winks at me, and I can't help giggling. I'm betting he was a real charmer when he was young.

"I think you might have a message." Beatrice hands me my purse. "It made a little vibrating noise a few minutes ago."

My heart launches into my throat as I clutch my purse to my chest. Oh my fucking god. I can't believe I was so careless. I debated whether to bring my cartel cell with me today, but Mom and I were both punished the last time I left it behind, and as we were attending a very public wedding, where his goons would be following me, I didn't see how it was overly risky bringing it. I was so sure I'd put it fully on silent, but I must have fucked up.

"What's wrong?" Josef asks, his face instantly awash with concern.

"You are really pale," Beatrice adds.

"I just felt a wave of nausea." I place a hand on my stomach. "Maybe it was something I ate or too much wine."

"You didn't drink too much," his mother says. "Perhaps something you ate didn't agree with you."

"I'm gonna go to the bathroom. I can meet you outside."

"We'll wait for you in the lobby," Josef says. "It's best we all stick together."

I flee to the bathroom with beads of sweat dotting my brow.

Once inside the stall, I sit on top of the closed toilet seat and rest my head in my hands, taking measured breaths in an attempt to calm down. I'm an idiot, and my idiocy is going to give the game away or get my mother killed. My fingers tremble as I remove my cell and open the message Pablo sent.

All the blood drains from my face when the photo loads. It was taken recently. Cristian and I are on the dance floor, holding one another tight, our brows pressed together, and our mouths scant inches apart.

Fucking hell.

Pablo's mole must be here.

My heart rate skyrockets as the organ thumps frantically against my rib cage. Sheer panic charges through my veins as I struggle to breathe.

A new message arrives, and I almost throw up all over my expensive dress when I read it.

Good girl. Now take him home and fuck him.

Chapter Twenty-Three
Sloane

Cristian is waiting for me outside the bathroom when I emerge sometime later. I don't know how long I was in there, panicking and hyperventilating, before I pulled myself together and found the strength to put one foot in front of the other.

"I was about to send in a search party," he says, gently tilting my head back. "You're very pale."

Yeah, no shit. "I'm not feeling so hot."

"Let's get you home." Cristian puts his suit jacket around me before sliding his arm around my shoulders. He keeps me close to his side while escorting me down the hallway toward the lobby, and I'm grateful for the warmth emanating from him because I'm chilled to the bone. I am not cut out for spying, and I don't know how much longer I can keep pretending. I don't know what to do; I have no one to confide in, and it's killing me inside.

"Oh, sweetheart." Beatrice lightly clasps my clammy face in her hands when we reach them. They are waiting just inside the doors, protected from the chilly February weather outside.

A sleepy Elio is in his grandpa's arms, his head resting against his shoulder. "You feel feverish." Cristian's mom looks over at him. "You should all come stay with us tonight. It's closer, and I can look after Sloane."

"You don't have to do that," I protest, hoping no one hears the hysteria in my tone. I don't want to lead Pablo directly to Cristian's parents' house, yet it's not like I can dispose of the damn cartel cell.

"Thanks, but we'll head home," Cristian says, and I hope the relief isn't evident on my face. "We've got Sunday lunch plans tomorrow, and it's best we sleep at the penthouse. Maybe next weekend?"

"Sounds good," Beatrice agrees as six bodyguards appear outside to escort us.

The front of the once-stately home that is now a luxurious golf hotel and resort is closed to vehicles, but it's only a short walk to the large parking lot at the side. Umberto lifts Elio from Josef's arms. The little guy is fast asleep, tuckered out from all the excitement today. Umberto and Clint walk ahead while we hang back, strolling at a more leisurely pace as we talk. I cling to Cristian's right side, my eyes darting wildly around the place. I'm on edge and probably imagining the eyeballs I feel on my back. I'm only half paying attention to the conversation as I scan the surroundings while we walk.

The grounds are stunning here. Miles and miles of woodland border lush lawns and manicured gardens. We pass by neat flower beds, enclosed behind decorative beige low stone walls. The area is well lit, though largely unoccupied as most all the guests are still inside enjoying the celebrations.

Up ahead, Umberto closes the back door after securing Elio in his seat. Clint is just rounding the front of the car as we approach when a flash sparks in the dark sky. I only notice because I'm avidly scanning our surroundings. I'm opening my mouth to say something when a pop rings out, and something whizzes over our heads.

It's instant pandemonium.

"Get down," Cristian yells, shoving me to the ground as his father does the same with his mother. "Papa!" Cristian roars, jumping over me to lunge at his dad, slamming him to the ground and covering him with his body as more shots pepper the air. The bodyguards have opened fire, but I don't know what's going on as I'm curled into a ball, shaking and terrified, with my hands covering my face. Is this Pablo? Is he done waiting, and he's taken matters into his own hands? But then why send me that text?

"Is my son protected?" Cristian shouts.

"He's safe, boss," Umberto hollers.

"This way, Don DiPietro," an unfamiliar male says. "They're fleeing toward the southern woods, heading for the back road, but we can cut them off."

"Go, Cristian," his father says. "I'll call for backup, but don't let them get away."

"Sloane." My hands are peeled back from my face. Cristian peers over me. "Go with my parents. Clint and Umberto will take you to their place. You'll be safe there."

Terror has shackled my tongue, and I can only nod.

"Protect my family with your life," Cristian snaps before he takes off with a gun in his hand.

Pounding footsteps resonate behind us as I push myself into a seated position on the ground. I'm still trembling, and my heart is racing like crazy.

"Over there." Josef points in the direction Cristian and a few other men have already gone. They are in hot pursuit of three blurry forms running toward the woods. At least ten men, all wedding guests, run around us. In the commotion, I dig out my cartel cell, switch it off, and smash it repeatedly against the asphalt before stuffing it in a nearby bush.

"Here, let me help you up," John Angelo says, materializing at my side.

Mr. DiPietro helps his wife to her feet. "Sloane and Elio are coming home with us," Josef explains as I extend my hand, letting the bodyguard help me to stand.

My left side throbs with pain I'm only now feeling. John Angelo rushes me to the SUV, climbing in beside me, while Josef and Beatrice get into the second vehicle.

"Buckle up," Clint says from the driver's seat when I lean over to check on Elio. "He's still sleeping. The vehicle is sound-proof," he adds, answering my silent question.

"It's also bulletproof," Umberto confirms, slamming his door shut as I fumble with my seat belt.

"I've got it." John Angelo places my hands gently on my lap before clicking my belt into place. He nods at the front seat.

"Hold tight, Sloane," Clint warns, putting the pedal to the metal as we floor it out of there. Looking over my shoulder, I spot two similar SUVs following hot on our heels.

Adrenaline is coursing through my body, my ears are ringing, and my heart is pounding like it wants to escape. "Will Cristian be all right?" I ask, pressing my nose to the tinted windows as we pass by the field where all the men are. Cristian grabs one of the assailants and slams the butt of his gun into his temple. The guy crumples to the ground as the other mafia men round on the other two, pummeling them with their fists.

"The boss will be fine," John Angelo says. A smile creeps over his mouth as he watches things going down outside. "They have it under control." He turns to look at me. "Try not to worry. Cristian knows what he's doing."

"Feeling any better?" Beatrice asks when I enter the homey kitchen of the old castle-type mansion she calls home, ninety minutes later.

"A little," I lie. Though soaking in the bath helped to ease my aches and pains, I'm sick to my stomach with worry for Cristian and fear for my mother. Ditching my cartel cell might not have been the smartest decision. Pablo probably already knows where this house is, but I reacted on instinct, fear for Elio and Cristian's family driving my actions. Now, I feel sick with guilt because there's no way Pablo will not punish us for this. I plan to lie and say it got smashed in the shootout. It doesn't even matter if he believes me. He'll still take it out on us.

"Is Elio still sleeping?" I helped her put him to bed before my bath.

"Josef checked on him again. He's fast asleep. Don't worry. He's fine."

"I'm so glad he slept through everything."

"That is a blessing," she calmly replies, and I can see where Cristian gets his unflappable manner from. "Come sit." She gestures toward the long, solid wooden table. "I heated up some chicken broth for you. It cures all ails."

Oh god. I don't think I can stomach anything right now, but I don't want to be rude.

"I'm glad the clothes fit." Her warm smile settles on me like a security blanket as I claim a seat. She places two bowls on the table. "Sabina isn't quite as tall or thin as you, but a close enough match." The silk pajama top is a little loose, the matching pajama shorts a little tight, but I'm grateful for them. My beautiful dress is ruined, dirty and torn in a few places. Not that I'm complaining. I'd rather a ruined dress than a bullet in my body.

A shudder works its way through me. Beatrice notices,

leaning down to hug me. I sink into her embrace as the magnitude of everything that's happened tonight fully hits me. A sob rips from my throat before I can stop it. I could have died. Elio could have been hurt. Or Cristian's parents or Cristian. "We could have died," I whisper as I shiver and shake.

"Cristian would never let that happen." She rubs her hands up and down my arms. "I'm sure you are frightened, but I promise you're safe here. We have the best security, and no one is getting near us." With one last squeeze, she lets me go, sliding into the seat beside me. "Drink up. Trust me, it will make you feel better."

I surprise myself by drinking it all, and she's right; it helps to settle my stomach. Though my nerves are still on edge.

We wash and dry the dishes side by side in quiet companionship. After, she hands me a hair tie and a tub of aloe vera from the refrigerator. "That will help with any soreness."

Tears stab my eyes. She is so kind, and I'm not sure I'm worthy of it. "Thank you." I tie my long hair into a loose ponytail and clutch the aloe vera in one hand.

"You're welcome, sweet Sloane." She hugs me once before lifting one shoulder. "Come."

Beatrice leads me out of the kitchen and down along the winding hallway toward the back of the house. Ornate staircases spiral above us on both sides, leading to the upstairs level. Large, heavy-looking gold frames house oil paintings on the walls alongside the polished mahogany banisters. "Are they relatives?" I ask as we pass under the grand stairs.

"Yes. Generations of the DiPietro family have walked these halls. We remember them by hanging their portraits."

"You have a beautiful home."

"Thank you. We have spent a lot of time and money restoring and maintaining it over the years, but it's an important legacy we want to pass down to our children and grand-children."

Beatrice guides me into a stunning room with a vaulted glass ceiling and floor-to-ceiling dark wood shelving. There must be thousands of books in here. The sturdy old desk by the window is clearly an heirloom, the chunky mahogany legs gleaming under the dim lighting in the room. Healthy plants occupy large sage-green pots dotted around the room. Several tabletop lights are lit around the space, and it smells of paper, leather, and peppermint. Thick green and gold brocade curtains cover the windows, blocking the view of the gardens outside and helping to keep the heat in.

The roaring fire in the corner of the room beckons to me like an old friend. Cristian's dad rises from one of the leather-backed chairs in front of it. "Come join me, my dear," he says.

The old floorboards creak as I walk across the study-slash-library in my borrowed slippers. I'm not sure if I'll ever get to meet Cristian's sister, but I hope she doesn't mind I borrowed some of her things. A thick, patterned rug blankets the floor underneath the seating area, helping it to feel extra warm and cozy. "Sit." Josef pats the base of a brown leather couch. "Warm your frozen bones."

"I'm heading to bed, Sloane," Beatrice says, kissing me on both cheeks. "Press the service button in your room if you need anything during the night." Plucking the aloe vera tub from my cold fingers, she sets it down on the end table.

"Thank you so much for your kindness and the yummy broth. It was delicious."

"You're welcome."

"Goodnight, my love." Josef embraces his wife, kissing her passionately on the lips, and I look away, not wanting to intrude on their private moment. "I'll be up in a while."

The only sounds in the room after Beatrice leaves are the

crackling of the fire, the rhythmic chiming of the old grandfather clock, and the silent racing of my heart. Anxiety flutters in my chest as I tuck my feet up under me and cover myself with the soft blanket. Josef climbs awkwardly to his feet before walking toward the liquor cabinet. I watch as he pours two generous measures of neat whiskey. When he returns, he hands one to me. "It'll help with the shock."

"Thank you."

He reclaims his seat, nursing a tumbler in his hand as he stares into the dancing flames.

I take a sip of my drink, and the whiskey burns as it glides down my throat, but it settles warmly in my stomach, helping to heat me from the inside.

"I am sure you have many questions, Sloane."

I lift my head, my gaze connecting with Cristian's father. "I do."

He nods slowly. "That's to be expected. I know my son, and he will want to explain it to you himself. I just didn't want you to go to sleep being afraid. You are safe here. Safe with Cristian. We will not let anything happen to you. Family means everything to us, and you are family now."

I can tell he's sincere, and a lump forms in my throat. How I wish it could be so.

Josef takes a healthy mouthful of his drink. "Italian American families have lots of secrets and traditions. We don't allow many outsiders into our world, but those we do are treated with kindness, respect, and loyalty. We only ask for the same in return." He knocks back the rest of his drink and staggers to his feet. I move to help him, but he waves me away. "I don't spring back as quickly these days after a knock to the ground, but I can still walk unaided."

"Do you want to take this?" I offer him my aloe vera.

He curls my fingers around the tub. "I think my wife has

shares in this stuff. We have tubs of it everywhere." He presses a kiss to the top of my head. "You should get some sleep, but if you want to wait for Cristian, this is the best place."

"I'll wait a little while."

"Sleep well, Sloane," he says, walking stiffly out of the room. The door snicks shut after him.

I sip my drink and try to quiet my mind as I snuggle on my side on the couch, staring into the boisterous flames of the fire. I fully intend on waiting up for Cristian, but I guess I doze off because the next thing I'm aware of is the creaking of the floorboards as someone enters the room. The couch conceals me, and I hold my breath for a few beats, my pulse throbbing painfully as fear sprouts goose bumps on my arms until Cristian speaks, and I relax knowing it's him. "You should be in bed."

Pulling myself upright, I fight a yawn as I look over at him. He's propped against the front of the desk, looking weary as he scrubs his hands down his face. "I was worried," I admit, kicking the blanket aside and standing. "I wanted to make sure you were okay," I add, pushing messy strands of hair out of my tired eyes.

"Fuck, Sloane." His eyes graze over me slowly, from head to toe, and I'm hyperaware of the hunger burning hotter and hotter on his face as he drinks me in. "Are you scared of me?"

"What? No." I shake my head before taking a step toward him. "You don't scare me, Cristian. That is the opposite of how I feel."

"Thank fuck," he says, quickly pushing off the desk and striding toward me.

He holds my face in his hands like I'm precious as his lips descend, and he claims my mouth in a searing-hot kiss that curls my toes and kindles an inferno inside me.

Chapter Twenty-Four
Cristian

I devour her, holding her stunning face in my hands as I worship her lips like I've been longing to for the past two weeks. Sloane kisses me back with the same passion, readily parting her lips and letting my tongue slip inside. One hand leaves her face as I band my arm around her back and pull her flush against my body. Tilting her head back a little, I sweep my tongue around her mouth as my lips take and take and take. My blood heats, and my cock jerks against my zipper as I gyrate my hips and grind against her.

I want to strip every item of clothing from her gorgeous body, lie her down on the rug in front of the fire, part her tempting thighs, and slide home. Precum leaks from the tip of my dick as I make love to her mouth, needing more, more, more. My hand creeps under the back of her pajama top, and sparks fly across my skin the instant my fingers meet her satiny-smooth flesh.

My need for her is at an all-time high, and I couldn't stop this if I tried. Pushing her back until her ass hits the side of the couch, I continue perusing her warm skin, circling around to her stomach and moving higher. Our tongues tangle as our kissing grows frantic, and she's meeting me every step of the way, her fingers digging into my ass through my dress pants.

When I brush the underside of her tits, she moans into my mouth, arches her back, and thrusts her breasts forward. The hard peaks of her nipples crush against my chest as she squeezes my ass and whimpers. "Cristian."

Palming one tit, I roll my thumb around her stiff nipple and grip her waist on the other side, freezing instantly when she winces. I rip my swollen lips from hers and remove my hands from her body, struggling to get my breathing under control. "You're hurt," I pant.

"It's only a little bruising," she says in a breathless tone.

What the fuck was I thinking throwing myself at her like this after everything that's happened tonight? I was pretty rough when I threw her to the ground as gunshots rang out, and it's obvious she's injured but downplaying it.

Pulling her over to the desk, I angle the desktop lamp so we're bathed in light.

Sloane gasps, and her eyes widen in alarm. "You're bleeding!" Panic is etched upon her face as she tentatively raises a hand to my left arm.

"It's nothing. Just a scratch."

"It is *not* nothing," she protests, straightening up. Stretching my arm out, she frowns at the large pool of blood staining my white dress shirt. "Hold still," she demands, removing my cuff link, unbuttoning the cuff, and carefully rolling the sleeve up. I close my eyes as my skin tingles from her touch. My cock is digging into my zipper painfully, silently screaming in need.

So much for staying away from the nanny.

I barely lasted two weeks.

She sucks in another gasp when she reaches the wound.

"Oh my god. You were shot." Horror splays across her face as she examines the bloody gash on my upper arm.

"It only grazed me. It looks worse than it is."

"I need to clean it and put some antiseptic on."

"It's fine, Sloane. I can handle it."

"Shut up, Cristian." She glares at me, and it only turns me on more. "Where can I find a first aid kit?"

I peer into her determined eyes before my gaze drops to her mouth. Her lips are all red and swollen from my kisses, and I like it a lot more than I should. "Fuck." I drag a hand through my hair. "I shouldn't have pounced on you like that."

"Don't." She moves a step closer, and fire blazes in her eyes. "Do not say you regret it. I'll give you a matching wound in your other arm if you do."

A chuckle rumbles from my throat. "I wasn't going to say that," I truthfully admit. "But I didn't give you a choice, I just—"

"Shut. Up. Cristian." That seems to be her new mantra. She prods one finger into my chest. "I wanted it. You know I did. Now stop trying to change the subject and tell me where the first aid kit is."

"You should find one in the bottom drawer of Dad's desk," I say, glancing over my shoulder.

"That's a strange place to keep it." She rounds the desk and bends down.

"Not really." I have a lot to tell her. There's no keeping who we are—who I am—a secret any longer, but it's not a conversation I want to have at three a.m. when we're both sore and tired. "I'll explain everything tomorrow."

Hugging the box to her chest, she nods before walking back around to me. She sets the kit down on the desk and takes my hand, pressing the cuff link into my palm. "I'll get some water and a cloth." She takes a couple of steps back, and her tongue darts out, wetting her lips. "You, ah, should remove your shirt," she blurts before spinning around and racing out of the room.

I chuckle to myself as I remove my shirt, tucking my cuff links into my pocket so I don't lose them. While I wait for her to come back, I stare into the dying embers of the fire and wonder what the hell I'm going to do now. I shouldn't have touched her. Now I've had a taste, I can't tame my inner beast or continue denying what's been blatantly obvious from the moment I set eyes on Sloane.

I want her. Under me. Over me. On all fours. In every way imaginable.

And it's problematic on many levels, but especially because she might not want me when she realizes exactly who she's been kissing.

A heavy sigh escapes my lips, and my bones feel weary. Thoughts of earlier return, and I scrub my hands down my face, ignoring the pinch in my arm with the motion. The discovery is not a welcome development, and it doesn't bode well.

Sloane returns, interrupting my thoughts. Her footsteps falter as she comes closer. Her eyes are like heat-seeking missiles where they roam every inch of my bare chest. Shivers dust over my flesh in every place her gaze lingers, and my dick is about ready to bust from my pants.

Tension bleeds into the air when she stops directly in front of me. Her hands shake as she places a bowl of water down on the desk alongside the medical kit. Sparks crackle in the air, and it's taking every molecule of self-control not to strip her bare and impale her on my aching cock. I long to bury myself deep inside her and stay there for the rest of the night.

Gripping the edge of the desk, I remind myself she's vulnerable as the tension twists and tightens, ready to snap at any second. Sloane dips the cloth in the water and wrings it out. Her head lifts, and her gaze ensnares mine. "You're beautiful, Cristian," she whispers, dragging her eyes over my broad shoulders and down over the ink on my chest and along one side of my body.

"I can say the exact same. I don't think you realize how completely stunning you are."

Heat crawls up her neck and onto her face, and she can't contain her shy smile. I don't move a muscle as she lifts her arm, moving it tentatively toward me. Reassuring her with my eyes, I hold myself perfectly still as the tips of her fingers trace over the ink on my arms and my chest. I bite on the inside of my cheek, trapping a groan, when her fingers explore the dips and grooves of my abs, and I'm clinging to my sanity by a thread. Sloane doesn't explore any lower, but she must see the bulge straining my pants and know it's all for her.

"Like I said—beautiful," she whispers as her cheeks turn a deeper shade of red. She kisses me softly on the lips before switching her attention to my wounded arm. "This might sting." Sloane presses the damp cloth to my skin, and my heart thumps steadily as I watch her carefully clean and dry my wound. I'm completely mesmerized by her. She has bewitched me, and I like being under her spell. The bullet only grazed my arm, so it's not serious, but it still stings like a bitch when she dabs it with an iodine-based antiseptic. Then she applies an aloe vera salve before bandaging it. "You should get a doctor to look at it. You might need some butterfly bandages."

"I'm sure it's fine." It's not like it's the first scar to adorn my body. I have plenty of war wounds, but most are covered by ink and not visible unless closely examined.

"Your turn." Picking up the tub, I stab her with a purposeful look. I haven't forgotten she's hurt too. "I see my mother is trying to convert you to the wonders of aloe vera." I can tell it's from Mom's stash because she's been buying her products from the same local salon for years. Swearing by its healing properties, she has oodles of the stuff all over the place. I'm not surprised Mama was mothering Sloane in my absence. Nurturing is second nature to her, and I can tell she's already very taken with Elio's nanny.

I inwardly groan at the thought. I was supposed to keep things professional, and I've really fucked it up now.

"She doesn't need to convert me. I'm already a fan." Sloane snatches the tub out of my hand. "You don't need to do that. I can do it myself."

I put myself all up in her space. "Shut. Up. Sloane." I smirk as I turn her words back around on her. "Lie down on your stomach on the couch and lift your top," I instruct, plucking the tub from her slim fingers.

She nibbles on her lip, and my blood sizzles. "Sloane," I growl, seconds from throwing all my self-made rules out the window, tossing her over this desk and having my wicked way with her. "Lie the fuck down."

Her gaze dips to my mouth for a fleeting second before she pivots around and walks over to the couch. I discreetly adjust myself in my pants and caution myself to behave. Despite her bravado, Sloane has got to be freaked out over everything, and I won't take advantage of her vulnerability. Not any more than I already have done, at least.

My mouth turns dry as she lies down and pulls her top up to her upper back. The sleep shorts she's wearing barely cover her ass, and my fingers itch with a craving to fondle her shapely cheeks. My lips long to drop a line of kisses along her spine. Her tan skin is flawless and begging for my touch.

I'm going to hell, I think, as I drop to my knees at her side. Soft warmth from the dregs of the fire heats my back. Sloane's trusting eyes meet mine as I move closer to examine her side. Discoloration is already showing from the top of her ribs down to her hip bone, and she's going to be black and blue tomorrow. Remorse is instant. "I'm so sorry." I unscrew the lid and plunge my fingers into the cold gel.

"Don't be," she quietly says. "You protected me, and I'm grateful. I'd rather a few bruises than a bullet."

"I would never let that happen," I say, bringing my fingers to her skin.

She flinches when the gel hits her flesh. "Fuck, that's cold."

"Mama likes to keep it in the refrigerator, though I'm not sure it makes any difference to the effect."

"My mom always kept it in the refrigerator too. She used to put it on me when I was little if I got sunburned," she says, her gaze instantly tearing up. "The coldness was always soothing."

"I'm glad you have lots of good memories of her," I say as I gently coat her bruised skin.

"She was the best mom." A tear rolls down her face, and my heart hurts for her.

"I think you should speak to someone," I suggest, mopping up the tear with the pad of my thumb. "I can get the name of a good therapist, and I'll cover the cost."

"Thank you for offering, but it's too soon," she whispers before turning her head to the opposite side, away from me.

We don't speak as I continue to cover her sore skin with the aloe gel. My fingers edge low, brushing against the waistband of her sleep shorts. She squirms a little as I carefully rub the gel in. I could do this all night. I'm addicted to the feel of her velvety-soft skin, and my hand is tingling every time I touch her. Moving my hands back up, I work the gel in with soft strokes so I don't hurt her. When my fingers brush against the underswell of her breast, I snap myself out of it and yank my hand back. "I think that should do," I croak, putting the lid back on the gel and jumping to my feet. I adjust myself again in my pants, willing my hard-on to back the fuck down.

"Thank you." Sloane curls her arms around me from behind, and I close my eyes, savoring the feel of her warm body pressing against mine. My hands cover hers at my stomach, and we don't say anything as we embrace. I don't know how long we stand there like that, but when she yawns, the spell is broken.

We separate at the same time, and I slowly turn around to face her. I tuck her hair behind her ears. "Are you doing okay with everything that happened tonight?" My fingers caress her face of their own volition.

"I was terrified," she admits.

"I can imagine." My thumb brushes against her lower lip. "I'm sorry that happened, but I promise I will keep you protected and safe."

"I trust you," she quietly says, but she looks troubled.

My thumb traces her lips. "It's late. You should go to bed."

She opens her mouth to speak, and my thumb slips between her lips without thought. Heat flares in her eyes as her lips wrap around it, and I am going to hell. With my free hand, I tug her body flush against mine. "Go to bed. Please," I say, groaning as she sucks my thumb while fucking me with her eyes. "Fuck, Sloane." I remove my thumb and lower my head, needing to kiss her so badly. My lips brush against hers just as my cell rings.

I step back, creating distance between us. Pulling my cell out of my pocket, I quickly glance at it. "I've got to take this." Leaning down, I kiss her soft cheek. "Go to bed, Sloane. I'll see you in the morning."

Chapter Twenty-Five
Cristian

The door snicks shut behind Sloane. "Fuck," I say into the phone when I answer Caleb's call.

"That bad, huh?"

"Goddamn it." I slump onto the couch and sigh. "I just kissed Sloane, and I was about to do a whole lot more if you hadn't interrupted."

"Screw my shitty timing. I'll hang up, and you can pretend like this never happened."

The line dies, and I stare at my cell for a few seconds before laughing. I love that my best friend is still the same crazy goofball I've grown up with. I call him back, but he doesn't answer the first two times. On the third time, he picks up. "Dude, this can wait. Go get your girl."

"She's not my girl, and I've sent her to bed. Alone."

Caleb heaves out a sigh. "You're your own worst enemy, DiPietro."

"Don't I know it."

"I heard about tonight," Caleb says, and all trace of humor

is gone from his tone. "Wanted to check in and ensure you were all okay."

"We're fine. We were well protected, and the idiots were massively outnumbered."

"I want in on the interrogation. I haven't had any fun in a long time."

"There won't be an interrogation." I swing my legs around, lying lengthways on the couch with my feet dangling over one side. "When we got to Staten Island, we found all three dead in the back of the van."

"Poison pill?" Caleb accurately guesses.

"Yeah. We should've checked them more thoroughly."

"Cartel men?"

"They were *Cosa Nostra* but could've been put up to it by the cartel." I lean my head back and sigh. "Our own men tried to take us out at a fucking family wedding."

"Fuck."

"Yeah."

"You recognize them?" my buddy asks.

"No, but we'll ID them in time. Ben is already on it. He might even have an update in the morning." Our president has called an emergency sitting of the board first thing.

"Okay. We'll talk more then."

I hover outside Sloane's bedroom for a few minutes, silently arguing with myself. I want to crawl into bed beside her and offer her comfort, but I don't trust myself to keep it PG, and I can't take advantage of her. She's had a big shock, and me making moves on her when she might not be fully in control of her actions would be a mistake. So, I force myself away from her door and go to my room.

I jerk off in the shower, imagining Sloane's in here with me, and I come in record time, something that is becoming the norm these days. I dry off, grab some pajama pants from the dresser, and conk out the second my head hits the pillow.

It feels like I've just closed my eyes when my alarm goes off, and I smother a yawn as I throw back the covers. Dressing quickly in jeans, a black sweater, and boots, I borrow one of my old man's coats and then head out.

It's still dark out when I walk into the large garage. Half the vehicles inside are mine. I've been storing them here because parking spaces are limited at our place in the city. I only have the Lexus SUV and my BMW Series 8 Coupe at the penthouse, but I'll be moving everything to Connecticut when the new house is ready. Now, more than ever, I'm very keen to leave The Big Apple behind. It's safer for Elio and Sloane in Glencoe.

I grab the keys to my black Maserati and slide behind the wheel. Then I set off for the forty-minute drive into the city. I don't usually take bodyguards with me if I'm out alone because I can handle myself. But with the current situation, I think extra backup is smart, so a few of my guys are trailing behind me in an SUV.

The sun is rising when I pull into Commission HQ, arriving the same time as Don Maltese. We walk to the elevator together. "Glad you're all safe. That's some bullshit to pull at a wedding."

"I'm furious," I admit as we step into the car. Fiero presses the button for the top floor, where the conference room is. "They took aim at Papa too." They tried to take both of us out.

"We'll get to the bottom of it."

"We'd better." I crack my knuckles, incensed to have missed the opportunity to beat the truth out of the three traitorous pricks.

"You still okay for later?" he asks as the numbers climb on the panel.

"Yeah. Elio's looking forward to it. He was telling Sloane all about Armani yesterday in the car on the way to the church."

Fiero's face lights up at the mention of his one-year-old son. "He's into everything now he's walking. I spent yesterday putting locks on all the cabinet doors."

"I can't wait to see the little guy," I say as the doors open.

"We have additional guests," he supplies as we step out into the hallway. "Rowan and Tullia."

I arch a brow. "They patched things up?"

Last I heard, Mazzone junior was tapping the older Maltese sister, but no one considers it serious. Apparently, they've been fucking around, on and off, for years. According to Joshua, Ben isn't overly pleased his eldest son is messing around with Sofia. She's known to be a ballbuster and fiercely independent, with stated intentions to never settle down. She's a good few years older than Rowan, and they certainly set tongues wagging when they first started hooking up when he was nineteen.

The Mazzone heir has been good friends with the youngest Maltese daughter since they were kids. If he was going to hook up with anyone, we all thought it'd be Tullia. Rumors are she thought so too, and it's why she hasn't been speaking to either of them in recent times. Sounds like it's a bit of a mess, but it's nobody's business but their own.

"Seems like it, but I didn't ask." Fiero shrugs. "I stay well clear of my sisters' love lives and the resulting drama."

The rest of the New York dons are in the room when we enter, as well as Agessi from Philly. Most of us are casually dressed. Formality is usually the standard, but early-Sunday-morning emergency meetings are the exception. We grab coffee and pastries before taking our usual seats around the table.

Massimo dials in Mantegna, Volpe, and Pagano and starts the meeting by explaining what happened last night.

"What can you tell us about the guys?" Agessi asks, directing the question at me.

"They were all under thirty, and my guess is they were relatively new recruits because I didn't recognize any of them."

"They might not be DiPietro *soldati*," Mantegna says.

I nod. "True."

"Did they have tracking devices?" Joshua asks.

"Yeah, but they'd been cut out recently. All of them had stitches and bandages on their upper arms." I take a sip of my coffee. "It's how we knew they were one of us." In recent years, our loved ones had an additional tracking chip installed at the back of their necks. The general masses are not aware of it, and it's extra peace of mind for our families.

"It's got to be the cartel," Caleb says, drumming his fingers on top of the table. "They must have put them up to it."

"We can't afford to make assumptions," Ben says, brushing crumbs from his fingers. "The obvious conclusion is it's the cartel, but what's the motive? They knew coming for us at a family wedding was a suicide mission."

"It could've been a warning shot," Volpe says.

"Seems silly to show their hand like that if it was," President Greco says.

"No one said they were smart," Pagano adds.

"What happened with your *soldato*?" Ben asks Fiero. "Has he made any progress? Could he possibly identify if the cartel were involved or not?"

"He was made, and I had to send him and his family into hiding for their protection," Fiero says.

"Shame that's a dead end, but whoever planned this knew it was a suicide mission for sure," I agree. "It's why they were given pills. They probably hoped they'd succeed before they were taken out or taken in. Either way, they were ensuring the guys didn't talk."

"What action is being taken to ID these guys?" our president asks Don Mazzone.

"The team is already running their photos through facial recognition software. Hopefully we'll get a hit on at least one of them, and we can go from there," Ben replies.

For years, we had full online personnel records for everyone, but we stopped the practice because it was too dangerous. If the intel fell into the wrong hands—like a rival mafia, a hacker, the cartel, or the authorities—it could jeopardize the entire *Cosa Nostra*.

"I don't need to impress on you how serious the situation is." Massimo drags his gaze over the table. "I want each of you to personally meet with your capos this week and see if anyone is missing. Files will be emailed to every don in the US today. Show the pictures around. Ask questions at the ground level. Someone knows something."

"We should share the intel with O'Hara," Fiero says. "See if his crew has heard anything."

We've been working with the Irish for years on drug distribution in the city. Between us, we've driven out the other competitors, but new ones pop up all the time, and we're continuously dealing with some threat.

The Irish mafia is mostly based out of Boston, but they have a division here. It was initially managed by O'Hara's brother but after he double-crossed all of us, O'Hara took direct control. He has a few men managing it who report to him, but he closely watches proceedings. He splits his time between New York and Boston and maintains family homes in both cities.

While the Irish and Italian operations are completely separate entities, there is crossover between our teams at the street level in New York, and it's possible the Irish might have heard something.

"I'll call him," Joshua says. "See if he can put out a few feelers."

"We need to contain this threat," Massimo says. "We know the cartel is sniffing around, and even if this is unrelated, they are looking for ways in. Don't give it to them."

I return my sister's missed call from the car as I drive back to my parents' place after the meeting. "Pipsqueak, how are you?" I ask, grinning as I imagine Sabina's face scrunching in displeasure. My sister loathes that name.

"If you were here, I'd knock you flat on your ass, jerkface."

I chuckle. "I'd like to see you try."

"I've been working out, and I've put on muscle. I wouldn't be too cocky, brother."

"I'll have to come visit to test your theory."

"Bring the new nanny. Mom said she's super sweet and super pretty and that you're clearly obsessed with her. Fair warning, she's already checking out mother-of-the-groom outfits."

"She is not, and don't go putting notions in her head."

"I notice you don't deny it."

"Sloane *is* super sweet and pretty, but I'm not obsessed with her. Good enough for you?"

"I'll be the judge of that," she retorts. "You should come visit. You haven't been here in years. Get out of the city until shit blows over. Mom told me what happened, and it doesn't sound safe for any of you right now."

"I can't abandon ship, and Mom and Dad are safe at the house. No one is getting near them, I promise."

"Mama said they shot at you and Papa. I'm worried."

"I'm not letting anything happen to them, sis. Don't worry. Let me handle it."

"I want to see them, but Nolan can't abandon work right now."

Her husband is a heart surgeon at a top hospital in North Carolina. Sabina hates *La Cosa Nostra*. As soon as she was old enough, she flew the nest, attending college in California and then eloping to marry her college boyfriend when she was twenty-one. Papa was disappointed she wanted nothing to do with the *mafioso*, but her happiness meant more, so he eventually came around.

Sabina and Nolan have been married for almost seven years but no grandbabies yet, much to Mama's disappointment. They're both focused on their careers, and as Sabina just got a promotion at the architectural firm where she works, I can't see that changing anytime soon.

"We have the same security here," Sabina reminds me, though there's no need. I organized and paid for it. Even though she's not actively involved in *La Cosa Nostra*, it doesn't mean she's safe. Cruz put a target on all our heads. "And you can send a ton of bodyguards with them if you like. The guesthouse is finished now, and they can stay there. Getting them out of the state might be the best option while you figure this out. Send Elio too. I miss his handsome little face."

It might not be a bad idea. It was already shaping up to be a busy week at work before this additional burden. Knowing Elio is safe and out of harm's way will ease my mind, and it'll give Sloane and me time to figure things out. "I'll think about it and talk to Papa."

"I expect you to come visit another time, Cristian, with the new nanny you're not obsessed with."

I roll my eyes as I take the next exit. "You should come here sometime. You hardly ever visit anymore."

"I hate New York. I go home once a year for Mama, but I truly hate being back around all that shit," she grits out. "I'd rather chop off a tit than step foot in The Big Apple any more than is necessary."

"You kiss your husband with that mouth?" I tease.

"Nolan is well aware of my flaws," she drawls, and I detect an edge in her tone.

I can't say I'm overly fond of my only brother-in-law, but it's not really a fair comment. They live in NC, and I live here, so it's not like we can meet regularly to bond over a game and a beer. He's always seemed a bit strait-laced, but all I care about is that he treats my sister right.

"Is everything okay between you?" I ask, taking the next left turn.

"Everything is fine. We're just busy with work. I'll take a few vacation days if Mom, Dad, and Elio come. We can take Elio to that Discovery Science place in Uptown Charlotte. He'll love it. It's got all kinds of interactive things for kids to do."

"He would love that."

"Talk to Pops and let me know. Oh, and by the way, I told Mom it's fine for Sloane to borrow my things. Tell her to take whatever she needs."

My nostrils twitch when I enter my childhood home, and I follow the smells to the kitchen. Standing in the doorway, I observe the activity within with a growing smile. My mother and Sloane are loading trays filled with different baked goods into the oven while Elio is licking chocolate off the back of a wooden spoon. Sloane laughs at something my mother says, brushing wispy strands of hair off her face and leaving a few chocolate dots on her cheeks.

"Daddy, you're back!" Elio hops up when he sees me and runs across the room.

I scoop him up into my arms before he can muddy my jeans with his chocolatey hands. I only keep a small supply of clothes here, and I'd rather not have to detour back to the penthouse before heading to Long Island. It makes more sense to go directly from here. "Someone needs to clean up," I say, tickling his tummy. I'm so glad he slept through everything last night and he's none the wiser.

"I've got him." Sloane smiles softly at me, opening her arms for my son.

Elio leaps into her arms, and she giggles as she almost loses her balance. She props Elio on her uninjured hip.

"We need to talk," I say, wiping the chocolate off her face with my fingers.

"Sure." Her eyes probe mine as my fingers linger on her face. "Let me just clean Elio up first."

"Don't lick the bowl, Daddy!" Elio calls out as Sloane walks off. "That's all mine!"

I stare at the doorway as they disappear through it. Mama appears at my side, looping her arm through mine and smiling. "I approve. She's perfect for you, and everyone already loves her."

I open my mouth to argue, but what's the point?

Mama pulls my face down, kissing my cheek. "Stop letting your head rule your heart, Cristian. I know Aliya hurt you, but Sloane isn't her. You deserve to be happy. Stop fighting your feelings. Let her in and see where it takes you."

Chapter Twenty-Six
Sloane

"Let's walk and talk," Cristian says after we've left Elio and Beatrice to put the finishing touches on the baked goods in the kitchen.

"Okay." The grounds are huge here, and I wouldn't mind exploring. I borrow Sabina's coat and boots. My feet are a bit squished as she's a size smaller than me, but I'll manage. "I hope your sister won't mind I've borrowed so much of her stuff," I say as we head outside through a back door.

"I spoke to her earlier, and she said to take whatever you need."

"That is kind of her."

"Sabina's great." Cristian threads his fingers in mine. I'm not sure if he's realized he's done it. Heat warms my palm, and I get a little thrill inside just from holding hands with him. I'm truly pathetic, or maybe just starved for genuine human touch. "I think I'm going to send Elio to stay with her this week."

"How come? And will I need to go with him?" Separation from Cristian would not be good for me. I'm already terrified of the consequences of ditching my cartel cell. As much as I want to bury my head in the sand, I know I'll need to go to the diner tonight after we get back to the city and try to reason with Pablo and his goons. I'm not looking forward to a repeat of last week, and I feel sick to my stomach.

"It ties into what I have to tell you. As for needing to go with him, I don't think it'll be necessary. My parents are going to take him."

Relief powers through me. A week alone with Cristian is perfect. "What will I do?"

"Perhaps you can plan ahead. Do some meal prep. Organize new artwork projects, and you can take it easy and maybe catch up on some sleep. I'd also like you to talk to Natalia and Sierra, if you agree. Both are family friends. Nat is a doctor and Sierra practices alternative medicine. They might have some suggestions for things you can try to fix your sleep issues."

I cling tighter to his hand as tears prick the backs of my eyes. Cristian is so thoughtful, so caring. I honestly cannot fathom how some woman has not snapped him up yet. Cristian's brow puckers as he stares at our conjoined hands. I expect him to pull away, but I'm pleased when he doesn't. "Sierra already gave Elisa some essential oils for me, but if either of them has suggestions, I'm all ears. I'm sick of feeling so tired all the time."

"Good," he says, leading me out from the main garden and across a stone path toward a small forest. "I'll set that up."

"What happened yesterday, Cristian?" I ask, staring directly into his face. I want to get this secret out in the open so it's one less thing for me to fuck up. "Your friends and family have been really nice to me and very welcoming, but there have been lots of cryptic comments, and I'm sensing there is something I don't know. The way Isotta's father stopped to acknowledge you and your parents during the walk up the aisle was strange. Then people were taking potshots at us, and I saw you and others run after them with guns. What is going on? What don't I know?"

Cristian guides me over to a bench positioned just outside the small wooded area. "I'm going to level with you, Sloane, because there is no sugarcoating the truth." He pulls me down onto the bench and turns so he's facing me. He takes my hands in his. "Before I explain, you need to understand I am still the same guy, and you don't need to be afraid of me."

"I'm not afraid of you, Cristian."

"You might be when you hear what I have to say."

I touch his arm. "It's not going to change how I feel."

"About that." His thumb rubs circles over the back of my hand as we talk, and it's wonderfully soothing.

"Please don't push me away again. Not after last night."

"It would be smart to. Us starting something complicates things, but the truth is I can't fight my feelings for you any longer."

My heart thumps like crazy, and the goofiest smile spreads over my mouth. "I was so sure you were going to tell me it was a mistake."

"I thought about it, but I don't play games, Sloane, and as much as us being together concerns me for Elio, I'm done living in denial. The truth is, I've been attracted to you from the moment you walked into my office. I offered someone else the position over you purely to try to avoid this situation."

"I didn't know that." I move in closer, and our knees touch.

"I don't want our relationship to interfere with your job as Elio's nanny, but I'm not sure how we separate them. But we have this week to figure it out."

I lean in and kiss him, and I'm relieved when he kisses me back without hesitation. Cristian pulls me closer and tilts my head so he can deepen the kiss. This time is different than the frenzied kissing from last night. Cristian kisses me slowly, deeply, passionately, and thoroughly, and I get lost in him and the way he makes me feel.

When we break apart, we're both breathless and smiling.

"You're so beautiful." Cristian tucks wayward pieces of my hair behind my ears. "Far too good for me, but I'm too selfish to stop this."

I circle my arms around his neck. "I don't want you to stop, Cristian. I want to be with you."

"I'm too old for you, and you still don't know everything about me."

"Like I already said, I'm older than my years, and your age doesn't bother me." I run my fingers through the ends of his dark hair.

"It should," he murmurs, closing his eyes as I toy with his hair. "Damn, that feels so good."

"You take care of everyone, but no one takes care of you," I softly say, pressing my brow to his. "I want to take care of you. Being with you like this feels so natural to me. I can't imagine being with anyone else." I speak no lie, even if he's not aware of the full truth about me either. But my feelings for him are real. I'm not doing this because I *have* to—I'm doing this because I *want* to. Right now, I want to feel everything he's making me feel, and I'm ignoring everything else. I can feel guilty later. For now, I'm soaking up the excited buzz thrumming throughout my body and equally giddy as the butterflies swooping through my chest.

"I don't want to be with anyone but you," he says, scooping me up and placing me on his lap. My arms wind tighter around his neck as we meet in another toe-curling kiss. We kiss for ages, and I'm floating on a cloud. Every nerve ending in my body is wired, and delicious knots coil low in my belly as my core tightens and spasms with every breathless kiss.

When we finally break apart, we're both panting and

flushed and grinning like fools. Cristian nuzzles into my neck. "You make me feel young again." His arms tighten around me. "I haven't felt like this about anyone before, Sloane, and that scares me."

"It scares me too." I dot kisses into his hair.

"I still haven't told you what I came out here to tell you."

I cup his face and tilt his head back. "So tell me. I promise I'm going nowhere."

"I hope you mean that." The backs of his knuckles caress my face. "Prepare yourself. This won't be easy to hear."

"Just tell me, Cristian," I softly plead. "I don't like being kept in the dark."

He maintains eye contact and says, "I'm one of the leaders of the Italian American mafia in the US, and my family is one of the five New York families."

I respect his bluntness, and though it's not a surprise to me, I react appropriately, hating I must pretend. I give him my full attention as he explains it further, staring directly into my eyes and giving me a no-holds-barred account of the violence and danger he's a part of.

"So now you know, do you want to change your mind about anything?"

I slowly shake my head. "Nope."

His answering stare is incredulous.

"I'm not saying I'm not shocked, and obviously it's a lot to take in, but it doesn't change who you are to me."

"It might when you've had time to process it."

"I really don't think so." I brush my lips against his before resting my head on his shoulder and my hand on his chest. "It makes so much sense now. All the security and bodyguards."

"I didn't lie when I told you we had enemies."

I sit up straighter. "You also said your brother had made enemies. Is that who came after you last night?"

"We're still gathering intelligence. The men were *Cosa Nostra,* but they could've been put up to it by the Mexican Cartel. My brother had made a deal with them before he died. A deal he didn't fulfill, and now they want revenge."

Blood rushes to my ears, and my stomach lurches painfully. "You think this cartel wants to hurt you because of something your brother did?"

"They want to hit back at all *Cosa Nostra,* but they have a big hard-on for the DiPietro *famiglia* thanks to Cruz. None of us is safe."

A full-body shudder works its way over me. At least I've found out why Pablo has planted me in Cristian's life.

"You're scared." His arms band tighter around me. "I won't let anyone hurt you. I'll protect you. I swear."

"That's why you wanted John Angelo to go everywhere with me."

He nods. "It's a precaution, and I'm glad you agreed."

"I definitely want to learn how to use a gun."

"I will get that organized this week too. Women in our circle know how to defend themselves. Traditionally, enemies targeted loved ones, and it continues to this day. Most all the women you will meet through me have endured kidnappings or attempted kidnappings at one time."

My eyes widen, and prickles of fear crawl up my spine. I know exactly how that feels, and the thought that more women might get kidnapped by the cartel sends a fresh wave of terror rolling through me. Images of the women in that file flash before my eyes, and pain flays me on the inside. Is that what they did or what they're planning? Is this more than just Cristian?

"That frightens you, and honestly, I'm glad to see it. You've been taking this so well, nearly too well. A healthy dose of fear is natural and welcome. It will keep you on your toes. I don't want to scare you, and I'll do everything in my power to protect you, but you need to always be vigilant. Like I said before, if your gut tells you something is off, trust it."

I nod, wetting my suddenly dry lips.

"Have you changed your mind now?" Cristian calmly asks.

I shake my head. "No, Cristian. I'm definitely scared, but it'll take a lot more than that for me to walk away from you and Elio. I will learn to protect myself, and I'll be more observant, and if anything seems strange, I'll tell you immediately."

"You are truly remarkable, Sloane." Pride and something deeper shine behind his eyes as he takes my hands to his lips and kisses my fingers. "I'm more than a little smitten."

I beam at him. "That's good because I'm more than a little smitten too."

We meet in a soft, slow, sumptuous kiss, and I melt against him, feeling safe and protected despite the precariousness of my situation.

We smile at one another when we break the kiss. "We need to make tracks," he says, looking apologetic as he traces my lower lip with his thumb. His eyes blaze with heat, and I'm sure mine look the same. "If you need time to think about everything, I can organize some of my men to take you back to the penthouse, and Elio and I can go to Sunday lunch alone."

"You can't get rid of me that easily," I tease, running my fingers along the back of his neck. "I'm excited to meet more of your friends, and I don't want to go back to the penthouse alone."

"Are you sure?"

"Absolutely." Reluctantly, I climb off his lap and extend my hand. "Let's go get your son."

Cristian bundles me into a hug. "I'm so grateful you came into our lives, Sloane."

A messy ball of emotion clogs my throat, and I wrap my

arms around him as I squeeze my eyes shut, trying to ward off the wave of guilt threatening to engulf me. "I'm the lucky one," I whisper.

He tips my chin back. "Until we've talked more, we need to keep this under wraps. Especially around Elio."

"I understand," I say, shucking out of his embrace.

He folds his hand around mine as we start the walk back to the house. "But know this much, Sloane." His gorgeous green eyes bore into mine with an obsessive intensity that sends shivers of desire racing through me. "As soon as we have it all worked out, I will be shouting about you from the rooftops because you're *mine,* and I want everyone to know it."

Chapter Twenty-Seven
Sloane

"This is Sloane," Elio says, tugging on my hand and dragging me down the hallway of Cristian's friends' house on Long Island. "She's my new nanny, and she's awesome at basketball."

Cristian chuckles as we enter a large, homey kitchen that smells like every food lover's dream. "Sloane is setting the benchmark high."

Delicious aromas scent the air, and my stomach rumbles appreciatively, which is a miracle because I've felt ill all day thinking of how furious Pablo must be now he's lost contact with me. My nerves are stretched tight, my chest a twisted mass of anxiety, and it has effectively slaughtered my appetite.

"That's high praise indeed," an older guy with white-blond hair says. He smiles and extends his hand. "I'm Fiero. This is my wife, Valentina, and our son, Armani." His arm circles Valentina's shoulders. She's stunning with wavy black hair, piercing green eyes, and the most incredible flawless skin. A cute little dark-haired boy is propped on her hip, wriggling and trying to get down.

"It's lovely to meet you, Sloane," she says. "I've heard lots of wonderful things about you."

"Here, I'll take him." Fiero reaches for the little guy, instantly setting him down on his feet.

"El, El," he babbles, wobbling toward Elio on chubby legs.

"He's walking! Look, Daddy!" Elio shrieks. "Armani can walk now."

"I can see, buddy. It won't be long before he's shooting hoops with you."

Elio hugs the little guy. "Good job, buddy," he says, gently patting Armani on the head.

Valentina and I trade matching smiles. It's too cute for words.

Cristian crouches down and holds up his hand. "Hey there, Armani."

Armani emits a high-pitched screech, then a few babbles before softly slapping his hand against Cristian's in a high five.

"He's adorable," I tell Valentina.

"He's the best." Her eyes radiate love and affection as she stares at her son. "We must be insane, but we'll have another little bundle of joy in a few months." She smooths a hand over her softly rounded tummy.

"Congratulations. You'll have your hands full."

"I wouldn't have it any other way," she says as the doorbell chimes. "Excuse me while I let our other guests in." She walks off, heading out of the kitchen to answer the door.

Cristian explained in the car that Fiero's youngest sister, Tullia, was joining us for dinner with her friend Rowan. Apparently, Rowan is the eldest son of Don Bennett Mazzone, who is husband to Sierra, the lady who gave me the essential oils. I'm grateful he's not hiding things from me now, but it's a lot to take in. Everyone seems to know one another, and they all seem close. It must be nice.

Cristian's hand brushes discreetly against mine as if he's read my mind and knows I'm a little out of my depth. "You'll like them," he says, attempting to reassure me with his eyes.

"They're close to your age," Fiero says, earning a daggered stare from Cristian. Fiero laughs, slapping him on the back as he keeps one eye on his son and Elio, who are tossing a soft ball back and forth. "Down, boy. I didn't mean anything by it." Fiero winks at me, and I fall into a little bit of a daze. He is superhot for an older dude, and I can see why Valentina fell for him. He oozes natural charm, and his personality seems fun. Clearly, his wife is much younger, and he was just trying to make me feel at ease. Not sure why Cristian feels threatened by what he said.

"Hey everyone."

We all whip our heads around at the sound of the bubbly female voice.

"Lia. Come here and give your big brother a hug." Fiero sports a wide grin as he walks toward the petite brunette.

"Ro. Missed you." Tullia removes the camera from around her neck, passing it to Valentina, before throwing herself at Fiero and squeezing her arms around his broad back.

"Sup, little dudes," a man with a deep, gravelly voice says, and I turn around to face the other new arrival.

Trying not to stare is challenging because he has a charismatic presence that is tangible. Rowan Mazzone is well over six feet tall with broad shoulders, a muscular physique, and a devilish glint in his big blue eyes. His dark hair is shorn tight at the sides and longer on top, and he has exquisite cheekbones and lush, full lips. He's extremely good-looking, and I bet he knows it too. Hot guys my age tend to be cocky, bordering on arrogant, though it's unfair to judge him before I've got to know him.

"Rowan!" Elio screeches, dropping the ball and running toward the man.

Rowan chuckles as he bends over, offering his arm to Elio, and they do one of those elaborate handshakes that isn't really a handshake. Tattoos sneak out from under the cuffs of his shirt, covering his hands. More ink creeps up the side of one neck. He's a seriously sexy guy, but he's not in Cristian's league.

Cristian exudes sexiness without trying or acknowledging it. Confidence and maturity set him apart from other men. Combined with his nurturing side and that underlying dark intensity he's shown me, he is the definition of my perfect man. Strong, capable, caring, sexy, self-assured. He ticks all the boxes.

"Hi there." Tullia lands in front of me, instantly pulling me into a hug. Her petite stature belies her fierceness as she squeezes me in a warm embrace. She steps back and smiles. "I'm Tullia, but friends call me Lia. It's really good to meet you, Sloane."

She's super pretty with deep-blue eyes and dark hair pulled into a high ponytail. She's not wearing much makeup, and she's dressed casually in skinny ripped jeans and a lace-trimmed tank under a half-zipped hoodie. Black-and-white retro Nike sneakers adorn her small feet. Everything about her is fun and dainty, and I feel like an out-of-place, overdressed giant in my borrowed black dress and gold sandals. None of Sabina's shoes fit comfortably, so I had to wear my wedding outfit shoes. "Good to meet you too."

"You have exquisite bone structure," she says, taking her camera back from her sister-in-law. "Mind if I take a pic?"

My brows climb to my hairline. This is a first. "Ugh, I guess so."

"Not everyone likes getting their picture taken, Polly," Rowan says, flashing me a dazzling smile. "I'm Rowan."

"Sloane." I extend my hand, and he clasps it in his much larger palm. "What's up with Polly?" I inquire, letting my gaze bounce between them.

Tullia rolls her eyes, feigning indifference as Rowan raises my hand to his lips. "He thinks he's funny. He started calling me Polly Pocket when we were kids, and he keeps it up 'cause he knows how much I freaking hate it." Her lips pull into a tight line when Rowan presses a kiss to the back of my hand.

"Knock it off." Cristian rips my hand out of Rowan's and glares at the younger man.

"Dude, what's your problem?"

"Behave, Mini Mazzone." Fiero pins him in place with a pointed look.

"You can take my pic," I blurt, purely to break the rising tension.

"Great." Her infectious smile returns. "Let's go outside. There's too much testosterone in here." She shoots Rowan an agitated look before looping her arm through mine and pulling me away from the brooding men.

"Lunch will be on the table in ten," Valentina calls out after us as Tullia drags me out of the room.

"Don't mind him," she says as we walk through double French doors that lead out to a side patio. "Rowan is the biggest flirt. He just can't help himself unless it's me," she adds with a sigh.

"Oh?" I ask, admiring the gorgeous grounds set across three levels. Various shrubs and flower beds are dotted around the property, the colors muted this time of year. Below us is an infinity pool with an adjoining pool house, and I spot a cute cottage on the lower level, facing toward the dock where a couple of high-end boats are moored.

Crime clearly pays well. It's funny, but when I'm with these people, I never think of them as criminals. They're some of the nicest, most welcoming people I've ever met. Yet I can't deny at least some of what they have has come from illegal means. Cristian told me everyone runs legit businesses, and while they used to be a front for their mafia-run enterprises, they are successful in their own right these days.

It must be nice to have so much money you never have to worry.

"I've been in love with him forever, but he only sees me as a friend," Tullia confides, steering me toward a small seated area with neat flower beds housing shrubs with pretty yellow and white flowering buds.

"That must suck."

"It sure does. What's worse is he's been hooking up with my older sister on and off for years."

My mouth hangs open, and my jaw trails the ground. "No way."

"Yeppers." Pain splays across her face. "I haven't spoken to Sofia in years, and I've only recently patched things up with Rowan, though things are still a little strained."

"Does your sister know how you feel?"

She nods before pointing toward the seat. "She's known all along."

I shake my head before sitting down. "I have no words." What kind of sister would do that? I'm heartsick on Tullia's behalf.

"She doesn't even care about him, and he follows her around like a dog begging for scraps. It's pathetic."

"Sounds heartbreaking," I say as she snaps a few pics.

"I'm used to living with the pain."

"You should screw his brother. Give him a taste of his own medicine."

She almost chokes on her tongue. "Rhys is only eleven."

I cringe. "Shit, okay, definitely don't do that." I arch my

head to the side. "Screw his best friend. Hell, screw all of them. Really mess with his head."

Laughter tumbles from her mouth. "I like you. You talk a lot of sense." She moves in closer, snapping away. "I wish I could, but they're all like brothers to me. Just thinking about it gives me the ick."

"Well, I hope you're at least dating. Make him jealous, and he might see sense."

"He's never going to see me like that." She shoves her glasses up the bridge of her nose. "I'm the opposite of the girls he picks and a pale imitation of my gorgeous older sister."

"You're so pretty," I truthfully say. "And really friendly. Any guy would be lucky to date you. It's his loss if he doesn't see what's right in front of him."

She sits down beside me. "That's sweet of you to say."

"It's the truth. You need to get out there and date, sister."

"I've tried dating, but no one measures up to him. It's hopeless."

"Just have fun then. No-strings-attached one-night stands can do wonders for a girl."

"Is that right?" Cristian asks in his familiar, deep, sexy voice.

My cheeks flush as he walks toward me, arching a brow. "I was speaking metaphorically, and eavesdropping is rude."

"It wasn't intentional. Dinner is ready, and Valentina sent me out to get you." Cristian stares at my lips, and I think he's remembering our kissing the same way I am. My blood heats, and longing stirs low in my belly. Cristian offers me his hand, and I let him pull me to my feet. My heels dig into the soft grass, and I get stuck, stumbling forward as I lose my balance. But he's there to catch me before I face-plant the grass and ruin myself.

The instant my body brushes against his, fire blazes hot and heavy inside me. Cristian's eyes lock me in place as his arm winds around my back. My heart is spinning like a whirlwind as we stare at one another. My hands land on his chest of their own volition, and the craving to kiss him is almost insurmountable.

The clicking of a camera snaps us both out of it, and we quickly pull apart. My cheeks heat again.

"Wow, that is one seriously hot photo," Tullia says, looking at the preview screen of her Nikon.

"Let me see." Cristian takes the camera from her and stares at it. "Email me all those, including the ones you took of Sloane on her own."

"Yes, *boss*," Tullia sasses, and I cringe a little.

"You didn't see that," Cristian warns.

Tullia makes a zipping motion across her lips.

Cristian leans in and claims a quick, hard kiss before walking off, leaving me staring at his retreating form with my heart in my mouth and my panties on fire.

"Damn, girl." Tullia threads her arm through mine. "I need all the tea."

Chapter Twenty-Eight
Cristian

I've always liked Rowan. He's ten years younger, so he wasn't part of our friend group until recent years. He's quite close to Caleb now, and he sometimes tags along on nights out. As Don Mazzone's successor, he'll be a fellow Commission board member in the future, so it's important we get along. But right now, I am imagining several creative ways to remove his head from his shoulders.

I detoured to the bathroom after I went to get Sloane and Tullia. When I returned, everyone was seated around the table, and Rowan had strategically placed himself on Sloane's left. Elio is seated on her other side, and Fiero is at the top of the table, meaning I had no choice but to sit across from my son. Tullia is beside me with Valentina to her right, and Armani is in his high chair at the other end of the table.

I've had a front row seat to Rowan hitting on my girl any chance he gets, and my patience is currently in limited supply. Sloane looks hugely uncomfortable, and she's not encouraging him, but he's either oblivious or deliberately ignoring the vibes she's putting out.

"You can't kill anyone in leadership or an heir," Fiero says, speaking in a low tone. "Just remember that."

"Didn't stop you," I say before popping the last piece of succulent roast beef in my mouth. Valentina is a superb cook, and she served up a delicious lunch, but it sits in my stomach like a rock. I haven't been able to relax and enjoy the meal because I'm so wound up about Rowan and Sloane.

"Extenuating circumstances, my friend." Fiero waggles his brows.

Tullia leans in close, whispering to both of us. "You could mess up his pretty face though. Maybe if we're on a level playing field, he might finally notice me."

"You're beautiful, Lia," Fiero tells his sister. "And you shouldn't put yourself down. I suggest you forget about Rowan, at least for a few years. He's not a bad guy, just young and dumb. We were all there."

"Speak for yourself." I pin him with a cool stare.

"I said what I said." Fiero grins.

There's no point arguing, even if I want to protest, I was not like most of my idiot friends at that age. Steam is practically billowing out of my ears as I watch Rowan lean closer to Sloane, and honestly, if Elio wasn't in the room, I'd be all up in his face right now. I purposely eavesdrop on their conversation.

"A few of us are heading to a club tonight. You should come," Rowan says.

"I've already got plans," Sloane replies, instantly shutting him down.

I drill Rowan with a look that I hope screams "she has plans with *me*."

"Surely the boss gives you a night off." Rowan smirks as he looks across the table at me.

"I'm not Sloane's keeper," I calmly reply. "Sounds to me like she doesn't want to go."

"You didn't mention any club to me," Tullia says.

Rowan grimaces a little. "We're hitting up Club H. I know that's not your scene."

"Club H? Are you fucking kidding me right now?" I snap, gripping the edge of the table.

"Calm down, Cristian. We're going to the lower-level club. What kind of man do you think I am?"

"I'm beginning to wonder," I mutter under my breath, only marginally less angry.

Club H is one of the clubs run by the Mazzone *famiglia*. It's a popular sex club among wealthy VIPs in the city. There are various levels to the club, with various activities, but the ground level is a normal club and very busy most nights of the week. Still, I don't want Sloane going there. At least not without me.

"Thanks for the invite, but I'll pass." Sloane pushes the remaining food around her plate, and I notice she's only picked at her meal.

Rowan's face drops, and Tullia notices. "See? I might as well be invisible," she whispers with pain lacing her words, and I feel for her.

We continue talking in hushed tones.

"You're a great catch, sis. It's Rowan's loss if he doesn't see it."

"You're my brother. You're biased."

"I'm not your brother, and I agree," I say, raising my voice before adding, "Rowan is an idiot."

"I heard that." Rowan frowns as he jerks his head up and looks over at me.

"Good. I meant for you to hear it." I drain the rest of my red wine in one go. I hadn't planned on drinking much, preferring to drive rather than be driven, but this day is testing my sanity. One of my men can drive us back home if need be.

"You get out of bed the wrong side today or something, DiPietro?" Rowan asks, sliding his arm around the back of Sloane's chair.

"It's Don DiPietro to you," I snap. "And learn to read the room, Mini Mazzone." I'm being petty, but I can't help it. I pointedly stare at Sloane as Valentina silently watches while spoon-feeding Armani.

Elio has long since given up sitting. He's currently under the table racing some of Armani's toy cars, chattering away to himself and hopefully oblivious to the painful conversation around the table.

"I need the bathroom," Sloane blurts, rising so suddenly her chair almost falls to the floor. Her cheeks are inflamed as she strides out of the room.

"So much for having a lovely meal with family and friends," Valentina says, imploring her husband with her eyes.

"What's a meal without some drama?" Fiero jokes.

"Keep an eye on Elio, yeah?" I ask as I stand.

"Sure thing. Go. I'll try to offer some words of wisdom to the young and dumb."

I ignore Rowan as I leave the dining room and head toward the downstairs bathroom to check on Sloane. I lean against the wall outside as I wait for her to emerge. When the lock turns a few minutes later, I straighten up, meeting Sloane's eyes when the door opens. Her hand flies to her chest. "Shit. You startled me."

I seem to do that a lot. Either I'm too stealthy or Sloane has a jumpy disposition. "I wanted to make sure you're okay."

"I'm okay," she lies. "It's just a little awkward."

I move toward her, drawing her slowly into my body. "It's more than a little awkward. I'm sorry. I thought we'd have a pleasant afternoon with my friends, but Captain Oblivious ruined that."

Sloane giggles, circling her arms around my neck. "I can't work out if he's actually oblivious or only pretending. Either way, I don't like it. He seems like a nice guy, but he's way too similar to other guys I've met his age. Cocky to the point of ignorant arrogance."

"Is that so?" I tighten my arms around her back and nuzzle my nose against hers.

"I prefer older guys. They're sexier and more mature."

"Older guys plural?" I say, dropping a slew of kisses along her jawline. "Or anyone in particular?"

"Are you fishing for compliments, Don DiPietro?"

Blood rushes to my dick hearing her say my name. "What if I am?" I purr, grabbing her ass and pulling her flush against me so she feels what she's doing to me.

"You don't need to fish for them, Cristian. You've already reeled me in. Hook, line, and sinker."

Our mouths meet in a fiery kiss that hardens my dick to steel behind my pants. I can't get enough of her, kissing her hungrily as I push her up against the wall and ravish her skillful mouth. Sloane whimpers, opening her lips and letting me in, as I continue kissing her like my life depends on it.

"Now it all makes sense," Rowan says, interrupting the moment.

I hold Sloane close as I angle my head and stare at the younger man. "It should've made sense an hour ago," I reply, sliding my arm around Sloane and tucking her into my side. "Like I said, learn to open your eyes and read the room." He seems genuinely oblivious to Tullia too, which sucks for her.

"You should've said something." He walks up to us. "If I'd known you were together, I'd have toned it down. I hope you can forgive me." Sincerity bleeds into his tone as he stares at Sloane.

"It's not me you should be asking forgiveness of," Sloane

cryptically replies, and Rowan frowns. For a smart guy, he sure is clueless when it comes to Tullia Maltese. Does he honestly not see it?

"We're keeping it under wraps for the moment," I explain.

"Elio, right." He nods before thumping me in my injured upper arm. If I didn't know him, I'd think he did it deliberately. "Sorry, man. I didn't mean to interfere. No hard feelings, yeah?"

It's hard to stay mad at Rowan. He's not a bad guy. Just hyped up on hormones and making the most of his twenties before he has to shoulder all the responsibility coming his way. While I went about it differently, I understand where he's coming from. "It's already forgotten."

"Sweet." Rowan winks at Sloane. "If you ever get tired of the old guy, you know where to find me."

"Punk," I call after his laughing form.

"Poor Lia," Sloane says, resting her head on my chest. "She's got it bad for him, and he's completely blind."

***

The rest of the evening is much more enjoyable, though not without further drama. Tullia leaves early, clearly upset over something. When Rowan returns from taking a call, he's surprised to discover she left without him. I have no clue what went down, nor do I have any desire to find out. After Cassio Greco shows up to collect Rowan, we stay a little while longer, and it's a calmer environment now the source of the drama is gone. Before we head home, I pull Fiero aside and update him on how the search is going for Cruz's kids, promising to keep him informed when we have more news.

Sloane is in her room taking a shower after reading Elio his bedtime story, so I use the opportunity to call my mom and make the final arrangements for the NC trip. I'll meet them at the private airfield in West Harrison in the morning, where my plane will be ready to fly them to Charlotte. Elio is excited for his mini vacation with my parents and looks forward to visiting his aunt and uncle. I'm gonna miss him. We are rarely apart for long.

I have just finished plating the charcuterie board when Sloane appears, wearing her coat and boots. I frown. "You're going out?"

"Yes. I did say I had plans."

I fold my arms over my chest. "Stupid me. I thought you meant plans with me."

"Don't be angry," she whispers, cautiously approaching me. "I'm only meeting him to break it off."

I work hard to leash my anger, but today has been a trying day, and my patience is practically nonexistent at this stage. "I thought you did that last week."

She averts her eyes, shoving her hands in the pockets of her pink Moncler jacket. "Something came up, and he didn't make it."

"You mean he stood you up," I say in a clipped tone. "I don't know why you're showing him any respect when he clearly doesn't respect you. I thought it was only casual. You could break up with him by phone."

Her gaze connects with mine. "That's not who I am. I get why you're mad, but I promise I'm not interested in him. I just want to do this the right way." Her eyes lower again, and I hate to see her suffering.

A heavy sigh trickles from my lips. "Come here."

She shuffles toward me, sniffling, and I bundle her in my

arms. "I'm sorry. I'm jealous, and I wanted you all to myself tonight."

"We have all week and every night afterwards when Elio goes to bed," she says, clinging to me with a desperation that equally concerns and consoles me.

"Take John Angelo with you," I say, tipping her chin up. Pain shimmers in her eyes. "I'd offer to go myself, but I can't promise I won't kill the guy." I expect horror, fear, disappointment, but she looks like she almost wants me to. "I don't like this, but I respect your decision." I kiss her deeply, wanting her to remember who and what is waiting for her at home. "I'll be waiting."

Chapter Twenty-Nine
Sloane

I'm shaking like a leaf as I set foot in the diner. What little I ate at dinner is threatening to make a reappearance when I spot Diego waiting in a corner booth for me. His back is to the window, and he's wearing a cap with a hoodie over it so John Angelo can't see him. His eyes never leave my face as I walk toward him on wobbly legs.

Wordlessly, I slide into the seat across from him. He licks his lips as his gaze rakes over me, and it's like being dumped in a bucket of ice-cold water. I shove my hands between my knees to try to stop the trembling. "You've been a very naughty girl, Sloane."

"It isn't my fault the phone is out of action." I hate how much my voice quakes, and I tell myself to get my shit together. Dragging up my alter persona, I try to remember my acting skills. "I got caught in the crossfire, and my cell broke when Cristian slammed me to the ground. Maybe next time, try not shooting at me," I snap.

A flicker of something glints in his eye, but it's gone before I can decipher it. Tension is thick in the air. "That wasn't a sanctioned hit," he coolly replies after a few beats, poking his teeth with a toothpick as he studies me.

"What?" I lean forward a little, setting one hand on the table. "What do you mean?"

"Where did you go today?" he asks, ignoring my question.

"What?"

Grabbing my hand, he pulls it across the table. He ducks his head a little, angling his body so he's not seen from outside as he glares at me. "Don't play dumb. We had to detour crossing the bridge so they wouldn't make us, and then we lost you. Where did you go?"

"I don't know. He made me wear the blindfold again."

Diego threads his fingers through mine and digs his nails into my palm. "You're lying."

"I'm not." I yank my hand back. "My bodyguard is watching, and you're going to ruin everything. I'm with Cristian now. The plan is working."

"It doesn't sound like he trusts you much if he's blind-folding you everywhere you go."

"And what, you wouldn't do the same with newcomers? Come on. You know who he is. He's not just going to trust me until I've earned it. Which means I can't meet you again like this. It'll make him suspicious. I told him I was coming here to break things off with you."

Diego drums his fingers on the table. "Is that so?"

"I told him previously we were casually dating. Figured I'd need a cover story in case anyone saw you."

"Maybe I should call the boss and tell him to slit your whore mother's throat right now."

I lean forward, pinning him with wide, panicked eyes. "No. Please no. Diego. I swear I'm telling the truth." I gulp nervously. "I'll have intel for Pablo in two weeks. I swear. Please don't hurt my mother."

His stabbing stare feels like tiny pinpricks slashing me everywhere. "Fine."

I almost slump over the table in relief.

"Here's how this is going down." He grabs my head, pressing my brow to his. His rancid breath turns my stomach, and I hate him being all up in my face. "You're going to get up, go outside, and pull your bodyguard away from the door. Act visibly upset."

His grip tightens on the back of my head, but I barely feel the pinch. I'm stunned he agreed. At least it's bought me a reprieve.

"Say you need to go to the bathroom. I'll slip out while you occupy him. Alvaro is waiting for you with your new phone and a little gift."

All the blood leaches from my face at his smirking tone, and nausea swims up my throat. My entire body starts trembling again. "I can't go back to Cristian upset. He'll be suspicious. Please tell Alvaro not to hurt me," I plead.

"You know the rules, slut. You disobey, you and your precious mama get punished." Those were not the initial rules, but they seem to twist them whenever it suits them, and I can't do a damn fucking thing about it. His smirk kicks up a notch. "Tell that Italian prick I was cruel and my words upset you. He'll buy that." Releasing my face, he nudges my foot under the table. "Go. Pablo doesn't like to be kept waiting."

I walk outside on autopilot, and I don't even have to act upset when I pull John Angelo away from the door and play my part. I'm so tempted to tell him the truth, to beg him to shoot Diego in the back as he slinks away into the night, and to rescue me from the ordeal waiting in the bathroom. But I can't. *I can't.* Mom needs me. She didn't mean what she said. She wants me to save her, and it's my duty to do it.

So, I go to the bathroom, listen to Pablo reciting all

manner of threats as Alvaro strips me to the waist and paws at me while assaulting my mouth with his vile cock. Pablo watches, and I'm grateful there's no sign of my mother, if it means I'm taking the punishment this time for both of us. The assholes laugh as I vomit the second Alvaro is finished, throwing up his cum all over the floor. Alvaro crawls out the window, leaving me holding myself and rocking on the dirty bathroom floor.

It's a miracle I can pull myself together after being violated, but I manage to do it before my bodyguard comes looking. Hiding the new phone inside my coat, I fix my clothes and gargle with tap water. I stare at my reflection in the mirror in a kind of numb, shocked state. I look as dead as I feel on the inside. My legs feel heavy as I force them to move, exiting the bathroom and heading outside.

John Angelo sends repeated concerned looks my way as we walk back to the penthouse. I know I should do better, but I don't have it in me to pretend right now. Feeling eyes glued to me the whole way home, I try my best to hold it all in. I won't give those sick fucks the satisfaction of knowing how much they've broken me this time.

Cristian is waiting in the hallway when I enter the penthouse, and it's clear John Angelo messaged him. His troubled eyes drift over my pale face. "What happened?"

"I don't want to talk about it," I say in a voice that sounds dead to my own ears.

"Did he hurt you?" His voice is lethally quiet. "I want his name."

"He was cruel with his words, and he upset me, but it's done. I won't be seeing him again, and I just want to put it behind me."

"I don't like the sound of this guy. Let me handle him."

Oh, how I wish he could. I stare straight ahead, not looking at him, as I speak. "No. He's in the past, where I want him to stay. Please drop it. I don't want to talk about him ever again."

Cristian moves to hug me, but I shake my head, hold up my palms, and take a step back. "Don't. I got sick. I think I might be coming down with a stomach bug. I felt ill last night at the wedding too." It's a pathetic excuse, but it's all I've got.

There's an awkward pregnant pause for a few beats. "Go to bed. I'll make you some peppermint tea. It should settle your stomach."

I don't have the energy to argue, so I merely nod and shuffle off. I'm shaking all over as I strip out of my clothes, shoving them in the laundry basket. Turning the shower on to the highest setting, I get in and try to wash the memory of unwanted touches from my body. But no matter how hard I scrub at my skin, I still feel dirty, broken, and damaged on the inside.

This feels like an insurmountable task, one I'm failing at every turn. I can't see any scenario where this ends well for anyone. Tears don't fall this time, even though I'm torn into shreds on the inside. I think my tear ducts are broken too.

When the water turns cool and I notice my red, wrinkled skin, I finally get out and wrap myself in one of the big, fluffy towels.

Cristian is sitting on the bed when I enter my bedroom. He looks up, concern puckering his brow as his gaze roams over my red-raw skin. "I need privacy to get dressed," I say in the same nonemotional voice. I can only imagine what he must be thinking. I wish I could do better, but I'm all out of juice. I just want to turn off the lights, crawl under the covers, and never resurface.

"Of course." He stands. "I left a bottle of water and some peppermint tea by your bed. Let me know if you need anything else."

"Thank you."

He approaches me cautiously, hesitating for a beat before he presses a lingering kiss to the top of my wet hair. "Try to get some sleep."

I nod, though I doubt there is much sleep in my future.

"You're scaring me a little." With great tenderness, he angles my face so we're staring into one another's eyes. "Come get me if you need anything during the night." He hugs me softly and gently, like I'm made of glass. "I mean it, Sloane. I don't care if I'm asleep. Wake me."

"Okay."

"Are you sure nothing else happened?" he asks again. I'm not surprised he doesn't believe me.

"I'm sure," I lie.

He seems reluctant to leave, but thankfully, he does, sending one last concerned look my way before he closes the door.

I dress in leggings, fluffy socks, and a long-sleeve top because all my sleepwear is too flimsy, and I'm chilled to the bone. I drink my tea before turning off my bedside lamp and curling into a ball under the covers. Circling my arms around my middle, I tuck the covers around me like a human burrito, but nothing stops the persistent shivering that originates from deep in my fractured soul. I can't form logical thoughts. My mind is a dark, dark place, and my heart is covered in the heaviest invisible scars. I just want it all to stop. The pain, fear, guilt, and worry are tearing me apart, and I fear there will be nothing left of Mom or me at the end.

Cristian

"I need to find him," I say to John Angelo, talking in hushed tones in case Sloane reappears and overhears. "He did something to her. She's traumatized, and it's got to be his fault."

"I don't know what else to tell you, boss. I didn't get a good look at him, and he slipped out while I was talking to Sloane. We have nothing to go on unless she gives you a name."

I swirl the Scotch in my glass and grip the crystal tight. "I know she's not telling me the truth. Something happened tonight."

John Angelo tries to hide it, but he looks at me like I'm losing it. Maybe I am, but it's the only explanation. Unless he threatened her with something. I guess that's a possibility. "I watched them the whole time. He held her hand for a bit and then put his forehead to hers, but he didn't hurt her. It's like she said. He cut her with his words. Emotional pain can be just as damaging as physical pain, boss."

"I can't do nothing." I knock back my drink. "She's hurting, and I feel helpless."

"Like she said, he's out of her life now. Best thing you can do is show up for her. Take care of her and show her you are nothing like that asshole. She's young, and he was obviously toxic for her. A few days with you, and he'll be a distant memory."

"I hope you're right."

***

Sloane looks like she hasn't slept at all when she surfaces early the next morning in Elio's bedroom. Her face is pale, her eyes are bloodshot, and she seems unsteady on her feet. "Go back to bed," I say. "I've got this."

"Are you sick, Sloane?" Elio's face scrunches in concern.

"It's just a stomach bug."

"Okay." He grabs his bag, trying to lift it up by the straps, but it's way too heavy. "I'm going on vacation with Grandma and Grandpa."

"I know. Have the best time. I'll miss you." Sloane kneels and Elio strangle-hugs her.

"Careful, bud."

"Want me to rub your sore tummy?" Elio asks her with wide-eyed innocence.

Tears fill Sloane's eyes as she brushes hair off his brow. "You are the sweetest, kindest little boy."

"It's okay, Sloane." He gently pats her stomach. "Daddy'll get you medicine to make you better. Won't you, Daddy?"

"I will do my best to help Sloane feel better. I promise."

"See." Elio beams at her, planting his hands on his hips. "You'll be all better when I get home."

Sloane climbs to her feet. "Of course, I will. Have an amazing time, my little prince. I can't wait to hear all about it."

Chapter Thirty
Sloane

I'm lying on the couch in my pajamas, huddled under my comforter, with my head on a pillow, attempting to watch the frivolous reality show playing on the TV screen, but my mind can't focus. Too many thoughts are terrorizing my brain. Images of last night have been playing on a loop in my head, and inside I'm screaming and clawing at my body, wishing I could eradicate every horrific touch, every haunting memory.

As if that's not enough to give me nightmares for years, Pablo sent a photo of Mom this morning. She was curled in a ball on a dirty floor, her body so badly beaten I could barely see any pale skin through the multitude of bruising and discoloration. I'm so scared, and I've never felt so alone. The urge to reach out to Rory is hitting me hard again. My bestie would know what to do, but I've already placed enough people in harm's way.

Noise in the hallway cuts through my thoughts, and my heart speeds up as footsteps approach.

"It's just me," Cristian calls out, saving me from a full-blown coronary.

Before, I would've said no one can get to me here. But that pic sent to my cartel cell Saturday night has freaked me out. Pablo's contact is real, and he's *close*. For all I know, he could be one of Cristian's trusted men, meaning I'm not as safe here as I thought I was.

"Hey." Cristian's deep voice softens at the edges when he materializes in front of me. Crouching down, he gently brushes hair out of my eyes. "How are you feeling?"

"I'm okay."

"No, I don't think you are."

Tears prick my eyes, and I silently plead with him to drop this. I have never wanted to tell someone something so badly before, but I can't risk it. Mom already looks like she's on death's door. I don't know if Pablo's contact has access to Cristian's high-tech cameras and audio so everything I do and say is monitored, and I have no choice but to play it safe. That sobering thought dries the tears waiting to fall. "Like I said before, being around you, your family, your friends, reminds me of all I've lost. Don't get me wrong, I love you have that, but it only highlights how alone I am in the world." There is no lie in what I've just said, but it's a deception all the same. However, I need to give him a reason for my current sorry state so he'll let go of last night.

Cristian kneels before me, taking one of my hands and bringing it to his lips. "You have people who care about you, Sloane. You have me, Elio, my parents, my friends. You're not alone. Not anymore."

I can't speak over the massive lump wedged in my throat. I know he means that, and I wish it could be true, but no one will want anything to do with me when they discover the depths of my betrayal.

"Don't cry. Please." Cristian climbs onto the couch and repositions us so my head is resting on his muscular thigh. His fingers weave tenderly through my hair. "Natalia is coming over soon. She's going to check us out. Ensure our injuries aren't serious." His piercing green eyes skim over my face. "You can trust her completely. Doctor-patient confidentiality means she can't discuss anything you say. If you need to unburden anything, unburden it to her."

She's not my official doctor, so I'm not sure how true that is. Either way, I won't be unburdening anything because I can't. "Is that why you came home? I thought you were going straight to the office after dropping Elio off."

"I'm going to work here today in case you need anything. I also have more of Mama's chicken broth if you can stomach it."

"I would love some."

He leans down and kisses my brow. "Stay here and I'll heat some up for you."

Pulling myself upright, I watch Cristian walk out of the room, admiring how good he looks in a charcoal-gray suit. He's worried about me; that much is obvious. How amazing would it be if this was all real? If he was mine? I've only had a tiny taste of what it'd be like, and I'm already falling hard for him and his son. How incredible would it be if his family was mine? If I was truly a part of his circle. Pain presses down on my chest at the thought. It's foolish because it won't ever be my reality, and I feel so disloyal to my mother even thinking it.

Cristian returns a few minutes later, carrying a tray with a bowl, a glass, and a bouquet of colorful flowers. My eyes widen as he sets it down on the coffee table before swiping the flowers and handing them to me. "I thought these might help cheer you up."

I want to cry. No, drop to this man's feet and worship the ground he walks on. "I love them. Thank you," I croak before burying my nose in the pretty petals and inhaling the delicate scent.

"I'll put them in water while you eat."

I hand the flowers back, and he leaves the room again. I gobble down the broth, and it helps to settle my stomach a little. Cristian returns, holding a thick crystal vase with my flowers. He puts them down on the coffee table and stays with me until I've drunk every morsel of broth and drained my glass of water. Then he wraps his arms around me and holds me close. I sink into his comforting warmth, and for a few fleeting moments, everything feels right with the world.

Cristian goes to his home office to work while I doze on the couch until Dr. Natalia Messina arrives. Caleb and Joshua's mother is a stunning woman in her late forties or early fifties. Glossy dark hair tumbles in waves over her shoulders, and her broad smile is warm and friendly. Cristian introduces us before stripping out of his shirt and taking a seat while she removes the bandage wrapped around his upper arm and examines his injury. "You did a good job cleaning and treating the wound, Sloane," she says, smiling over her shoulder at me.

My cheeks heat at being caught ogling Cristian's impressive chest. His toned abs and all the ink covering his skin are so freaking hot. I've never been more tempted to lick any man. Cristian's eyes darken with obvious pleasure as he stares at me. His lips twitch, and I think he likes knowing I was checking him out.

"Glad my first aid training came in handy at long last."

Natalia applies some butterfly bandages to his arm, and then she comes with me to my bedroom to examine my side. Stripping off my pajama top, I cover my hideous fake boobs with my arms as she gently probes the bruising that stretches from my rib cage to my hip bone. "Nothing is broken," she confirms. "Keep applying the aloe vera, and I'll give you a prescription for anti-inflammatories. Take Tylenol to relieve pain, and I'd recommend a warm compress for a few days. It'll help to ease the ache and will support reabsorption of trapped blood. Warm baths would be good too."

"I'll do that. Thank you."

I pull my robe on, intending to shower and dress and maybe go out for a walk. Some fresh air will do me good, and I can visit the pharmacy while I'm out.

"Can we talk?" she asks with a soft smile.

Bile crawls up my throat, but I can't be rude to her. "Okay." I sit on the edge of the bed, and she joins me.

"Cristian is concerned about you. He thinks something might have happened with your ex last night. I understand if you don't want to talk about it, but I'm a good listener, and anything you say to me will be confidential."

It's nice of her to care, but I can't tell her the truth. Still, it's an opportunity I can't pass up. "It was a toxic relationship, and I downplayed it to Cristian before. I was a little freaked out last night because he made some veiled threats, but I'm okay. It's behind me now, and he's out of my life."

Natalia peers deep into my eyes as she takes my hands in hers. "If you're in trouble, Cristian will help."

"I'm not." It's hard to look her in the eye and lie, but I do. "My ex is full of hot air, but his threats are empty. I wouldn't have been so emotional if I wasn't so freaking tired all the time. I'm fine, though, I swear."

"Cristian mentioned you've been having trouble sleeping. I can write you a script for sleeping pills, and I believe my sister-in-law plans to offer you a few acupuncture sessions too."

"You're both very kind, and I appreciate it."

She squeezes my hands. "I lost my mother when I was a teenager. It was one of the worst times of my life. I still remember how excruciating the pain was, so I understand a little of what you might be going through. Grieving is normal, and it's different for everyone. Be kind to yourself and let yourself feel. Healing is different for everyone, but in time, it will get better." Her hand lands on her chest, right over her heart. "I still feel her loss acutely, every single day, but I can talk about her now without bursting into tears or feeling like I'm having a heart attack. Right now, it's all so raw for you, but it will get better."

Tears roll down my face unbidden. Though my mother isn't dead, it already feels like she is. I'm already grieving the life we shared.

Natalia hugs me, rubbing a soothing hand up and down my arm. "You'll be okay, Sloane."

When my tears eventually dry, I feel a little better, but I'm embarrassed as hell. "Sorry." I sniffle, accepting the tissue she offers me.

"You have nothing to be sorry about, honey." Opening my free hand, she presses a business card into my palm. "That's the number of a therapist I know, should you ever decide to talk to anyone. Marjorie is wonderful and a very kind lady."

"Thank you so much. Everyone has just been so nice to me."

"Family means everything in our world," she says, rising to her feet. "You're part of Cristian's family now, which means you're one of us." She hands me a second card. "That's my number. Call me if you need anything."

"Thanks, Natalia."

She pulls me into a quick hug. "You take care of yourself, and let that man outside cherish you. He will treat you like a queen if you let him."

Chapter Thirty-One
Cristian

Lying flat on my back in bed in the dark, I stare at the ceiling and wish Sloane was here with me. The craving to comfort her is at an all-time high. I just want to bundle her in my arms and kiss all her troubles away. She's been quiet all day, appearing even more introspective since Natalia left. After FaceTiming Elio, we had takeout for dinner and watched a movie together. Sloane snuggled against me on the couch, but I was afraid to do more than hold her because she seems so fragile right now. Natalia wouldn't tell me what they discussed—not that I asked—only saying to look out for her.

My head lifts as the door opens and Sloane slips into my room. She nibbles on her lip as she approaches the bed, wearing pink silk pajamas. "Cristian?" she whispers.

"I'm awake." I prop up on my elbows. "What's wrong?"

"Could I sleep in here with you? I don't want to be alone."

I pull back the comforter and turn on my side, stretching out my arm. "Come here."

Sloane crawls into the bed, setting her head on the pillow and pulling the covers over her body.

"Closer," I say, willing my dick to stay down. I'm only wearing boxers, and I don't want to scare her away.

Sloane scoots closer, tentatively resting her head on my bare chest as my arm winds around her back. "Is this okay?" She peers up at me.

"It's perfect." I brush a tender kiss to her lips. "Sleep, baby. I've got you."

I hold her long after she falls asleep, watching her chest rise and fall as she reaches for me in slumber. My arms hold her a little tighter, careful not to squeeze too tight, and my dick approves when she curls into me, sliding one pajama-clad leg over mine.

It's a miracle I manage to fall asleep at all, but the next thing I know, my alarm is going off. Reaching back, I switch it off before Sloane wakes. We're tangled in the sheets and one another, and sometime during the night, my hand slipped under her pajama top, resting on the middle of her back. Her skin is warm and soft under my palm, and I covet every part of her silky-smooth skin. Her cheek rests on my chest, her warm breath fanning across my flesh, heating my blood. One hand is flat on my lower stomach, and her fingers rest dangerously close to the bulge straining the cotton of my boxers. Her leg is straddling both of mine, like she tried to climb me during the night. I have zero complaints, and I wish I could stay here like this with her for all eternity, but duty calls.

With military precision, I slide out from under my Sleeping Beauty, somehow managing not to wake her. Sloane needs her sleep. She mumbles something before curling into a ball and nestling deeper onto the pillow. I could stare at her all day and never grow tired of it, but unfortunately, I don't have that luxury today.

After showering and dressing, I make myself a coffee to go before scribbling a quick note for Sloane. I grab a pink rose from the vase and tiptoe back into my bedroom, setting the note and rose down on the pillow beside her. Snapping a pic of her with my phone—because she looks too beautiful not to—I then press a soft kiss to her hair and leave. It's an effort to drag myself away, and I really wish I could take the day off, but I've got a heavy schedule of meetings, and I won't be home until late.

Making a pitstop at the bodyguards' apartment, I talk with John Angelo and Vincenzo, the second *soldato* I've assigned to watch over Sloane, telling them to stick to her like glue today and to let me know if she needs anything.

The day is a blur of meetings, but I find time to check in with Sloane to ensure she's okay.

I'm just getting ready to wrap things up and head home when I get a call from our president. Punching the button, I accept Massimo's call and slump back in my chair. "Don Greco."

"Cristian. No need to stand on ceremony with me."

"It's called showing respect, Massimo."

"It's not necessary."

"Were you calling to discuss *mafioso* etiquette, or is there another reason?"

Massimo chuckles. "Such a wiseass." He clears his throat. "There's been a development. I sent a team over to the wedding venue today, and we found a cell phone. It's most likely a burner, and it's smashed to fuck and won't turn on, but I've passed it to the IT team to see if they can work their magic. It might not be anything, but I wanted you to know."

"Thanks for the heads-up."

"Gia said she'd liaise with the team and advise you if anything crops up."

"Good. Have we had any hits with facial recognition yet?" I stretch my legs out under the desk.

"Not so far, but you know these things can take time."

"I'm meeting my capos tomorrow night, and I've already preempted things with a few of my men," I explain.

"We'll figure it out. Until we do, increase your personal security."

"Already done." I have four men going everywhere with me now, and I sent a team of eight with my parents and Elio, most from my father's crew, with Clint and Umberto. I'm taking no chances.

"Call if you learn anything."

"You got it," I say before hanging up.

Entering my penthouse, I'm accosted with a host of delicious smells that tickle my nostrils and rumble my stomach. "I'm home," I call out while unbuttoning my coat. Hanging it on the coat stand, I keep hold of my laptop bag as I stride toward the kitchen. I had breakfast and lunch on the go, but it's been hours since I ate, and I'm starving. "Something smells really good," I say when I step inside my large kitchen. Salty, lemony, tomatoey scents linger in the air, and my mouth waters.

Sloane is peeking into the oven, but she straightens up at my voice. "I hope it tastes as good as it smells." She smiles, and there isn't a hint of the previous melancholy on her face. "It's my first time cooking it."

"What's on the menu?" I ask, dumping my laptop bag on top of the island unit.

"Chicken piccata with baked ziti."

My eyebrows climb to my hairline. "That's my favorite dinner."

Her smile widens, and her eyes light up. "I know. I called your mom, and she told me. Your sister helped her use the computer to email me the recipes."

I reel her into my arms. "You didn't have to do that."

"I wanted to." Her arms glide around my neck. "You've done so much for me, and I wanted to thank you. I thought cooking your favorite meal might be a good place to start."

"It's a very sweet gesture. I feel like a gratitude kiss is in order."

Her eyes flare with heat as they drop to my mouth. "I wouldn't say no," she says in a breathless tone.

My lips descend in a searing-hot kiss as I pull her body flush against mine. Tilting her head, I deepen the kiss and slide my tongue between her lips. Sloane kisses me back with the same energy, her tongue dancing seductively against mine, and I can't remember the last time I enjoyed kissing so much. Maybe never. Floral notes from her perfume wrap around me, enclosing us in a heady embrace. We hold one another close, arms firmly bound around each other as we kiss, and I can't get enough of her. She feels so perfect in my arms, and the way her lips mold against mine makes it seem like she was made just for me.

All too soon, she pulls back, breaking our kiss. A pretty flush decorates her flawless skin, and her eyes dance with the same exuberance I feel. It's good to know I'm not in this alone. My heart seems like it might explode out of my chest it's so swollen with everything I'm feeling. "I need to rescue our dinner from the oven before it burns."

"Rain check, beautiful." Tipping her chin up, I press a soft, barely there kiss to her full lips. "Is there time to grab a shower?"

"Make it quick, boss."

I quirk a brow, and she giggles. It's my new favorite sound, and I silently vow to make her laugh and smile more.

"Go before you distract me again." She playfully swats my chest.

I grab my bag and walk off, adjusting my hard-on in my pants with what I'm sure is the biggest, goofiest smile. A guy could easily get used to this.

"Cristian."

I turn around when she calls after me.

"Thank you for yesterday and last night, for the flowers and the note and the rose." Her eyes shine with unshed tears. "It means a lot, and it helps."

"You don't need to thank me." We haven't had a serious discussion about us yet, but I can't not say what I'm thinking. "You're *mine* now, Sloane. Mine to worship and adore, so get used to it because this is only the start."

"This is absolutely delicious," I say after swallowing a few mouthfuls of my dinner. "Every bit as good as Mama's."

She positively beams at my praise. "It doesn't taste too bad."

"It's perfect." I lean in and kiss her quickly. "Thank you for going to all this trouble."

"It wasn't any trouble." Two dots appear on her cheeks. "I had the best sleep in months last night, and I feel like I could climb mountains today."

"Maybe you should sleep in my bed every night." I shovel a piece of the moist breaded chicken into my mouth, and as I chew, I fix her with a salacious look.

"I don't want to take advantage."

A chuckle rumbles from my chest. "That's an impossibility, trust me."

"You make my heart sing, Cristian," she blurts before burying her face in her hands. "Oh my god." Her face is inflamed when she lowers her hands. "I can't believe I said something so cheesy."

"I don't see anything wrong with it if it's how you feel."

"It is."

Cupping her stunning face in my hands, I admit, "You make my heart sing, too, beautiful."

We move as one, and our mouths meet in a ravenous kiss I can't get enough of. Entwining my fingers in her hair, I hold her neck at the nape, taking control and directing our kiss as I fall deeper and deeper. This time, I'm the one to pull back first. Reluctantly, but if I don't stop it now, I won't be able to stop it at all. "Damn, baby. I can't resist you."

"The feeling is mutual." She runs her fingers gingerly through the scruff on my face. "I've been wanting to do that since day one."

"That feels so good." I'm practically purring as I nuzzle my cheek into her palm. "But we should eat before it gets cold."

She sends me a flirty look before picking up her silverware.

I shovel a forkful of ziti into my mouth and moan. "So, so good," I add after swallowing. "I think you may have found your true vocation in life."

"I've never been that interested in cooking," she says, cutting her chicken. "But I love cooking for you and Elio."

We continue chatting in between eating.

"I spoke with him earlier. He's having a blast."

"I talked to him on the phone when I called your mother. He was so excited telling me all about the Discovery Museum."

"I miss him," I admit.

"I miss him too. It's much quieter around here without our little prince." Her chair scrapes as she pushes it back. "I need to show you what I got for him today." She rushes out of the room, returning a few minutes later with a bag. My heart is in my throat when she removes a kid's astronaut costume. "I've been researching fun things we can do, and I thought I could build a space station in the playroom as a surprise for when he returns next week. I found an article online about how to recreate one, and I bought supplies today. Then on the walk back, I saw this in the front of a costume shop, and I had to buy it." She pulls out two adult costumes. "Call me crazy, but I couldn't resist buying us matching ones." She giggles, but her smile slowly fades as she looks at me.

I can't imagine what is showing on my face but fuck it. I'm not holding back anything anymore.

"Unless you think it's a really stupid idea and then—"

"He will fucking love it." I swivel in my chair, and she shrieks when I pull her down onto my lap. Taking the costumes, I set them on the table and reposition her so she's straddling me. "I love how much you love my son." My voice comes out darker, threaded with the potent desire flowing through my veins. "I love how much thought you're putting into activities." My hands move to her ass, and I squeeze her cheeks through her jeans before grinding her down on my erection. "But mostly I love spending time with you, and I'm done holding back, Sloane."

Moving my lips to her jaw, I dust a slew of drugging kisses along her neck. "Tell me you feel this too." I thrust against her as my mouth travels up and down the column of her elegant neck. "Tell me you want me as much as I want you."

"I feel it, Cristian," she pants, gyrating her hips and sliding back and forth against my hard length. "And I want you too."

Fisting her hair, I tug her head back a little as I stare into her face with barely any space between us. "How much do you want me?" I growl, lightly biting her exposed neck.

"Badly, Cristian." She gasps when I tug her sweater down and suction my lips to her chest. "Fuck me, please. Make me yours."

A squeal parts her lips when I stand and fling her over my shoulder. "You're already mine, Sloane," I confirm, swatting her ass as I stride with purpose across the room. "This will just make it official."

Chapter Thirty-Two
Sloane

My heart is careening around my chest like a race car spinning turns on a loop as Cristian storms toward his bedroom with purpose. Butterflies swoop into my stomach when he throws me down on the bed and looms over me with fire burning in his eyes. "If you don't want this, tell me now." His rich, gruff voice twists the knots already coiling low in my belly.

"I want this."

Leaning over me, he cages me between his arms and stares deep into my eyes. "There is no going back after this, Sloane. Once I have you, *you are mine.*" He punctuates the words, making his intent crystal clear.

Reaching up, I palm one side of his face. "I'm already yours, Cristian, and I don't want to go back."

Though you might when you discover the truth.

I punt the devil on my shoulder into oblivion. Nothing is going to ruin this. I'm taking this for myself, damn the consequences. I'll deal with the aftermath another time because I have never wanted any man as much as I want Cristian, and I'm promising myself I'll be fully present in the moment with him. "Have me. Take me. I'm yours." No truer words have ever been spoken.

"Fuck." His lips descend in a claiming kiss that causes fiery tingles to detonate all over my body. Cristian literally sets my entire being on fire. My hips buck, and I whimper into his mouth as he slays me with a slew of hypnotic kisses that melt my body and fry my brain. I'm putty in his arms, and it's exactly where I want to be.

When he pulls back, dark desire radiates from his eyes and his face is alight with wicked intent, and I. Am. Here for all of it. Nerves mix with excitement and longing as his hungry gaze rakes over me. "I want to take my time. To worship every inch of you with every part of me, but I can't wait, Sloane. My need to fuck you is all-consuming." He pulls my slides off my feet and throws them away. "I can't do gentle right now," he adds, popping the button on my jeans.

"I'll take whatever you want to give me and fucking love it." Lifting my hips, I help him roll the jeans down my legs, and they join my slides somewhere on the floor. Cristian divests me of my shirt next, leaving me in only my underwear. I'm wearing a sexy white lacy bra and matching panties, and from the look on his face, he approves.

"Damn. You're even more beautiful than I imagined." His fingers brush softly against my bruised side. "Does it hurt?"

"I'm not made of glass, Cristian. A few bruises are not stopping this."

His lips curve into a sultry grin as he deftly unclips my bra and tosses it aside. His nostrils flare as he stares at me with molten heat, and there's no denying he wants me as much as I want him. I hate he's not seeing my normal breasts, but I promised myself nothing would ruin this moment, and my hatred for my fake chest is top of that list. Cristian hooks his thumbs in my panties and slides them down my legs until I'm lying underneath him completely bare while he's still fully clothed.

My hands travel down my body as I spread my thighs for him. "What are you waiting for? Take me." Parting my folds, I let him drink his fill, almost coming on the spot when he looks at me like he wants to eat me alive. A squeal flees my mouth when he kneels between my legs and immediately buries his face in my cunt. His tongue goes to town, licking a vicious path along my slit. When his tongue shoves inside me, I almost lift off the bed, but he holds me down with one large hand as he works me good. Pressure is rapidly building in my core because it's been so long since anyone has worshipped me like this. "Cristian," I pant, a strangled moan drifting into the air when he sucks on my clit and plunges two fingers inside me.

"Hush now, sweetheart," he rasps in between fucking my pussy with his tongue and his fingers. "Let me take what's mine." Large, warm callused palms stretch my thighs wider, and then he feasts like a man who's been starved for a very long time.

Lying back, I close my eyes and just *feel*. It's sheer heaven, and I give myself fully over to this beautiful, sexy man. All manner of sounds are coming from me as he drives his tongue inside in relentless, firm strokes while his thumb circles my bundle of nerves. My thighs tremble as pleasure keeps mounting in my core, traveling to my stomach and my legs as the sensation builds. My pussy clenches and unclenches as the spiral grows and deepens, climbing to the ultimate peak. I'm whimpering, pleading, and writhing as Cristian uses his hands to hold me in place while he eats with possessive hunger glinting in his eyes.

"Let go for me, beautiful," he commands. "Take everything

I'm giving you." His fingers twist and curl inside me, hitting the perfect spot, and I cry out. Stabbing me with smoldering eyes, he sucks hard on my clit, hurling me through the sky on the crest of the most incredible climax of my life. It zips through me like lightning, illuminating me from the inside out, as wave after wave of delicious bliss remakes me.

Tremors shoot along my thighs, shaking my flesh as my body starts to descend from the high. Cristian stands, watching me with confident satisfaction as he rips his shirt off one-handed. My greedy eyes latch onto his chest, traveling with his fingers down his toned stomach to the button on his pants. Breathing becomes challenging as he slowly lowers the zipper. He smirks as I clench my thighs while waiting for the big reveal. Evidence of my arousal drips down my inner thighs, and my pussy pulses with aftershocks.

When Cristian shoves his pants and boxers down over his muscular thighs in one expert move, I swear I stop breathing for a few beats. Big doesn't even come close. Oh my. Licking my lips, I study his thick, long girth, jutting proudly from his body, rock hard and leaking precum at the tip.

"Keep looking at me like that, baby, and this won't last long." His eyes don't stray from me as he removes the rest of his clothes and shoes and kicks them away.

"I want you," I pant as fresh need courses through my body, pooling in my core.

"You can have me." Setting one knee on the bed, he fists his cock and wantonly strokes it. "Knees to your chest, Sloane."

A little shiver ghosts over me at his instruction. He's bossy, but I like it. I oblige and get into position. My heart is pounding frantically as his gaze dips to where I'm exposed before him. "You're so fucking beautiful." His fingers trail through the slick arousal coating my pussy. "Perfect in every way." Two fingers push into his mouth, and he groans as he tastes me while jerking his dick faster. In a superfast move, he crowds my body, putting his face all up in mine. "I'm going to devour you, Sloane. Remake you. Change you forever." His lips set a punishing pace as he ravishes my mouth in a succession of hungry kisses that stamp his claim all over me. Heat from his body warms my pussy, and I groan into his mouth when the tip of his cock nudges my entrance.

Cristian stops to roll on a condom, and watching him do it is so freaking hot. Adrenaline courses through my veins as excitable butterflies run amok in my chest. The anticipation is almost too much, and I squirm on the bed, breathless and needy and primed for what's coming next.

"Breathe for me, baby. Relax and let me take care of you." Spearing me with a savage look, he brutally thrusts inside in one hard stroke. A scream rips from my mouth unbidden as insane fullness surrounds me. Cristian is everywhere, and all thoughts flee from my head. I'm reduced to my baser desires, arching my back, pressing my chest against his, and digging my nails into his shoulders as he rams inside me like a madman. I'm careful to avoid touching the bandage around his arm as I feel him up in every place I can reach. His skin is firm, ripped, hot, and like silk under my fingertips. Each new thrust goes a little deeper until he's buried so fully inside me I can't feel anything but him and the pleasurable sensations he's coaxing from my body. The way he's making me feel is unlike any intimate experience that's come before.

Cristian kisses me as he destroys me for every other man. Curious hands roam my body, joining his lips as he worships every bit of flesh he can reach while he pounds into me over and over. Grazing his chest with my teeth, I swirl my tongue around his nipples before sucking on them. Cristian groans, throwing his head back and moaning as he ruts into me in deliberate, punchy thrusts while holding the backs of my knees in a firm grip. "Fuck, you feel so good." Enlarged pupils pin me in place as he fucks into me. "I won't ever get enough, Sloane. This is everything."

I lift my hips, and he hits deeper. "Yes, Cristian. Yes. More," I plead, arching my hips more and crying out at how incredible it feels from this angle. Leaning down, he tugs on my hard nipples with his teeth, and I cry out. His mouth suctions over one breast, and he sucks deep on my sensitive flesh. He continues to slam in and out, and I'm cresting a new peak, completely lost in the touch of his hands, the reverence of his mouth, and the utter ruination of my pussy for anyone else.

Flipping me over, he puts me on all fours and thrusts back inside. A loud moan tears from my throat, and black spots flash before my eyes. "Fuck, yeah, baby." His hand moves to my neck, applying soft pressure as he lowers my face down to the pillow and angles it to the side. Cristian pivots his hips as he moves in and out of me, and I can only hold on for the ride. Pure, unadulterated pleasure cascades through my body as he owns me completely, and my mind is blissfully empty.

I'm suddenly pulled upright, and my body is pressed against his as he kneels behind me with his cock buried deep in my pussy and my knees on the bed. Fucking me slower, he turns my head around and claims my lips in a heady kiss that has me seeing stars. Our hungry kisses are synchronized as we fuck in perfect alignment, and I'm feeling so many things. One hand attends to my clit while his other toys with my breasts.

"You undo me, beautiful," he pants against my lips, his eyes boring into mine with clear devotion. "Come for me like this," he adds, rubbing my clit harder as he fucks up into me and gropes a boob. "Cover my cock in your cum. I want to feel you come undone while I'm inside you." Cristian drags my bottom lip between his teeth as he pinches my clit and rams deep inside.

Another climax sweeps over me like a tsunami, detonating sparks of pure pleasure all over. Bucking and writhing on top of him, I am lost to the heavenly bliss he's wrought from my body and completely in awe of his prowess. Cristian is the most incredible lover, and we're only getting started.

He rubs my clit and continues thrusting throughout my orgasm, only pausing when my shuddering body quiets. I slump against him as I luxuriate in the most exquisite release. I'm boneless, floating on air, and putty in his hands. Cristian kisses my neck before turning me over onto my back. Spreading my legs wide, he slides home with clear intent. "Look at me, Sloane," he pants, moving his hips as he picks up speed. "Watch me fall apart for you."

Veins in his neck strain as he ruts into me in quick, hard, deep thrusts that jostle my body on the bed. My hands land on his stomach, stroking and worshipping as I stare at him in awe. He's like an otherworldly god as he hovers over me, all glistening, tan, inked skin, and rippling muscles. Power exudes from his pores as he lays claim to me in the most intimate way. A guttural groan precedes a gruff shout as he lets go, releasing his seed in a series of skillful, deep-seated thrusts.

Cristian collapses on the bed beside me, throwing his arm around my body and curling me against him. Gentle fingers brush sweaty strands of hair out of my eyes. "Are you okay?" he asks in a breathless tone.

A satisfied smile rolls slowly across my mouth, and I slide my leg between his, bringing us closer. My arm curls around his back, stroking the rippling muscles I find there. "I'm more than okay, Cristian." I kiss his swollen lips softly. "You just blew my mind and rocked my world."

Adoration swims in his eyes. "Ditto, beautiful. God, Sloane." He kisses me passionately and hungrily, pulling back before I can prolong it. "When I said it was everything, I meant it." Hauling me against his chest, he hugs me tight. "You're everything to me." He dusts kisses into my hair as he holds me close. The thrumming of his heart is steady under my ear. "I'm never letting you go. You're mine now, and that's the way it will always stay."

Chapter Thirty-Three
Cristian

I don't want to get out of bed. I *never* want to get out of this bed. I want to stay here forever with her. My eyes squeeze close as I cradle a sleeping Sloane against my chest. Her warm body has been curled around mine since we both fell asleep, exhausted, sometime in the early hours of the morning, after multiple rounds of fucking and lovemaking. It was, hands down, the best night of my life, and I want a repeat of it every night from now until my dying breath.

It replays continuously in my mind, and my dick is hard as steel and leaking precum at every delicious memory. Being with Sloane like this is a dream. She's everything I have ever wanted, and I was such a fool to push her away at the start. I should have claimed her the instant I set eyes on her because some innate part of me recognized her immediately. She's the missing piece I've been seeking. No one can convince me otherwise.

With Aliya, I thought I'd found "the one," but I was wrong. So very wrong. I never felt this way with my ex, and I'm so glad she showed her true colors and we broke up, paving the way for me to meet my true soulmate. Opening my eyes, I stare at the woman sleeping soundly in my arms, marveling at the way fate works. I had given up hope, resigned myself to never having love, and when I least expected it, it popped up and slapped me in the face. Some might say I should take it slow, but screw that —I'm all the way in already.

I love her.

I love her with my entire being.

She looks so perfect nestled against me, like she was made to fit there. I'm convinced she was. An almost overwhelming urge to protect her and always keep her close crests over me. I just want to bundle her in my arms and never let go. I don't know if her age is the reason I feel such strong protective instincts or if it's just her because I have never felt like this with any woman who has come before.

They all fade into nonexistence now I have found the other half of my soul. Sloane and I were meant to find one another, and I'm going to do everything in my power to make this work. We have a lot of talking to do, but right now I must get up or I'll be late to the office. I have back-to-back early-morning meetings I can't get out of.

Very carefully, I extract myself from Sloane without waking her. She seems to sleep better in my arms, and I plan to make her a permanent fixture in my bed. Elio goes to sleep before us and wakes after us most days, and he's a sound sleeper, rarely waking in the night, so I don't think it's risky moving Sloane into my bed before we make things official in front of my son.

I leave Sloane another note and a rose, explaining Sierra is dropping by at lunch. Then I press a soft kiss to her brow, snap another sneaky pic, and reluctantly tear myself away.

After eating lunch at my desk, I make a few quick calls, checking in with John Angelo first. Sloane's bodyguard confirms Sierra is at the penthouse and Sloane is safe. I Face-Time Elio, and he talks excitedly about the zoo they visited this morning and their plans for the rest of the day. Papa reassures me everything is fine and security is alert and watchful. Tullia sends me the pics she took on Sunday, and I forward them to Sloane. There are several gorgeous ones of her, and that stunning one of the two of us I make my new screensaver.

Massimo calls in the early evening as I'm packing up my laptop bag, ready to head to the meeting with my capos. "This is becoming a habit, Don Greco."

"Not deliberately." Frustration underscores his tone.

My tone sobers. "What's happened?"

"We got an ID on one of the shooters." A heavy sigh trickles down the line. "He's part of the Accardi crew."

"Fuck." Caleb will not take that lying down. Traitors in their ranks almost brought all of us to our knees a few years ago. "Active or not?"

"Active but new. He was the youngest son of a seasoned capo. I'm meeting with Joshua and Caleb now to discuss it. I'm sure they'll update you."

"What about the other two men?"

"We have nothing. The investigative team will do a full background check on the other guy and see if we can identify these two through mutual contacts. Chances are they were friends or friends of friends."

"Let's hope. Did O'Hara have anything to add?" I inquire, placing two folders in my bag before zipping it.

"He's putting feelers out. Maybe something will turn up."

"I hate we are back to this." I grab my coat and switch off the main light in my office.

"It's the nature of the game. No matter how careful we are, there will always be a few rotten eggs."

"Whoever it is, he's mine." I'm gonna enjoy torturing the fucker who set this all in motion. No one tries to take me and my father out and gets away lightly.

"Of course. Talk later, Cristian. Be safe." Massimo hangs up, and my thoughts are troubled as I drive to the meeting at the warehouse.

"It's only me, Sloane," I call out a few hours later when I enter the penthouse.

"In the kitchen," she shouts back as I hang up my coat and walk to meet her.

Depositing my laptop bag on the island unit, I hand her the flowers and chocolates I picked up on the way home. "For you. I missed you," I say before dropping a kiss on her lips.

"You just bought me flowers," she splutters when we break apart.

"So?" I shrug. "Is there a law that says I can't buy you flowers whenever I want?" I inquire, opening a cabinet door to extract a vase. I set it down, smiling as Sloane practically ingests the flowers.

"You are the most thoughtful man." Putting the flowers and chocolates down, she flings herself at me. "Thank you. I adore you."

My heart soars at her words. "Right back at you, sweetheart."

Sloane's arms wind around my neck as we kiss, and gradually, I feel the stress leaving my body. The meeting with the capos, my *consigliere*, and underboss was tense. The thought we might have a spy or spies doesn't sit well with any of us. My men couldn't think of anyone who stood out as a potential traitor, but they have sworn to question the lower ranks and keep a closer eye on our *soldati*. Dano, my underboss, is going to talk with the men in groups and set up surveillance. I hate we have to do this, that I can't trust everyone, but I won't compromise when it comes to my family's safety.

"By the way, I missed you, too, lover." Her cheeks flush, and her eyes dance with emotion as she smiles shyly at me.

"Any regrets about last night?"

"Nope. Not a single one." She presses a kiss to the underside of my jaw, and I hug her closer, relishing the comforting warmth of her body snuggled against mine.

"You?" she asks, peering up at me.

"Zero regrets." I kiss her gorgeous mouth. "You're stuck with me now, beautiful."

"I don't deserve you," she whispers as pain flits fleetingly across her face.

"Stop that. You are more than worthy." I kiss the tip of her nose before straightening up. My nostrils twitch as I cast a glance around the kitchen. "What culinary delights have you whipped up tonight?"

"I was going to make your mother's lasagna, but Sierra gave me the recipe for Mazzone meatballs earlier and convinced me it was yummy and really easy to make, so that's what's coming up."

I chuckle. "A staple in every *Cosa Nostra* household in New York. I've been telling Natalia for years she should publish a cookbook instead of giving all her recipes away for free." My arms band around Sloane's waist as I gently sway us. "Natalia uses all her mama Rosa's recipes, and they've been handed down for generations."

"I love that, and she should definitely do a cookbook." She

shucks out of my embrace. "I need to finish dinner. Go shower or whatever. It'll be ready in ten minutes."

Dropping my laptop bag in the bedroom, I strip out of my clothes and grab a hot shower before redressing in jeans and a designer hoodie. I slip my feet into slides and return to the kitchen, where Sloane has dinner waiting. The flowers occupy center stage in the middle of the table, and I decide to buy her flowers regularly because she gets so much enjoyment from them. My mission in life is to make her happy today and every day for the rest of her life.

Chapter Thirty-Four
Cristian

"How did your session go with Sierra?" I ask as I twirl spaghetti and a chunk of meatball with my fork.

"It was great. She was great, so nice and full of advice. I've never had acupuncture before. I thought it would hurt, but it was really relaxing. I even fell asleep for a while."

"That's good." Flavors explode on my tongue. "This is too," I add after swallowing, pointing to my bowl.

"I think I might've found a new passion and a new sleep remedy." She sweeps her fingers across my face, smiling expansively. "That's two nights in a row I've had decent sleep with you."

I arch a brow and grin. "I think I fucked you into a coma last night."

"I think you did." Devilish delight glints in her eyes. "You might have to take one for the team every night if it means I sleep soundly after."

"Mission accepted, beautiful." I lean in and kiss her. "I love this."

She tilts her head, urging me to continue with her eyes.

"Coming home to your gorgeous smile, eating your delicious food, you curled around me on the couch and sprawled on your back in my bed as I love you into a deep sleep."

Heart eyes glimmer in her gaze. "Sounds like my ultimate fantasy."

"Mine too." I cup her face and kiss her deeply. "I'm so glad you came into our lives, Sloane. It feels like we've both been waiting for you to show up."

"Cristian." Her tone is all choked up. "You say the sweetest things."

"I've never been one to play games. You will always know where you stand with me, and I will only ever speak the truth."

"Like I said," she whispers. "I don't deserve you."

"Of course, you do." I kiss her quickly before easing back. "Eat." I point toward her half-eaten dinner. "You need to keep your strength up." I flash her a flirty wink, and she giggles before picking up her fork.

"We haven't talked about us properly yet," I say, before taking a drink of my water. "How should we play it? What are your thoughts?"

"I'd love to buy a billboard to broadcast it to the world that you're mine, but it might be a bit excessive."

Chuckling, I lean in to kiss her because it seems I can't stay away from her. "Maybe a little, but I like the idea."

"We're together, right?"

I clasp her pretty face. "There is no question, Sloane. I'm enchanted by you. You're mine. I'm yours. End of."

Tears well in her eyes. "You're like every Prince Charming I've ever conjured in my mind, Cristian, only better."

"Keep talking like that, sweetheart, and I'll have you stretched out over this table in record time."

"You shouldn't tease a girl like that." Her slim hands circle my wrists, and her flirty tone gives way to a more serious one. "I wish everyone could know, but they can't. Elio is the most important person to both of us, and he's just undergone a big transition. This could unsettle him, so we should keep the status quo around him. He can't know we're a couple yet."

"I'm on the same page. We need to ease him into this gently when the time is right."

"Now that's settled, I think we should get to the table-fucking part." Sloane whips off her top, revealing bare tits, and blood hardens my cock in a split second. Quickly tapping into the security system on my phone, I switch off every camera except for the one by the front door.

No one gets to see Sloane like this but me.

After shoving her yoga pants down her slim legs, she tosses them aside and crawls into my lap in only her panties. "I can't stop thinking about last night. I've been horny for you all day," she admits.

"You should have led with that," I quip, standing with her in my arms. Placing her on the empty side of the table, I lay her flat on her back before ripping my hoodie off and flipping the button on my jeans. "I've gotten hard every time I think about how amazing it feels to be inside you." Bending over her, I kiss her deeply and fondle her tits. She flinches a little, and I ease back, frowning. "Did I do something wrong?"

"No. It's not you." She skims her fingers through the stubble on my cheeks, and I lean into her touch like a needy child. "I hate my breasts."

My frown deepens as I study her chest, not seeing what she sees. "What's wrong with them?"

"They're not mine." Chewing on the corner of her lip, she sits up, placing her hands at my waist and eyeballing me. "My natural breasts are small, but they were perfect." She glares at her chest. "These are hideous and all wrong for me. I plan to rectify the situation when I get the chance."

"Baby." My fingers wind through her long, wavy hair. "You're perfect with big tits or small ones. It doesn't matter to me as long as I have something to play with. But if it bothers you, we can book an appointment and get them fixed. I'll pay." I'm guessing the reason she hasn't had the implants removed is because she can't afford it.

"You are too good to be true, Cristian." Sliding her hands into the opening of my jeans, she curls her hand around my erection. "Thank you for offering, and I'll think about it." She kisses me slowly before pulling back. "I'm sorry for ruining the moment." She waggles her brows. "Now, where were we?" Sloane works me in her hand with skill, and I lose myself to her touch, thrusting against her palm as she jerks me off. But I want to come inside her again, so I retreat before I reach the point of no return.

"Stay there while I get a condom. Don't move." Her laughter follows me as I pull my jeans up and sprint out of the room. In my bedroom, I grab a condom and lose all my clothing. She's not laughing when I return fully naked, primed, and ready to rock her world.

After rolling on the condom, I remove her panties and lower myself to the apex of her thighs, enjoying all the glistening pink flesh on display. *Mine.* All mine. Now and always. My tongue darts out, licking a path up and down her slit as my cock jerks in anticipation. "You're drenched," I say, straightening up and adding one finger inside her. "Soaked and ready for me."

"Told you I've been horny all day," she pants as I add another finger and glide them slowly in and out of her warmth.

"What do you need, Sloane?"

Hungry eyes pierce into mine. "You, Cristian. I need your

cock buried so deep the only thing I'm thinking is how incredible you feel inside me."

"Fuck, Sloane. You're perfect." Stretching her arms over her head, I clasp her hands together. "Keep them like that," I instruct, slowly caressing her face, her neck, over her collarbone, and across her tits. I tweak her taut nipples and move lower, palming her flat stomach before I meet the Promised Land. "Your pussy is my nirvana," I proclaim, cupping her most intimate area. My eyes darken with heat. "This is mine. Only mine."

"Only yours," she agrees, whimpering as I push three fingers inside her and work them hard and deep.

"This is yours," I say, removing my fingers and taking my cock in my hand. "Only yours."

Emotion pools in her eyes again. "Take me, Cristian."

"Happily, my love." With one confident stroke, I fill her to the brim, and we both moan as I settle myself fully inside. Our eyes connect as I hold myself still, and my heart swells to bursting point. "You're my everything," I say, pulling out and then driving back into her in deep, slow, rhythmic thrusts while kissing her lips and touching her skin everywhere.

Sloane wraps her legs around my waist, and when she digs her heels into my back, I lose all restraint, fucking her like a crazy man who needs her pussy like he needs air to breathe. The table shakes as I take her ruthlessly, savagely, gripping her hips in my hands to control her body while I plunder her pussy, pounding into her over and over and over. The only sounds in the room are our mutual moans, the slapping of our skin, and the subtle creaking of the table.

"Come with me," I grunt, moving one hand to her clit when I sense she's close, and my balls lift, ready to release their load. We fall apart together, and I'm almost blinded by the most intense, earthshattering orgasm. It crashes into me, nearly dragging me to my knees. After we ride it out, I lift her into my arms and sit in a chair, hugging her to me. Rocking her gently, I dot kisses in her hair and memorize her curves with my free hand.

"Every time just gets better and better," she says in a satiated tone.

"Sex has never been like this for me." I plant a lingering kiss on her cheek.

"Nor me," she quietly replies.

"We belong together." The truth of my words resonates deeply.

We stay like this for a while before I carry her to my bathroom and run her a bath. "Don't fall asleep," I tease when she's submerged in the scented water with her head resting on the back of the tub. I'm so fucking tempted to join her, but I want to call Caleb for an update. Returning to the bathroom a few minutes later, I hand Sloane a glass of champagne before pressing a feather-soft kiss to her lips. "Want to watch a movie before bed?"

"Yes. Something romantic." With the way she's looking at me now, I'd do anything she requests.

"Your wish is my command." I kiss her again, trailing my fingers across her collarbone, silently rejoicing when visible goose bumps sprout across her damp flesh. "Take your time. I'm going to clean up, and I have to make a call."

Sloane grabs the back of my head and kisses me hard and fast. "Don't take too long. I already miss your arms around me."

This girl slays me in all the best ways, and I'm already so in love with her. I'm smiling to myself like a loon as I quickly clean up the kitchen and cover the leftovers with Saran Wrap. Then I make my way to my home office to call Caleb.

"I'm with Joshua and Gia," Caleb confirms. "I'm putting you on speaker."

"Do you know the guy?" I ask, swiveling in my chair so I can look out the window. It's dark out and raining.

"Barely," Caleb confirms. He manages that part of the Accardi *famiglia* while Joshua co-manages the street trade with Fiero, and they jointly run their official company enterprise, which has several different interests. They're both busy, so it's not possible to know every single man who initiates.

"He comes from good stock," Joshua says.

"His father will be shocked and disappointed," Caleb adds.

"We'll dig deeper, and Gia will liaise with the internal team on the investigation," Joshua says.

"I'll update you as and when we discover intel," Gia says.

"I appreciate it."

"There's more bad news, Cristian," Gia says, and I'm instantly on alert.

"Give it to me."

"I hired a local PI in Georgia to track the first woman down, like we agreed, but she's disappeared, Cristian. Her son too. Her family filed missing persons reports three days ago."

"Fuck."

"It could be a coincidence—"

"Except none of us believe in coincidences, especially not with anything related to Cruz," I say, cutting across her.

"I'm worried for the other women," she says.

"We need to get someone on the ground in France and Switzerland ASAP. I don't care what it costs, Gia, find the best and find them now."

"I figured you'd say that, and I'm already on it."

"Thanks." I rub a hand over my chest. "I have a real bad feeling about this."

"Same. I hope we're wrong."

"If we're not, it means we're not the only ones searching, and that's a big problem."

"The Commission will have to step in and help," Joshua says.

"Like they should've done from the start," Caleb supplies with ire in his voice.

"They won't have a choice anymore," I say. "Time could be running out to protect these children and their mothers. These kids are my flesh and blood, and I'm not letting anything happen to them."

Chapter Thirty-Five
Sloane

"What's troubling you?" I ask Cristian an hour into the movie when it's clear he's distracted. He's been staring at the screen as if he's looking through it, his fingers idly playing with my hair as I lean against him.

"What?"

"You totally spaced out." I rub my hand up and down his arm. "Anything I can help with?"

"Sorry." He kisses me softly. "I've got a lot on my mind this week."

I'm about to press, to encourage him to speak to me, when I think better of it. I don't want to know. I don't want Cristian to tell me anything important I would be expected to pass on. So, I shut my mouth and snuggle back into his side.

When the credits roll fifty minutes later, he turns off the TV and takes my hand, leading me out of the living room and into his bedroom. He kisses me softly as he slowly undresses me, and I cling to him with a desperation that is only mounting with each passing day. I'm wholeheartedly embracing the fantasy of us because I'm so in love with him, and I'm not ready to face reality yet.

Placing me on the bed on my back, Cristian covers me with his naked body, propping himself up on his elbows so he doesn't crush me. His lips worship my mouth before moving down my body, gently kissing and caressing every inch of bare skin until I'm a writhing mess of need and longing. When he parts my thighs and blows on my sex, the moan that leaves my mouth is nothing short of sinful. "Cristian, please. I need you inside me now."

"Let me make sure you're ready." He sucks on my inner thighs before swiping his tongue along my slit. "You're always so wet for me," he adds, driving one thick finger inside. My pussy clenches around his digit, coating his skin in a layer of my juices, before he removes it. Cristian kneels between my thighs, positioning his straining length at my entrance as he makes a meal out of sucking his finger while fucking me with his eyes. "I love the way you taste. It's my new favorite thing in the world."

My core pulses painfully, and my hips buck up of their own accord. "Please, Cristian."

"Baby." When he leans forward to kiss my lips, the tip of his dick pushes inside me. "You don't have to beg. You need me, you have me," he confirms, sliding home in one slow, deep drive.

Something settles deep within me as he fills me up. A sense of completion, of being whole. Like a puzzle piece that's always been missing now slots into place. Contentment and belonging bloom in my chest, and I never want to stop feeling like this.

Cristian makes sweet, sweet love to me this time, and this tender exploration is equally as intoxicating as the more frantic wild monkey sex we've been having up to now. Hands touch and mouths meet as we move in perfect harmony in the most intense, intimate way. My legs wrap around his waist, and my hands trail over his shoulders, down his back, and over his sculpted cheeks. His gaze spears me with a host of emotions as we move closer to the finish line, and it matches everything I'm feeling inside. We maintain eye contact as we come together, and I have never felt closer to any man in my life.

I am so, so in love with him, and it terrifies me.

Cristian falls asleep first tonight, and I spend far too long staring at him. He has quickly become my entire world, and I don't want to lose him, but it's inevitable. Closing my eyes, I force these thoughts from my mind because I don't want to think like that. Not after what we've just shared. If we only have this week, I want it to be the best week of my life.

Cristian is in the shower when I wake the following morning, so I tiptoe to my bedroom to retrieve the gift and card. I'm in the middle of wrapping the framed photo when my cartel cell vibrates with an incoming message. Acid crawls up my throat. I'm tempted not to look, but it will only be worse for Mom if I leave it unread. My fingers tremble as I open the message, and tears instantly spring to my eyes. Pablo has been sending a daily photo. A reminder not to forget my mission or the reason I agreed to it. Slapping a hand over my mouth to muffle my strangled cry, I stare in abject horror at the screen. Mom is naked, lying sideways on the bed as multiple men violate her in different ways. Her battered body seems slow to heal, her skin still mottled with bruises and cuts. The glazed look in her eyes is the only comfort I glean from the picture. I'm glad she's drugged and not fully conscious. The pain must be unbearable.

How will my mother ever come back from this?

The trauma of what she's endured will remain with her for the rest of her life.

Knots pinch in my gut as pain pokes holes all over my body. This is too much—for her and for me. Silent tears roll down my face as the cell vibrates with a text.

> I want information by Sunday or your mother dies.

My fingers fumble over the keypad as I type a reply.

> I have a week from this Sunday and I need that extra time.

His response is swift and brutal.

> This Sunday. Time is up.

That bastard never sticks to his word, and I know he does it on purpose to add to the torment. I hate him, and I want him to die a gruesome death. Anger rears up inside me, and I'm imagining killing that prick a hundred different ways as I finish wrapping Cristian's gift. It's not long before my anger gives way to the usual gamut of emotions: fear, guilt, remorse, and an abundance of pain. I'm grateful I wrote the card last night, as there's no way I'd be able to hold a pen and write anything that would make sense right now.

Heading to the bathroom, I splash water on my face and dry it before applying tinted moisturizer to disguise my blotchy skin. After spritzing on some perfume, I grab the gift and card and return to Cristian's bedroom, where I find him in the middle of dressing. He's got pants, socks, and shoes on, but he's bare-chested as he clasps one of his expensive watches on his wrist.

"Good morning, beautiful." His instant smile fades a little as he looks at me. "What's wrong?"

I force myself to be cheery. "Nothing is wrong." I smile widely as I walk toward him and hold out the gift. "Happy Valentine's Day, Cristian."

He looks stunned, glancing between me and the gift with wide eyes. "You didn't have to get me anything."

"Of course, I did. You're my man, and it's customary to exchange gifts on Valentine's Day." Truth be told, I'm usually pretty cynical when it comes to the annual event, but it's probably because I hadn't found a man I wanted to celebrate it with until now. "It's only something small, though I am going to make you breakfast if you're not in a rush."

"I can make time." Threading his fingers in mine, he pulls me over to the edge of the bed. We sit side by side as he rips through the gift wrap to get to his gift. "Sloane." His tone is full of wonder. "This is perfect. So perfect." His fingers trail over the photo Tullia took of us with reverence.

"I had one printed and framed for me too. It's a great pic."

"Thank you." He kisses me deeply. "I love it." He gets up to place the picture on his bedside table before returning to haul me onto his lap. "Happy Valentine's Day, baby." Holding my face in his hands, he dots kisses all over my skin.

Hugging him close, I savor the strength and comfort he brings to everything.

"Stay here." He puts me down carefully on the bed and walks off into his closet, emerging a few minutes later wearing an unbuttoned dark-gray shirt and carrying a blue Tiffany's box and a card. "For you." He places them in my hands before sitting and returning me to his lap with my legs to the side.

My heart is jumping around my chest as I pry the box open, gasping at the beautiful pear-shaped aquamarine and diamond pendant. "The vibrancy reminded me of your eyes," he explains, lifting the platinum chain from the box. "Hold up your hair."

Bunching my hair in my hands, I lift it up and angle my head so Cristian can put the pendant on.

"Beautiful, like its owner," he says when it's nestled on my chest, glinting and glistening under the overhead light.

"This is too much," I croak, staring at it in awe as I let my hair down. I have never owned anything so special, and I'm sure it cost a fortune.

"I want to spoil you." He peers deep into my eyes. "And it doesn't end here." His lips kick up at the corners as his fingers sweep across my cheek. "I'm taking you out to dinner tonight, and I have some items being delivered this afternoon."

"You aren't real, Cristian," I whisper, swiveling on his lap so I'm straddling him. "Things like this don't happen to me."

"They do now." He claims my mouth in a heart-melting kiss I feel all the way to the tips of my toes. "You're precious to me, Sloane." His thumb swipes across my lips. "I want to take away your pain and put a permanent smile on your face."

I'm so close to blurting I'm in love with him, but how can I tell him when my deception lies between us, and he doesn't even know it? "You help more than you know."

"One day, you'll tell me all your secrets." He places my feet on the ground as he stands. "But until then, I can be patient." Lacing his fingers through my hair, he kisses me slowly, and my legs almost go out from under me. "I do believe someone promised me breakfast." His teasing smile coaxes one from me.

"Coming right up, *sir*." I flash him a flirty smile.

He groans, adjusting himself in his pants, but his eyes are still smiling. "I need to rearrange a couple of things, but I'll meet you in the kitchen when I'm done."

"Sounds like a plan. It won't take me too long to cook it." I did all the baking yesterday and hid the evidence so he wouldn't find it and ruin the surprise.

"You're spoiling me, too. I like it." He playfully swats my ass before leaving the bedroom.

I'm moving to follow when my eyes land on his laptop bag on the floor. It's unzipped, and a few folders peek out, silently beckoning me. Sticking my head out the door, I check to ensure Cristian is gone before running to his bag and removing the folders. I don't have time to think, only act, so I pull my cell out from the pocket of my jeans lying on the chair, and snap pics of the folder contents. It looks like schedules, something Pablo requested, but I don't know if these are the right ones. Blood rushes to my head and rings in my ears, and guilt is like a heavy weight pressing down on my chest. Returning the folders to the bag exactly how they were, I bundle up my clothes, then take my cell and head back to my bedroom.

Locking my door, I transfer the photos from one cell to the other, deleting all evidence from the cell phone Cristian gave me. Sweat beads on my brow as I hover over the message button, debating with myself over whether to send them. I have a bit more time, and I don't need to make the decision now, so I toss my cartel cell back in its hiding place in my closet, dress in jeans, slides, and a cute top, and walk to the kitchen to fix breakfast.

"Wow, this looks incredible," Cristian says fifteen minutes later when he joins me.

The table is laden with an array of baked Italian goods, including almond biscotti, which Beatrice told me is his favorite. There's also sliced fresh fruit, plain yogurt, bagels, and creamy scrambled eggs with crispy bacon. "It's an ode to Italy and the US," I joke, nudging him toward a chair. "Sit. I'll get the coffee and orange juice."

"I think I'll have to take some of this to go. I'll never eat everything."

"I'll make you a packed lunch," I holler over my shoulder as I fix his coffee the way he likes it. Cristian showed me how to use the coffee machine because that witch Isa was too much of a snake to do it. Pouring freshly squeezed orange juice into two glasses, I carry them with the coffee on a tray.

We chat casually as we eat, and I push everything else aside, pretending this is real and I'm not the absolute worst person in the world.

Cristian kisses me slowly at the door, and I cling to him, not wanting him to leave. It's easy to forget when his arms are around me, and I need that so badly right now.

"Fuck, it's so hard to leave you," he says when we finally break apart. "I wish I didn't have to go."

"I already miss you," I truthfully say, handing him the small bag. "Don't forget your lunch."

"A guy could get used to this." He squeezes my ass before planting one last kiss on my lips. "Have a great day, beautiful. Be ready at six for our date."

"Don't work too hard," I call after him, watching until he disappears into the elevator.

Closing the door, I flatten my back against it and draw deep breaths as everything I'm trying so hard not to think about resurfaces in my addled mind.

I clean up the kitchen on autopilot, my thoughts hugely conflicted as I walk toward my bedroom like I'm walking the plank to my doom.

I sit on my bed for eternity, holding my cartel cell in my hand, debating with myself, but I can't do it. I can't send those pics. Pablo asked for transport schedules, but I don't know what he plans to do with them. What if he hurts people to get back at Cristian? I already feel sick thinking of those women and kids in the files I sent him when I first got here. It feels like I made the biggest mistake sending those, and if anything has happened to them, I'll never forgive myself. What if this is another mistake? And how can I live with myself if I betray Cristian like this? I love him, and my need to protect him is riding me hard. Continuing to play Pablo's game will hurt others. How can I go on knowing Pablo intends to kill the man I love?

The simple truth is I can't.

I cannot let him hurt Cristian or Elio or anyone else.

Images of Mom's beaten body flood my mind, and an agonized scream tears from deep in my soul. If I don't do this, he'll kill my mother. I'm damned if I do and damned if I don't. Cradling my head in my hands, I rock back and forth as I argue nonstop with myself.

Make it stop.

Somebody, please, make it stop.

Picking up the cell, my finger lingers over the send button for ages until I throw it on the bed and flop down on my back. I can't make myself do it. It feels totally wrong. I want to save my mother, but not at the expense of other people. She wouldn't want that either, but how do I live with myself if I sacrifice her so others live?

Round and round it goes, driving me to the brink of insanity.

Like I told myself earlier, I don't need to make the decision now. I have until Sunday. So, I secure my cartel cell in its hiding place without sending anything to Pablo. This isn't the time to make rushed decisions. Too many lives are at stake. There is time to think my options through. Is there a way to protect everyone and save Mom? I don't know, but I'm going to try.

Chapter Thirty-Six
Cristian

Heels tip-tap across the floor as I shut the door to the penthouse behind me after a long day. I've only hung up my coat when Sloane appears, looking pretty as a picture in the pink and black minidress I chose for our date tonight. Kate helped me pick matching shoes and a clutch purse. "Oh my god, Cristian." Throwing her arms around my neck, she envelops me in a cloud of spicy perfume as she peppers my face with kisses. "You are freaking insane, but I'm crazy about you."

My arms band around her back as she peers up at me, her eyes brimming within smoky lids and thick black lashes. She can't fully hide the pain she's desperately trying to hide, but I don't question her about it. She will talk to me when she's ready. Until then, my job is to distract her and worship the ground she walks on. To make her feel safe, secure, and loved so she knows she isn't alone. "I take it you liked the gifts?" I ask, flattening my palms over her shapely ass.

"You bought me an entire new closet, Cristian. It is far too much, and I don't deserve it."

"I'll be the judge of that." It put a smile on her face, and she looks incredible. Whatever is troubling her, I plan to take her mind off it tonight.

"Before you get changed, I want to show you something." Linking her fingers in mine, she guides me forward. Golden-blonde hair falls in straight sheets down her back, and she looks elegant and sexy in her new outfit. Predictably, my cock jolts to life, hardening the longer I stare at her long slim legs encased in black peep-toe shoes.

"Cristian, did you hear what I said?" Sloane stops at the door to the playroom, planting her hands on her hips. "You haven't heard a word, have you?"

"Guilty." I smirk. "I was too busy imagining a hundred different ways I can ravish you after I peel that sexy dress from your body."

"Fuck." She slumps a little against the doorway, fanning her face with her hand. "You can't say things like that when we have plans."

"I can when I'll be making my fantasy a reality *after* we get home from our date." I reel her into my arms and slam my lips against hers, uncaring she's wearing lip gloss. Sloane doesn't disappoint, sinking against my chest and kissing me back with the same intense need. "You're too sexy for your own good," I say when I break our lip-lock. "You make me want to toss all our plans and spend the night in bed."

"I see nothing wrong with that plan." She arches a brow.

"Tempting as it is, I'm taking you out and showing you off." Standing back, I drag my gaze up and down her body. "You are so beautiful. I'll be the envy of every man in New York tonight."

Her features soften as she closes the gap between us, placing her palms on my chest. "I'm proud to be on your arm, but it's me women will envy. You're the hottest man on the planet, and I'm the luckiest woman alive."

I kiss the tip of her nose. "I made reservations, and we need to leave shortly. Show me now."

"Close your eyes," she instructs, giving me the stink-eye until I do as I'm told. "Keep them closed until I tell you."

"Yes, boss."

She pinches my ass. "Very funny." Her fingers clasp mine as she pulls me through the door. "It's not fully done yet, but open your eyes and tell me what you think."

I blink my eyes open, and my mouth trails the ground. Sloane has transformed the playroom into a space-filled world my son is going to love.

Black coverings scattered with stars and hand-drawn planets drape the four walls. Overhead, the ceiling is hidden behind another black layer with string lights stretching across the length, their twinkling brightness illuminating several hanging planets and floating spaceships. A pile of plastic rocks in one corner hosts the flag of the United States. Beside it is a handmade rocket with a triangular tip sporting a NASA sign. The round table in the middle of the room contains maps, plans, and several different rocks and mock planets. Two separate areas, cordoned off on either side of the room, are constructed of movable screens covered in silver foil. Astronaut School hangs over the entrance to the one on the left. Inside is a desk and chair.

"I've got books, crayons, and tons of activity sheets to go in there," she says. "And I've got some computer games and educational short movies to project in the Space Control section," she adds, pointing at the other area that has warning signs pinned up on the outside.

"This is incredible, Sloane. I can't believe you got all this done today."

"It was a team effort. I roped John Angelo and Vincenzo into helping. I made most of the stuff while they assembled it and put up the lights."

I snort-laugh. "What I wouldn't give to have been a fly on the wall."

She laughs. "They did lots of bitching and whining, but secretly, I think they loved it."

"Elio is going to love it." I hug her to me. "He'll never let you take it down."

"That's A-okay with me."

"Thank you." Love pours from my eyes as I stare at her.

"Don't do that." She shucks out of my hold, stepping back and circling her arms around her waist. "You're paying me to do a job, and I want to do it well."

I don't know what's happened to alter her mood, but it's as if a switch went off in her head. "Did I say something wrong?"

"No, Cristian. Of course not." Her voice cracks.

"I wish you'd tell me."

"I want to," she whispers.

Closing the space, I stand in front of her without touching her. "I'm right here, and you can tell me anything." My pinkie locks around hers. "I know something is wrong. Let me help."

Pain contorts her face, and my concern cranks up a few notches. But I don't push her. Whatever it is, she's got to tell me when she's good and ready. I still think this is connected to that prick of an ex. If he has hurt her, threatened her, I will fucking end him without hesitation.

Tears cloud her eyes before they disappear as if I've imagined them. "I'm fine. It's just grief. It hits at the weirdest moments."

She's lying. A heavy sigh spills from my lips. I can't force her to tell me, but it's disappointing she doesn't feel she can confide in me. I remind myself she's young and her pain is still raw. "Okay." I press a kiss into her hair, inhaling lavender and vanilla from whatever shampoo she uses. "Let me shower and change, and then we'll leave."

The next few days are some of the best of my life. Our Valentine's date night was incredible and a lot of fun, and when we returned home, I spent hours making love to Sloane as I promised. I left the office early on Friday so we could travel to Glencoe for the weekend. Between checking in regularly with Elio and my parents, I teach Sloane the basics of shooting at the private range on the Mazzone estate and demonstrate how to clean, handle, and store the small handgun I bought for her.

"You two look all loved up," Joshua says on Saturday night as we fix drinks for everyone now that Chiara and Niccolo are asleep and in bed. "I'm happy for you."

I haven't felt the need to hide from my best friends this weekend. Which is just as well because I can't keep my hands off Sloane. "I can't remember ever being this happy in any previous relationship."

"It's amazing how when you meet the right person, past loves become completely insignificant and you realize you had it all so wrong," he says, passing the beers to me while he puts three glasses and a bottle of chilled white wine on a tray.

I know exactly what he means. "Truth."

"She looks at you like you hung the stars in the sky," he says as we walk toward the living area where the women and Caleb are gathered.

"It's scary how quickly she's become my everything, but it feels right."

"That's how you know. I hope it all works out," he adds as we join the others.

Sloane nestles against my side with my arm thrown casually over her shoulders as we chat with our friends. I love how easily she has slotted into my life. Gia, Elisa, and Sloane get on famously, and it makes me happy to see her making friends. Hopefully, in time, she will realize she has more than just Elio and me. There have been moments where she's slipped away from me, lost in her troubled mind, but I've been keeping her busy and distracting her.

Gia gets up when her cell rings, leaving for a few minutes to take a call. Concern is transparent upon her face when she returns. "What is it, love?" Joshua asks, instantly pulling her onto his lap. His fingers smooth the creases in her brow.

"I have an update on those European women." Gia stares at me before her eyes flicker to Sloane. "Do you want to talk in private?"

"We can talk here." I didn't say anything to Sloane the other night because she's got enough on her plate, but I won't disrespect her by leaving the room as if I don't trust her enough to hear this.

"It's not good news, I'm afraid." Gia drags her hands through her hair.

I sit up straighter. "Don't say they are missing too."

She nods. "They're all missing, Cristian. Someone is targeting them."

"Who could know?" Caleb frowns, shaking his head as he plays with Elisa's hair. "We only know because Cruz told Valentina. It's not like he was broadcasting his plans."

"I'll need to update Fiero. Valentina will want to check on Leandro." Her son with Cruz was adopted in Sicily. After finding him safe and well cared for, she chose not to come forward and upset his life. But Fiero hired a couple of local guys to watch over the family in secret for this very reason.

Joshua nods, swallowing a mouthful of beer before speaking. "We can't know for sure Cruz wasn't broadcasting his plans. Think about it," he adds after a few beats. "Cruz was a narcissist through and through. Of course, he'd brag about it. He couldn't do it within *Cosa Nostra* for obvious reasons, but he could totally boast about it to outsiders. It's not impossible that somehow someone who shouldn't know knows."

An awful thought pops into my head, and my stomach twists into knots. "What if it's the cartel?"

"What if what's the cartel?" Sloane asks, lifting her head from my shoulder. "What are you talking about?" She nibbles on her lip and knots her hands in her lap.

Putting my beer down, I haul her into my lap and wrap protective arms around her. This is all new to her, and it's no surprise she looks frightened. Talk of mafia and cartel would be scary to anyone not brought up in our world. "We found out after my brother died that he had purposely knocked up different women as part of a plan to infiltrate *La Cosa Nostra* with his offspring."

Her eyes blink successively, and fear gives way to shock. "What the fuck?" A strangled laugh bursts from her chest. "You're kidding, right?"

"I wish I were."

Horror washes over her face. "It's like this documentary I saw on Netflix last year. This sperm donor deliberately impregnated hundreds of women all around the world. All these kids have siblings everywhere, and it could have serious implications."

"It's why we're trying to find these women and children," Gia says.

"How many are there?" Sloane grips a tight fistful of my shirt.

"We don't know," I explain. "Gia has only started investigating. We recently found three women who had children with DNA that matched mine."

"We were planning on talking to them," Gia continues. "But they've all gone missing."

"Oh God." Sloane is shaking and pale. "That is awful. What—" She breaks off, looking sick to her stomach.

Maybe I should've spoken to Gia in private. As shocking as this is, it's not the worst thing we've all dealt with. Perhaps we've become immune to the horrors taking place in the world today because we're confronted by so much of it. To an innocent like Sloane, this would be a massive shock. It's no wonder she looks ready to pass out.

She clears her throat before speaking, looking directly at me. "What do you think has happened to them?"

"We don't know." I hug her tighter, resting my chin on her head when she presses her face into my neck.

"It's nothing good," Gia says, and I shoot her a warning look. "But don't worry, Sloane. We intend to find out, and if anyone has hurt them, trust that we will make them pay."

Chapter Thirty-Seven
Sloane

"This. Is. Awesome!" Elio races around the playroom Sunday evening with his eyes bugging out of his head. Having arrived back at the penthouse a little after four, I had just enough time to finish the space station before Cristian returned with his son. "This is sooooo cool." Elio stops beside the flag with the rocks. "Daddy, take a pic of me and send it to Nonna and Nonno, and Grandma and Grandpa."

Cristian chuckles as he takes out his cell phone.

"Hold that thought!" Pressing my mouth to Cristian's ear, I whisper, "I'll get the astronaut costumes."

I race to my room to grab them. Walking into the closet, I deliberately avoid the hiding space where the cartel cell is. I didn't send the schedules, deleting every pic so the decision is final, and I couldn't change my mind. Not that I would. It's the right call. I cannot place anyone else in danger. My stomach lurches as the thought lands in my mind. Sleep evaded me last night, despite the comfort of Cristian's arms, because I couldn't stop thinking about those missing women and kids.

I did that.

They are missing because of *me*.

I know the cartel has done something to them.

I haven't eaten anything all day because I'm sick to my stomach thinking of what could be happening to them right now. Maybe they're dead and I'm an accomplice to murder. I deserve to be locked up because I've done everything all wrong. I've made the worst decisions, and now other innocent people are paying the price. I've considered using the handgun Cristian gave me to end it now, but that'd be the most supremely selfish act of all. Taking my life without trying to right my mistakes would be cowardly, and I've got to try to fix things.

Cristian needs to hear the truth.

He will hate me, but he's the only one who can possibly help now.

Hindsight is torment of the highest degree. It's easy to look back now and see the situation more clearly. I should've taken a risk and told Cristian from the start because the harsh truth is Mom and I were never getting out of this alive. Pablo played me like a finely tuned instrument, pulling all the right strings to make me do his bidding. If I'd succeeded, he still would've killed us or used us as cartel playthings until we no longer served any purpose. Our lives were fully over the moment we were kidnapped in Cancun. I know that now.

Bending over, I clutch my aching stomach as wracking pains assault me from the inside.

I'll never see my mother again, and she'll have died because of me. Slumping to the floor, I raise my knees to my chest as I stare straight ahead. I can't even cry. Something intrinsic is broken inside me, and I'll never be the same again.

All day, I've tried to find the courage to tell Cristian, but the words wouldn't come out. So, I'm giving myself this last night before I bring everything crashing down around us.

The fantasy ends in the morning.

The stakes are too high, and there can be no more delays.

On autopilot, I climb to my feet, retrieve the costumes, and walk back to the playroom.

"I'm an asonaut!" Elio proclaims, puffing out his chest and glancing at his reflection in one of the silver foiled panels. Thankfully, the costume fits, and he looks so cute. "This is the best day of my life." Turning around, he throws himself at me, hugging my legs. "And you're the best nanny ever." I lift him up, and he circles his legs around my waist and flings his arms around my neck. "I wish you were my mommy," he whispers before burying his face in my neck and squeezing me tight.

I can't stop the tears as they silently glide down my face.

Can a broken heart break all over again? Because that's what it feels like inside my chest right now.

I can't even see Cristian through my blurry vision to note his reaction. When his arms envelop us in a group hug, I cling to my little family, wanting this to be my reality more than anything. How I wish I had a time machine so I could go back and do everything differently.

"Sloane." Elio's cute little voice snaps me out of it.

"Yes, my little prince?"

"Why are you crying?"

I swipe at my eyes as Cristian holds us steady while gently rubbing my shoulders. "Sometimes adults cry when they're happy, and you make me happy, Elio."

"Oh." His brow puckers for a few seconds before smoothing out. "You make me happy too." He plants a light kiss to my lips before shimmying down my body. "Can we play space station now?" He grabs my hand as Cristian presses a kiss to the top of my head.

"Absolutely." I dry my eyes, refusing to ruin this last precious night together. Grabbing the remaining costumes from the bag, I thrust one at Cristian. "Time to suit up, handsome."

***

I stare at Cristian in the dark like I've been doing for the past few hours since he fell asleep after making love to me several times. He's so beautiful. The best of men, and I'm so lucky I got to share these last few weeks with him and his adorable son. My biggest regret is never telling him I love him. I couldn't say it because it wouldn't have been right, and even if I did, he wouldn't believe it once he learns the truth. Cristian will doubt my feelings are real, and that guts me because none of it was fake.

Daylight won't be long now, and the fantasy will be over. I've had a taste of how perfect my life could've been. It was more than I ever dared to dream of. Hoping for forgiveness is futile, as is hoping Cristian can get my mother out alive. I have missed Pablo's deadline, and she could already be dead.

My eyes squeeze shut as pain rattles through me, and I curl into Cristian's warmth in one last act of selfishness. His arms pull me close, even in sleep, and I silently fall apart while he cradles me to his bare chest.

When slivers of light creep through the blinds, I slowly extract myself from Cristian's safe embrace and pull on my robe. Padding in my bare feet to Elio's room, I am careful as I open the door so as not to wake him. This little boy has come to mean the world to me, and I am going to miss him badly. Pain ruptures my heart as I kneel beside his bed, snapping a picture of him so I can remember him like this, looking angelic, happy, and peaceful in sleep.

My heart won't be the only one breaking after today, and it's killing me.

I'm numb as I pack a bag, leaving all the clothes Cristian bought me on the hangers. After storing my bag in the closet, I grab jeans, underwear, and a hoodie and take a quick shower.

Cristian is still asleep when I return to his bedroom. He'll wake soon with his alarm, but I can't wait any longer. He needs to know now. Perched on the side of the bed, I lean over and whisper, "I love you, and I'm so sorry," before kissing him softly on the lips. I will never forget how amazing it feels to be loved by this man, and I'll never stop missing him.

The pressure in my chest is so intense it feels like I might rupture into billions of atoms and disintegrate into nothing. A choked sob rips from my lips before I can trap it. It's a miracle it doesn't wake him, but he's still sound asleep. It takes effort to compose myself, but I swore I wasn't going to cry or beg. I've got to own my mistakes, accept the consequences, and I can't be an emotional mess. There will be time to fall apart later. I lightly shake him. "Cristian, wake up."

He murmurs, reaching for me automatically, and pain pummels me from the inside, but I force myself to be strong. "Cristian," I speak louder. "I need you to wake up. I have to talk to you." Running my fingers through the stubble on his face, I call his name again, and this time, his eyes pop open.

"Sloane," he rasps in a sleep-heavy voice. "You're dressed." Concern is instant as he rubs his eyes and sits up against the headrest. "What's wrong?"

"Everything," I whisper, struggling to keep my emotions at bay when I look at him.

"I've got you, beautiful." He reaches out for me again, but I scramble off the bed, shaking my head, and folding and unfolding my hands.

"I need to tell you things, Cristian. Important things, and I need you to get dressed." I can't do this with him naked in the bed where we've shared so many intimate moments. "I'll make coffee and wait for you in the kitchen."

I don't wait for a reply, turning around and walking off, praying my nerves hold because I'm already a mess. I fix two coffees on autopilot while shivering and shaking. I'm so cold inside, and it feels like I could throw up any second. Nerves jump around my chest, and my stomach twists painfully as I wait for him to appear. Cradling the mug in my frozen hands, I take little sips, praying I keep it down.

Footsteps approach, and my entire body locks up. This is it. The moment when I lose the only man I've ever loved.

"Our talk will have to wait," Cristian says, still buttoning up his shirt as he enters the room. "There's an emergency. I have to go."

"What emergency?"

He leans in, kissing me quickly. "I'll tell you later. Kiss Elio for me."

The front door slams a few seconds later as I stand in shock in the kitchen. My entire body convulses as I slump over the island unit, my heart racing so fast it feels like it might jump out of my chest.

"Sloane."

My head lifts at Elio's sleepy voice. "Good morning, my little prince." My smile is instant despite my heartbreak. It looks like I'm getting one more day with this little guy, and I refuse to waste it being glum.

"Is Daddy gone to work already?"

"He is." I scoop him up and place him on the counter. "How about pancakes for breakfast?"

"But it's not pancake day."

Pancakes are usually only served on Saturdays, but I'm throwing out the rulebook today. "I won't tell if you don't."

"Deal." He holds up his hand for a high five, and I vow to give him the best last day ever.

I'm on edge as I watch Elio run around the playground in Central Park, keeping one eye on him and watching for any sign of Diego or Alvaro with the other. I didn't take my cartel cell—I've been afraid to even look at it today—but that doesn't mean we weren't tailed. Trying to keep Elio in all day didn't work because he's not the kind of kid who can be cooped up inside. He was begging me to come to the park for ages, and I relented after lunch. With four armed bodyguards protecting us, it should be safe. Especially when we're in public, in a crowded part of the park, in the middle of the day. Still, I can't relax, and I won't until we are safely back indoors. I don't know how long it will take the cartel to come for me, but I plan to be far away from Cristian and Elio when they do. My fingers curl around the Glock in my jeans pocket, and it offers a modicum of comfort. "Five more minutes," I call out when Elio looks my way.

"I wish I had a tenth of his energy," John Angelo says, chuckling as Elio whizzes down the slide for the umpteenth time.

"You and me both. He's a live wire."

"He's a great little guy."

"He is the best. It only took about three seconds for him to claim my heart."

"How long was it for the boss?" John Angelo asks with a wink.

"Instant." I don't even hesitate to offer him complete honesty.

"He's crazy about you too. We can all tell."

His words are meant to reassure me, but he might as well have taken a dagger and shoved it straight through my heart. It's said there's a fine line between love and hate. I wonder how long it will take for Cristian's love to blacken and transform into hate?

John Angelo frowns as he looks at me, but he doesn't pursue the conversation, and I'm glad.

I have to practically drag Elio out of the playground a few minutes later. "Please, Sloane. Five more minutes," he begs, and I hate disappointing him, but my nerves can't handle being outside any longer. I want to get him back indoors where he's safe.

"I'll have to start making dinner soon, and I've got a surprise for you."

"What is it?" he asks, clasping my hand and grinning as we exit the park with two bodyguards behind us and two in front.

"Want to learn how to make paper airplanes?"

"You can do that?" His eyes widen.

"Yep."

"Yay. I'm gonna make one for my daddy."

Screeching tires skidding on asphalt claim my immediate attention, and my pulse races in my veins as I whip my head around. My heart thumps wildly against my chest wall as a black van stops at the curb a few feet behind us. The back door slides open, revealing six armed men clad in black, wearing balaclavas. Our four bodyguards pull out their guns as screams echo around us. "Give us the kid, and no one gets hurt," one of the men shouts as they jump out of the van and start walking in our direction.

Reacting on instinct, I scoop Elio into my arms. "Hold on tight, and don't let go."

"Get Elio and Sloane out of here," John Angelo bellows at Umberto and Clint as the kidnappers come closer.

"Go, Sloane." Clint places his arm behind me and prods me forward.

My legs are pounding the sidewalk before I've even processed the motion. Adrenaline is coursing through my veins as I push my limbs faster, desperate to get away from the men who wish to do Elio harm. I will die before I let them take him. More screams pepper the air as gunshots are traded behind us. Elio is crying, clinging to me with his head buried in my neck. His entire body is trembling.

"Shit," Clint says. "Run, Sloane." Warmth fades as he falls back.

"Aim for the front entrance," Umberto says, dropping back into Clint's vacant position. "Get out onto the main road where it's busy. They won't follow."

My feet pound the pavement as I run, hugging Elio tight to me.

"Fuck," Umberto shouts, still running behind me. Alarm bells ring in my ears, but I don't look back. My sole focus is getting Elio out of here to safety.

"Keep going, Sloane," Umberto adds. "Get to the main road and call for help."

I scream as gunshots sound closer, and I feel the loss of Umberto behind me. Bile swims up my throat, but I try to stay calm. Elio is counting on me, and he's not getting hurt on my watch.

"I'm scared," Elio cries.

"I know, sweetie. Keep your head down." Up ahead, throngs of parkgoers are causing a traffic jam at the main arch in their haste to get out of the park. I'm praying some police officers show up soon. Surely, someone has raised the alarm by now? The woman running beside me screams, tumbling to the ground with blood gushing from her leg.

I don't stop to think; I dart left, taking the side path that circles around to the information kiosk.

Elio screams when a shot whizzes over our heads, and warmth trickles down my leg when he wets himself. I'm panicking as I race forward, cradling Cristian's son to my body, begging someone up there to help me.

"You can't run from this, Sloane," a man with a horribly familiar voice says, and my legs almost go out from under me. I look behind me at the man in the mask chasing me. He's eating up the distance between us, but he appears to be the only one. Farther down the road, bullets are crisscrossing through the air, flying over a few prone bodies on the ground.

Making a split-second decision, I dart behind a cluster of trees out of sight and put Elio down. "You need to run to the nice lady in the kiosk." Elio makes a point to say hello to the volunteers who man the information kiosk every time we come here, and they all dote on him. Hailey is on duty today, and she can hide him inside. I point toward the path ahead, in the direction he needs to go. "Run as fast as your legs will carry you, Elio, and don't stop for anyone or anything. Run to Hailey, and tell her to call the police."

"Sloane, I'm scared."

"Be brave like a superhero. I'll be right behind you." I give him a gentle push. "Go now, Elio. Run fast, and don't look back. Keep running. Go. Go."

He takes off crying, pushing his little legs, and I pray he makes it. I flatten my back to the tree and swipe a thick fallen branch from the ground as I wait. A modicum of relief settles when Elio rounds the bend up ahead out of sight.

"I'll kill him, Sloane," Diego taunts, his voice so close it causes goose bumps to sprout on my arms. "I don't care if Pablo wants the kid alive. I'll kill him and make you watch."

No one is hurting Elio. If I only get to do this one thing, I will make sure Elio is safe. A snap to my left spurs me into action, and I swing the branch, putting every ounce of strength I have into the motion.

Diego curses as the branch hits him, and he falters. His gun clatters to the ground. I move to kick it away, but his hand wraps around my ankle, and he tugs. Screams rip from my lungs as I end up in a tangled heap on the ground with the bastard. I kick out and swing my fists as he tries to grab me. We roll around for a few beats, and I lash out, kicking, screaming, and clawing at his mask. Pain skitters across my jaw when his fist connects with my face, momentarily stunning me. Climbing onto my legs, he pins me to the ground, flashing me a savage grin.

"You stupid whore." He grabs my neck and squeezes as I attempt to reach my gun without him noticing. "You had one job, and you couldn't even do that right. It's your fault your mother is a dead bitch and El Rey changed the plan." I try to buck him off, panicking as I struggle for air. My fingers find my jeans pocket and slip inside. "Killing DiPietro is too easy." His fingers loosen a little as he brags about the new plan. "Taking his kid will torture him forever, especially when we groom him to be a cartel killer." My finger curls around the trigger as I slowly slide my gun out. "Killing his whore is an added bonus," he adds, retightening his fingers around my throat.

I shove the gun into his stomach and pull the trigger.

Diego's eyes flare wide, and he releases me when his hands automatically gravitate to the bullet wound leaking blood from his gut. My hands shake as I shoot him in the stomach again and push him off me. "I'm not the one dying today." I shoot him a third time for good measure, watching the blood pooling around him with sick satisfaction.

Then I remember Elio, and I shove my gun in my back pocket and take off running in the direction of the kiosk. Please be safe. Please be safe. Please be safe. I repeat it over and over as I run.

Excruciating pain rips through my calf, and I scream before face-planting the grass, eating a mouthful of dried leaves. Sobbing, I push off the ground, grab my gun, and sit up. Scooting around on my butt, I point my gun straight ahead, ready to fight to the bitter end, but there's no one chasing me. The injury to my leg was Diego's dying shot. He's lying face down, unmoving, his arm outstretched with rigid fingers curled around his gun.

Ignoring the pain, I smother my sobs and stagger to my feet, hobbling toward the kiosk, praying I find Elio there.

Chapter Thirty-Eight
Cristian

"**I** should've listened to you," Isa sobs, clinging to my arm and crying into my shoulder.

My head pounds, and I'm about done with all the drama. I left Sloane for this shit, just as she was about to confide in me. So, my patience is stretched thin. I want to be done with this so I can go home. My thoughts are not charitable, but I don't care. Sloane and Elio come first, and I'm regretting not asking Dano to handle this when Isa called this morning, screaming hysterically, claiming her life was in imminent danger. "Isa, you need to stay in your seat. I'm trying to drive." It takes effort to keep my tone soft and low, and my touch gentle, when I push her back into the passenger seat.

When she called earlier, Isa made it sound like Carmine was about to murder her. Except when I got to the small two-bedroom apartment she shares with her new husband, he was nowhere to be found, and Isa was a sobbing mess, pawing at me and begging me to save her. I'm not completely unsympathetic. That prick forced her home early from their honeymoon and then beat her bloody for no apparent reason. When that abuser shows his ugly face, I'm going to beat the shit out of him before throwing him in a cell at our interrogation center on Staten Island where he can stew for a few days before I decide what to do with him.

Isa called her parents from the private *mafioso* hospital where Natalia tended to her injuries and administered a sexual assault kit. She has contusions everywhere, a split lip, a busted nose, and two cracked ribs.

"Are you sure you want to go back to the apartment?" I ask when we're around the block from the building. "I can take you to your parents' place and arrange for someone to pack your things. You don't have to face him. I can handle it."

"I want to be there when you kill him." Vengeance burns in her eyes.

"I need to discuss the next steps with Dano, but you can watch me beat the bastard if that'll help."

"It will." Removing a tissue from her purse, she blows her nose and straightens up. "Thank you, Cris." She touches my arm as I drive into the underground parking lot. "Thank you so much for coming straight to me. It means a lot."

"You're family, and I hate men who hurt women." Truth is, I did it for Elio mostly. He would want me to help his aunt.

After parking the car, I help her out, glancing at my watch as we walk across the parking lot, hating how I've lost most of the day. I haven't had a chance to check in with Sloane since lunch, and I'm desperate to speak to her.

"He's home." Isa points to where Carmine's black sedan is parked in a space in the corner.

"It's okay to change your mind." I slow my steps and face her. "Wait in the car, if you like."

"I'm not changing my mind. I want to see the look on his face when he realizes how much trouble he's in."

Carmine is a goddamn fool, and he deserves everything coming his way.

"Carmine," Isa roars when we enter the apartment. "Show yourself, you fucking coward!"

Eerie silence greets us, and my instincts kick in. I'm instantly on high alert. "Stay here," I whisper as I take my gun out. Isa nods, covering her mouth with her hand, as I stealthily creep through the main living area to the bedrooms and bathrooms at the back, checking every room with my gun pointed and ready.

"Fuck," I mutter to myself when I enter the main bedroom and discover Carmine slumped over the bed with his throat slit. Blood is fucking everywhere.

A scream almost bursts my eardrums when Isa appears in the doorway. So much for staying in the kitchen.

"Isa, calm down." Tucking my gun away, I walk to her side and circle my arm around her shoulders. She's gone into shock, crying and shaking as I steer her out to the main living area.

Pouring her a stiff whiskey, I force her to sit on the couch with a blanket and the drink. Then I step out onto the small balcony to make a few quick calls to her mother, her father, and Dano, telling the latter to organize a cleanup crew ASAP.

"Cristian, you need to see this," Isa says when I step back into the living room. A folder is open on her lap.

"What is it?"

"I just found it on the coffee table. It wasn't there before, I'm sure of it." Horror floods her eyes as she stares at something. "No!" She hops up, clutching a photo, and dropping her empty glass on the patterned carpet as the blanket pools at her feet and pictures and papers fall out of the folder. "I knew it! I knew she was up to something!"

A sense of dread washes over me as I pluck the photograph from her hand. My brain rebels at first. The woman in the picture looks like Sloane, but also doesn't. It's not simply that her hair is dark, not blonde, or her face looks different, and she's heavier—still slim but not as slender as she is now. No, it's how she looks so much younger and more carefree than the Sloane I know. There's a light in her eyes, a warmth in her smile, an innocence in how she holds herself that I rarely see in the troubled young woman I'm in love with.

But it's still her.

There is no doubt in my mind it's my Sloane.

Pain mushrooms in my chest the longer I stare at it, as all kinds of hideous theories sprout in my mind. "What the fuck is this?" I question out loud, only now noticing Isa scrambling at my feet, gathering the rest of the folder contents.

"It's all about Sloane. Look." Isa thrusts the folder at me, and I flip through more photos and copies of Sloane *Barton's* driver's license, passport, and college exam reports from Yale. Other paperwork is included, and some of the documents are the ones supplied as part of the recruitment process when I hired Sloane *Clark*.

My heart is racing as all manner of thoughts run through my mind. "Why is this here?" I ask in a lethally cold tone.

"I don't know, but Carmine's name is on the envelope." Isa plucks one of the report statements out. "She's a fraud, Cristian. She took this job under false pretenses." She jabs her finger at the report, lifting it to my face. "Fuck! Look. She was studying *drama* at Yale, not early childhood education at NYU. She's been acting. She was totally faking it all along. Oh my god." Isa's gaze widens. "Where is Elio?" she cries. "Please say he's not alone with her!"

I'm reaching for my cell phone just as it vibrates with an incoming call.

"Cristian! The cartel ambushed us!" Umberto pants into the phone. The folder drops from my hand as I rush from the apartment with the phone on speaker. "Where is Elio?" I roar, not waiting for the old elevator, taking the stairs two at a time in my haste to get to my car.

"He's safe, boss. He's safe. Don't panic. Sloane's quick thinking saved him."

Mention of her name ignites rage unlike anything I've felt before. I don't know what the fuck is going on, but it can't be a coincidence that Carmine is murdered, a folder is deliberately planted in his apartment, and the cartel tries to take my son all on the same day. "Keep her away from my son!" I bark. "I think she's involved in this."

"Sir?" Confusion underscores Umberto's tone.

"Keep Sloane away from Elio until I get there, but don't let her leave. I want eyes on her at all times until I arrive."

"Move, motherfuckers!" I yell, slamming my palm on the horn and keeping it there for a few beats. I do not have time to deal with Manhattan's usual bullshit traffic. I'm frantic to get home and lay eyes on my son. I can't relax until I do. Sitting in traffic also allows me too much time to think, and my head is a fucking mess of epic proportions. Everything I have learned is churning through my mind, and I'm struggling to make sense of it. The one thing I know for sure is Sloane has been lying to me. This is what's been troubling her, and I want to know what the fuck is going on. She will tell me the goddamned truth, or I'll fucking torture it out of her.

Pain stabs me in the chest at the thought. Resting my head

on the steering wheel, I fight to contain the tsunami of emotions spinning me upside down. I *love* her. I gave her my whole heart, and I've been imagining our future with her in it, and it was all fucking *lies*. I fucking love her, and she played me so skillfully I didn't see any of this coming.

I don't know the full extent of her involvement, but the betrayal already cuts deep.

I lift my head when my cell rings through my car system. Accepting Gia's call, I try to tame the rage rampaging through me. My buddy's wife doesn't deserve to be on the receiving end of my anger. I'm reserving all that for Sloane. "Gia."

"Cristian. Where is Elio right now?"

A fresh wave of apprehension ghosts over me. "He's safe at the penthouse with Umberto. What don't I know?"

"You might need to sit down for this."

"I am sitting. I'm in the car en route home."

"One of the team got into that smashed cell phone we found at the wedding venue. It's a burner, and everything had been wiped except for two messages." She clears her throat. "This is going to hurt, Cristian. Prepare yourself."

"Spit it out, Gia," I say through gritted teeth, already assuming this is more evidence of Sloane's guilt.

"The cell belongs to Sloane, Cristian." I swallow over the painful lump in my throat as I wait for the rest. "The first message is a picture, taken at the wedding, of you and Sloane dancing, followed by a message that says, verbatim, 'Good girl. Now take him home and fuck him.'"

Pain lays siege to my entire body, and any smidgeon of hope I was clinging to is smashed into sharp pieces that embed in my skin, drawing blood and killing parts of my soul.

"We can't trace the burner to an individual or even get a number," she continues, "but we have verified that the cell was purchased in Mexico."

All the blood drains from my face as my worst fears are realized. "It's the cartel." My voice cracks before I compose myself. "Sloane is working with the cartel. It's the only explanation that makes sense."

Chapter Thirty-Nine
Sloane

"**I** should be with Elio," I protest, trying to get up from the bed, but John Angelo shakes his head. "Please, I need to make sure he's all right. He was so scared yet so brave." My little prince ran to Hailey like I told him, and he was sobbing and shaking when I found him hidden in her kiosk. I hugged him close, dotting kisses into his hair and rubbing his back, his arms, his legs, trying to get warmth into him because the poor child was freezing and clearly traumatized. I whispered reassuring words, trying to comfort him until he was forcibly taken from my arms by Umberto.

"Umberto is with him," John Angelo reminds me for the umpteenth time from his position on the floor. My jeans have been cut to my knee, and I'm lying on my side while he's holding on to my lower leg as he searches for the bullet in my calf. "Hold still."

I purposely let my mind wander to distract me from the pain as he probes my bloody wound. It was chaos at the park, and police were swarming all over the place as we left. I don't know how we got away without giving statements, but it wouldn't surprise me if the cops were on the mafia's payroll. Isn't that usually how things work in gangster movies?

Briefly, I wonder if I'll be arrested for Diego's death. I wouldn't even contest it. Like I said before, I deserve to be locked up. Truth is, it might be the safest option now I know the cartel will be gunning for me. I have to get out of here before they make a follow-up move. I won't risk Elio and Cristian any more than I have.

"I think I see the bullet." John Angelo looks up at me. "You know what to do."

Stuffing the rolled-up cloth in my mouth, I bite down hard on it, using it to muffle my screams of agony as the bodyguard rummages around in my bloody calf.

"Got it." He holds up the tweezers containing a mangled bullet as I slump forward, breathing heavily as my calf throbs.

"She's going to bleed out all over the floor." Vincenzo's suspicious gaze fixes on the hole in my leg that's now gushing blood. His arm is in a sling from a bullet injury he picked up in the park. John Angelo removed that one first.

"Leave it." I shrug. "I'll just clean it and wrap a bandage around it."

"You'll do no such thing." John Angelo stands. "It could get infected." He glances over his shoulder at the other bodyguard. "Grab me some more cloths, a bowl of warm water, and the first aid kit from the kitchen. Check with Umberto while you're out there. See if we've had any update from the hospital."

Pain has a vise grip on my heart, but tears don't come. I don't think I have any more tears left to fall. I'm weirdly numb. It's probably shock, because I'm remarkably calm as I wait for Cristian to return. It's quite possible he might kill me. I can't find it in myself to care. I deserve to die. Elio was almost kidnapped by the cartel today, and it's all my fault. If Clint doesn't pull through his life-saving surgery, his death will be on my conscience too.

Vincenzo looks like he wants to argue, but he leaves my bedroom after a tense face-off between both bodyguards. John Angelo goes into the en suite bathroom, returning with a wet cloth and a towel. I grit my teeth as he mops up the blood, cussing under his breath. "You should be at the hospital." His brow puckers as he stares up at me from his position on the floor. "But I'll have to do. You need stitches, girl. It's going to hurt a lot."

"Good." I nod but offer nothing else.

"What's going on, Sloane?"

I feel dead on the inside as I stare at him. "Do you ever wish you had a time machine so you could go back and do everything differently?"

"Doubt there's a human alive who hasn't thought that at one time or another."

"I wish I could go back to June of last year and not step foot in that bar."

"What bar?" he asks, frowning as Vincenzo slips back into the room carrying the requested items.

Vincenzo stalls, looking between me and his colleague with fresh suspicion. From the moment I was carried into my bedroom, he has stalked my movements with mistrustful eyes, almost like he wishes I'd do something so he has an excuse to shoot me. Perhaps I should give him a reason. He whispers something in John Angelo's ear as he off-loads the supplies. John Angelo nods, proceeding to clean my cut without uttering another word.

I almost pass out as he stitches the wound, and I'm panting and sweating by the time he's done. "Take these." He drops two pain pills into my hand along with a bottle of water, waiting until I swallow them before saying, "The boss will be here in ten minutes. You should freshen up."

The pain is incredible when he helps me to my feet, but I push him away, hobbling toward my closet to grab clean clothes.

"Going somewhere, Sloane?" Vincenzo hisses when he spots my packed bag on the floor of the closet.

"It's not what you think," I mumble, opening the bag and pulling out a pair of sweats, a hoodie, clean underwear, a ball cap, and my purse. I can't leave without my wallet and ID.

"Isn't it?" he snarls, glaring at me like he wants to snap my neck.

I could try telling him, but what's the point? He's not the one who deserves the truth, and I only have enough strength in me to tell it once. Concealing the purse under the clothes, I limp past a scowling Vincenzo and walk into the bathroom, slamming and locking the door behind me before he can come in.

Instant shouting tickles my eardrums as the bodyguards go head-to-head, but I can't make out what they're saying through the door. It's obvious Cristian already suspects me of something. There's no other explanation for the way I've been separated from Elio, had my gun confiscated, and been forcibly confined to my room. Once again, I have fucked up. I should've demanded Cristian stay this morning and listen to me. If we'd talked, everything would have gone down differently today.

There isn't time for a shower, so I wash my face and body with a cloth, careful not to get the bandage wet. After drying myself, I redress in clean clothes and brush my hair back off my face, smoothing it into a high ponytail that fits in the gap at the back of the ball cap. I stuff my wallet and passport in the pocket of my sweats and discard the purse.

"Sloane." Fists pound on the door. "Time to come out. Don DiPietro is here."

Drawing a deep breath, I face myself in the mirror, hating what I see. Whatever happens now, I deserve everything that comes my way. My fate lies in Cristian's hands. If he kills me, then it's meant to be. If he lets me go, I could give myself up to the cartel, let them torture me or kill me as an apt punishment, but I know Mom wouldn't want that. She'd want me to survive, so I'll give it my all if I live through this day. I will fight to survive—even though I have lost the will to live—for my mom. So her sacrifice isn't in vain.

Steeling my nerves, I walk out of the bathroom, dragging my aching leg behind me as the two bodyguards escort me to the kitchen.

Cristian is waiting by the island unit. His lethally cold gaze snags mine, and I stop breathing. Cristian has always had this magnetic presence that has called to me, comforted me, and protected me. But not now. Now, the molecules around him twist into sharpened daggers ready to strike me down upon his command. Tension is rife in the air as he stalks toward me like a hunter primed to make the winning kill.

The pain in my leg is nothing compared to the pain in my heart as his dark glare shreds me on the spot. His fingers grip my chin painfully, and his nostrils flare as eyes that once looked at me with so much love and compassion pierce me with nothing but vicious contempt. "I'm going to ask questions, and you're going to answer truthfully."

I try to nod, but his grip on my chin is too firm and my head barely moves.

"Did the cartel send you here?"

"Yes."

A muscle clenches in his jaw, and his eyes burn with pure malice as his fingers dig into my skin.

"Why?"

"They wanted information on drug distribution routes, and they wanted me to seduce you and then help them to kill you."

I'm not surprised when the muzzle of a gun is pressed into my brow. Cristian forces my back to the refrigerator, curling his finger around the trigger of his gun as he glares at me. For a fleeting second, the darkness fades, and I see the pain he's trying so hard to hide.

"Do it," I whisper. "I deserve it, but you should know I couldn't let them hurt you. I—"

"They tried to take my son!" he roars, pressing the gun harder into my brow.

"That wasn't part of the plan. I would never let them take Elio. I—"

"Shut your lying fucking mouth." His free hand covers my lips. "You faked your way into my home, my *bed*. You were very convincing. I'll give you that."

I try to tell him it wasn't fake, but my words are muffled by his hand.

"Should I write to Yale and tell them you deserve your degree because you delivered the performance of a lifetime, or should I riddle your deceiving body with bullets and toss your carcass into the Hudson?"

"Shoot me," I say with my mouth and my eyes. At least all the pain would end.

"Were you planning to slit my throat while I slept, or did the cartel want the honor of killing me themselves?"

Staring straight at him, I beseech him to see the truth in my eyes. That I love him. That I could never kill him. That I failed and signed my mother's death warrant to protect him and Elio. But even if I could speak, there's no point. He wouldn't hear it, and I don't blame him.

If the tables were turned, I'd kill me too.

His finger curls a little tighter around the trigger as he continues prodding my forehead with the gun while turmoil spreads across his face.

"Do it, boss," Vincenzo says.

"Shut the fuck up," Cristian snaps, never taking his eyes off mine.

A strange sense of peace settles over me, and my body relaxes. If I'm going to die, I'd rather it be at Cristian's hands than the cartel's. At least my love will make it quick.

I try to convey everything I'm feeling with my eyes: It's okay. I understand. I forgive you. I love you. I hope, in time, you won't hate yourself for this. Tell Elio I love him and I'll miss him, but he'll have a guardian angel watching over him from now on—if God doesn't boot me out of heaven.

Sweat beads on his brow as he stares at me. His Adam's apple bobs in his throat. Indecision flickers in his eyes. "Fuckkkkk!" he yells before lowering the gun and his hand from my mouth. He steps back, grabbing fistfuls of his hair as he paces in front of me. "I trusted you," he yells, glaring at me. "I trusted you with my son, with my heart. How could you do this?"

"I'm so sorry. I had—"

"No." His fingers pinch my lips closed. "I'll hear no more lies."

Emotion disappears from his face as icy darkness swallows him whole. He's every bit a dangerous mafia killer when he levels me with a malevolent look that lifts all the fine hairs from my arms. "Get out and stay out. If I see you again, I won't hesitate next time. Show your face in New York, and you're dead, Sloane."

Chapter Forty
Sloane

Vincenzo volunteered to escort me out of the building, but Cristian assigned John Angelo instead, and I was relieved. I think my other bodyguard might have killed me. John Angelo leads me to a rear exit at the back of the ground-floor parking lot, and apprehension washes over me. Darkness encroaches on the sky overhead as we emerge in an alleyway. Dumpsters overflowing with trash line one side of the grim space while empty crates are stacked in a tall pile on the other side.

"Take this." John Angelo stuffs a wad of cash in my hand.

I open my mouth to ask why, but movement in the alley traps the words on my tongue. Lights flash from a dark SUV a few feet in front of us, and the terrified scream that rips from my mouth is instinctive.

"Shush, Sloane." John Angelo clamps a hand over my mouth. "It's okay. It's not the cartel. It's my brother, Rob."

"Your brother?" I choke out as the driver's side door opens and a tall, muscular man with cropped dark hair steps out.

"He'll drive you to the farthest bus station and purchase you a ticket." John Angelo holds my shoulders in a gentle grasp. "Get far away, Sloane, and keep running. If you've crossed the cartel, they won't stop hunting you. Change your appearance. Get a different ID. Only use cash. Rob will take you to an ATM. Take out everything you can, and then rip up your card. Never stay in the same place for too long, and don't trust anyone. Do you hear me?"

I nod over the messy ball of emotion in my throat. "Why are you helping me?"

"Because I see what the boss can't right now."

Tears well in my eyes. Guess I'm not quite as broken as I thought I was. "I couldn't do it! I couldn't do what they asked of me. I love them, John Angelo. It wasn't fake. It's real." The words rush out of my mouth in a desperate plea.

"I know, sweetheart. I know."

When he hugs me, I have to choke back my tears. I'm literally running for my life now, and I can't break down. I need to harden my heart and act smart if I'm to survive. "Protect them, please." I shuck out of his embrace as his brother bends down to retrieve my bag. I have no idea how it even got there, but I'm grateful. "Pablo Fuentes won't stop trying to hurt Cristian and Elio because of Cruz. I couldn't bear it if anything happened to them."

"Worry about yourself, Sloane. Cristian has the resources to protect his family. You're all alone." He presses my Glock into my hand. "I put extra bullets in your bag. All untraceable. Keep this with you at all times, and don't hesitate to use it." A soft kiss lands on my brow. "Good luck, young Sloane. I'm sorry I can't do more."

"You've done enough." He's gone behind his boss's back, and that could get him killed. "I won't ever be able to thank you."

"Thank me by staying alive." He nods at his brother. "Godspeed, Sloane. Be safe."

Chapter Forty-One
Cristian

"Cristian," Gia calls from the hallway, and I slide off the bed, making my way to the door of her guest bedroom. Elio and I moved here six days ago, fleeing the penthouse the day after the attempted kidnapping and shootout. Gia and Joshua welcomed us into their home until our house is ready. I've spoken to the construction crew and told them to move the timeline up. I don't care what it costs. I just need it ready ASAP. I don't want my son in the city. It's too dangerous with the cartel still on the prowl. They won't get to him here, and it's the best way of protecting him.

Our guys took three of them out, and Sloane...Sloane killed one of them. I only discovered that truth after I'd kicked her out of my house and my life. Not that it changes anything significantly. My heart still burns with the pain of her betrayal, but she killed him to protect Elio, proving that her feelings for my son were genuine.

I yank the door open. "What's up?"

"There is something you need to see." She lifts one

shoulder in a gesture for me to follow her. "We're worried about you," she adds as we walk side by side along the hallway.

It's late, and the kids are all asleep, so we talk in hushed whispers.

"Don't be. I'm fine."

"You're not, and no one expects you to be. You don't have to hide from us, Cristian. We're all feeling the pain of her betrayal."

I bark out a bitter laugh as we descend the stairs. "No offense, Gia, but none of you know the sting of betrayal the same way I do."

"That's not what I'm saying." Stopping at the bottom of the stairs, she places her hand on mine. "If we're feeling this so hard, I can only imagine how much pain you are in. Don't feel like you can't let it out, Cristian. It's not good to let it fester inside."

"I don't want to talk about it," I say, like I have every time one of my friends has tried discussing her. I'm still licking my wounds, and I need time. Sloane has crushed me. Far worse than Aliya did. I'll talk to them when I can make sense of the mess in my head.

I stride across the large living area toward the couches where Caleb, Joshua, and Elisa await. They're standing in front of the TV, wearing similar troubled expressions. "What is it?" I ask, pushing my way through my friends so I can see the screen.

"Listen to the report," Joshua says, and we're all quiet as the CNN reporter speaks from outside the US consulate building in Hermosillo, Mexico.

"The US State Department has issued a statement tonight confirming that a dead woman left outside the gates of the embassy here in Sinaloa two weeks ago has been identified as a US citizen. While her name has not yet been released to the press, the authorities are making the necessary arrangements to fly her back to the US in the absence of next of kin. We'll update you as we receive more information on this breaking story."

I turn to face my friends. "You think this is one of the women Cruz impregnated?"

"No." Joshua scrubs a hand along his jaw. "Let's sit."

I sit beside Gia and Joshua on one couch, with Caleb and Elisa occupying the other couch across from us.

"Tell him, Gigi." Elisa's face splays with concern as her gaze darts between Gia and me. Caleb slides his arm around her shoulders, and I hate how the familiar affection serves as a reminder that the last time we were all here, Sloane was snuggled into my side, clinging to me like I was the air she needed to breathe. But it was all a ruse. A trap I fell headfirst into. How easy it was for her to lure me in. I'm so fucking weak and so fucking done with women. Screw love. All it does is make a mockery of me. Rubbing my hands up and down my face, I'm unsure if I can handle whatever news they have to share. I doubt it's anything good.

"I didn't want to say anything until I'd gathered more evidence." Gia gently squeezes my hand. "The folder Dano gave me was very helpful, and I've been compiling more background on Sloane. I think I have a pretty good picture of what went down now."

I could have investigated myself, but I chose not to. I don't give a fuck if Sloane Clark is Sloane Barton. I know enough to hate her without needing to know everything. All week, I've been like a bull charging around the ring, and Sloane is the red flag. I've chosen to focus on my son, prioritizing his needs.

The shootout has traumatized him, compounded by Sloane's absence. He's had nightmares this week, and I've heard him calling out for her on more than one occasion. It breaks my heart, and I hate her even more for dragging my son into her sick agenda.

"Just lay it on me. It can't break me any more."

"I wouldn't be too sure about that." Joshua grimaces a little.

Caleb has been uncharacteristically quiet, and that troubles me.

"I think we were right," Gia says. "Sloane gave the cartel the information on those women and kids. I'm so sorry, Cristian. It's all my fault. I left the envelope on the counter in the kitchen the Sunday we left Sloane here alone. She must have opened it and taken copies of the files. It's the only explanation that makes sense."

"You don't need to apologize. You opened your home to her, and she's the one who betrayed that trust. It's not on you."

"Doesn't make me feel any better. I should never have left the envelope in plain sight."

"Don't do this, love." Joshua wraps his arm around her. "It's not a crime to leave a sealed envelope out in your own home for a trusted friend. A home that is impenetrable because we have the best security system. You couldn't have known."

Gia turns to her husband. "You're missing the point. Our home is only impenetrable if we trust every person we let into it. Sloane was a stranger, and I should've been more careful. I can't help feeling guilty. If the cartel has those women and children, and it's our best guess now, they're as good as dead, and I contributed to their situation."

"A stranger who was vetted *twice*," Joshua reminds his wife. "What happened to those women is not your fault."

"Your actions were natural, and you shouldn't blame yourself, Gigi. But you're getting sidetracked. Cristian needs to hear the rest. Tell him the other things you've discovered," Elisa prompts.

"There's no need to be so enthusiastic, Lise."

My eyebrows lift at Gia's caustic tone, and I sit up straighter. Those two rarely argue, but I'm definitely not imagining the strained tension in the air between them tonight.

"Don't be like that," Elisa quietly says.

"You're too soft, Lise. You're—"

"Darling. This isn't the time." Joshua rubs his wife's arm. "Tell Cristian. He needs to know."

Gia wets her lips and turns to face me. "When Sloane stayed behind that Sunday, she asked to borrow a tablet. I didn't think anything of it until everything went down. She tried to hide her tracks, but it wasn't too hard for me to recover her activity. It confirmed her identity without question." Gia sets a tablet on my lap. "Sloane set up a fake Gmail and Insta account for the sole purpose of looking up this profile."

"Rory Simmons," I say, reading the name on the profile and staring at the woman with long, wavy, blue hair. I don't recognize her at all. "Who is she?"

"Sloane's best friend from Yale. She has campaigned relentlessly since Sloane and her mother disappeared while on vacation in Cancun."

Chills tiptoe up my spine. "Say that again?" I ask, scrolling through post after post appealing to the authorities to do more to find Sloane and Robin Barton.

"Sloane was kidnapped by the cartel, Cristian," Elisa says with tears in her eyes.

"We think they targeted Sloane to use as bait," Caleb says. "Her mother was how they forced her to do their bidding."

"Carmine was their man on the inside," Joshua says.

"I still think Isa was involved," Gia says.

"Darling, she loves Elio," Joshua says. "She would never agree to any plan where the cartel would take him. Same for Rafaelo. Don Greco personally interrogated them both, and there is no evidence confirming they had anything to do with it.

Rafaelo was sickened to discover Carmine was in debt to the cartel and colluding with them to kidnap Elio. As much as I hate that man, he would never hand his grandson over to our enemies. They fought so hard to gain custody of him because they love him. He's their last link to Bettina. None of the Da Rosas would place him in harm's way."

"I don't trust the Da Rosas either, Gigi. I agree with you there, but what Joshua said makes sense. I can't see them hurting Elio. They adore him," Elisa says.

The whole time I'm listening to my friends talk back and forth, I'm reading Rory's posts with a lump in my throat. Sloane was kidnapped nine months ago, yet she only showed up at my door a month ago. What were they doing to her all that time?

Fuck. Putting the tablet down on the coffee table, I prop my elbows on my knees and clutch my head in my hands. I squeeze my eyes shut for a few beats and concentrate on breathing. My mind is a confused mess, and I veer between so many differing emotions all the time. I don't want to feel pain for Sloane after what she's done, but she's a victim too, so how can I not? Round and round it goes until it feels like my sanity is about to snap.

I jerk my head up and ball my hands into fists. It doesn't matter if Sloane was kidnapped. She still had choices, and she chose wrong. I won't ever forgive her for placing Elio in danger, irrespective of what happened to her.

"Cristian." Gia places her hand on my shoulder. "There's one more thing you need to know." Her hand drops off my shoulder as she leans into her husband for support. "I put out alerts for any mention of Sloane or her mother, public or otherwise, and I got a hit. I don't need to wait for the official news report because the body dumped at the embassy in Sinaloa is Robin Barton, Sloane's mother."

Chapter Forty-Two
Cristian

"You're sure it's her mother?" I ask, smoothing a hand across my chest.

"Yes. I've seen the coroner's report. It was gruesome reading." Gia flattens a hand to her stomach. "She had been badly beaten and horrifically assaulted. Not all her injuries were recent. There was evidence of older abuse, older injuries."

"The poor woman." Elisa's eyes flood with tears. "What she must have endured. Sloane too."

"Don't paint her as a victim," Gia snaps. "Sloane had choices. She knew what she was doing."

"How can you be so cruel, Gigi?" Elisa cries. "You were kidnapped and traumatized also!"

"I don't need a reminder, Lise." Gia cracks her fingers. "The difference is I fought back, and I didn't put innocent lives at risk."

"What if they'd taken your mother?" Elisa says, getting to her feet. "What if they were beating and raping Frankie if you didn't do what they asked? What would you've done then?"

Gia stands. "I wouldn't have risked a little boy I professed to love no matter what!"

"She took a bullet for Elio, and Cristian said she didn't know they were going to target him. How can you not see she did what she could to protect them?"

"Gia is right," I say. "Sloane had choices. All she had to do was tell me, and I would've helped her."

"I'm sure she wanted to," Elisa says, reclaiming her seat. "But she was clearly terrified. We could all see she was troubled. We should've tried harder to get to the truth."

Gia barks out a laugh. "Hell no, Lise. We're not putting this on us. We were her friends. She had ample opportunity to confide in us. She knows Cristian is a good guy. There was no reason to hold back from telling him."

"You're forgetting she wasn't brought up in our world. She was a college student on vacation taken by the goddamned Sinaloa cartel. They had her for months! Think about it! What do you think they were doing to her to make her comply?"

"Stop." Bile churns in my gut. "I can't hear this."

"You need to, Cristian," Elisa softly says. "Sloane was obviously traumatized, terrorized, and depressed. We know they were watching her, sending her regular threats to comply. She wasn't sleeping, and she was exhausted. I can't imagine what she must've gone through." Elisa sniffles. "How could anyone make sound decisions with all that stress and pressure?"

"She still had options, Lili. She should've trusted the man she was sleeping with," Caleb says, speaking up for the first time.

"I don't understand any of you." Tears spill down Elisa's cheeks. "Maybe it's because I remember what my mom was like when she was married to that prick who hurt her all the time. I haven't forgotten what she was like back then. She's spoken to me about it. How fear and stress immobilized her. How she did things because he threatened to hurt us. You can't know how Sloane was thinking or feeling. She was thrust into a trap, caught between a cartel and the mafia. Can you at least try to imagine what it must be like for someone sheltered from the evils of this world to be thrown headfirst into a living nightmare? She must've been so scared, and now she's running for her life."

"Stop it," I shout, unable to hear this. "Just stop, Elisa." I get up and pace, thoroughly conflicted.

"Watch your fucking tone, Cristian," Caleb warns.

"How can you defend her, Elisa?" I ask in a calmer tone because my best friend is right. I can't take this out on his wife even if her soft heart is pissing me off right now.

"How can you not?" Her eyes probe mine. "I thought you loved her."

"I did and she fucking betrayed me! She played me, used me, and put my son in danger. The cartel could've taken him, Elisa. Would you defend her if they'd succeeded?"

"There is no way she played any part in that. Sloane loves Elio. She'd never have allowed anything to happen to him. She loves you too."

"It was all an act, Elisa. She was doing what she had to do to save her mother."

"Her mother is dead because she crossed the cartel," Joshua says.

"We can't know that for sure, and it seems like her mother was killed before the attempted kidnapping," Gia says. "Why was Sloane still doing their dirty work?"

"She wasn't." Elisa is holding steadfast to her conviction.

"Sloane doesn't know, honey," Joshua replies. "The news has only broken, and the cartel wouldn't have been truthful. They were using her mother as bait right up until the last moment."

"Sloane chose you and Elio over her own mother, Cristian," Elisa says. "Doesn't that count for anything?"

"All of this is supposition," I say, clinging to the threads of sanity. Truth is, I don't know what to think now, and I'm very confused.

"You could have asked her," Elisa quietly says.

"I was doing everything in my power not to riddle her manipulative ass with bullets!" I shout as my anger returns like a clap of thunder streaking through the skies.

Caleb glares at me, and I draw deep breaths, trying to calm down.

"I'm sorry, Elisa. I know you mean well, but I'm too angry to find forgiveness in my heart. She jeopardized my son's safety. I can't get past that. Everything could've been avoided if she'd talked to me. I think she planned to, that last morning, but it was already too late. I gave Sloane no reason to doubt I would've helped. The truth is, she didn't trust me with anything, and now we're all paying the price for her poor deci-sion-making skills."

"She is as much a victim as her mother, Cristian. She's probably hating herself for the things she's done, and she's all alone now. Don't you care what happens to her? Because the man I thought you were wouldn't have tried to kill the woman he loves without getting all the answers."

Her words try to penetrate the thick wall I've renewed around my heart, but those walls are rock solid now. "I only have enough strength to care for my son. This has devastated Elio, and he's my priority now. He needs my full devotion, and he's getting it."

"Then you never truly loved her." Elisa's eyes pierce mine with a fierceness that speaks to the core of her personality. "If you did, you'd be tearing the world apart to find her before the cartel does. I hope you can live with yourself with her death on your conscience."

Elisa's words are still tormenting me a week later. I'm all cut up. Torn to shreds with all manner of conflicting emotions. Sleep evades me at night, and I'm functioning on fumes. This must be what it was like for Sloane.

Upon reflection, Elisa spoke a lot of truths, but how can I forgive Sloane when the betrayal runs so deep? Maybe she was trying to protect Elio, but she still put him in a position where he was almost kidnapped. Every time I think about it, I break out in a cold sweat. I could have lost my son. The cartel could have their hands on him now. The only thought that terrifies me more is the thought of Sloane out there alone, being hunted by the cartel.

Fuck. I'm a certifiable mess, and I don't trust myself to make the right decision.

All these thoughts churn through my brain on the helicopter ride to the city, making mincemeat of what's left of my heart. Joshua, Gia, and Caleb are pensive too. We've had several conversations, and it's safe to say we're all troubled.

Elisa is taking care of Elio for now, but I'm going to have to start looking for a new nanny soon. Isa is begging me to come back as Elio's nanny. While it might make the most sense for my son, my trust in her is shaken too. I don't think she had anything to do with Sloane or the cartel. She was vehemently opposed to me hiring her, and she did everything she could to drive her away. I also don't believe she'd do anything to hurt Elio. But I'm mistrustful of everyone now, and the truth is, I don't want her living at Glencoe.

A child psychologist friend of Natalia's from the hospital

came to the house a couple of times to talk with Elio. I'm hoping she can help him through this. I'm also trying to find the right words to explain the world we live in. I'd hoped to avoid this conversation for another few years, but Elio needs to know now.

Fuck the cartel for forcing my hand.

Resting my head against the window as we fly over The Big Apple, I acknowledge that a large part of me still pines for Sloane. I would never say it out loud, but I miss her. Precious memories are tainted now, and I can't believe every smile, every laugh, and every moan of pleasure was all fake. Is it possible some of it was real? Or am I still clinging to delusions?

Sloane made me look weak in front of everyone, like Aliya did. I've always prided myself on being smart, level-headed, and dependable, but these past two weeks, I've been an emotional, indecisive mess, and it's time to pull myself together. Leaving Elio today was hard, but we both need to get back into a more familiar routine. Starting today, I'm pulling my head out of my ass, getting down to business, and putting Sloane behind me.

Dano is waiting for me when we land, and this can't be anything good. He'd only be here if there were some kind of emergency. "What is it?" I shout over the noise of the helicopter as it takes off after we've disembarked.

My underboss ushers me inside the building with my friends at my back. "We found something at the penthouse you need to look at."

"We're coming too," Caleb says. His expression tells me not to bother arguing.

When we reach the penthouse, John Angelo is there, wearing a stern look. Wordlessly, he hands me a tablet, and we crowd around it, watching Vincenzo enter Sloane's bedroom door a few hours ago. "I cropped the video," John Angelo explains as it flips forward fifteen minutes to the point where Vincenzo steals out of the room. "By pure chance, I was in the control room earlier when this happened, and I copied the video to my phone. Vincenzo wiped it from the official log, and I didn't say anything to him, so he's none the wiser. I filled Umberto in. He's with Vincenzo in the apartment now. He'll ensure he doesn't leave."

"Well done. That was smart thinking."

"His reaction to Sloane that last day has been preying on my mind, so I've been watching him."

Remorse fills my mouth. I kept Vincenzo back to rip him a new one for interrupting me when I was questioning Sloane that Monday, and I should have suspected something. Since all this went down, I'm definitely off my game, and I can't afford any more fuckups.

"What was he doing in her room?" I ask.

"Come see." Dano leads the way to Sloane's bedroom. I hesitate for a second before stepping inside. The room smells like her perfume, and acid burns my throat when my gaze lands on the slight stain on the hardwood floor where she bled.

"This was lying on the bed." Dano points to a cell phone enclosed in a clear ziplock bag.

"It wasn't there before," John Angelo adds. "I came into her room after she left it, and there was no phone on the bed."

"I dusted it for prints and already sent it to the lab," Dano confirms.

"I'll make a call and get them to prioritize it." Gia leaves the room to talk in the hallway.

"Did you try to switch it on?" Joshua asks.

My number two shakes his head before looking at me. "I didn't want to touch it until I'd talked to you."

"The lab has moved it to the top of the pile," Gia says, coming back into the bedroom. "From the initial inspection, it looks like there are several different prints on it." Donning a pair of plastic gloves, Gia removes the phone from the bag.

Tension is palpable in the air as she switches it on. There is no security, which in itself is strange, and the message inbox loads automatically, displaying three recent unread messages.

"That prick must be working with Carmine and the cartel," Caleb hisses. "He wanted you to find this."

"If he's watched the cameras, he knows I haven't stepped foot in here since the day Sloane left. He assumes I'll think she left this here for me to find." I crack my knuckles, prepping them for the beatdown that's coming when I get my hands on the rat.

"It's all video messages," Gia supplies. "Let's watch from the top down."

I brace myself as she presses play on the first video, but nothing could've prepared any of us for this. No one speaks as we watch Sloane's mother being beaten and viciously assaulted by Pablo Fuentes and multiple other men.

"Maybe you should sit this one out, honey." Joshua implores Gia with his eyes as her finger hovers over the second video.

"I won't shy away from this." She presses the button, and the next video plays.

"Oh fuck." My hand covers my mouth, and pain spears me through the chest as I watch Pablo beat the life out of Sloane's mother, Robin. Horrified expressions are traded around the room as we watch his men defile her body long after the light is gone from her eyes.

I've seen a lot of vile things in my life, but this is pure evil. Thank God, Sloane didn't see this.

Gia thrusts the phone into Caleb's hand when Pablo starts fucking the corpse and dashes into the bathroom. Joshua runs after her. Sounds of throwing up filter into the bedroom as the four of us watch Pablo grinning at the camera like the psycho he is.

"I want his head," Caleb snarls when the video dies.

"He's mine," I grit out. Panic sluices through my veins as thoughts I've worked so hard to ignore rush to the surface of my mind. This prick cannot get his hands on Sloane. Fear for what he'll do to her squashes every other thought in my head.

Caleb hits play on the last video.

"DiPietro." Pablo's guttural tone rings out around the room. "I hope you enjoyed the show. Your son might have slipped through my clutches for now, but we'll get him. We'll get all of them. Cruz will be turning in his grave when he sees what we plan for his offspring. But you." He puts his face all up in the screen. "You'll be living a nightmare when I get my hands on your pretty whore. What you witnessed is nothing compared to the plans I have for my little American Barbie. I'm going to cut her, fuck her, break her. Let my men use her. Bring her to the brink of death over and over, but never let her die. If you're a good boy, I'll send you some videos. Something to jerk off to on cold, lonely nights."

A roar tears from my mouth as everything I've tried to keep contained breaks free, ripping me apart from the inside as I lose it.

Chapter Forty-Three
Cristian

My fist slams into the wall, and I go to town on it. My friends hold Dano back, knowing I need this. I'm yelling and cursing as I pummel the wall, breaking through the drywall, the jagged ends shredding my knuckles, making them bleed, but I barely feel the pain. Inner turmoil charges through my veins as I continuously beat my fists into the wall, berating myself for all my failings. What the fuck have I done?

"Save some of that for the rat." Joshua places his hand on my arm, pulling me back. "You're no use to anyone with a broken hand."

"I swore I'd protect Sloane, and I failed her." Tears stab my eyes as I let my friend pull me back. "What kind of monster convicts the woman he loves without letting her explain?"

"You were under a lot of stress," Caleb says. "It's a natural reaction. We all would've done the same."

"No." I wrench free of my friends, grateful to find Dano and John Angelo gone and the door closed. Gia's pale face looks haunted as she stares silently at me with her back pressed to the door. "No." I shake my head as crippling pain destroys me. "Neither of you would've tossed your loves out on the street like trash." I yank on my hair. "I held a fucking gun to her head, for fuck's sake! I almost killed her!" I slump against the nearest wall, struggling to draw enough air into my lungs. "I sent her away when she was hurt. She took a bullet defending my son, and I refused to see what was right in front of me." Scrubbing my eyes, I let loose another roar, hating myself for instantly thinking the worst of her. What have I done? What have I done? I didn't even give her a chance to fully explain, deciding I'd heard enough. I hang my head. "I'm so ashamed of my actions. I was so cruel. So cold."

"What happened with Aliya clouded your judgment," Joshua says. "I know my past clouded mine when I was with Gia at first."

"It's no excuse. Elisa is right." I eyeball Caleb. "Everything she said is right. I was too hurt, too angry, to see it last week, but she's right. Sloane is a victim, and I know—" I slap a hand to my chest, "—deep down, I know she would never have hurt Elio or me." A bitter laugh tumbles from my chest. "She was a terrible actress. Her blatant attempt to seduce me was so transparent. God, hindsight is a bitch." Air blows out of my mouth as I drag my fingers through my hair. "She stopped faking it." It seems so obvious now, and I'm a fool. "I pushed her away because I thought it wasn't real, but I was wrong, I was so fucking wrong." It all comes back to me in full technicolor, and I see it for what it is. I wasn't in it alone. She loves me as I love her.

Pressure builds behind my heavy eyes as my gaze bounces between my two best friends. "I never even told her I loved her. Now she thinks I hate her. She has nothing and no one, and the cartel is after her. Oh God." I straighten up and pull myself together. I've got to become the man she needs me to be and pray it's not too late. "I've got to find her before they do. I can't let them hurt her any more than they already have."

"Tell me the plan starts with ripping that backstabbing motherfucker to pieces?" Caleb asks.

Clamping a hand on his shoulder, I flash him a savage grin. "Great minds think alike, my friend. Let's grab the rat and introduce him to our fists."

Vincenzo spills his guts with little motivation. Turns out, his stepmother is a distant cousin of Carmine's, and Carmine used blackmail to force Vincenzo to spy for him. It seems Carmine threatened the first woman I offered the nanny job to, and she lied when she told me she'd accepted another offer. Until Carmine's death, Vincenzo had no direct contact with the cartel. His phone records unearthed messages sent after the shooting, demanding he silence Sloane or hand her over to them. His family was threatened when he failed to comply, so he readily accepted their new offer to work for them, and he planted the cell on their instructions.

Caleb and I took turns torturing him for hours, but we chose not to kill him. We can use him to beat the cartel at their own game. Killing Fuentes will be at the top of my priority list after I find Sloane. Rescuing Cruz's offspring and their mothers is also on the agenda, as well as finding any other kids before the cartel does. The latest developments mean The Commission has changed its tune and given us approval to accelerate the investigation as a matter of urgency.

Gia is now heading up an official task force to find these children and their mothers and take them into protective custody. It's most likely going to be an ongoing investigation, spanning years. It's not an easy task, but at least the appropriate focus is being applied now.

———

The following morning, I meet with John Angelo at my office in the DiPietro Freight Management & Logistics building to find out if he knows anything about Sloane's plans. He was the last person to interact with her, and I'm hoping he might have some clue as to where she went.

Guilt threatens to smother me when he eyeballs me with zero regret and tells me what he did. He helped her when I pushed her away like she meant nothing to me. Right now, I don't feel worthy of the legacy passed down to me. I have never been more disgusted with myself.

"I understand if you need to punish me, boss, but I stand by what I did."

"There will be no punishment." I level John Angelo with a solemn expression. "I'm glad she had help. I'm ashamed of how quickly I judged her. You knew she was true, didn't you?"

"When you've been around as long as I have, you learn to recognize the good'uns from the bad'uns. Sloane loves with her whole heart, and I don't doubt what she felt for you and Master Elio was true. That girl couldn't hurt a fly. Anything that happened wasn't intentional. I'll go to my grave believing that."

"I made the wrong call, and I need to fix it fast because she's in danger. If anything happens to her, I'll never forgive myself. Call your brother and get me the details. I need to retrace her steps and see if I can find her."

After he leaves, I call Dano and request he promote the man. He has more than earned it. Then I call the bank and transfer a large deposit into Sloane's bank account—the one the cartel doesn't have access to. Rage resurfaced when I learned the second bank account we thought was being used to pay off debtors was actually being funneled to an offshore account owned by the cartel. The fuckers were making sure she was desperate with little money and totally beholden to them.

I've asked Don Mazzone to run a covert investigation into how the cartel was able to hide all of this so effectively. Our teams should have uncovered the truth. Gia personally oversaw the second background check, and she's thorough. Someone with specialist knowledge helped the cartel to cover their tracks, and I want to know who they've got in their pocket.

I'm about to call Gia to tell her to set up the trace on the money when my secretary buzzes to say she's here to see me. Getting up from behind my desk, I stride to the door, reaching it as Gia does. "What's happened?" I know she wouldn't show up here unless it were important.

"I didn't want to risk emailing you," she says as I usher her inside and over to the couch in the corner. "In case we have a mole on the tech team."

"You think it was someone inside the *Cosa Nostra* IT team who helped the cartel?" I glance over my shoulder as I make coffee.

"I hope not, but it's a possibility." She removes a tablet from her briefcase and swipes her finger across the screen. "Until Don Mazzone has concluded the investigation, I'm taking no chances, and you shouldn't either. We'll have to do this the old-school way. Leave no trace if you can."

"Understood." I hand her a mug and sit beside her. Gia angles the screen so I can see. "What am I looking at?" I ask, cradling my mug in my hands.

"This came into my personal email ten days ago. I rarely check that account anymore. It landed in my junk folder, and I almost deleted it because I didn't recognize the email address, but something made me open it. It's from Sloane."

Putting my coffee down, I take the tablet and read the email.

> *This is Sloane. I know you probably hate me, Gia, with due cause, but please don't delete this message without reading it. It's important. You need to tell Cristian he has a mole. I don't know who it is, only that this person is working with the cartel.*
>
> *The other thing you should know is it's my fault those women and children were taken. I'm sure the cartel has them. I hate that I've placed them in danger, and I hope you can find them. I didn't understand what I was sending when I sent those files. It's not an acceptable excuse, so I don't even know why I'm saying it, only that I didn't do it deliberately.*
>
> *I gave them nothing else, so put Cristian's mind at ease. They don't have the location to your house or Cristian's parents' house, and I never sent them any schedules. I didn't know they were planning to kidnap Elio, but I was nervous going out that afternoon, and I should've listened to my instincts. I'll never forgive myself for putting him in so much danger. I love that little boy like he's my own, and I would gladly have given my life for his. I hope you believe it because it's the truth.*
>
> *There is lots more I could say, but you probably don't want to hear it. Like Cristian doesn't want to either. Please warn him. Contrary to what he thinks, I have never wanted to hurt anyone, especially him or Elio. I love them both so much, and I hate that I*

*caused them pain. I'm sorry for deceiving everyone, and
I truly wish things could be different.*
Keep them safe, Gia. Thank you.

I didn't think I could hurt any more, but a fresh wave of pain pokes new holes in my heart. Sloane didn't even attempt to defend herself, offering no explanation for why she did the things she did. "She's running from the cartel, and yet she's trying to protect us. I really fucked up this time."

"I feel bad for being so judgmental, so I can only imagine how you must feel."

"I jumped to all the wrong conclusions." I drink a mouthful of hot coffee. "I love her, and I've let her down in the worst way. My love was supposed to be unconditional, and I forgot that when it mattered most."

Shards of pain scrape my throat raw. Why was my first instinct to presume she was guilty instead of asking my love to tell me the full truth and listening without interruption? Instead, I cut her off before she could fully explain, deciding I couldn't trust anything out of her mouth.

"Elio would be so ashamed if he was old enough to comprehend things," I admit. "Sloane needed me to see what I should've seen all along. Everything was a cry for help, and I should've pushed her to tell me what was wrong instead of backing off and letting her tell me in her own time. But there's no point looking at all the what-ifs and should-haves. This is the reality, and I'm going to find her, bring her home, and pray we can forgive one another and start over. The cartel is not getting their fucking hands on her again. I'll blow their entire operation sky-high if they touch her, so please, Gia, tell me you got some lead from this email."

She bobs her head. "The email account is deactivated, but I

was able to trace the IP address to a small café in Alton, Illinois. I hacked into the traffic cam across the street." Her fingers fly over the keyboard. "Watch."

My heart is in my throat as I watch a woman exit the café, tipping her head forward and pulling a ball cap down firmly to cover her face. She's wearing nondescript jeans and an over-sized gray hoodie, and she's walking with a noticeable limp. A muscle pops in my jaw as I watch her dragging her injured leg and trying to disguise the obvious pain.

"Wait for it," Gia says, and I hold my breath.

At the crosswalk, Sloane stops on the sidewalk and purposely lifts her chin. Strands of short dark hair peek out from under her cap as she tips her face directly in front of the camera. Blue eyes shine with regret as she stares into the camera for a few seconds. Gia pauses it there, and I drink in every beautiful feature.

A pang of longing rushes through me, and I wish I could project into the screen, scoop her up, and run away with her. But this was days ago, and I'm doubting she's still there. John Angelo told her to keep running, and I know she'll have listened to him.

Still, this was a bold, reckless move. One she risked to warn me. If I have any lingering doubts, they're fully eviscerated now. Sloane loves me and Elio. She sacrificed her mother to protect us, and I'm the prick who repaid her with cruelty instead of kindness and love. As long as I live, I will never forgive myself for the mistakes I've made, and I won't stop looking for her. Rubbing a hand across the pain spreading in my chest, I silently offer up my soul to whoever is listening, begging them to keep her safe until I can find her.

Chapter Forty-Four
Cristian

Five Years Later

"Please tell me you're not seriously considering it." Caleb drills me with a pointed look as he lifts a beer bottle to his lips.

Giggles and high-pitched screams pierce the air as the kids run around the garden, playing and chasing one another. It's the weekend, and Elisa decided to throw an impromptu alfresco lunch when the early June day dawned bright and sunny. Us five adults are congregated around the patio area, enjoying a cold beer and a chilled glass of wine under the shade while we keep an eye on our rambunctious offspring.

Gia and Elisa cradle their sleeping babies in their arms as we chat, gently rocking them or dotting kisses on their cute faces. I'm happy my friends have expanded their families over the years, but it only serves to remind me of everything I've lost through my own stupidity and weakness.

"I'm thirty-seven, and Elio will be ten in December. He

needs a mother, and I promised Pops on his deathbed I would give up chasing a ghost and take a wife."

"We hate seeing you like this, and we want you to move on. It's what Sloane would want too," Joshua says. "But a marriage contract isn't your only option."

"It *is* the only option." I knock back a mouthful of beer. "You, of all people, should understand."

Elisa clutches my hand. "It's so hard to see you hurting. Has it gotten any easier?"

I shake my head, letting the pain loose to run free inside me. "Every month that passes without any sighting or news of her kills me a little more inside." I scrub my hands down my face. "Sometimes, I wonder if I'm legit insane because I only knew her for three weeks, but I still miss her every second of every day, and there is no one else for me. Sloane is the love of my life. There won't be another."

"Time is irrelevant when you find the other half of your soul," Gia says, smiling lovingly at her husband from across the table. "My parents were engaged less than a month after meeting, married a few months later, and they are still blissfully happy all these years later. You're not crazy, Cristian."

"Some would say I am because I found the one, and I didn't protect her the way I promised. I pushed her away and told her she was dead if she ever came back to New York. She's gone, lost to me forever, because of my actions." The usual pressure sits on my chest, but I'm used to living with the pain. It's been constant throughout the years, when each new lead winds up going nowhere.

"You weren't the only one who handled it badly." Gia reminds me, snuggling her babe against her chest. "I'm ashamed of how I reacted. Elisa was the only one who saw it clearly without any doubts."

"There's no point looking back, and no one could've done

more to find her than you," Joshua says, directing his comment in my direction. "You've been relentless, and you've tried everything."

"Yet it wasn't enough." I slap a hand over my heart. "She's in here. Sloane will always own every piece of me. Which is why a marriage contract is the only way forward. I don't want any other woman." Even the thought of it turns my stomach. "I only want her, but I promised myself I'd draw a line when five years were up. There hasn't been any sign of her in over a year, and I can't keep chasing a ghost." I can't verbalize the crippling thoughts that sometimes creep into my brain, telling me I was too late getting to Fuentes and he got to her first. I don't want to believe the shit he said before I ended the psycho bastard were truths, and not purely the taunts of a man who knew his time was up.

"Maybe Sloane realized she could finally stop running," Caleb says.

"She is most likely settled somewhere under a new identity living a new life," Gia says, but I can tell, like me, she can't discount the possibility my love is buried in a nameless grave somewhere.

"I want to believe it so badly," I say over the lump in my throat. "I want to think of her happy out there somewhere living her best life, even if it's not with me. I'd have closure if I got confirmation, but not knowing either way is slowly eating me alive."

"Perhaps she's out there thinking the same thing of you, Cristian." Elisa's features soften with compassion. "She wouldn't want you to live your life without love. You might just need more time before you're ready to date again."

"I know what I want, Elisa, and it will always be her. If my punishment is to live without love, so be it. It's what I deserve for betraying the woman I love, for not being there for her when she needed me most. But I won't let Elio suffer. He doesn't deserve to be punished for my failings."

Genuine affection mushrooms in my chest as I smile at my best friend's wife. "I'm so grateful to you, Elisa. Natalia, Serena, and Sierra too. You've all showered him with love, but he needs a permanent guiding light in his life."

Elisa babysat the kids for part of the day every day for years, while her mother, mother-in-law, and Gia's mother took the kids the rest of the time so she could work for her graphic design clients. It has made life easier for all of us, and I'm so grateful for the support.

Elio was troubled for months after Sloane left, and I didn't want to hire a stranger to care for him, so Elisa's selfless offer was a lifesaver. Now he's older, he doesn't need a full-time nanny, but he does need a mother.

"And you think Isotta Da Rosa fits the bill?" Gia's tone is laced with disbelief. I've been waiting for her to cut in. She hates Elio's aunt even more than she used to.

"She's been consistent in his life, and he adores her." They have weekly sleepovers, and she shows up for every school play, every basketball game, every event, and activity. No one can convince me she doesn't love Elio as much as she'd love her own child.

"That won't change if you marry her," Caleb says. "Let her have more access to him if that's what Elio wants, but don't saddle yourself with a woman you'll never love."

I knew my friends would react like this when I told them of Rafaelo's proposal. Elio's maternal grandfather is retiring this year, and he's keen to tie up loose ends. His spinster daughter being top of the list. He has approached me about it a few times in the past couple of years, and I get it. There is already a blood bond between our families and a shared commitment to Elio's well-being. Isa never remarried after the shame of Carmine's treachery, and I haven't recovered after losing Sloane. We both crave a family but haven't found love.

On paper, it makes a lot of sense.

"Love has nothing to do with it," I say. "Isa knows I will never love her and never be her lover. We'll have separate bedrooms and use IVF to have children. It's a mutually beneficial business arrangement where both parties know exactly what they are getting out of the union."

"You cannot genuinely be this naïve." Gia shakes her head. "Come on, Cristian. Wise the hell up. Isa has always wanted you. I don't care what bullshit is in the contract, mark my words, as soon as your ring is on her finger, she'll be doing her best to seduce you. The woman is a snake, and I can't believe you are giving this any consideration! You will never convince me she didn't have some involvement in what went down. I don't care if everything pointed to Carmine and Vincenzo, and nothing tied her to it. My gut says there is more to it, and I always trust my instincts."

"Gia, I love you, but you're totally biased when it comes to her."

"You're a blind fool if you go ahead with this," she clips out. "I'm not sure I can ever speak to you again if you shackle yourself to that cunt."

"Tell me how you really feel." I drain my beer and snap my fingers, gesturing at Elio to come. I don't want to say something I'll later regret, and it's clear we'll never see eye to eye on this subject. "I promised my father I'd marry, and it's time."

"Your old man was a sly bastard on his deathbed." Caleb pins me with a look that dares me to challenge him for speaking ill of the dead. "He did a number on you and poor Sabina. Just because you told him what he wanted to hear before he passed away, doesn't mean you have to go through with it. It's a conversation you should have with your sister too."

"It's called honoring a promise. Something both of us feel a duty to fulfill."

"Maybe you *are* legit insane," Caleb adds, "because you're throwing your life away without even trying to find love again."

Elio runs across the grass as I stand abruptly, letting my chair fall to the ground. "You don't get to lecture me." I work hard to leash my anger because I know my friend's words come from a place of concern. "You have a beautiful wife, a beautiful family, and life is perfect. I gave up my one and only chance at that kind of happiness." I thump my clenched fist against my chest as Elio approaches, slowing his steps and frowning at the obvious confrontation. "I don't get to have that now, but I've got to find some way of moving forward, and this is my only option." So what if I'm miserable? Maybe it's the price I have to pay for fucking up so spectacularly.

"Why not wait and find someone else to enter into a marriage contract with?" Joshua suggests. "You'd have no shortage of offers."

She'd be a stranger to Elio, but I'm not stating that out loud when he could possibly hear. "I'll think about it," I lie. Crooking my fingers, I gesture Elio forward. "Thanks for a lovely lunch, Elisa." Bending down, I kiss her cheek before kissing her baby son's brow. "I'm gonna stay in the city tonight, but you can tell Natalia we'll be back tomorrow in time for Sunday lunch." Elio is staying with Isa tonight at her Manhattan apartment, and I plan to drop by my mother's house to see her and my sister. I'll either sleep there or at the penthouse.

"We only say this because we love you so much and want you to be happy," Elisa clarifies, squeezing my arm.

"I know, and I'm grateful to have friends who have my back." It's no word of a lie, but we're never going to agree on this, and ultimately, it's my life, my decision.

Elio hugs his aunts and uncles, then trots alongside me as we make our way around the side of the house. "Why were you arguing?" He frowns as he stares up at me. He's shot up a lot this past year, and I can already tell he's going to be taller than me.

"It's nothing for you to worry about."

His brow creases in concentration, and he nibbles on his lip as we walk to where the bodyguards are waiting. Nodding in acknowledgment at John Angelo and Umberto, I stride toward my BMW as my men climb into the SUV. Even though Pablo Fuentes has been dealt with and a tentative peace deal is in place with his much more reasonable brother, I still take zero chances, insisting bodyguards come everywhere with us.

John Angelo turned down the capo promotion I offered him five years ago, requesting instead promotion to head bodyguard. I readily agreed, and it was a good decision. As well as being my personal bodyguard, he manages the bodyguard team that protects me, my son, my mother, and my sister. He's kept us safe, and I'm grateful. He's approaching retirement, and we've already begun discussion on succession planning. I will miss the guy who's become a quasi-father figure as much as a valued employee.

"Dad," Elio says when we're on the road a few minutes later. "Are you going to marry Auntie Isa?"

I arch a brow. "Where'd you hear that?"

"I overheard Auntie Isa talking on the phone last weekend."

The contract has only been drawn up, and nothing is signed, so Isa should not be talking about it to anyone. Goddamn her. I rub at my throbbing temples. Fuck, maybe my friends are right, and I should look for someone else to enter into an arrangement with.

"I am considering entering into a marriage contract with

your aunt, but nothing has been agreed yet." Elio is aware of his heritage and the traditions associated with *Cosa Nostra,* so he knows what this means. My son has embraced our world, and he's already told me he wants to initiate at thirteen. Taking my eyes off the road for a second, I look at my son. "How would you feel about it if I did marry her?"

He doesn't answer immediately, thinking about it. "Will it make you happy?"

I never want to lie to my son, but how the fuck do I answer truthfully? "It's not about me being happy. It's about my responsibility as a don. It's time I took a wife, gave you those siblings you long for, and a mother."

He's pensive again, and I give him time to think about it as I take the exit for the highway. "I love Auntie Isa, and I'd like a little brother, but the only thing I need is my dad." My chest swells with love for my son. It's been the two of us for so long, and in a lot of ways, I don't want that to change. But that's the selfish side of me speaking. We have a tight bond; one I worry might change if I bring others into our huddle. Elio glances at me, and he looks and sounds more mature than his years when he says, "Grandma says life without love is only half a life. She says your love for me is really big, but your love for Sloane is big too, and you're sometimes sad because you miss her."

My heart is a shredded, bleeding mess that has robbed my senses of normal functionality, but I somehow manage to force a response. "I didn't know Grandma had spoken to you about Sloane." Elio missed her a lot at the start, crying for her at night on so many occasions. I wasn't the only DiPietro to fall hard. It hurt him every time her name was brought up, so I stopped mentioning her. He was only four when she came into his life, and I assumed he'd long since forgotten about her. "Do you remember her?"

"Not much," he admits, leaning his elbow against the car

door and propping his head on his hand. "She built me a space station," he adds, looking wistful.

"She did."

"And she was an amazing basketball player."

Tears prick the backs of my eyes. "She was."

"I know you have pictures of her in your drawer," he says. "I found them one day. She's very pretty."

"She's beautiful," I choke out. "Inside and out."

"You should marry Sloane," he says with confidence, shrugging like the decision is no biggie.

It's a miracle I don't crash the car. It takes several minutes to compose myself because my son has left me speechless. Elio pulls out his tablet and begins searching through his movie database as I finally find my voice. "I would if I could, but she's gone, buddy. I tried finding her, but she disappeared without a trace." It takes effort to keep things lighthearted when it feels like my heart is splintering inside my chest. I will never be able to think about Sloane and not feel heart-crushing pain.

"Well, that sucks," he says equally casually as he turns on a movie. His head lifts briefly. "But maybe you should keep looking for her. That's what I would do."

Wise words from a wise little man. I'm still mulling over it when we enter Manhattan. I think I'm only now realizing how grown-up Elio is getting. He's smart and kind with a big heart, and I'm so proud of him.

The main streets are congested with traffic, so I take a shortcut, zipping along narrower side streets, heading in the direction of Isa's apartment. The bodyguards keep pace with us, staying close to the rear.

Thoughts of Sloane rotate through my mind, and the more I think about it, the more I realize everyone is right. I can't marry Isa. She will push for more, and it'd be a disaster. But mostly, I can't do it for Sloane. She'd hate for me to marry the woman who was so cruel to her. She'd hate for me to marry without love.

One more year.

I'll give it one more year.

I'll forget about marriage contracts for now and continue the search for Sloane. I'd know if she were no longer of this world. My heart would tell me, and right now, my heart is telling me not to give up. Someone out there knows something, and I'm determined to find them.

"Dad, watch out!" Elio shouts, and my foot instantly slams on the brake as a person darts across the road in front of me, seemingly out of nowhere. The next few seconds shave years off my life. It happens as if in slow motion. My mouth widens in horror as the person clad in a black hoodie and black sweatpants rolls over the hood of my car before dropping to the ground in a heap.

I'm out of the car on autopilot, vaguely conscious of other car doors opening and closing.

The person is lying on their stomach, but thankfully, moving. "I'm so sorry. I didn't see you," I say, approaching cautiously as they scramble slowly to their feet. Their back is to me, and I can't make out if it's a man or a woman through the shapeless clothing. "How badly are you hurt?" I ask, stopping behind them. "I can take you to a hospital or call an ambulance."

"That won't be necessary," the woman says, her voice barely a whisper. Tucking her chin into her chest, she starts walking forward as I fall into a daze.

"Dad! You need to go after her." Elio lands at my side with John Angelo on his left.

They stare at me and my lack of action, unaware of the turmoil spiraling inside me.

Goose bumps sprout all over my arms, and prickles of

awareness coast over my skin as I watch her walking off with an obvious limp. That innate pull I only ever felt in her presence springs to life, shooting imaginary strings toward her retreating form.

It can't be, can it? Things like this don't happen in real life.

"Dad." Elio tugs on my arm. "She's hurt. You need to go after her." Elio's words snap me out of my fugue state, and I start running, anxious to catch up to her before she disappears for another five years.

"Wait!" I call out as she reaches the end of the road. "Sloane! Stop!"

Her head whips around, and she stares at me in blatant terror for a few seconds before she takes off running.

But I saw enough.

She looks different, but it's her.

It's Sloane.

I've finally found her.

Chapter Forty-Five
Sloane

My body is wracked with aches and pains as I push my limbs harder, willing them not to give up on me now. But I'm so tired. Tired of constantly running, constantly being chased. I had no intention of stopping in New York, but my damn car broke down, and I literally had to flee for my life, abandoning all my belongings as two men came after me. Perhaps fate has brought me back here on purpose. Maybe this is where it all ends.

How fucking ironic that in a city of millions I almost get run over by the one person I need to avoid. Cristian warned me he'd kill me if I ever came back, and I think Lady Luck is about to run out.

"Sloane, stop."

Panic crashes into me at how close he sounds, and I force my limbs to move faster, but my gimpy leg wobbles, the old injury throbbing from the inside, and I falter, stumbling on my feet, screaming as I fall. But I don't faceplant the asphalt because familiar arms are there to catch me. Briefly, I close my eyes, letting Cristian's warmth sink into my bones one final time.

If this is the way I go out, it's not the worst way to go.

"Sloane," he whispers, slowly turning me around in his arms.

Swallowing over the sudden lump in my throat, I lift my head as my heart flips somersaults and butterflies swoop into my chest. Our eyes connect for the first time in years, and we stare at one another, drinking each other in as the five-year drought ends.

Cristian looks the same. Like he hasn't aged at all. He's still drop-dead gorgeous with this intense charisma I can't help being drawn to. I struggle to believe any part of this man was ever mine. His piercing green eyes still hold enormous power over me as his gaze roams my face. Dormant longing stirs inside me as I get lost in him. Guess some things will never change. Don DiPietro always captivated me in a way no other man ever has. The stubble on his chin and cheeks is thicker than he used to wear it, and his face is more tan, but otherwise, it's as if time stood still.

"My god. It is you." Keeping one arm around my waist, Cristian pushes the hood down off my head with the other before releasing my hair from its ponytail. Dark, messy waves cascade over my shoulders as I steel myself for what comes next.

"Make it quick." I'm pleased my voice doesn't tremble and my stupid leg doesn't give out when I awkwardly kneel before him. "Do it now before I have time to be afraid." Committing his face to my eternal memory, I close my eyes and relax. There's a sense of peace in knowing I don't have to run anymore. I'll finally be reunited with my mom in a place where there's no suffering, no pain, only joy, love, and light. I'm ready for that.

"Sloane, no."

My eyes open, and I frown as he helps me to my feet.

"Fuck." Tears fill his eyes. "I didn't mean those horrid words I said that last day." His fingers dive into my hair, clasping the back of my head. "I'm not going to kill you, Sloane. God, even saying that destroys me." He winces as if in pain. "I could never hurt you. I've spent five years looking for you, just wanting to bring you home and protect you, but I couldn't find you." His voice breaks, and I barely resist the urge to tug at my ears, sure they must be deceiving me.

"You were looking for me?"

He nods. "I hadn't stopped, but I thought...I thought you might be dead," he whispers before pulling me into a hug.

I'm frozen in his arms, shaking and a bit dazed as I try to make sense of what he's said. I've missed him so much, and the pain was worse because I thought he hated me. Knowing he didn't mean it, that he's been searching for me all this time, blows my mind.

"I was so angry that day, Sloane, and I couldn't think straight. I didn't even let you explain. I didn't stop long enough to realize the woman I loved would never hurt me or my son. I—"

"Dad?"

We break apart at the young voice, and emotion builds at the back of my throat as I face the boy sheltered at his father's back. "My little prince," I whisper, my voice cracking with emotion as I stare at Elio.

Unlike his father, Elio is completely changed. His head reaches Cristian's chest now, and he's sporting the same dark hair, vibrant green eyes, and strong features as his father. No one looking at them would ever doubt they were father and son, despite Cristian being his uncle and adopted father. No longer a cute baby-faced little kid, Elio is a handsome young man in the making. I'm stunned speechless.

"Sloane?" He stays close to his dad as he looks at me with confusion.

"It's me." I clear my throat. "You're so grown up, Elio."

"I'm nearly ten now." His chest puffs out proudly as he stares at me. "You look different."

"I do. I didn't expect you'd remember me."

"I remember some things. You saved me from the cartel," he softly says. "I used to have nightmares about it," Elio explains, and my heart hurts for all he must have endured. "But at the end, you were always there, in the kiosk, hugging me and kissing me and telling me I was safe, that the police were coming, Daddy was coming, and you weren't letting anyone take me."

"I'm sorry. I—"

"Sir, we should get off the street."

"John Angelo?" I'm only noticing the broad-shouldered older bodyguard now.

"It's good to see you again, Sloane." There's no mistaking his welcoming smile.

I'm only alive because of him, of that I'm sure, but I don't know if Cristian is aware he helped me, so I don't throw myself at him and thank him like I want to, merely saying, "You too."

"Will you come back to the penthouse?" Cristian asks.

"Why?" I cross my arms around my chest.

"To talk, maybe get something to eat. Please, Sloane."

My eyes dart wildly around the place as I remember the men chasing me. There is no sign of them, but I don't relax. They could've taken off when they spotted Cristian, but most likely, they're hiding close by, watching our interaction. "I can't go with you. It's not safe. I won't bring the cartel to your door again."

Cristian frowns. "The cartel is no longer a problem. Pablo Fuentes is dead, as are all his men, and his brother is now in charge. He doesn't give a fuck about his brother's vendetta. He's all about business. We brokered a peace deal with them, so you're safe now, Sloane. You can stop running."

"No." I shake my head, instinctively moving in closer to Cristian. "They're still after me. I was fleeing from two men when my car broke down a few blocks away. I had to abandon it because they were chasing me."

Cristian whips out his gun at the same time John Angelo does. "Get Elio back to the car now!" he barks before tucking me against his side. John Angelo grabs Elio's hand, and they start running.

"What are you doing?" I ask, protesting as Cristian pulls me with him, striding purposely back down the street after his son and bodyguard.

"What I should've done that day." He peers into my face as he threads his fingers in mine. "Protecting you."

"But—"

"No buts, Sloane. You've dealt with shit on your own for years, and it ends now. I don't want to force you to come with me, but I'm not letting you go. Not ever if I have my way, or at least until we figure this out."

"I don't understand." Surely, he can't be saying what I think he's saying?

"I know you're hurt, but can you run? It's too open here. We need to get off the street."

"Nothing is making sense."

"It will when we talk. Don't fight me on this. Please." His eyes blaze with steely determination. "No one should be after you, Sloane. But someone clearly is, and I'm not letting you out of my sight until I find the threat and eliminate it. I'm protecting you now the way I always should have. Now, am I carrying you, or are you running?"

Chapter Forty-Six
Sloane

Standing in what was once my closet is like stepping into a time warp. All the clothes Cristian bought me five years ago are still on hangers. Most of them I didn't even have an opportunity to wear. They all smell freshly laundered, and I can't believe he didn't toss everything out with my lying ass. Apart from a fresh layer of paint, the room is exactly how I remember it too. Even the body wash and shampoo I just used in the bath are the same brands I used when I lived here. It's like this entire room is a shrine to me.

Dropping the towel, I pick out clean panties, a pair of jeans, and a white tank top for under the pink silk blouse. All my old bras are way too big now, so I'll have to go braless. After dressing, I slip my feet into my old comfy slides and head out to find Cristian.

It's surreal being back here and seeing Cristian, Elio, and John Angelo again. We dropped Elio at Isotta's apartment even though he begged his dad to cancel the sleepover so he could come with us. Cristian warned him to keep my reappearance a secret before escorting him to his aunt's place alongside

Umberto. It gave John Angelo and me a chance to talk privately for a few minutes.

I'm still mulling over everything he told me about the desperate lengths Cristian has gone to over the years to find me. I don't understand it. I betrayed him in the worst way. He should hate my guts. He certainly did the day he held a gun to my head and basically told me I was dead to him. John Angelo reassured me he doesn't mean me any harm, and I'm safe here. I've learned to listen to that inner voice and trust my instincts, and it tells me to accept the help Cristian is offering. At the very least, we are both owed a conversation.

"Hey," I say when I enter the kitchen to discover Cristian unpacking a large takeout bag.

"Hi." He stops removing cartons, letting his gaze rake over me from head to toe. It feels like a sensual caress, and I shiver all over.

My body certainly hasn't forgotten the way he used to make me purr with pleasure. No lover before or after has ever matched up to him.

Cristian's eyes briefly linger on my much smaller chest, and I'm not surprised he's noticed because it's a big change—pun intended. "I had the implants removed a couple of years ago." I don't mention the reconstructive surgery needed to tighten my overstretched skin because it's private. "Fuentes forced them on me, and I hated everything they represented."

Cristian nods, his expression pained.

"John Angelo said you pieced together my story. That you know the cartel kidnapped me and my mother when we were on vacation."

"Yes, but a lot of it was guesswork. I'd like you to tell me if it's not too difficult."

"Can we eat first? I'm starving."

"Of course." He unloads the rest of the bag. "I hope takeout is okay. We live in Glencoe now, and I only stay here a couple days a month, so the refrigerator hadn't been restocked, and the pickings were slim."

"I'm not fussy, and it smells delicious."

"I wasn't sure what you wanted, so I got a ton of different things."

"Thank you."

We don't talk as we open cartons and heap food on our plates, but we're both sneaking glances at one another, and I wonder if butterflies are swooping through his chest the same way they are through mine. Not that I'm under any illusion about what this is. Cristian obviously feels guilty for not protecting me, and this is his chance at redemption. It doesn't mean we get to live out the fantasy we got a taste of. I'm a very different person, and I'm sure he is too. It's not like we could pick up where we left off, even if we wanted to.

"By the way, I located your car. It's been impounded, but I'll process the paperwork to have it released. Then I'll get it towed to the garage and repaired. John Angelo will arrange one of my men to pick up your things."

"I appreciate it, thanks." It'll be good to have my stuff. All I took when I fled was my gun and my wallet.

"Wine?" Cristian asks, reaching for two glasses.

"I'll pass in favor of water and some pain pills."

His face instantly dissolves into concern. "You need to be checked out. I'll call Natalia."

"Don't bother. Nothing is broken, and a few bruises won't kill me."

"For me, please."

"It's Saturday night. Let the woman enjoy her downtime."

"She's on shift in the city, and I know she won't mind dropping by on her way home."

I shrug. "Okay then. If you insist."

I carry our plates and glasses of water to the table while Cristian calls the doctor.

We eat in uncomfortable silence for a few minutes until I crack. "Well, this is super awkward."

"I still can't believe you're here," he says, pushing his plate away. "I feel like I should keep pinching myself to know it's real."

"I know the feeling. It's very surreal." I pop a shrimp in my mouth and chew. "Why are all my clothes still in the closet? Why does my room look like a shrine?"

"Because I never stopped hoping you'd come back to me."

"What changed? You almost put a bullet in my head, and I know you hated me. I saw it in your eyes."

"Eat and I'll talk," he says, jabbing his finger at my dinner.

Lifting my fork, I shovel a mouthful of noodles and shrimp between my lips.

I listen as he explains his thought process that day and in the weeks that followed. I continue eating, trapping my words inside as he outlines the steps he took to find me and his frustration at being thwarted every time they came close to locating me. By the time he's finished, I've cleared my plate and drank all my water.

"Tell me Pablo suffered," I say through gritted teeth after he's explained how they lured El Rey into a trap so Cristian could kill him.

"Trust me, the bastard suffered." A muscle clenches in his jaw. "Caleb, Joshua, and I tortured him for weeks. He was begging for death by the end. I watched him bleed out and die like a coward. Then we hacked him up and burned his remains. Nothing is left of that prick, and I hope he's rotting in the fiery pits of hell."

Emotion has me tied in knots, and it takes several minutes before I can speak. "Thank you. I have dreamed of avenging my mother every night since we were taken. It helps to know he can't hurt anyone ever again." My mind drifts, as it so often does, to the innocents I put in danger. "What about the missing women and children?" I'm terrified of his answer, but I need to know. "Please tell me you found them."

"This can wait for another time. You must be exhausted, and it's already been a lot."

"I won't shy away from this, Cristian. Tell me."

"It's not your fault," he rushes to assure me.

"We both know that's not true."

"Sloane, listen to me." Swiveling his chair, he faces me, taking my cold hands into his warm ones. "The only people responsible are my brother and the cartel."

"Tell me." I brace myself because I know it's going to hurt.

"We found two of the children. A boy and a girl. They're safe and being well cared for."

"What about their mothers and the other mother and child?"

Pain glimmers in his eyes. "We were too late to save the women, and the boy is missing, but we haven't given up searching. He's high on our priority list."

I rest my head on the table and breathe deeply as pain whittles through me.

"Sloane." Cristian's warm hand lands on my back. "Please don't blame yourself. I could easily blame myself or Gia for finding them. If we hadn't, the cartel may never have known about them. Or I could point the finger at The Commission for not immediately prioritizing the search. There is lots of blame to go around, but the real blame lies with Fuentes and the cartel."

My eyes sting when I lift my head. "I set it all in motion, and I'll never forgive myself."

"I can't tell you how to feel, but please don't take that burden on. I'm begging you. You have taken on enough."

"Guess we'll have to agree to disagree." I rub at my throbbing temples. "Not a day has gone by where I haven't worried about them or thought about you and Elio."

"It was the same for me." His fingers thread through mine. "We found eighteen other kids. All Elio's half-siblings."

My eyes pop wide.

"They're safe, and the search is continuing because we believe there are more."

"That's a lot to process."

"It is."

Silence descends as we're both locked in our thoughts, until Cristian breaks it a few minutes later. "How about we grab a bottle of wine and move into the living room?"

"You haven't eaten much." I glance at his half-eaten plate, the food cold by now.

"Elisa made a big lunch, and honestly, my stomach is in knots. I can't eat another thing."

"How is everyone?" I ask. "John Angelo told me Clint survived but had to retire early from his injuries. Before I leave, I'd like to see him to apologize."

Cristian scowls, opening and closing his mouth. "You have nothing to apologize for. You didn't shoot him. The cartel did, and we made them pay. Everyone is doing great." A big smile lights up his face. "Elisa and Caleb had a little girl four years ago, and they have a new baby son. Gia and Joshua welcomed another daughter five months ago. You should know Elisa immediately defended you. She didn't for one second ever blame you. She cried a lot of tears, and everyone's been extremely worried about you."

"Elisa is a sweetheart through and through." I stand,

reaching for the plates when Cristian wraps his fingers around my wrist.

"Leave those. I'll clean up later. Go into the living room, and I'll bring the wine."

The doorbell chimes just as I've sat on the familiar couch, and then Natalia is there, hugging me repeatedly and marveling at how well I look, before whisking me into the bedroom to check my injuries.

"You're right. Nothing is broken. You're lucky," she says, gesturing for me to get dressed.

"The car had almost stopped when I hit it, so I kinda rolled over the hood," I say, pulling my tank and blouse back on. "All the bruising is from hitting the ground at an odd angle."

"Does this give you much pain?" she asks, gently probing the jagged skin on my calf.

"On and off. I don't think it healed right."

"I'd like to have strong words with whoever did your sutures." She frowns as she prods more firmly around the messy scar.

"John Angelo did it, but he saved me from bleeding out. A little pain and an ugly scar don't bother me when it could've been much worse."

"I think there are bullet fragments still under the skin. It's why you get intermittent pain. We should schedule surgery to remove them. We have a great cosmetic surgeon at the hospital, and I'm sure he could do something to make the scar less obvious."

"I'm not sure what my plans are, but I'll consider it," I say, pulling my jeans up my legs.

"I'm going to suggest something. Cristian asked me to ask you, but it's entirely your choice." She holds up a small, thin silver chip. "This is a high-tech tracking device. A lot of *Cosa*

Nostra have these, families included." She lifts her hair up. "Prod the back of my neck, see if you can feel it."

I do as she asks, and when I press in firmly, I can feel it, but you wouldn't know by looking at her neck.

"How does it work?" I ask as she lowers her hair.

"Once inserted, it can be tracked either locally by a loved one or centrally via our IT team. It's added security. If you'd had one of these five years ago, you wouldn't have been lost to us for so long."

"Cristian wants me to have this?"

She nods. "For your protection, but it's your choice, which is why he left it to me to ask you. He doesn't want you to feel pressured."

"If it's for my protection, I don't see the harm. You can put it in."

Numbing the area first, she then makes a small incision and pushes the chip in before applying a few butterfly bandages.

"Keep it dry, and I'd like to check it in a week."

"Thanks, Natalia."

"You're welcome." She packs up her bag. "We're all having dinner at my house tomorrow, and I'd love you to come. I'm sure everyone would love to see you."

"Thanks for the invite, but I'm not sure yet what my plans are. I'll talk with Cristian and let you know."

She draws me into a bear hug. "I'm so happy you're safe. It took strength and smarts to survive."

"My mother died so I could live, and I never forget it. I have fought with everything I have to make sure her sacrifice wasn't in vain."

"I'm so sorry for what you both endured. Losing your mother like that is horrendous. We were all so worried about you. Especially Cristian. He's been a shell of himself since you left."

"It hasn't been a picnic for me either."

Her expression turns grave. "No, I don't expect it was." She kisses my cheek. "Do you remember what I told you the last time I saw you?"

Wracking my brain, I draw a blank and shake my head. "Some of my memory is patchy from that time."

Compassion splays across her face. "Trauma does that. I gave you the name of a therapist, and Marjorie still takes on new clients. If you want to talk to her, call me, and I'll pass on her details. The other things I said that day were you're family, we take care of our family, and Cristian would treat you like a queen if you let him." She squeezes my hand. "That is all still true. I know he messed up, but he hasn't stopped looking for you. It's always been you for him. There has been no one else. I thought you should know that when deciding where you go next."

Chapter Forty-Seven
Cristian

"Before you explain, can you tell me anything about the men following you?" I ask when we are settled on the couch after I said goodbye to Natalia at the door. If Sloane is still being hunted, I want to get a handle on it ASAP. I swear if Rodrigo Fuentes is double-crossing us, I'll personally see his blood spilled. "Think carefully. Even small details could help to identify them. What do they look like? What vehicle were they driving? How long have they been chasing you? I have a team looking at the traffic cams in the area where your car was abandoned, and if we can pinpoint them from camera footage, we can use facial recognition software to track them down."

"I didn't see their faces, and I can't even be sure it's the same men who have almost found me a few times." She says it so calmly with no trace of fear, almost like she's resigned herself to a life of always looking over her shoulder. Sloane pours the chilled Sauvignon into two wineglasses and hands one to me. "But it was two men. One was about six feet tall, the other shorter and stockier. They were in a dark-green SUV with tinted windows. Texas plates. Most likely fake. They've been following me for a month, all the way here from Kentucky. It didn't matter how often I ditched them, rotated my plates, or switched cars, they always found me. It hasn't been this intense since the early days. I'm wondering if they messed with my car. If maybe it was intentional that I broke down here of all places?" She shrugs casually as she sips her wine. "Maybe I'm reading more into it, but I've learned the hard way not to ignore my instincts."

"You've changed."

"I had no choice." She looks straight at me, not shying away from anything. "It was either fall to pieces and the cartel would find me, or pick myself up and fight for my life. I chose the latter, and I haven't stopped fighting ever since. But it was touch and go at the start. The first few months after I fled, I was a mess. Especially after I saw the news reports about my mother." Pain glints in her eye for a few beats before she shakes it away. "I went off the grid. Found an abandoned cabin in Montana and hid there for months, only venturing out to get food. I wanted to die. I was all alone, and I knew they were hunting me, and it was probably only a matter of time before they found me."

"I will never forgive myself for leaving you to fend for yourself." Placing my glass down on the coffee table, I turn to face her. "I am so sorry, Sloane. My biggest regret is not trusting you." I fist a hand over my chest. "Deep down, I knew you wouldn't betray me or Elio. I should've helped you, but instead, I tried to kill you before pushing you away. I have hated myself every day since."

She sits forward and cups my face. "Forgive yourself, Cristian. I have never blamed you. You were protecting the person you loved most in the world."

"Elio was only one-half of that equation." Keeping her

hand flush against my face, I nestle into her touch, marveling at the tingles ripping across my skin as if no time has passed at all. Every part of me still craves every part of her. "You were the other half. I never even told you I loved you, but I did. I still do."

"How can you say that after everything I did?"

"Forgiveness works both ways, Sloane. You were a young woman trapped in a nightmare, and you tried to do your best. I know that now. Like I know you tried to protect me and Elio the best way you could while trying to save your mother's life. I'm so sorry you lost her, Sloane. She didn't deserve to suffer and die like that."

"It was you, wasn't it?" she asks, moving closer. "You arranged the funeral and the gravestone."

"It was the least I could do."

Her eyes turn glassy for a few beats. "Thank you for doing that, and for the deposit you put in my bank account."

"When I realized you had no money, I knew I had to act, but it wasn't entirely altruistic," I truthfully reply. "I thought it'd be how I'd find you, but you outsmarted us by withdrawing it in cash immediately, closing the account, and disappearing."

"That money was the difference between life and death. I bought a car and met a couple of guys who helped me buy different fake IDs, set up multiple bank accounts in different countries, and taught me how to live off the grid. At the beginning, I tried to find work in some towns where I stayed for more than a few weeks at a time. But it was too visible, too risky, so I studied foreign currency trading, did an online course, and found I had an affinity for it. I've traded wisely and never gone hungry, always had a roof over my head. It enabled me to travel around easily and often to avoid being found. None of that would've been possible without that money, so you did protect me, Cristian. You did help. And you took care of my mother when I couldn't. I didn't find out you'd done that for months after, but it gives me peace to know she's at rest now."

"I pay a man to keep her grave neat and tidy and to place flowers on it weekly. I wasn't sure if you'd ever visited."

"I wanted to, but it was too dangerous."

"I'll take you there," I promise. "As soon as I find these pricks and kill them, I'll take you to Ithaca. You can visit the grave and the house."

Her brow puckers as I lower our hands to my lap and link our fingers. "The house?"

"I bought your mother's house off the bank, and I've ensured its upkeep has been maintained. I didn't know if you'd want to move back there or sell it or whatever. But it's yours to do with as you please."

"Cristian." Her face floods with warmth. "I can't believe you did all that for me." She doesn't even know the rest yet.

"It's quite simple." I stare deep into her eyes, holding her hands more tightly. "I love you. I would do anything for you, Sloane."

"I was so sure you still hated me."

"Never." Tugging her into my chest, I hold her close to me. "It was anger speaking that day. I have never hated you, Sloane. Far from it. I hope you can find it in your heart to forgive me someday."

"There is nothing to forgive." She eases away from me. "I have never hated you for anything you did that day. I deserved it and more."

"No. You were a victim too."

"I was, but I still made a lot of bad choices. I've read a ton of self-help books during the years we were separated, and I went to therapy during a six-month period where I was settled in a small town in Switzerland. Sylvie helped me to realize how much trauma and stress impacted my decisions back then. She told me to forgive myself, and I'm trying, but it's not easy knowing different choices might have meant different outcomes."

"You were put in an impossible position. Thrown headfirst into a world you knew nothing about."

"I wish I'd told you. I wanted to, Cristian. I really did, but every time I came close to telling you, that bastard would send me another picture of my mother and send me reeling. My head was such a mess." She gulps back a mouthful of wine and kicks off her slides, lifting her knees to her chest. "If I'd been able to think more clearly, I would've realized there was never any way to save my mother. She knew it. In the last live video, she told me to save myself. That was the time to tell you, but guilt was eating me up and screwing with my head. It was only much later I realized Pablo had already killed her before I missed his deadline. He'd been toying with me all along, and I feel so fucking stupid for not seeing it."

We stay up for hours talking. Sloane fills in the rest of the gaps, and I listen as she tells me everything, stuffing my fist in my mouth when she explains the abuse she endured while in Mexico and here in New York. It's hard not to hate myself for not realizing what was going on right under my nose. Sloane asks a bunch of questions about Elio, and I scroll through photos on my phone, talking her through all the milestones she missed.

By the time the clock chimes one, we're both all talked out and exhausted. We haven't discussed what happens next, but it'll have to wait until the morning. All I know is I can't lose her again. I want her back in my life, fully, in every way possible, and I have zero doubts. I truly hope she feels the same way. "I left some pain pills and a bottle of water by your bed," I say before we part ways in the hallway. "If you need anything during the night, come wake me."

"Okay. Thanks, Cristian. Sleep well," she says before disappearing into her bedroom.

I stare at her bedroom door for way too long before I force my legs to move, walking into my room. I grab a shower before climbing into bed, and though I'm tired, I'm too wired to sleep. Knowing Sloane is across the hall is the worst kind of torture. Today feels like a dream, and I'm afraid to sleep in case I wake to find it was all a figment of my imagination.

After an hour of indecision, I say screw it and fling the covers off. I stalk out of my bedroom in my pajama pants and bare feet, like a man on a mission.

Five years.

Five fucking long years I have waited to know if Sloane was even alive.

On so many nights, I ran through scenarios in my head of what I would say and do when I found her, and not a single one involved us sleeping in separate bedrooms when we reunited.

This isn't about sex—though every part of me craves intimacy with her—but connection. For years, I lay lonely in bed, remembering how incredible it felt to hold her in my arms. I'm fucked if I'm sleeping alone tonight.

"Sloane," I whisper, tiptoeing into the room. "Are you awake?"

Covers rustle as she props herself up on her elbows. "Yes. You can't sleep either?"

"Not without you." I pad to the bed. "I swear I don't have any expectations, but I spent years sleeping alone, missing you so much it felt like I was dying every night. Let me sleep here with you. Only to hold you. To reassure myself you're real and you're not going to disappear overnight."

Wordlessly, she peels back the covers and pats the empty space.

I waste no time getting in and wrapping my arms around

her. A deep sense of serenity settles over me when she curls into my side and presses her cheek to my bare chest.

We don't speak, but words are not needed.

This. I just need this.

The ministrations of her fingers tracing light circles on my chest lull me into sleep, and I'm dozing off when she lifts her head. "Cristian," she whispers, and my eyes instantly flicker open.

"What is it, baby?"

Her hand flattens over my heart. "I need to tell you something else."

"I'm listening," I promise, tightening my arm around her waist.

"Everything we shared back then was real. None of it was a lie. My feelings for you were always pure and true."

"I know, beautiful. I know." Pressing a lingering kiss to her brow, I wish it were her lips, but I can't push any agenda. We still have a lot to work through, and I won't do anything that might scare her away. My biggest fear right now is that I can't hold on to her. It will devastate me all over again if she decides not to stay.

"I had a lot of regrets," she says, holding my face trapped in her gaze. "But my biggest regret was never telling you I loved you."

My heart soars hearing it. I hoped her feelings were as strong as mine, but hearing confirmation of it is *everything*.

"Like you, I never stopped." She peers deep into my eyes as she says, "I love you, Cristian. I love you so much, and that will never change."

Chapter Forty-Eight
Sloane

"Please say I can kiss you." Cristian stares at my mouth with ardent longing.

"If you don't, I will," I reply with zero hesitation. One key lesson I've learned these past few years is to grasp the happy moments when I can, because they've been few and far between.

I want Cristian, and he still wants me. Everything else can be figured out later.

"I love you." He holds my face like I'm precious before his lips descend in a searing-hot, claiming kiss that heats me all over. Cristian kisses like a man starved of oxygen who can finally breathe. I can relate. With every sweep of his lips, every plunge of his tongue, he breathes life back into me.

The marriage of our mouths is greedy, possessive, almost bordering on violent, as we devour one another with years of pent-up longing. I never thought I'd have this again, and I'm desperate for him. Teeth clash and tongues tangle as we frantically kiss, drawing moans and pants from one another as hands find bare skin, touching, tasting, wanting.

Then we're ripping at our clothes in a competitive race to get naked and seal our reunion.

"Fuck, you're beautiful." Cristian's gaze roams my bare flesh when we're both naked. Propping on his side, he pulls the covers back and lets his hands explore.

My body has changed. I'm healthier with more meat on my bones and sculpted muscles. Daily gym workouts and regular runs keep me fit, and self-defense classes and practice at the range ensure I'm always prepared for the unexpected.

"You're perfect," he adds, cupping one breast while tracing the dip at my waist with his free hand.

"This is the real me this time," I say, letting him drink his fill.

"I didn't think you could be more beautiful, but you have proven me wrong." There is nothing but desire and adoration in his gaze, and relief courses through me.

"I need you inside me, Cristian."

Rolling on top of me, he presses his body onto mine, careful to keep some of his weight back so he doesn't crush me. "Do I need a condom?" he inquires, dusting kisses along my collarbone.

"I have an IUD, and I'm clean." We never made love without a condom previously, but this feels right. I want to feel him inside me with no barriers, no obstacles in our way this time.

"I haven't been with anyone since you."

My eyes widen. "You haven't?"

His fingers draw circles around the hard points of my nipples as he shakes his head. "I couldn't bear the thought of being intimate with anyone but you." My guilt must show on my face. "Hey, that was my choice." His fingers brush over my lips. "It's okay if you haven't been celibate. I gave you no reason to believe I was waiting for you."

"There were only a few," I truthfully admit. "I was all alone, and sometimes I needed human contact. None of them meant anything more than a warm body to temporarily chase the pain away."

"I understand." He kisses me softly. "I hate the thought of anyone else touching you, but you did what you had to do to survive, and I'll never hold it against you because the path led you back to me. Promise me one thing."

"Anything. It's yours." I pant, wrapping my legs around his waist and arching my hips as his mouth closes around one breast.

"No other man is ever touching you again. You are mine, Sloane. Forever mine."

"That's what you really want?" I place my hand over his heart, and the steady thrumming against my palm is a balm to my soul.

"Yes. I know we have a lot to work through, but we'll figure it out." He places his hand on top of mine on his chest. "Together." He kisses me. "We're a team. You'll never be alone again."

I attack him, forcing him onto his back and straddling his thighs. "I love you so fucking much," I say before crushing my mouth to his and sliding my body back and forth across his erection. Cristian groans into my mouth, grabbing handfuls of my ass and controlling the rocking motion of my hips.

When I can't take it anymore, I rip my mouth from his, hold his dick steady at the base and position myself over his hard length. "Yours," I say, slowly lowering onto his cock. "Forever," I promise, seating myself fully.

"Oh fuck." Cristian's eyes gleam with heat and so much love I almost cry.

I thought this was lost to me, and I can't believe he is finally truly mine.

"You feel so incredible, and I will never get enough of you, Sloane. *You. Are. Mine.*"

I didn't dare to dream of this in recent years, but my earlier fantasies were filled with hot, sweaty nights spent fucking and making love to Cristian, and days full of light and laughter with father and son.

I start moving, setting a fast pace, desperate to ride the ultimate high with the only man I have ever loved. Cristian sits up, winding my legs around his back and thrusting into me in hard, punishing strokes, setting a relentless pace as he worships my lips, kisses my tits, sucks my nipples, touches me everywhere, and tells me over and over again how much he loves me and desires me.

Tossing me flat on my back, he pushes my knees into my chest and fucks me with no mercy, and I'm loving every second of it. I'm grateful Elio isn't here because my shouts and screams could raise the dead. Cristian drills into me in powerful thrusts, pinching my clit when he feels I'm close, and that's it, I'm gone, shattering in the most blissful way as wave after wave of ecstasy pulses through me.

Cristian finds his own release seconds after mine, and we're both panting, sobbing, laughing, and clinging to one another when we come down from the best high.

"I love you. I fucking love you." He dots kisses all over my face while hugging me to his sweaty chest.

"I love you so much, Cristian. It's only ever been you for me," I admit as tears stream down my face.

"Ditto, baby." His strong arms almost crush me. "I've got you. You're safe, and I love you. Sleep, sweetheart, and know I'll be right here when you wake up."

Waking up in Cristian's arms is truly the stuff of dreams. "Good morning, beautiful," he says before cupping my face and kissing me.

"A girl could get used to this," I say, snuggling closer.

"Get used to it because I'm never letting you go."

"You'll need to let me go for a few minutes." I drag my fingers through the stubble on his face, remembering how I always loved touching him like this. "I need to use the bathroom."

We clean up together before falling back into bed and making slow, sweet love. After, we take a shower together, and Cristian fucks me against the tile wall, holding me up as he pummels into me with an insatiable passion that coaxes intense pleasure from my body.

He orders breakfast while I blow-dry my hair and get dressed.

"Come, baby," he says, lounging in the bedroom doorway with his arm extended. "Our food is here."

We eat at the island unit, touching and kissing the whole time because we can't keep our hands off one another. "Your stuff will be here shortly," he says, reading a text on his phone. "Or if you prefer it, I can get it sent ahead to Glencoe? We'll have to leave soon to pick up Elio and head to Nat and Leo's place."

"About that." I loop my fingers through his belt. "Would you mind if I stayed here? I'm still processing everything, and though I want to meet everyone again, I'm not sure I'm up for a big family dinner." Cristian explained there'd be over thirty people at Sunday lunch, and it's a lot. "I'd also like to go through all my stuff and decide what I'm taking to the house."

"Are you sure that's it? You're not going to run off?"

"Cristian." I smooth out the furrows in his brow with my thumbs. "I know we need to build trust, but I swear I will never lie to you again, and I won't play games. I vow to always be honest. Open communication is the key to building a long-lasting relationship, and I want that with you." I stretch over and kiss him. "I'm not going to run away. I want to be with you and Elio. It's the only thing I've wanted from the moment I met you. But this is all a lot, and I need a little time."

"Okay. Of course. I won't ever pressure you." His fingers toy with my hair. "I'd prefer if you didn't go out. Not until I know more about this threat against you."

"I have no problem staying here. If that's what you need to set your mind at ease, you've got it."

"I can drop Elio at Natalia's and come back to the city straightaway. Elisa or Gia will take Elio tonight and get him safely to school tomorrow."

"Stay and have dinner with your friends. I'll be packing anyway." My hands land on his ass and I pull his body against mine. "But come back tonight. Let's see how many more times you can make me scream your name." I flash him a flirty grin. "We can leave in the morning for the house, if that suits?" I know he probably has work, but he's generally good at rearranging things for family priorities.

"I like this plan a lot." His mouth lowers to mine, and he drops a slew of drugging kisses on my lips that have me seeing stars when we break apart. "I'll pick up a phone for you when I'm out too," he offers, knowing I ditched my last burner cell.

John Angelo arrives then, overseeing the delivery of the boxes and bags from my car. After they're all stacked in my bedroom, Cristian's men leave, and I go with him to the front door.

"Promise me you won't go outside," Cristian says, hovering in the doorway. I know he doesn't want to leave, and he's worried.

"I promise. I'll be here when you return." Flinging my arms

around him, I plant a firm kiss to his lips. "Tell everyone I said hi and I'll see them soon."

"Love you," he says, reluctantly tearing himself away.

"Love you too." I wiggle my fingers and moon at him like a lovesick teen, only closing the door after he's disappeared into the elevator.

Chapter Forty-Nine
Sloane

Spending a couple of hours going through my things, I sort them into different piles. Stuff for storage and items to take with me. A lot of the belongings I've accumulated over the years are household items I won't need any longer. I'm sure Cristian's house is fully equipped, and his stuff will be much better quality. Excitement bubbles inside me at the thought I'll get to live in the home he built after all. I have often wondered what it looks like and whether Cristian and Elio are happy there.

Humming to myself as I rummage through my things, I'm relieved everything seems intact and untouched. I'm skimming through my photo album and sketch pads when the doorbell chimes. I'm not expecting anyone, but it's possible Cristian arranged a food delivery.

Sounds of arguing tickle my eardrums when I approach the front door, but the voices are muffled, and I can't hear what's being said. Using the peephole, I check to see who is outside, instantly scowling when I recognize the woman arguing with

John Angelo. Cristian said his new head bodyguard was also his personal guard, but it's no surprise he made him stay here to watch over me. That's a totally Cristian thing to do.

The arguing stops the instant I open the door. "What's going on?" I ask, my gaze bouncing between them.

"You." Isa seethes, her nostrils flaring, gaze burning with hostility. "So, it's true. You are back." If looks could kill, I'd be ten feet under by now.

"Yes, not that it's any of your business."

"Oh, it's my business all right," she says, shoving past me into the hallway.

"I can make her leave," John Angelo says.

"No, it's fine." I have dealt with much worse than Isotta Da Rosa, and the inquisitive part of my brain wants to know why she's here.

"You don't have to talk to her," John Angelo adds as the annoying woman huffs in outrage behind me.

"I know I don't, but I'll humor her. Don't worry." I shoo him away when he moves to come inside. "We're going to attempt a civil conversation, and then Isotta will be on her way." I'm not concerned. I can handle the jealous bitch.

"I'll be right outside," John Angelo cautions. "Shout if you need me."

"Oh, for God's sake," Isa hisses, stalking forward. "I'm just going to give her a piece of my mind, not riddle her with bullets, so there's no need to look at me like that." She slams the door shut in his face as if this is her place.

Thrusting my shoulders back, I stand tall and level her with a sharp look. "Let's not pretend we like one another. Say what you came to say and then leave."

"You don't call the shots," she snaps, digging something out of her purse. "And I'll decide who is leaving." Thrusting a square card in front of my face, she smirks as she says, "If you've come back for Cristian, you're too late."

Bile crawls up my throat as my gaze skims over the wedding invitation. It's for her impending wedding to...Cristian. What the fuck? My heart thuds painfully against my chest wall as I stare at the offensive invite.

"Cristian is mine, and you need to fuck off back into whatever hole you crawled out of," she snarls, putting her face all up in mine.

"I don't believe you." I'm hurt and confused, but this has got to be a trick. A last-ditch effort to get rid of me by a woman who has always wanted my man. Young me would probably have fallen for it. But I'm not the same naïve girl anymore. Cristian wouldn't lie to me, and I'm going nowhere until I talk to him. Pushing her back out of my face, I rip the invite into pieces and throw them at her. "Get out, you malicious bitch, and stay out."

"You can't throw me out!" she shrieks. "I won't let you ruin this for me again."

Anticipating her move, I thrust my fist out and punch her in the nose before she can touch me. Isa screams, tripping over her feet and falling flat on her ass on the floor. With more calmness than I feel, I open the door and request John Angelo to escort her from the building. Isa is screaming threats and expletives as John Angelo tries to wrangle her out the door. More bodyguards show up, and together they get her into the elevator.

Closing the door, I lean back against it and try to slow my racing heart. My eyes drift to the tattered remnants of the invite on the floor, and uneasiness settles on my chest. Isa is a conniving cunt, but how could she produce a professional wedding invite mere hours after Cristian and I reunited? I can't even blame Elio for blabbing the secret to his aunt because he's only a child, and he didn't mean any harm.

A knock on the door drags me from my troubled thoughts. After checking the peephole, I let John Angelo in. "We put her in a taxi and sent her home. She won't bother you again. Are you okay?"

"Is something going on with her and Cristian?" I ask, not mincing my words.

"That's a question for the boss," he replies, averting his eyes.

"John Angelo." My voice is stern. "Tell me what you know."

"Sloane." He squeezes my hands. "Cristian loves you. He was the happiest I've seen him in years earlier, so forget whatever that woman said and wait until Cristian gets back. He'll explain it."

"Explain he's marrying her?" I snap, losing the tenuous hold on my composure as anger rears its head. John Angelo grimaces, and I stagger back. "It's true?"

"Aw. Fuck." He scrubs his hands down his face. "Look, I've heard rumors, that's all."

"What have you heard?" Crossing my arms around my waist, I already know I'm not going to like this.

"That Cristian signed a contract to marry Isa."

"No," I whisper. "Hell no. It can't be true."

"I'm sure it's not." John Angelo tips my chin up. "Rumors have a habit of becoming embellished as they get passed around. The boss hasn't said anything to me, and I've heard nothing official. Perhaps it's a complete lie. I wouldn't be surprised if that woman started the rumors. She's always had a thing for the boss, but I swear to you, Sloane, Cristian has never shown any interest in her."

"She had a wedding invite. The date is set and everything."

Sympathy splays across his face and I hate it. "You need to talk to Cristian. Don't do anything rash until you know the truth."

"Right." I bark out a laugh, wondering if this is Cristian's cruel way of exacting revenge. Maybe last night and this morning have been a lie, and this is his way of punishing me for the things I did. Dangle the fantasy in front of me again and then rip it away. "I'm such a fool."

Rushing to the bedroom, I start plucking things off the bed, tossing them back into boxes. I'm fuming. Hurt. Angry. Feeling like a stupid, naïve, young college student all over again.

"Sloane." John Angelo comes into the room, holding out his cell. "Cristian wants to talk to you."

Snatching the phone from his hand, I press the speaker button and let him have it. "I assume John Angelo told you about my little meet and greet with your fiancée?" I spit out the word, and it fucking hurts. I'm so enraged, I want to hit something. Preferably her smug face. She got off lightly with a busted nose.

"She's not my fiancée, and I'm not marrying her."

"She had a fucking wedding invite with your names on it!" I yell.

A pregnant pause ensues before he speaks. "She had what?" His lethally cold tone sends chills up my spine.

"Don't pretend you don't know," I hiss.

"Listen to me, Sloane. I don't know what the fuck Isa is up to, but I am not marrying her. When I get married, it will be to you. *You*, Sloane. Not her. *You*. Now, I will handle Isa, and I'll explain it properly when I get back, but do not run. Please." Fear laces through his words. "You promised. Don't do what I did because we've both paid a high price for that mistake. Give me a chance to explain. If you still want to leave, then I'll help you leave safely, but I swear to you, Sloane, the only woman I love is you. I don't want her. Not at any time and certainly not now. This is a ploy to drive you away. Nothing more."

Air whooshes out of my mouth. "Okay. I'll wait for you to explain it, but I'm angry, Cristian. So fucking angry. You should've told me."

"I wish I had, and you have every right to be mad, but I promise I can explain it. Just don't leave."

After John Angelo leaves, I change into yoga pants and a crop top and tie my sneakers before heading to Cristian's gym to work out some of my frustration.

Switching on the treadmill, I start running, gradually increasing the speed as my limbs loosen. As I stare out the window at Manhattan, I barely see the buildings, Central Park in the distance, or the crowds on the sidewalk below because I'm lost in my head.

There's obviously some grain of truth to the story, but I'm choosing to put my trust in Cristian and waiting to hear what he has to say. Running away would not have been the answer. I can't tell Cristian we need to openly communicate and then revert to knee-jerk reactions. I probably wouldn't have gone through with it, but I'm glad for John Angelo's quick thinking. I guess Cristian and I have a long road ahead of us. Past mistakes and everything that has happened will undoubtedly color both our judgments. I can only hope in time we navigate successfully through all the obstacles in our way.

Cranking the speed a notch higher, I pound the treadmill as I physically vent my frustration. Sweat rolls down my back and beads on my brow. The fucking nerve of that bitch to show up here like that. If I'd left, it would've played straight into her hands. I'm mad at myself for letting her get to me. I'm better than this. But I'm also pissed that Cristian facilitated a situation where I was blindsided.

I'm so lost in thought, I almost miss the reflection in the

glass, only spotting the man creeping up on me from behind a split second before he reaches me.

Jumping off the treadmill, I duck under his arm before he can grab me, racing for the door and screaming for help. Yanking on my ponytail, he pulls me back with force, and I fall to the ground. His body covers mine before I can roll away, but I fight back, swinging my fists and getting a good jab in before he grabs both wrists and stretches them over my head. He's clad head to toe in black, and his face is shielded by a balaclava, but I have never forgotten those dark, evil eyes or the derisory tone in his accented voice when he speaks.

"Good to see you again, slut. I've missed your pretty mouth."

I try to buck him off, but he straddles my thighs, pinning me in place. "It's Alvaro," I shout, knowing Cristian has a camera somewhere in here. "He's—"

When his hand covers my mouth, I bite hard through his glove, digging my teeth into his flesh like a wild animal.

Alvaro roars before backhanding me, but I have one hand free now, and I reach between us, hating I have to do this, but it's the smartest option. Grabbing his junk through his pants, I squeeze hard, digging my nails in for added displeasure.

Tears fall from his eyes as he clutches his groin and yells. Using both hands, I shove him hard in the chest, catching him off guard. He falls to the side, and I kick at his legs before climbing to my feet. Sprinting toward the door, I notice the open air vent panel lying on the floor for the first time. As I run, I scream his name repeatedly, stating he's cartel, hoping someone is watching the live feed in the control room and they're coming to my rescue.

I'm halfway through the door when his hand wraps around my ankle. I scream as I face-plant the floor, pain rattling across my brow as I crash into the hardwood floor.

Black spots mar my vision as Alvaro sits on my back, restricting my breathing.

"Fucking whore," he hisses as a sharp prick stabs the side of my neck.

"Cristian," I slur as my vision blurs. "I love you."

Then I black out.

Chapter Fifty
Cristian

"Why isn't she waking up?" I ask Natalia for the umpteenth time since she arrived last night. Perched on the side of my bed, I gently brush strands of dark hair off Sloane's brow as she sleeps, oblivious to everything that's happened in the past few hours or the torment I'm in, waiting for her to resume consciousness.

"She was given a strong sedative." Natalia squeezes my shoulder. "Her vitals are all good. Try to relax, Cristian. She'll wake when she's ready."

Thank fuck for John Angelo's quick thinking. That prick Alvaro was seconds from shoving Sloane through the air vent when my men arrived. My fists twitch with an urge to beat the shit out of him and the other prisoners waiting in the interrogation center on Staten Island. No doubt Caleb is having fun, but he knows to keep them alive for me.

"You should sleep," I tell her. "Take the spare guest room."

"You should sleep too."

"There's no point even trying." Lifting Sloane's hand to my lips, I kiss her warm flesh. "I shouldn't have left her. I almost lost her again. I'm not sure I'll ever be able to let her out of my sight."

Compassion is etched upon her face. "I understand, but you can't be everywhere for everyone all of the time, and you're no good to anyone if you're exhausted."

"Watch me." There is nothing I won't do for Sloane and Elio. Nothing.

"I think it ends now." Her features harden. "Gia and Joshua never trusted the Da Rosas."

"I should've listened. Dug deeper. I think they must've been involved from the start, and they had help covering their tracks."

"You wanted to see the good in them for Elio, and that's not a flaw, Cristian."

"It sure feels like one."

"You have them now." She fights a yawn. "After it's handled, you can draw a line and move forward with your life." She smiles at the woman fast asleep in my bed. "I'm happy you have her back, Cristian. Elio is thrilled too."

"I only need to convince her to stay now." She might want nothing to do with me when I tell her I'd been considering a marriage contract with the woman who tried to have her kidnapped again. I want to punch myself in the face for ever letting that bitch into our lives. Isa's betrayal will hurt Elio so much. I don't know how I'm going to explain it.

"At least get into the bed and try to rest a little," Natalia says before slipping out of the room.

Following her advice, I strip down to my boxers, crawl into the bed, and position Sloane in my arms where she belongs. Cradling her to me, I dust kisses into her hair and promise her over and over again that this is the last time anyone tries to take her. If I have to bundle her in bubble wrap and hide her away to ensure she's safe, I'll do it so she doesn't worry about anyone coming for her ever again.

Early-morning sunshine is trickling through the blinds in my room when I wake, conscious of fingers caressing my face and a pair of big blue eyes staring at me while I sleep. "I didn't want to wake you, but I have questions," Sloane says. "How did I get here? What happened?" she asks in a croaky tone.

"Are you feeling okay?" I ask, tenderly touching the goose egg on her brow.

"My throat is dry. I have a bit of a headache, and my limbs feel tired, but otherwise, I'm fine. Where is Alvaro?"

A growl rips from my mouth unbidden. "In an interrogation cell waiting for me," I confirm as I sit up straighter, resting my back against the headrest and settling her under my arm.

"You caught him?"

"We caught them all. It's over, Sloane."

"Until the cartel sends more men."

"It wasn't the cartel."

She bolts upright, ripping out of my arms. "What do you mean?"

"I don't have all the missing pieces yet, but I'll tell you what I know." I stretch my arm wide. "Now get back here. I almost died last night when I got the call. I was terrified I might lose you again, and I need to hold you. I'll probably be stuck to you like glue from now on."

"I won't complain," she says, snuggling into me. "I happen to love your arms around me. Now fill me in, and don't hold anything back."

"Isa was a diversion to enable Alvaro and another man to sneak into the building through the ventilation shaft. Alvaro went to get you while the other guy planned to hijack the system. They were going to use poison gas to knock everyone out so they could take you, but John Angelo foiled them. A group of men got the guy before he could inject that shit into the vents while a second team rescued you." Holding her tighter, I press a lingering kiss to the top of her head. "If you hadn't fought him, he might've gotten you into the vent before they arrived."

"I will always fight back," she says. "I swore to myself no one was ever taking me again, and I meant it, but they nearly had me." Her fingers move to the tiny prick mark on the side of her neck.

"He didn't get his hands on you, and there are no long-term side effects from the sedative. That's all that matters."

"So, Isa was working with the cartel all this time?" she asks, peering up at me.

"I believe her father is the mastermind." Rage barrels through me. "En route to you, I got a call from Gia. The tech team got a hit on Alvaro from the facial recognition system. They caught footage of him meeting Rafaelo Da Rosa. I've since heard they have captured evidence of other meetings between the two."

"Does she hate me so much her father would consort with the cartel to kidnap me?"

"Alvaro doesn't work for the cartel any longer. Same with the other guy. Don Greco spoke to Rodrigo Fuentes. Alvaro went rogue when Rodrigo took control. They're disgusted his actions have jeopardized the agreement in place between them and us. The cartel has washed its hands of them. Told us to handle it. Gia is working on the evidence now, but it looks like Isa's father was bankrolling the two men. I think this is the piece of the puzzle we've been missing all along."

Sloane sits up straighter, looking me straight in the eye. "I want in on the interrogation. Don't even think of dissuading me. I deserve answers as much as you do."

"I agree. If you want to be there, fine, but it'll get bloody. Are you sure you want to witness that?"

"If they're as involved as you think, then fuck yes." Sloane flings the covers off and slides out of my arms. "Come on." She glances over her shoulder. "There's no time like the present, and while we're on our way, you can tell me what the fuck that wedding invite was all about."

I'm officially in the doghouse. Sloane is furious with me for even briefly considering marrying Isa. Surprisingly, her biggest issue is the fact I had given up on love. That seems to have angered her more than anything. I have some major groveling to do, which I'll happily concede to. I'm just grateful she believed me, and she's still planning to stay.

"Wait a sec," I say when we've stepped inside the interrogation building, halting at the stairs before we go down. "Drink this." I thrust the bottle of water infused with electrolytes into her hand. Natalia checked her over before we left. She'd have preferred Sloane to stay in bed and rest today, but there aren't any major reasons to deny her this. She is owed answers more than anyone.

"Stop fussing, Cristian. I already drank a bottle in the car on the way here."

"Natalia said you need lots of fluids and to eat well." My men are packing up the rest of Sloane's things and transporting them to Glencoe later. Even though it seems like the threat is over now we've captured Rafaelo, Isa, and the two ex-cartel men, I'd still rather get Sloane behind the secure compound until we've finalized the investigation and confirmed there are no other loose ends or threats.

"And I will. After we get answers."

"I love you," I remind her before kissing her, uncaring that the *soldati* on duty can see and hear everything.

"I love you too." She bites my lower lip, and it stings a little. "I'm still mad though."

"I deserve it."

"You so do." She presses her mouth against mine, and her tongue darts out, licking the little bead of blood her teeth drew. "But I forgive you only because you'd already decided not to go through with it. That was your saving grace, Don DiPietro."

"I thought you'd make me grovel for ages," I admit, hauling her against my body.

She barks out a laugh. "I said I forgave you, Cristian, because life is too short to hold stupid grudges, but I said nothing about you not groveling." Her hands slide under my jacket and land on my ass. "You will grovel to the ends of time if I command it."

"I will do anything you bid, my queen."

She's giggling as we descend the stairs, and I'll take that as a win.

Neither of us is laughing when we enter the cell a few minutes later. The three men are stripped to their boxers and tied to chairs by their hands and feet. All of them have been worked over, but they're still breathing.

"Cris!" Isa wails, fighting the restraints tying her to the end chair. "Tell them I had nothing to do with this!" She's fully dressed—because none of us wants to see her in her underwear —and her face and body are free of marks, except for the busted nose Sloane gave her. I'm probably sick, but watching the footage of Sloane laying Isa out made my dick hard.

No honorable made man is comfortable hitting a woman, though I might change my mind after I discover the full extent of Isa's manipulation.

"She's protesting her innocence nonstop," Caleb says,

walking toward us shirtless. Blood splatters coat his bare chest in jagged streaks, and his knuckles are torn. "I've been tempted to kill her at least ten times already."

Isa continues crying and calling out my name, but I ignore her while her father hisses at her to shut up. Dano arches a brow from his position by the wall. I asked my underboss to personally watch over them in my absence, not thinking Caleb would still be here.

Caleb's brows climb to his hairline when he looks at Sloane. "I didn't realize you'd be joining us."

"I want to know what they did," she says. Despite her bravado, she's nervous, clutching my hand in a death grip.

"Of course." Caleb nods solemnly before lowering his voice. "I'm glad you are safe, Sloane. You had everyone worried, but it seems you were smarter than some of the best tech brains, and you managed to keep yourself safe and hidden all this time. I'm impressed."

"Thanks, Caleb. I had to learn on my feet and constantly move around, but I managed okay."

"I'm really glad you're back, and I hope you're staying because this guy has been unbearable in your absence."

She looks at me and smiles. "I'm staying."

My arm goes around her, and I tuck her in tight to my side. Isa's sobs grow louder, and Caleb smirks, his gaze bouncing between me and Sloane. I know he's pleased for me. Everyone at dinner was thrilled when I told them she's back safe and sound.

"They're all yours, Don DiPietro." Dano slaps me on the back. "I'll be outside if you need me."

"I'm sticking around to hear this." Caleb presses his mouth to my ear. "Ben and Massimo went at Rafaelo earlier, but he refused to talk. Said he'd only talk to you."

I stand in front of Rafaelo Da Rosa with Sloane on one side

and Caleb on the other. Isa is quietly sobbing, but she's stopped appealing to me because she knows I won't help her. She made her bed, and now she can lie in it.

"You only want to talk to me, so talk," I tell the old man.

"I want your word that my family won't be harmed. None of them were involved. This is all on me, and I'll tell you everything if you swear you won't touch them."

"Lying is not a good way to start, Rafaelo," I reply, leveling a dark look at his youngest daughter. "We know Isa is involved."

"Isotta was a pawn. She didn't know anything about my plan or how I used her. The fool loves you. She'd never agree to help me kill you."

"What?" Isa's sobbing completely stops. "What are you talking about?" Her confusion seems genuine, but I'm reserving judgment until I've heard it all.

Rafaelo turns his head to look at her. "The DiPietro *famiglia* is scum, and they needed to pay the price for what they did to our family. His brother killed my Bettina, and then *he* took her son away from us." Rafaelo snarls at me. "You had no right to take Elio. He belongs with us."

Chapter Fifty-One
Cristian

"This was about Elio?" How fucking dare this bastard claim he did this for the betterment of Elio. Who the fuck is he to decide the fate of *my son*.

"It's always been about Bettina's boy. Did you truly think you could walk all over us, and I'd let it lie? You were always going to pay."

I don't bother telling him I only gave his worthless ass a promotion because he is Elio's grandfather or that I have let them see him regularly and ensured he's fully a part of their family too because the man won't listen. He's clearly been holding a grudge this entire time. "I give you my word, your family will be unharmed provided you tell the truth. If I find evidence anyone else in the Da Rosa family was involved, I will take the necessary actions. This is treason, and it will be dealt with accordingly."

"I swear, Cristian, I didn't know any of this," Isa cries. "I love you and Elio. I would never do anything to hurt either of you! Daddy told me Sloane had returned, and I needed to run her off. I didn't know there was some other plan in place. Please, you have to believe me."

"Isotta is innocent," Rafaelo repeats. "She didn't know."

"You honestly expect us to believe that?" Sloane says.

"It's the truth."

"Whether she knew or not, Isa was still involved," I say.

"Send her away if you must, but promise me you won't hurt her," Rafaelo pleads. "It would break her mama's heart."

Caleb snorts. "You have some nerve, Da Rosa. You have dishonored *omertà* and plotted to kill Don DiPietro, and you beg him to spare one of your own? Why should he? Applying your logic, anyone bearing the Da Rosa name is guilty and should be punished for the sins of one of their own. If it were up to me, I'd shoot the lot of you."

Rafaelo's chest heaves, but he doesn't even attempt to contest Caleb's words.

"Unlike you, I don't condemn innocent people for the actions of family members unless they played an active part," I say. "Whether she was party to the plan or not, Isa still facilitated it, and that deserves punishment. When I've heard it all, I will decide her exact fate. I'm already tired of this, so let's hear it." I glance at Sloane, and she meets my eyes, nodding to let me know she's okay. "Start at the beginning," I tell Elio's grandfather.

"I had everything handled years ago, but fucking Carmine and that stupid whore ruined it." His evil eye fixes on Sloane. "Then I get a new opportunity to make you pay, and that whore fucked it all up again."

I punch him twice in the face, relishing the sound of bone cracking when I break his nose. Blood gushes out of his nostrils, dripping over his chin. "Call her that again. Go on, I dare you. I'll slit your daughter's throat right in front of you if you disrespect Sloane again."

"You sicken me." Rafaelo glares at me.

"The feeling is entirely mutual, and I'm running out of patience," I grit out, ready to forgo answers and send his treacherous ass on a one-way ticket to hell.

"I vowed to take revenge on your family after your brother ruined my sweet Bettina and gunned her down in the street like trash, but that vengeance was stolen from me." He swings his glare Caleb's way. "I might have let it go, but you fought us for custody of Elio, and you had no right," he yells, staring at me with so much venom in his eyes I don't have a hard time believing he genuinely hates my family. "That is when I decided you had to die, your papa too, so no one could stand in our way."

"How did Carmine fit in?"

"He gave me an in with the cartel. He got into debt to them while vacationing in Mexico. They were going to kill him until they discovered he was *Cosa Nostra* and aligned with the DiPietro *famiglia*. Carmine knew I was out for blood, so he arranged a meeting. We agreed to help them so long as they killed you and nullified Carmine's debt."

"The nanny strategy was your idea," Sloane says.

"Yes." He looks only at me, refusing to direct his reply to Sloane. I don't want him looking at her anyway, but it's fucking rude, and I'm going to go to town on this prick when I get to the torturing part of the night.

"I knew you'd hire a new nanny when Isotta wed, so we planned for it," he continues. "She had the interviewee files in her bedroom. It was easy to copy them so we could threaten whoever got offered the position. The cartel had hired their own tech team to create a fake background for the...for *her*, and I placed the application among the others."

"Why did you even need her if you had Vincenzo?" I ask.

"Nothing could lead back to Carmine or me. She was the

fall guy. She was to make it easy for the cartel to get to you, but they wanted to fuck with your business as well."

"Was I targeted because I was from New York?" Sloane asks.

"You were merely in the wrong place at the wrong time. The cartel had men working at several resorts in Cancun. They told them to find a young, pretty American traveling with a friend or a relative. Someone that could be used as bait to force her into cooperating."

I want to throttle him, but I settle for punching him in the gut. Repeatedly. It barely takes the edge off the blistering rage charging through my veins.

Rafaelo coughs up blood, and he's struggling to breathe. Caleb shoots me a warning look, a silent reminder not to kill him before we get all the answers.

"I always suspected Thiago was involved." Sloane clenches her hands into fists. "At least I know now for sure he set me up."

"I'll find him," I promise. "If he's not already dead, we'll get him and make him pay."

"Good luck with that plan," Rafaelo snarls, and I've had enough.

Taking out my gun, I shoot him through the foot.

Isa screams, and Rafaelo howls with pain.

"You're running out of time, old man, and I'm losing my patience. One would think you didn't care about your family's welfare."

"We have a deal," he says through gritted teeth.

"Go on," I say in a clipped tone, pulling Sloane back a little as blood pools around our feet. Isa is back to sniveling again, and she's giving me a headache. "Shut her up," I tell Caleb, and he stuffs a dirty rag in her mouth.

In the corner, the other two assholes are stirring from the

beatdown Caleb gave them, and it's almost their time to meet their maker.

"We were to wait for the cartel to tell us when to make a move, but Carmine got greedy, thought he could take you and your papa out at the wedding, and the cartel would be in his debt. Except he fucked it all up, and the cartel was enraged. I believe that's when they decided to change their plan and target my grandson instead. Fuentes was screaming bloody murder, but I appeased him by promising to take Carmine out. It seems they used that as a distraction. While I was slitting that fat fuck's throat, they were trying to take Elio."

"You married that *fat fuck* to your daughter," Sloane says. "Why?"

"I didn't trust him not to shoot his mouth off at a later stage. Isotta marrying him was an opportunity to watch him more closely, and I didn't plan on keeping him around for long anyway. He was never good enough for her." He's answering Sloane's questions but still not looking at her. She doesn't seem bothered by it, but it's seriously pissing me off.

"You truly are evil," Sloane says. "I hope you burn in hell where you belong."

He opens his mouth to spit venom at her, no doubt, but I make a slicing motion across my throat that shuts him up.

"I had no more dealings with them after that," he says. "I wanted to gut that asshole for trying to take my flesh and blood, but my hands were tied. There was an unspoken agreement we couldn't rat the other party out without risking ourselves. So, I hatched a backup plan. To wed Isotta to you, so I could get close enough to kill you. Then Isa would legally be Elio's mother, and he'd belong to us."

Tears are streaming down Isa's face, and she's looking at her father like she doesn't even know him. I think her reactions are genuine, but whether she was a willing accomplice or not, she still played a part, and she will suffer the consequences.

"Except *you* were still getting in the way when you weren't even here." He doesn't shield his animosity as he glares at Sloane, so I put a couple of bullets in his other foot.

Isa pisses herself, and the smell of urine infiltrates the air.

The two cartel deserters are fully awake now, shouting something behind their mouth tape.

"Cristian wouldn't entertain any discussion of a marriage contract until recently," Rafaelo says, having no issue eyeballing Sloane this time.

"No need to look so pleased with yourself," Sloane coolly replies, shrugging. "Your daughter tried to rile me up with the same bullshit, but your taunts fall on deaf ears, you old fucker." Sloane grabs my head and smashes her mouth to mine, kissing me hard and fast.

Caleb chuckles, and my lips twitch when we pull apart.

I move my mouth to her ear. "You are so getting fucked later."

"Can't wait," she whispers back before refocusing her attention on the overweight old man tied to the chair. "Cristian has been mine from the minute we met. Your attempts to tear us apart didn't work because you can't destroy love when it's soul deep, bone deep, and it transcends time and separation. You were always destined to fail because you have no concept of what it truly means to love someone."

She jabs her finger in his face. "If you did, you'd never have tried to kill your grandson's dad. Elio loves Cristian completely, and you would've devastated his heart to the point he would never have recovered." She bitch slaps him across the face, and it's a complete insult, whether she realizes it or not. "You're a petty, narrow-minded fool with no honor and no loyalty." She turns to me. "Are we done with this because

I'd like to get out of here in time to collect our son from school."

"I fucking love you." I slam my mouth against hers in a possessive kiss.

"I fucking love you too."

"Okay, lovebirds," Caleb drawls, smirking. "Let's get this show on the road. I'm ready to go home too."

"I want to know one final thing," I say, checking the bullets in my gun. "Were you chasing after Sloane, or was it the cartel?"

"It was Pablo Fuentes. I was happy for her to stay gone. I assumed they'd kill her, but the fucker couldn't even do me that favor before you chopped him into little pieces. Alvaro and Manuel approached me a few months later. Rodrigo was cleaning house, killing any man loyal to El Rey. They knew they couldn't go home, so they offered their services. They had eyes on *her*, and when you finally agreed to have the contract drawn up, I told them to start pushing her toward the city. I knew she was holding you back. She was supposed to die when her car blew up, but the idiots fucked up. When they said you had her, I had to think fast, and here we are."

"You're a disgrace to *Cosa Nostra*, and you will die. I planned to do it today, but that'd be too easy. So, you'll remain here while I investigate every member of your family. I'll visit regularly to torture you, bringing you close to death only to bring you back each and every time. When I decide you've suffered enough, I'll slit your throat, piss on you, and set your bones on fire. All that will be left is ash, which will flitter away in the wind. You will die with no honor, no grave, and no legacy except for your betrayal. You will die a traitor and always be remembered as one."

"I will see you in hell, DiPietro. Mark my words, I'll be waiting for you."

Isa suddenly screams behind her mouth covering, and she's a sobbing, shaking, stinky mess. I think reality is only now dawning.

I move in front of her, stabbing her with a dark look. "Elio doesn't deserve this. He is the one who will suffer because of your selfishness. He loves you, but you couldn't let it go, could you? You might not have known you were being used, but you were vindictive and self-serving, and I want you out of our lives."

Opening the door, I call Dano back into the cell. "Isotta is banished. Have someone escort her home to pack up her belongings, but I want her on a plane to Sicily within twenty-four hours."

"I'll personally see to it, boss."

"Put that prick in the corner cell. He's getting special treatment."

Dano grins before instructing a couple of his men to move Da Rosa. The old man says nothing to his daughter as he's led away from her for the last time. No apologies. No regrets. No expressions of love. Sloane is right. The man has no clue how to love. It was about possession and vindication for him.

Standing in front of Isa as her binds are untied, I don't feel an ounce of pity in my heart. I let her into our lives in good faith. She had full access to Elio, and he loved her, but it wasn't enough. I have never, not for one second, led her on or given her any indication I was interested in her sexually or romanti-cally. I might've reached a different decision today if she showed any genuine remorse for the way she's treated Sloane, but she hasn't, and she won't. The potential for her to interfere in my relationship is too strong, and it's not like I will ever trust anyone with the Da Rosa last name again. So, this is the way it must be.

Isa has brought it upon herself, and my only emotion is

concern for my son because losing his auntie and his granddad will hurt Elio. "Show your face in New York again, and I'll kill you," I warn her. "As far as Elio is concerned, his aunt and his *nonno* died tragically in a car crash. He will mourn you, but Sloane and I will help him through it."

Isa stares at me with a haunted expression as Dano hauls her out of the cell. I hope I never set eyes on her again.

"Now, on to the last business of the day." Turning to face Sloane, I gesture at Alvaro and Manuel. "You get to decide their fate. What do you want to do?"

"Can I borrow your gun?" she calmly asks.

I hand it to her and step back as she walks over to the two men. Caleb arches a brow, and I shrug. If anyone deserves vengeance, it's Sloane.

"Can you take that off his mouth?" she asks, pointing at Alvaro. "No part of me is touching any part of him."

"Agreed." I stride forward and rip the tape from his mouth, grabbing a handful of his hair and yanking his head back. "You're lucky your fate is in Sloane's hands. If it were up to me, you'd suffer the same fate as that old prick."

"Your whore swallowed my cum. Think of that next time you fuck that pretty mouth." A knife is in my hand and pressed against his neck before I've even processed the motion.

"No, Cristian!" Sloane shouts. "He's baiting you."

"Should've fucked that tight pussy and virgin ass when I had the chance," Alvaro adds, and I dig the knife into his neck, drawing blood, the same time Sloane shoots him in the crotch.

The guy roars, over and over, his entire body convulsing as blood pumps from the hole where his dick used to be.

"I could torture you for days. Make you feel some of the torment I felt, my mother felt, but I don't need that. I get to live, and you don't. I will be the bigger person and extinguish your miserable existence in a merciful kill, but I don't forgive you. I will never forgive you." Sloane puts the muzzle into his mouth. "Move away, Cristian."

I walk over to Caleb, and we watch my girl exact her revenge.

"Burn in hell, Alvaro." Sloane pulls the trigger, and the back of his skull shatters, splattering the wall with brain matter.

Her hand shakes as she stares at him with a look of shock on her face. I gently pull her away and take the gun. "Baby."

Her eyes lift to mine, and a myriad of differing emotions flicker in her eyes. The enormity of what she's done isn't lost on me. This took balls, and my baby has them in spades. But it's clear she's in shock, and I need to take control. "You did good, beautiful, but let me kill this other asshole for you."

Slowly, she nods, and I keep a tight hold of her trembling body as I aim the gun and fire. A clean hole appears between the fucker's eyes as his head falls back, and his vacant stare points to the ceiling.

"It's over." Placing my gun down, I crush her to me, wishing I could absorb all her pain and make everything better. Sloane sinks into my embrace, and her entire body shakes as I hug her. She was so brave, but the hardest part of the journey lies ahead of us as we come to terms with everything that's happened. I hold her until she stops shaking and releases me.

She looks more composed when she asks, "Now what?"

"Now, baby." I link our fingers. "We wipe the slate clean and start over." Caleb holds the door open as we walk out into the hallway. "It won't be easy, but we will conquer every challenge together. Today is day one of the rest of our lives."

Epilogue

Sloane – One Year Later

"Happy, Mrs. DiPietro?" Cristian asks, twirling us around the dance floor as our guests surround us, clapping enthusiastically with the odd wolf whistle and catcall mixed in.

"The happiest, dear husband." The biggest smile spreads over my face. "That will never get old!"

Cristian grins, tightening his arm a little around my waist. "It feels like I've waited an eternity to call you my wife."

"The road has been rocky, but it's worth it to reach this point, this day. Imagining this kept me going during some of the darkest times, never believing it would happen, but I guess sometimes dreams do come true."

Cristian kisses me to whoops and hollers from our friends, and I'm bursting with happiness and pride. Couples join us on the dance floor, but I barely notice because I'm too busy smooching my man. "I love you, and I love our life," he says, sharing my joy.

As one, we turn and look at Elio and Yasmine dancing in a circle with Beatrice and Sabina. We sway in time to the music as we smile at our family. Cristian's mother and sister have helped us a lot this past year, and I'm grateful. Things haven't been smooth sailing. I had a lot of repressed emotions I needed to deal with, and Cristian and I had several issues to work through in our relationship. But we spent time in therapy and prioritized open communication and giving one another space when needed, and we built a stronger bond on an even deeper level.

He's my rock. My best friend. My lover. My biggest champion and supporter. My partner in life until I draw my last breath. No matter what life has in store, I know I can handle it with Cristian by my side.

I'm continuing therapy because I still struggle with guilt over Mom. Visiting her grave was emotional on a whole other level. Walking through my childhood home and sharing stories with Cristian and the kids was nostalgic, heartwarming, and painful all at the same time. I hate how her life was cut short, but I want to honor the sacrifice she made by living my best life. Not a day goes by when I don't think about her, and I know I will always feel her loss deeply.

She'd be thrilled I found a wonderful man who loves me openly and passionately, and I have an incredible family I adore and friends who mean the world to me, but I don't know if I'll ever be entirely free of blame. I guess I'm still a work in progress, but with Cristian's support, hopefully, I can find a way to overcome the remaining hurdles I must face.

For now, I'm focusing on the good things in my life, and today is a day to celebrate and look to the future.

Three months ago, we decided to adopt Yasmine. She's the little girl *La Cosa Nostra* rescued from the cartel. At ten, she's much smaller than her half-brother in part due to the neglect she suffered during some of her formative years. Although medically there is nothing wrong with her vocal cords, Yasmine is nonverbal except when she wakes from one of her regular nightmares, and her screaming confirms her lungs are in working order, and it's trauma that stops her from speaking.

PTSD is no picnic, and Yasmine's only surviving relative—her *grand-mère*, an older woman who lives in a tiny town in northern France—was ill-equipped to give Yasmine the specialist care and attention she needs. When the opportunity arose, we didn't hesitate to adopt her. Fiero and Valentina would've taken her in if we hadn't, but they already have their hands full with four little ones at home. There was zero hesitation for Cristian or me. Yasmine belongs with us, and we haven't regretted our decision even on very difficult days.

Elio is the most amazing big brother. There are only five months separating them, but in lots of ways, Yasmine seems so much younger. Elio is incredibly protective, and they formed a bond straightaway. Where one is, the other is almost surely to be found. Yasmine often shies away from touch, but she readily hugs her brother, and her obvious joy in his company is plain to see. We're hoping in time, with more specialist therapy and unconditional love, Yasmine will be able to overcome the trauma and learn to find more joy in the world.

"I've never seen our son look as emotional as he did walking you up the aisle." Cristian's eyes grow suspiciously glassy.

"It was a precious moment. It's a miracle I didn't cry. I am so proud of him."

Elio and I have rebuilt our relationship with ease. Sharing the photos I kept and the sketches I drew of him and Cristian over the years helped fill in the gaps in his memory, and I've enjoyed bonding with him again, albeit in a much different way.

News of his aunt's and his *nonno*'s passing was hard for Elio as is the fact none of the Da Rosas are here today. Investigation cleared anyone else in the family of involvement, but no one blames Cristian for being wary. Bodyguards go with Elio anytime he's visiting his maternal relatives, and though he's curious, he's accepted Cristian's explanation about taking extra precautions because of everything that went down with the cartel.

Rodrigo Fuentes reconfirmed he has no beef with anyone in *Cosa Nostra* and no one has been following me, but the peace deal is tentative at best, and Cristian doesn't trust any of them. Taking bodyguards with me anytime I leave our house is a small price to pay. I'd rather feel safe and Cristian feel reassured. Most of the time, I forget they're there anyway.

"I'm so glad we opened our home to Yasmine," my husband says, pulling me out of my inner monologue. "I know we have more rough times ahead, but I already love her so much, and seeing them together confirms it was the right decision."

My smile is automatic as I cup one side of his face. "Do you think we have room for one more?"

Cristian stops dancing, and his eyes pop wide as he stares at me. "Are you saying that you're...we're..."

It's not often my husband struggles for words. Emotion swells my chest to breaking point as I nod. "I'm pregnant. We're having a baby."

"Sloane," he whispers, pressing his brow to mine. "I didn't think my heart could get any fuller, but this is the best news ever. Oh my god." Lifting me up, he swings me around, laughing, his joy contagious and obvious for everyone to see.

"Put me down, you crazy man, before you give the game away," I say over my giggles.

"I love you so much," he says, setting my feet on the ground. "You're not the only one whose dreams have come true." His lips meld against mine in a passionate kiss, and I cling to him, deliriously happy and so, so grateful we found our way back to one another, and we finally get the life we've both wanted.

"Ahem." Rory clears her throat. "Can I steal a dance with the groom, or is that pushing my luck?"

"I think it might be," I tease, slipping out of Cristian's arms. "I'm so happy you're here." I pull my best friend into a big hug.

"I wouldn't have missed this for anything."

"I'm immensely grateful for everything you've done."

"Ah, stop it. You don't have to keep thanking me, and I've already cried buckets today. I know you'd have done the same for me."

After I disappeared, Cristian reached out to Rory, and they met up. He told her everything, and she wanted to be involved. So, she packed up her life and moved to New York to head up the nonprofit organization Cristian established to search for missing children. She also worked closely with Cristian and Gia as they looked for me and the missing DiPietro children.

I don't think I can ever repay her for everything she's done for me and the relentless campaigning she did when Mom and I were kidnapped. She's the very definition of a true friend, and I'm so glad we were able to resume our friendship as if the years apart had never happened.

I started working with the charity ten months ago, and we're in the process of collaborating with Moonlight, a charity run by Selena Kennedy to support trafficking victims with healing, recovery, and reintegration into society. Nothing means more to me than helping other victims caught in similar situations. Selena is keen for me to speak to some of their clients. She feels my personal experiences will offer them much-needed hope and inspiration for the future.

"We're glad to have you and Felicity in our lives," Cristian agrees, pressing a kiss to my cheek.

"Speaking of your wife, where is she?" My eyes search the room for the feisty redhead.

"Oh, she's around here somewhere. Most likely flirting with some poor, hapless man," Rory says.

We all laugh. "I'll check on the kids." I peck my husband's lips. "Don't miss me too much."

"Don't go far," Cristian says. "My arms already pine for you."

"Oh my god. You are such a lucky bitch, Slo. Your man is so romantic." Rory clutches her chest. "I think you need to give Felicity some tips, Cristian."

I'm smiling as I walk off to check in with the kids and my mother and sister-in-law.

Gia nabs me then, pulling me aside into a huddle with Elisa. "Spill the tea, sister."

Elisa's eyes gleam with excitement as she stares expectantly at me. I'm so grateful they were able to forgive me and that we have a special friendship. Living close to one another means we see each other every day, and they're the sisters I always wished I had growing up.

"What do you mean?" I feign nonchalance, but it's already been determined I'm a crappy actress.

"Ha." Gia loops her arm in mine. "We saw Cristian swinging you around with the goofiest smile on his face, and we have bets on what you told him."

"You do, huh?"

"I think you're pregnant." Elisa lowers her eyes to my flat stomach, grinning. "And Gia thinks you promised him some kinky sex act for later."

"Is your mind always in the gutter?" I tease, arching a brow at the gorgeous blonde.

"Oh, come on, you act like you've never had sex when you two can't keep your hands off one another."

"We have a very active sex life, but it's still pretty much vanilla."

I've confided in the girls about some of the issues I have with intimacy. Cristian and I have a lot of sex, but I'm still uncomfortable giving him blowjobs, and I don't think I'll ever be able to experiment with anal sex. My husband tells me he's extremely happy with our sex life, and he always checks in to ensure I'm enjoying it and comfortable, but sometimes, when I listen to my friends' exploits, I can't help feeling a little inadequate. Cristian reassures me, and I'm talking it out in therapy, but it'd be nice to let go fully of all inhibitions and give in completely to the pleasure my husband is so expert at delivering.

"There is nothing wrong with vanilla," Elisa says. "I often prefer missionary lovemaking to kinky fucking. It's more intimate, and I always feel closer to Caleb after."

Gia looks instantly remorseful. "I didn't mean to imply anything. Ignore me." Her lips twitch. "But I do think you're deflecting, so out with it."

I roll my eyes. "Having an intelligence analyst for a best friend is a pain in the ass sometimes." I lean closer and whisper, not wanting anyone else to overhear. "You cannot tell anyone. We haven't told the kids yet."

"Confidential is my middle name," Gia says.

My smile is radiant, like every time I think of the little human growing inside me. "I'm six weeks pregnant. I just told Cristian, and he's over the moon."

"This is amazing news." Elisa hugs me. "I'm so excited and really happy for you, and well, I'm pregnant too!"

"You are?" Gia says, quirking a brow. This is obviously news to her too.

"No way, seriously?"

"Yes. I'm eight weeks along."

I look to Gia to see if it's a trifecta, but she shakes her head. "Nope, don't look to me. We're not pregnant, and it's staying that way, at least for now. We have our hands full already."

"I think Caleb would continuously knock me up if I agreed to it," Elisa muses, and I don't doubt he would. He's like a big kid himself, and he's always saying he wants at least ten kids. I never know if he's joking or half serious because he's the kind of guy who goes all out in every aspect of his life.

"You can't seriously be going through with it," an angry male says, claiming all our attention.

We turn around en masse as our husbands approach.

"What's going on there?" Caleb asks, sliding his arm around Elisa as we look over at the heated conversation taking place between Tullia and Rowan a few feet away. We're not the only ones who've noticed, either.

"I'll kick him out if he causes trouble," Cristian says, hauling me around to his front. His arms go around my waist, and he kisses my neck. "I warned him to be on his best behavior."

"It's not like we couldn't invite Tullia's fiancé. She's my friend as much as Rowan is Cristian's."

"What I do with my life is none of your business, Rowan," Tullia says, glaring at her former crush and best friend.

"Fuck," Joshua says, looking at the corner of the ballroom. Tullia's fiancé is storming across the room, looking like he's ready to tear into the Mazzone heir. "Should we break it up?"

Caleb fails to hide his grin. "I say let them duke it out. What's a *mafioso* wedding without a little drama?"

"A fight is not a *little* drama," I say. "It's the potential to turn into a full-scale riot."

"That won't happen. I'll handle it, honey." Cristian removes his arms from around me.

"No need," Joshua supplies, lifting one shoulder. "Bennett is handling it."

Sierra is racing across the dance floor after her husband as Bennett approaches his eldest son with a look of thunder on his face.

Cristian embraces me again.

"I wouldn't want to be in Rowan's shoes right now," I say.

"Kids are always your responsibility, no matter what age they are," Elisa says as we watch Don Mazzone argue with his son while forcibly dragging him away.

Tullia looks pained, nestled in the shelter of her fiancé's arms, but her face quickly transforms into a scowl when Sofia dips out the door after the Mazzones. Tullia's older sister is a fucking bitch, and I can't stand her. I was opposed to adding her to the guest list, but Cristian insisted we couldn't insult Fiero by not inviting one of his siblings.

Mafia drama is right.

I've been busy with wedding planning and haven't had much time to catch up with my newly engaged friend. Something I plan to rectify when we return from our honeymoon.

"I told Caleb and Joshua," Cristian whispers in my ear. "I'm sorry, I know we should've discussed it first, but I was dying to tell someone."

I turn around and snake my arms around his neck. "It's okay. I figured you would, and Elisa and Gia wheedled it out of me too." Cristian's hands land on my lower waist as we gently sway to the music. "You better not have told Rory."

"I value breathing," he quips before adding, "I knew you'd want to tell her yourself."

"I do, but we should tell your mother, Sabina, and the kids first. But that's all for now until the twelve-week mark, which is in six weeks," I add before he can ask me how far along I am.

His lips descend in a slow, sensual kiss, and I melt against my husband, happier than I ever thought possible.

"You've made me the happiest man alive today, baby. Life doesn't get any better than this."

"It truly doesn't." I touch his face, tickling the fine layer of stubble on his chin and cheeks. "Thank you for making all my dreams come true, Cristian. I cannot wait to share the rest of my life with you."

The next interconnected stand-alone in the Mazzone Mafia world is *Claiming My Bride* – Rowan and Tullia's romance. It's an angsty, friends-to-lovers-to-enemies-to-lovers, sister's ex, second-chance romance with all the feels. There is no release date yet, but subscribe to my newsletter for all updates on planned new releases. Type this link into your browser: https://bit.ly/SDRomanceNewsletter

Start the *Mazzone Mafia Series* with *Condemned to Love*, a sister's ex, age-gap, secret baby/surprise pregnancy, second chance, dark, mafia stand-alone romance. Available now in eBook, paperback, alternate paperback, hardcover and audio.

Mazzone Mafia Reading Order

All these titles are free to read in Kindle Unlimited and available in model paperback, alternate paperback, hardcover, and audio.*

RECOMMENDED READING ORDER

Condemned to Love – Bennett & Sierra

Forbidden to Love – Leonardo & Natalia

Scared to Love – Alessandro & Serena

Vengeance of a Mafia Queen – Massimo & Catarina

Cold King of New York – Joshua & Gia

Cruel King of New York – Caleb & Elisa

*Taking What's Mine** – Fiero & Valentina

*Protecting What's Mine** – Cristian & Sloane

The next releases in the Mazzone Mafia universe will be:

*Claiming My Bride^* – Rowan & Tullia

*Claiming My Revenge^* – Cassio & Irina

*Audio coming 2025.

^No release dates are set yet.

Her teen crush is now a ruthless killer and powerful mafia heir. Will one life-altering night unite or destroy them?

Bennett Mazzone grew up ignorant of the truth: he is the illegitimate son of the most powerful mafia boss in New York. Until it suited his father to drag him into a world where power, wealth, violence, and cruelty are the only currency.

Celebrating her twenty-first birthday in Sin City should be fun for Sierra Lawson, but events take a deadly turn when she ends up in a private club, surrounded by dangerous men who always get what they want.

And they want _her_.

Ben can't believe his ex's little sister is all grown up, stunningly beautiful, and close to being devoured by some of the most ruthless men he has ever known. The Vegas trip is about strengthening ties, but he won't allow his associates to ruin her perfection. Although it comes at a high price, saving Sierra is his only choice.

The memory of Ben's hands on her body is seared into Sierra's flesh for eternity. She doesn't regret that night. Not even when she discovers the guy she was crushing on as a teenager is a cold, calculating killer with dark impulses and lethal enemies who want him dead.

Understanding the risks, she walks away from the only man she will ever love, stowing her secrets securely in her heart. Until the truth becomes leverage and Sierra is drawn into a bloody war—a pawn in a vicious game she doesn't want to play.

As the web of deceit is finally revealed, Ben will stop at nothing to protect Sierra. Even if loving her makes him weak. In a world where women serve a sole purpose, and alliances mean the difference between life and death, can he fight for love and win?

more pain. Until Jared rocks up to the art gallery where I work, with his fiancée in tow, and I'm drowning again.

Seeing him brings everything to the surface, so I flee. Placing distance between us again, I'm determined to put him behind me once and for all.

Then he reappears at my door, begging me for another chance.

I know I should turn him away.

Try telling that to my heart.

This angsty, new adult romance is a FREE full-length ebook, exclusively available to newsletter subscribers.

Type this link into your browser to claim your free copy:

https://bit.ly/TITMHFBB

OR

Scan this code to claim your free copy:

About the Author

Siobhan Davis™ is a *USA Today, Wall Street Journal*, and Amazon Top 5 bestselling romance author. **Siobhan** writes emotionally intense stories with swoon-worthy romance, complex characters, and tons of unexpected plot twists and turns that will have you flipping the pages beyond bedtime! She has sold over 2 million books, and her titles are translated into several languages.

Prior to becoming a full-time writer, Siobhan forged a successful corporate career in human resource management.

Siobhan currently lives with her husband in Cyprus while their two grown-up sons reside at the family home in Ireland.

You can connect with Siobhan in the following ways:

Website: www.siobhandavis.com
Facebook: AuthorSiobhanDavis
Instagram: @siobhandavisauthor
Tiktok: @siobhandavisauthor
Email: siobhan@siobhandavis.com

Books By Siobhan Davis

NEW ADULT ROMANCE SERIES
The Kennedy Boys® Series
Rydeville Elite Series
All of Me Series
Forever Love Duet
The One I Want Duet

NEW ADULT ROMANCE STAND-ALONES
Inseparable
Incognito
Still Falling for You
Holding on to Forever
Always Meant to Be
Tell It to My Heart

REVERSE HAREM
Sainthood Series
Dirty Crazy Bad Duet
Surviving Amber Springs (stand-alone)
Alinthia Series

DARK ROMANCE - MAZZONE MAFIA

Condemned to Love
Forbidden to Love
Scared to Love
Vengeance of a Mafia Queen
Cold King of New York (The Accardi Twins #1)
Cold King of New York (The Accardi Twins #2)
Taking What's Mine
Protecting What's Mine

YA SCI-FI & PARANORMAL ROMANCE

Saven Series
*Broken World Series^*

^Previously the *True Calling Series*

www.siobhandavis.com